The Don Juan Con

Sonia Williams

THE DON JUAN CON

A Novel By

Sara Williams

Copyright © 2003 by Sara Williams.

ISBN: 1-59507-011-7

Published by ArcheBooks Publishing,
a division of Gelinas & Wolf, Inc.
www.archebooks.com

ArcheBooks Publishing
9101 W. Sahara Ave.
Suite 105-112
Las Vegas, NV 89117

First Edition: November 2003

"Novelist Sara Williams delivers a thriller as compelling as a the romantic legendary Don Juan himself. Sara's sharp dialogue and succinct word pictures put you in the middle of a first-rate suspense novel showing what a woman can do with a proper mindset. Sara Williams is a superior new stylist who is charting her own course."

Barbara Oehlbeck
Renowned Columnist and Biographical/Historical Author
Author of *The Sabal Palm*

"Williams paints a vivid portrait of a slimy-but-fascinating antagonist readers will love to hate."

Ad Hudler
Author of *Southern Living: The Novel*

"We often choose the wrong partners so as to punish ourselves. That's The Don Juan Con. Here is a modern retelling of a classic theme in fiction."

Richard Fadem, Ph.D.
Professor of English, Emeritus

DEDICATION

For my mother, Dorothy Kincaid,
who first nurtured my voice.

PROLOGUE

Where were the chimes, the panpipes? Anthony heard none of the arty music that ordered Maria Whitman's life. Instead, he listened to the hum of the refrigerator and the blowing of the cold air return. Could it be that Maria had taken a day off from the New Age?

"Ria? Ria Mia?" He closed the back door and passed through the country kitchen, briefcase and long-stemmed red rose in one hand, paper bag in the other. He poked his head through the swinging doors, expecting to see her at work in the library that took up most of the main floor of her sprawling home. The tall windows that faced the Banks River were shuttered and locked. Her computer was draped in its Tibetan prayer shawl. The incense burner on her desk was cold, thank God. Maria's spicy incense made his eyes run.

But of course. The famous astrologer would be upstairs, packing. Anthony passed the marble planter in the foyer and the phallic orange flames of bromeliads in bloom. Maria had told him their Latin name, which sounded to him like some sort of disease. A venereal disease, he'd said, and Maria had laughed until she choked. Maria loved his racy wit.

He took the winding staircase up to the master suite built into a loft above the lower level. Maria's bags were spread out on the bed. Pre-

1

cious little—if anything at all—had been packed. The creeping shadows of sunset and fronds nodding in a potted palm on the balcony were the only motion in the room. Uneasiness crept into his stomach. Then he noticed light spilling through the doorway to her dressing room and crossed the room with relief.

"Ria, Darling, I'm back at long last," Anthony called out. "Depositions took much longer than I thought." He set the briefcase and the paper bag on the credenza.

Across the room a light clicked on, startling him. Maria sat in her wing chair, a sapphire caftan flowing over her bulk. Her brassy hair was wrapped in a matching turban.

"Oh ho. What a surprise, my queen," Anthony said. "You are stunning. What a sight!" He strode across the room, dropped to one knee and bent to kiss her cheek. "Did I ever tell you how sexy you are?" he murmured, handing her the rose. "And how your theatrics knock me out?" He nibbled at her ear.

"Thank you, Anthony," she said. Her voice sounded strained. Puzzled, he settled back on his haunches. Where was the melodic laugh? The cheery expression?

"Ah, *poor* Ria," Anthony murmured. He stroked her rouged cheek with the back of his hand. "You look exhausted, my dear. I've rushed you, haven't I?" He laced her plump fingers into his long ones. "Your Anthony promises he'll let his pet snooze on the plane, all the way to New York." He gave her cheek a final pat. "Wait until you see the surprise I brought you, Ria."

At the credenza, Anthony brought a bottle of Chivas Regal and two glasses from a paper bag. A bell note sounded from one of the glasses when he tapped the rim. "I found these at that little antique shop by the courthouse. Ten dollars each. Worth fifty." He checked the massive Rolex watch on his wrist. "Just enough time for a toast."

"Anthony," Maria said wearily. "I can't join you, and I don't want liquor in my house."

"Ria, darling. Just this once?"

Maria raised her pointed chin in that imperious way of hers. Her mouth hardened into a determined line.

"Right, pet. My last drink ever in this house. I promise." He poured a shot and downed it in one motion.

Maria got up, swept across the room, capped the bottle and shoved it toward Anthony. "Take this when you leave. Consider it a parting gift. I'm sure I paid for it."

"Maria—" he protested, backing away.

"Oh, you *are* good, Anthony, or whoever you are." She set the bottle down and stalked away, putting the bed between them. "I never suspected a thing. Until this morning, that is." She turned to face him. Her voice faltered as she fought back tears. "Three days I tried to work up a chart for you. The signs were haywire. Your personality was mush. All I could think of was, I must have gotten your birth date wrong. So I peeked into your wallet, just to check the date. What do I find? Several identities. Conflicting birth dates."

Anthony laughed. "Maria," he said, rounding the foot of the bed, attempting to approach her, but she cowered against the wall. "I'm a lawyer. I defend criminals, remember? Clients give me their I.D. for safekeeping."

"Who are you, Anthony?" Maria's arms were crossed and her brow was knotted.

He picked up the briefcase and glanced at his watch. "We have no time for this. None. We'll be late to meet my brother's plane."

He headed for the stairway. Maria rushed after him, clutching his arm. "Let's drop it, shall we? Both of us know your brother isn't flying in from Los Angeles for our wedding ceremony." As he turned to her, Maria's expression softened. "Listen to me, Anthony. Despite what you've done, there has to be a reason why our paths crossed. There are no coincidences. I truly believe that. If you'll tell me who you really are, I can help you."

Pulling away, Anthony started down the stairs. "Wedding jitters, hon. I'll go back to the inn and check out. I'll pick you up in an hour."

"It's the alcohol, isn't it?" Maria said, gathering the skirt of her caftan and trailing after him on spindly heels. "Drink, and your evil side surfaces, Anthony. Mine does, too. I've been through it. You can kick it."

As she rounded the first turn down the stairs, Maria caught up with him. There wasn't room for both of them. Maria pinned him against the delicate teak handrail that seemed to float above the treads. Anthony stared into her eyes, brown as old bottle glass and enormous, enlarged as they were by her thick glasses.

"Why steal from those who love you, Anthony? Someone must have hurt you terribly. But listen, dear, I know there's good in you. In the few days I've known you, I've never encountered a more sensitive man."

Anthony wrenched away from her and headed down the stairs.

"Run then, if that's what you choose to do. But not on my money," Maria shouted. "I'll have you arrested." She started back up the stairs.

3

Anthony froze. Arrest him? What a bizarre notion. "But Maria. Do you think that's wise? What about your reputation? A renowned astrologer jilted by her lover?"

"Jilted?" Maria said with a gasp. From the top of the landing, she laughed at him. "But Anthony, I found you out, remember? A complete vindication of my powers."

Damn the woman! His bad heart was beginning to grind. Nevertheless, he had to settle this. He plodded back up the stairs. He stopped to rest just short of the top.

"You win, Maria," he panted. "You want your money?" He braced himself on the handrail and taunted her, waggling the briefcase.

Maria started down the stairs, made a grab for the case, but caught the sleeve of his blazer instead. He yanked his arm back. It was shaking.

"Here, take it." Anthony said, swinging the case back at her, flat alongside her head. The force of the blow sent her over the railing. With a shriek, Maria hit her head on the corner of the marble planter below.

Anthony stared after her. "Jesus, the damned planter, Ria," he murmured.

She moaned. Blood seeped from the wound. Her hand reached up for her head, faltered, flopped back. Gripping the handrail to support himself, he crept down the stairs. By the time he made the foyer, Maria was ominously still. The color seemed to be draining from her face. There was no pulse at her wrist, none in the artery at her neck. A trail of blood spilled from the corner of her mouth.

Damn all the luck!

Gasping for breath, Anthony slumped down on the steps. His heart was tearing at his ribs. This was too much. What was wrong with the woman, attacking him like that? He was no killer. Had no heart for it. Neither physically, nor mentally. He was too old for stuff like this. But who would believe a swindler? It was all just a terrible accident. It took him some time before his heart calmed down enough for him to think. He must erase his presence. It would put him well behind schedule, but a thorough cleanup was essential. This was an accident that truly had to look like one. He patted his breast pocket and pulled out his cell phone. God. What was the number? He was too rattled to think clearly. Finally, the right combination occurred to him.

"Anthony?" He detected anxiety in the husky voice. "I just knew it was you."

"Sweetheart," he said. "Forgive me, my darling, but something has come up. A business emergency. A client is in terrible trouble and I'm running a little late."

CHAPTER 1

DeLeon, FL
Friday, August 21

It was always the same. *The ball of light. The deafening sound. The rain of debris. The flight. The fall. The water, swirling at her, choking her. The breath sucked out of her. Her chest crushing in. Gasping. Coughing. The acrid stench. The flames licking at her face.*

"No," Angie Reynolds sobbed, her body writhing. "*Noooo!*" She awakened, her face wet with tears.

"Angie? Are you all right?" It was Barbara Baquero, chief esthetician at Salon DeLeon. Barbara raised the lid of the long, clam-shaped steamer where Angie lay baking in a tight wrapping of seaweed.

Angie sat up, wiped her face, and looked around the small white room with the antique butterfly prints hung on the walls. There was a massage table covered with soft white sheets to her left and a shower at the foot of the steamer. The Armani suit her fiancé had bought her hung in a garment bag on the wall. Anthony wanted her hairdresser to see the sculpted neckline, so that he could make the right decision on her hair. Up or down? Last night he had toyed endlessly with her hair, pinning it this way and that. Barbara handed her a tissue.

Angie blew her nose. "I'm sorry, Barbara. It's a pesky dream. A nightmare, really. I've had it since childhood. For years it went away. Now it's recurring."

The Don Juan Con

Barbara sat down on the edge of the steamer and stroked Angie's arm. "You sure, honey? I thought maybe I had the steam set too high. You scared me to death."

Angie's fingers fluttered to her mouth, then drifted away. Here she was in the finest salon on the Florida Gulf, making a complete fool of herself. "No. Really. This is wonderful. It's just that I've been under such stress."

Barbara shook her head. "A wedding can be hell." Her brown eyes grew big, her perfect mouth dropped in wonderment. "And here you are doing it on three days' notice. No time to plan?" Barbara raised her shoulders and shook her head, the fall of her dark hair rippling. Then she smiled, showing off her perfect teeth. "But it's a heavenly kind of hell, isn't it?"

"It's madness, I know. The whole thing is crazy. I'm completely exhausted, but my fiancé wants nothing less than perfection. It's really his parents' fiftieth anniversary. A big do in Manhattan. Six hundred guests. We're to be married quietly in a private ceremony afterwards."

"I met your Anthony just awhile ago," Barbara said.

Barbara stood up to recheck the settings on her machine while Angie studied the flawless taupe of Barbara's skin, hoping she would look half as good as Barbara did when they got done with her makeover.

"He came in for a hairstyle with Roberto," Barbara said. "He personally went over with me every single detail of your treatment. Such a concerned man. You know what I think? I think he was checking up. To see you got the best. Such a nice man. So proud of you. He told everyone in the shop about the three-carat solitaire waiting for you when you get to New York. When he left he said he was going to the bank. He needed a suitcase full of cash to pay for the wedding." Barbara laughed, rolling her eyes.

"That's Anthony, all right," Angie said, shaking her head. It bewildered her that Anthony felt compelled to regale everyone with their wedding plans, even complete strangers. But Anthony said she had to get used to that. It was the Italian in him.

"What do you feel like, Angie?" Barbara said, squeezing her shoulders at the base of her neck. "Maybe we should cut short with the body bake and go with the massage?"

"I'll be fine, Barbara. The dream won't come back. Just let me finish the treatment."

"I tell you what. I'll reset the timer. You need an uninterrupted twenty minutes," Barbara said, resettling Angie between the paper sheets that lined the steamer.

6

Angie rested her head on the small, throwaway pillow as Barbara let herself out. She should consider herself lucky. So why the qualms? She was uneasy. That's what the dream meant. But why? What young widow wouldn't jump at what Anthony had offered her? The chance to become the wife of a prominent New York attorney; the option to continue her career in interior design. Live on Park Avenue in the same building where his parents had the penthouse. A second home right here in DeLeon. Jason was to have the finest prep school education money could buy.

Yes, Anthony was older, maybe fifteen years, possibly even twenty. He was a little vague about his age. But so what? He was a handsome, fun-loving man with great social presence and he absolutely adored her. There was no doubt of that. Still, Angie felt a little unsure of herself. She didn't think she could measure up to what he wanted her to be. Wasn't that it?

She was attracted to Anthony, infatuated with him, maybe, but it just wasn't what it had been with Alan. She'd adored Alan. He'd been her soul mate, her best friend. One day she was married to a rising young architect, working with him on a daily basis. The next day she was a struggling widow, trying to hang onto the business she and Alan had opened together. She never would have made it if it hadn't been for Dad. And then to lose Dad, so soon after Alan? She couldn't believe it. Thought it was some kind of curse.

Angie's face broke into a sweat as steam filled the booth where she lay. A miasma of seaweed and clay filled her nostrils. Her lips curved into a wan smile. The weedy scent must have touched off that ghastly drowning dream. She wriggled her body, hidden in its clamshell casing, reminding herself to relax. The battle was over, and Angie had won.

Even though Jane, her mother, had begged her to simply close up her shop and come home, Angie had persevered. She'd scrimped and cut corners at home, and worked so many long hours that Jason had suffered. There were times she hadn't seen how unhappy he'd been. But as of last week, she'd made it. She had accumulated just enough money to pay off the quarterly installment on her bank loan. Then she'd met Anthony at the art auction she'd installed to earn the commission that put her a few dollars in the black. Now she would put this bad time behind her.

Just like the prince in some fairy tale, Anthony had ridden into DeLeon in his white Lincoln, an attorney taking depositions. He'd come into her shop, bought one entire lot of antique Limoges figurines for his parents' anniversary, and the two of them had spent every hour he had available from that day to this.

Anthony had begged her to marry him on their second date, when they'd dined at the new restaurant on Sanibel, Junonia, named for that rarest of shells. They hit all the clubby nightspots afterwards, from Tarwinkles to 'Tween Waters on Captiva, where Anthony stole the show everywhere with his bawdy songs, gossip about movie stars, celebrities and politicians, and lawyer jokes. Then they'd gone for a long stroll on the beach along the causeway, and Angie confessed she wasn't over Alan's death.

Anthony had taken her in his arms. "Angie, I know how you feel. I was devastated when I lost my beloved Maria. I brought up my boys all alone. Twenty years slipped away from me. And now that I've met you, I know Maria would never have wanted that for me. There are no coincidences, Maria always said. And I know your dear one would want you to be taken care of in the way you so richly deserve." Angie heard the throaty rumble of his voice against the crackle of the surf and she began to relax in the long steamer. He told her, "I know it's too soon to expect you to love me as much as I love you. But the way I'll take care of you, I know love will come."

Within a matter of hours, the Gulf Stream jet would arrive bearing Anthony's brother, the software publisher, and his good friend, Nate Tamblyn, star of kick boxer movies, and Tamblyn's supermodel wife, Iona. Anthony had brought her in here so that she'd look, well, perfect, and so she settled back and forced herself to shut off her rambling thoughts. She drifted off to a peaceful sleep as she heard Paul Anka singing "Put Your Head on My Shoulder" on the salon's piped in music. Funny. Wasn't that the oldie that she and Anthony had danced to when he finally arrived last night, so sweet, so apologetic at being hours late for their date?

•

"Angie, darling, wake up Hon," Barbara said.

"Already?" Angie moaned. "I felt *sooo* relaxed."

"I'm really sorry, Angie," Barbara said, handing her a phone. "It's a Miss Waters at your bank. They are about to close and they need your approval for something."

8

CHAPTER 2

Friday, August 21, 4:47 p.m.

Anthony Abruzzi pulled his white Lincoln Continental up beneath the portico of the Florida Seaboard Bank, right where it said No Parking on the pilasters. Frowning, a security guard in a blue uniform approached the car to wave it off. Seeing who it was, his wizened face split into a grin. He came around to open Anthony's door.

"George, how you be, Buddy?" Anthony said as he emerged from the car to pump the guard's hand. "How's that grandson of yours?"

"Fine, sir. He pitched a no hitter last night."

"You tell him I said keep it up, George." Anthony thumped the guard on the back.

"Good luck at your wedding, sir," the guard replied.

Anthony checked his Rolex. "Just two hours and thirty-three minutes from now, my brother's Gulf Stream jet swoops down on DeLeon Field to steal Angie P. Reynolds and me off to New York."

"It couldn't happen to a nicer girl. Congratulations to you and good luck to you both."

Anthony flashed the watch, a Presidential model. "My fiancée bought this for me. What do you think of it?"

The guard bent closely to inspect the gold watch. "Outstanding."

At that moment the bank manager, Ned Wadlow, came rushing forward to take Anthony by the arm. "We're all ready for you, Mr.

9

The Don Juan Con

Abruzzi. I realize you are in a hurry."

"And here it is a quarter to five on Friday evening and I've put you to all this trouble, Ned," Anthony said, his hand on Wadlow's shoulder as they strode across the gleaming expanse of sea green marble, passing what seemed to be miles of walnut paneling. Spare and rangy, Anthony had chosen to look casually elegant. He wore his favorite light gray, Gianfranco Ferre suit over a Karesh turtleneck with a stretched out neck. Very witty—the perfect thing to set off his dark skin and prematurely gray hair. By comparison the fresh-faced, chunky Wadlow appeared to be trapped in a suit that was an entire generation too old for him.

"Angie's one of our favorite people. And her mother as well," Wadlow murmured.

Anthony raised a dark brow, pruned by Roberto at Salon DeLeon earlier this afternoon. The reference to Angie's mother startled him. "You've met Jane Pelham?"

Wadlow's eyes widened. "Why, yes. She was down last winter with her husband." As they reached the head teller's cage, a young woman appeared. "Tell Hilda Mr. Abruzzi has arrived," Wadlow announced.

Anthony leaned toward Wadlow. "I suggested to Angie that I send my brother's jet to fetch Jane for the wedding. But Angie declined. Unfortunately, Jane is under medication for depression. It's been very hard on her since her husband died."

"A shame," Wadlow muttered, his eyes sweeping the cages, where pairs of tellers were in the process of closing out. "David Pelham was only fifty nine. Died a week after a checkup showed he was in perfect health. He was going public with his company."

"Sea Escape Designs?" Anthony said.

Wadlow nodded. "A total shock. Lucky in everything but his genes, I guess."

"I'll have *both* the Pelham women to look after," Anthony murmured. He pulled a wafer of a gold lighter from his pocket and lighted his long cigar within shouting distance of a No Smoking sign.

Noticing Wadlow's raised eyebrows, Anthony showed him the label.

"A Cohiba?"

"Genuine."

"Cuban?" Wadlow's eyes went round. "I won't ask how you got that."

"A grateful client," Anthony said with a shrug. "So I'll send you a box."

"Oh, no. No, I couldn't let you," Wadlow said.

"Come on, Ned. I'm your grateful client."

"We don't finish this transaction in the next ten minutes, you might not be so grateful, sir."

Anthony raised his cigar in a kind of salute as Wadlow took up his pen. "After the wedding, we'll be taking off for one of the Greek Islands. One of my clients has offered us his villa. Once I get this trial thing out of the way, I'm going to devote a lot of time to Angie. Maybe her mother will join us in Greece."

"I hope you won't forget DeLeon," Wadlow said.

"And I hope you won't forget to visit us in New York, Ned," Anthony said. "I got an uncle runs a haberdashery just two blocks from Bloomie's. I'll get you into some Italian suits. *Capisce?*

The banker chuckled. "Wouldn't I be the talk?"

"Don't let me kid you, Ned. You've got it made here in DeLeon. The beaches. The sunshine..." Anthony paused a beat or two and added his punch line: "The dog track."

Wadlow guffawed.

"Anyway—and I mean this Ned—please get in touch if you find a good buy in one of the better condominium properties here. Maybe a Villa in The Pines. Or possibly something in White Heron. Nothing too expensive, certainly no more than a million. At the most we'd use it five—maybe six months of the year."

"I'll surely do that," said the banker, glancing around nervously. "Here's Miss Waters." A tall woman with a mop of dazzling gold dreadlocks and a mocha complexion spiked with tiny black freckles appeared with a file box full of cash.

"My land, Mr. Anthony. You are some sugar daddy in that outfit," she said, flashing teeth rimmed in gold.

Wadlow reddened, started to sputter, but Anthony laughed explosively.

"Counselor Sugar Daddy. How do you think the judge would like that?"

"I don't know, honey. Depends whether the judge be a he or a she." The shell beads of Hilda's myriad braids clicked as she swiveled her head and tossed him a sidelong glance.

Wadlow blanched. Seeing that Anthony was amused by Hilda's antics, however, he brayed right along, but abruptly got back to business. "We have only twelve minutes to get the counting done," he said. "Sorry to rush you, sir, but if we've miscounted we have only minutes to get back into the vault. Everything's on a timer." Wadlow rolled his eyes. "Frankly, bankers are slaves to their security systems."

"Well, we'll just take your word for it, Ned. Hilda wouldn't cheat me, I know. Just hand me your paperwork and I'll sign it. I wouldn't dare be late tonight—Say? Did I tell you Nate Tamblyn will be coming on the plane?"

Wadlow looked blank. Hilda got him off the hook. "The Karate Kid? Ohhhh, I love his movies," she said clapping her hands. "Do you think I could get his autograph?"

"Give me your address, Hilda. I'll take care of it," Anthony said. Hilda penned her address on the back of one of the bank's business cards. Anthony read it back to her before he tucked the card in his pocket, noticing Wadlow's increasing irritation out of the corner of his eyes. Wadlow pushed a teller receipt beneath Anthony's pen. Anthony scrawled his illegible signature, all squiggles and flourishes, then opened the attaché case he carried.

"Did you see this beautiful briefcase my fiancée bought me?" Anthony said as he stacked bills inside, filling an entire compartment.

Wadlow whistled, "Hermés, isn't it?"

By the time Anthony had packed the case and locked it with flicks of the combination dials, it was five minutes past closing. Wadlow escorted him back across the lobby and the guard unlocked the door.

Saluting, George said, "Be careful now. Hear?"

"The clients I have? I got no choice. They take it very unkindly if I lose their money."

George held the briefcase as Anthony punched in the door lock combination on the Continental. Wadlow hovered on the sidewalk. From his rearview mirror Anthony caught Wadlow's goodbye salute, which he returned with a two-fingered V for victory sign as he sped off.

"Goodbye Wadlow. Goodbye DeLeon," he murmured.

CHAPTER 3

Friday, August 21, 9:40 p.m.

Outside, a car door slammed. Angie darted to the rear window of her second floor condominium, wedged open a slat in the blinds and peered down into the parking lot. It was only her neighbor returning from his courier's job at the library. Embarrassed, Angie stepped back from the window. What if he thought she was spying on him? Angie checked her watch once again.

By their revised schedule, Anthony's limousine was exactly sixty-two minutes late. He would be furious.

She slipped out of the jacket of her Armani suit. With deliberate care she laid the jacket over the back of a chair. If she didn't look absolutely perfect when the limousine finally did arrive, he'd be annoyed.

The limousine bearing Anthony's brother, Salvatore, his brother's wife and the Tamblyns. Where could they be? They should have been here long ago. For two days, Anthony had planned obsessively for this meeting. Angie hated to think how terribly disappointed he would be.

From the Gucci handbag that Anthony bought for her yesterday, Angie pulled the typed schedule she had prepared at his insistence. A Gulf Stream jet was to arrive from Dallas-Ft. Worth at 7:30 p.m. Anthony was to meet the jet with the limousine. Deplane, fifteen minutes. Twenty-five minutes from the airport to Angie's condominium in The Glades, a golf club community just two exits off I-75, just south of

13

downtown DeLeon. Party to arrive no later than 8:15. A short reception, thirty minutes. Have in a few close friends. Stick to people who won't gush over Tamblyn.

At seven p.m. he'd called to say he'd just learned that the jet had left Dallas a half hour late. He advised her to call everybody and cancel out on this party. Luckily she'd reached everyone except her best friends, the Goldheims.

Angie looked at the evening watch with the single diamond Anthony had given her. It won a top design prize at an international jewelry show. It was 9:47. What could have happened? A flat tire? She absent-mindedly arranged her russet blonde pageboy in front of the hall mirror, perhaps for the twelfth time. Normally Angie could depend on her thick hair to hold perfectly. Tonight, even her hair had failed her, despite the fact that Maurice at Salon DeLeon had nervously put a pound of spray on it. Come to think of it, a pound of spray was probably what was wrong. Appalled, Angie saw that her hair lay flat against her head, limp as the strips of the O-Cedar mop she had used on the kitchen floor, not once but three times. What a shame. Maurice had worked so hard to get her thick hair to wave just so, to compliment the curving collar of the suit.

Angie jumped a foot when Jason slipped up behind her, clasping her around the waist, resting his chin on the top of her head. Although he was only eleven, he was already a head taller than she and loved to emphasize the fact.

"Mom? When are we going?" Jason said.

She smiled at her son. His big gray eyes were hers, silvery hubcaps in his narrow Pelham face. He was dressed in the stylish Gap jeans and Polo shirt Anthony had let him select for the plane trip. He had warned Jason, however, that he'd have to go blue blazer and gray flannel preppie for the big social events in New York.

"Any time now, darling," Angie said, stroking the weight line at the back of Jason's haircut. This lumpish skater cut drove Anthony wild. When Jason had rebelled, Angie intervened. When Jason was enrolled in prep school, then he could go with a preppie haircut.

"Tired of the Xbox?" Angie said, relaxing a little, allowing herself to be rocked in her son's arms.

"I beat all the games already," Jason said.

"I'm grateful you didn't fuss over the Xbox," Angie said, first stroking his arms, then gently prying Jason's grip loose. She was afraid he'd wrinkle her suit.

"It doesn't matter, Mom," Jason said. He released his mother and slumped on the sofa. Though Jason had his heart set on the PlayStation computer game system, Anthony had insisted on getting the Xbox from Microsoft. "Always go for the American product, kid," he'd growled.

Angie sat down beside him, pinching his earlobe. "Not ready just yet," she teased.

Jason's mouth lifted in a tried-for smile. It was an old family joke that Angie would fricassee Jason's tender earlobes and have them for dinner—when they were ready, which, of course, they never were.

"Honey, you've been awfully quiet these past few days. Is something bothering you?"

Jason's mouth turned down. He refused to look at her. "I know Anthony's a really rich guy, Mom, but sometimes I think he's got an attitude," Jason said. The pair had tangled again this afternoon when Jason came home with scratches on his cheek. Jason had been climbing in his pal's tree house and fallen out and cut himself.

Anthony fumed, lecturing Jason for carelessly allowing himself to get scarred up. "You'll need a retouch before we put you in your mama's wedding picture," Anthony groused. Jason hadn't said a word, but immediately headed for his room and locked the door. He hadn't emerged until Anthony left.

Angie stroked the scratch on Jason's cheek. "It's true, darling, I agree, and Anthony himself knows he's a little pushy, but that's the way these high-powered attorneys are. Can you forgive Anthony that?"

"If he makes you happy? I guess so, Mom. I'll try."

It was a little rocky between Anthony and Jason, but Angie knew things would work out. After all, Anthony did seem to recognize he had his faults. Last night, cuddled together in a restaurant booth, they had dined on squab and champagne in the exclusive Seminole Lodge. He'd kept her waiting two hours for their dinner date and seemed distracted during the first part of the meal. Then, sensing her irritation, he had brushed her fingers with his lips and apologized. "I do hope you can learn to be patient, my pet," he said. "I was brought up by a woman who was head decorator for Bonwit Teller. Things simply had to be done to perfection or not even attempted. Unfortunately, I get caught up in a consuming need to take meticulous care of my clients."

Angie pulled Jason close. "I always want you to remember. You come first with me, sweetheart."

She realized how painful it was to watch Jason growing up right now. Every day his hair got darker and his features took on his grandfather's masculinity. His face was going through an awkward stage. His childish jaw line couldn't seem to keep pace with the emergence of the

Pelham high-bridged nose. From day one, Jason took after the Pelhams, their height, wiry builds, open faces, thick, burnt-umber hair and sensitive skin.

Angie stared at her watch for the umpteenth time. Even under the revised schedule the limousine should have been here at least an hour ago, and it was very odd that Anthony, usually so considerate and meticulous, hadn't called.

"I tell you what, Mom, call the airport," Jason said.

"Oh, I don't know, darling, whether we should upset Anthony."

"Hey, Anthony's always on the phone. He's probably gabbing on his cell right now."

It was true. Anthony carried a phone in his breast pocket, even the afternoon he took Jason to a baseball game. He received constant calls from his office. He frequently consulted with his mother.

"I'll talk to him."

"Deal," Angie said.

This was a good idea. Let Jason call Anthony. Maybe the two of them would make up. It was a muggy summer night. Angie stepped outside to catch a bit of breeze while Jason phoned, her thoughts racing. Anthony insisted that Mama Regina would love her on sight. But what if Anthony proved to be one of those mama's boys wrapped around Regina's finger? Could that be why he had never remarried? Angie had given Anthony a conditional promise. Yes, she would let him go ahead and sweep her off her feet—but Angie had insisted that she have a right to delay the ceremony if she felt too pressured. Anthony himself had suggested she proceed on this basis. "Of course I'm too aggressive and pushy, darling. Every judge in New York has told me the same thing," he'd said last night.

The memory of Anthony's earnest confession brought a smile to her face as she sat on her deck, staring up through the screened porch at the full moon. She told herself to stop worrying and enjoy her romance. After all, Anthony had been late before. I am *soooo* lucky, Angie had said to herself. Thank you, God. She was amazed how—in what, less than five days?—a person's entire life could turn around.

Jason came out to the porch. The moonlight robbed his face of normal color. The Jason she saw in that eerie light was foreign to her. His trusting young face had become a pallid etching of bewilderment and loss.

"Mom? I don't mean to worry you, but something doesn't add up."

CHAPTER 4

Friday, August 21, 10:30 p.m.

The music on WOLZ, the oldies station he was listening to, was fading out. He punched around on the radio dial looking for a replacement, but nothing held. He hated having nothing to listen to, but the fadeout signaled progress. It meant DeLeon was well behind him and Sarasota was coming up.

"All right. We made it!" he said aloud, whacking at the steering wheel. He eyed the briefcase full of cash beside him on the seat. Angie's cash. And that of all the others. What sweethearts, one and all!

It was then that he noticed the patrol car in the shadowy tunnel formed by a freeway overpass. Within seconds he felt a tightening behind his breastbone. The white Ford Escort he was driving began to weave. Je-sus, not now! The cop would think he was drunk. He didn't dare pull over. Sweat rolled down his forehead as pain radiated in his chest. He gritted his teeth as he felt his fingers grow numb. He eased into the right lane and willed himself to keep a steady pressure on the accelerator, waiting out the pain. Why did his stupid heart have to act up now? He'd been so careful. No speeding. No passing. Jeez! He'd even taken his pills! Nothing like a corpse in your immediate past to make an honest driver out of you.

The blast of a horn on his right rear sent him into a swerve. Damn.

17

The Don Juan Con

He'd wandered into an entrance lane on the far right. As the offended motorist pulled past him shaking his fist, he caught a glimpse of himself in his own rearview mirror. His heavily lidded eyes were slits. His skin seemed shrunken down around his bald head, a ghastly sight, but at least a sufficiently disguised one. His elegant attorney duds were packed away, along with Anthony's piece. What a shame it was. Cousin Anthony in his silver mane would be a perfect spokesman for the Men's Hair Club. Dressed in Dockers, a baseball cap, and a blue and orange Gators' jacket, he had two tickets to the college football game in his wallet. It was something to gab about in case he got stopped. He now had everything under control except his own damned heart.

The pain in his chest subsided as he passed another patrolman. No doubt the guy was the second peg of a speed trap. Imagine him being relieved to see a cop. The cop—a kid—was on the radio, and he chuckled with relief. This was no road block set up for him, the way it had been that other time, when he'd been nabbed and sent back to prison. Due to that unfortunate accident in Banks, he couldn't afford to be stopped. Never again.

He studied the patrol car in his rearview mirror, slowing his pace as he did so. A looker blonde in the Corvette behind him tapped her horn in irritation. He had watched her off and on for the last five miles. Too bad he couldn't pick her up. Fortunately, the Friday evening traffic was awful—just as he had planned. The first freeway exit for Sarasota came up and he took it, glancing at his battered Timex as he passed under a streetlight.

Angie, sweet, faithful Angie, would be giving up her vigil about now, her dream shattered—and that was tough for her. He had the feeling she really saw him, or at least the lawyer he pretended to be, as something other than a meal ticket, which is what most women wanted from Anthony Abruzzi. He never felt bad taking from the gold diggers. They were out to con a rich attorney. So what if they got conned themselves?

Angie was a decent kid, however. Strange what life turned up. What amazing luck after all these years to encounter her, Angie Pelham Reynolds. She'd turned out to be a daddy's girl, touchingly grieving the loss of her father.

He lit one of the cheap Cleopatra cigars he always carried to complete his ordinary guy look. Now Cousin Anthony would never touch such a stogie. But his mind was on Pelham—dead by natural causes. How fortunate. David Pelham was a first class bastard if ever there was one. Talk about coincidence.

Only there was no such thing as a chance happening—that was what Maria Whitman had taught him before her untimely passing. The most meaningful events were the most coincidental. If he understood the astrologer's teachings correctly. It was something she called *synchronicity*—that is, when she was in one of her highfalutin moods.

He was on his third or fourth drag on the cigar he wasn't supposed to be smoking and a Road Warrior Inn was in sight, when he had a brilliant idea. What a genius he was. It was no accident that he had found the Pelhams after all these years. He laughed aloud. Cousin Anthony made sure he had Jane Pelham's address. He even had her phone number. Angie's mother was sorely in need of consolation and companionship.

Why not?

He'd been plenty ticked that Angie had never told her mother about her forthcoming wedding. Now Angie would never dare breathe a word about the fact that she'd been dumped. Her mother was too depressed. Bad news from Angie might be just the thing to push Jane over the edge. So perhaps a little romance was just the thing for Angie's mother. Cousin Anthony couldn't woo Jane, of course. That would be a little too awkward. As for himself, he was just an ordinary guy. No, a class ring salesman would never appeal to Jane Pelham. But suppose another cousin appeared on the scene? Someone worthy of Jane's affections?

As he drove along, his thoughts focused on Angie's mother. If only he'd won her away from David Pelham in the first place. For Jane, he might have been something. Without her, he'd wasted his life. As he pulled over in front of the Inn, he tried to calculate what Jane must be worth. Eight? Maybe ten million? Certainly more than enough to see him through his twilight years.

As he plunked down cash for his room, he was careful to remove his bald cap to flash his tonsured skull. He deliberately left the tickets to the Gators game on the counter as he dug the cash for his room out of his wallet. He made a show of coming back to reclaim the tickets after he was halfway out the door of the office. Then he turned around and made a big deal of asking the reservation clerk which exit to take to the stadium tomorrow and which bar in town had the Gators fan club. Nose around a little and he might find a bookie.

He'd had to settle for a second floor room and was soaked with sweat by the time he'd carried three heavy bags up the stairs. He stretched out on the bed, feeling depressed and wondering why. He should have been elated over the fact that Maria Whitman hadn't been found. Not yet anyway. There had been no news flashes on the radio.

The Don Juan Con

He pulled a lumpy pillow out from under a thin spread and yearned for the comforts of a Hilton or a Ritz Carlton, where the linens were crisp and the suites had mini bars with tidbits you could make a meal from. He didn't dare open cousin Anthony's Vuitton bag and get out his Chivas Regal. Integrity of character was the only way he'd stayed on top for so long. The way his heart was acting, he might have to check into the hospital at any moment, in which case he'd have to stay rational enough to take the suitably shabby Samsonite he'd found at a Goodwill store.

He used what remained of his energy to tune in the late news. There was nothing on Maria, and he was safe. If he wasn't too sick to drive tomorrow he'd soon be out of immediate danger. Of course, it would come up soon enough, the links between Angie and Maria. But in a case like this the next move would be entirely up to Angie. The police would discourage her. After two or three days the coroner would be hard pressed to rule Maria's death anything but an accident.

On the other hand, if Maria were found immediately, then Anthony was one dead cousin. He'd have to bury Abruzzi's effects in some dumpster and move on. As for wooing Jane Pelham, it was stupid. He had to put that idea right out of his mind. He'd had his revenge on David Pelham when he'd jilted Angie. To steal Jane's affections as well? No, it was way too risky, much too arrogant.

Cousin Anthony might dream of pulling off something like that. For sure he would consider it. But wily Anthony wasn't nearly as arrogant as he pretended to be. That was what had kept the bogus lawyer going all these years. He didn't have the strength to raise his arm to put out the bedside lamp. He put a pillow over his head to shut out the light instead.

It took considerable effort to put Jane Pelham out of his mind. He focused on car doors slamming down in the parking lot, the slapping sounds of children chasing past his room, and the clanking of the miserable room air conditioner, the sort of distractions he never heard in a full service hotel.

CHAPTER 5

Friday, August 21, 10:30 p.m.

Gina Goldheim rang the doorbell. She was answered by loud, hurried footsteps. Angie yanked the door open, her face filled with fury. Her expression turned to confusion when she saw who it was.

"Gina, how nice to see you," Angie said woodenly.

"Gosh, what a greeting." Gina said as she swept into the room, trailing her usual scent of Fendi, though she liked to think she was not her usual self, a tough little terrier-sized woman. She had traded in her tank top and jogging shorts for a clingy red jersey dress and strapped, spike-heeled sandals. Seeing Angie's stunned expression, Gina tried to jolly her along: "I know. You save your real enthusiasm for the Internal Revenue Service." She handed Angie a big silver box with yards of white ribbon on it. "Happy wedding darling."

"I love you for your thoughtfulness Gina," Angie said stiffly, passing the box right back. "Please don't be offended if I ask you to return this unopened." Angie turned away from her friend and sank into a club chair, leaving Gina marooned in the tiny hallway.

"What?" Gina said, confronting her in front of her chair, hands on hips, drill sergeant style. "A Laura Ashley bedroom set? Including the curtains? Something I've always wanted? You turn it down?" Gina sat down on the chair arm and reached for Angie's forehead. "Sure you're feeling okay? Maybe a touch of bride's remorse?"

Gina looked around Angie's exquisitely decorated apartment. It was just the right mix of modern pieces and antiques, and homey besides. Somehow, Angie could combine fancy, lah-de-dah items, like the filigree chandelier over the glass-topped dining table—the one she and Alan had found in Paris on their honeymoon—with the whimsical and ridiculous. For instance, the rusty sprinkler can filled with tulips on the Louis XV coffee table. Angie had rescued the can from a trash bin. Gina's eyes shifted to the paintings.

"Hey," Gina said. "New art. I like the one with the herons." It was always fun to visit Angie's stylish digs. She was forever moving items from her home to her shop. Angie never bothered to hang pictures for that reason. She simply propped them on various sideboards or tables. Who else could get away with anything like that?

As Gina looked around, the scene took on a strange emptiness. Everything was entirely too organized: the champagne was on ice, the glasses stood on Angie's antique pine sideboard, the canapés were under damp towels. There was a muted undertone of jazz coming from the compact disk player, but nary a soul was around.

She glanced at her watch. "I'm sorry I'm so late. Has everyone left?"

"Your timing is perfect, Gina," Angie mumbled, her shoulders hunched. "It's mine that's evidently off. Don't mind me. I mistook the event. I thought I was getting married. This event turns out to be a jilting."

With her face crumpling, Angie got up and rushed into her small kitchen. Gina caught up with her as she hunched over the sink splashing water from the running tap on her face.

"I don't believe it," Gina said. She shut off the tap, took Angie's arm and led her around the bar counter to one of the tall swivel stools.

"There's no jet," Angie murmured.

"Are you sure?" Gina said.

"I last spoke to Anthony at seven. He told me the plane had been delayed by twenty-five minutes, forty at the outside. I expected to hear from him by eight at the latest, but at any rate, he told me that they'd be late and to cancel the party. I reached everyone but you. He's obsessive about schedules. By nine-forty I was frantic." Angie took the embroidered linen towel Gina handed her from across the counter and dabbed at the corners of her eyes.

"I should have known something was really wrong right then, when Anthony stopped calling. He was forever on the phone, always checking in." Angie hunched over the counter, hands to her mouth. "Then, all of a sudden, nothing. No calls."

"Let me check with Len at the hospital. He had an emergency. I don't mean to alarm you but—"

"Don't bother, Gina," Angie said, sitting up. "This was no accident. Finally, after I'd stood around worrying myself to death, Jason convinced me to call the airport. My kid has more sense than I do. The airport manager told me there was no Gulf Stream jet on the field. Never was."

"You have got to be kidding," Gina said.

"I wish." Headlights flashed across the window blind, Angie leaped up and rushed to the window. Seconds later she was back in front of Gina, shaking her head.

"There was no flight plan for any Gulf Stream whatever filed out of Dallas. That's where Anthony's brother was supposedly coming from. He was to meet a United flight from Los Angeles. The Tamblyns were supposed to be aboard." Angie shrugged, spreading her hands wide. "My guess is, Anthony got cold feet and just couldn't tell me."

"But why would he call and say the plane was delayed?" Gina asked. "That's not change of heart. That's heartless."

"All I know is, the airport manager was very nice. I suppose he felt sorry for me. He checked every small airport in the South. There was no Gulf Stream anywhere." Angie's shoulders sagged. Her expression was drawn.

"Where is Jason? How's he taking this?"

"In his room, packing. I'm going out to look for Anthony. Jason's staying with his buddy, the kid who lives one building over. I could understand it if Anthony wanted to call it off. After all, we don't really know each other that well. It's the way he backed out that kills me. It isn't just me. He had to drag Jason into this. My son must be totally confused. Every man in his life has disappeared. First his dad, then his grandfather, now Anthony." Angie rose and went down the hall to knock on the door of Jason's bedroom. "Don't forget to pack your toothbrush, sweetheart," she said.

"Hi, Hon," Gina said as Jason appeared, a backpack slung over his shoulder. He was dressed in a flannel shirt and faded soccer shorts. Wordlessly, Jason bent to give Gina a hug.

"Oooooh," Gina sighed. "Tell me. How many inches did you shoot up this week?"

"I think I shrank," Jason said, his shoulders drooping, bearing his mother's defeat.

The Don Juan Con

Gina hugged him around the waist. He refused to look her in the eye. "Hey, this is the pits. Anthony's been rotten to you both. But none of this is your fault," Gina said.

Mouth crimped, feet dragging, Jason headed for the door.

"Gina, I apologize. I didn't even offer you a drink," Angie said. "Please help yourself while I walk Jason over to Danny's. I'll be back in ten minutes." As Jason preceded Angie out the door, she murmured, "Thank God for Danny. Those two have been inseparable ever since we moved in here," and her gray eyes filled with tears once more.

CHAPTER 6

Friday August 21, 11 p.m.

Gina eased her new Lexus sedan, a present from Len, into the street. The leathery odor of it, mingled with Gina's spicy Fendi, created a glitzy redolence that made Angie feel soiled and despondent.

"Hotel or hospital?" Gina said in her New Yorker's imploded voice.

"Forget the hospital. It was no accident. The first thing I did was check the emergency rooms."

"Now Angie, you know that's not what I meant," Gina said, pushing a mop of wiry hair off her freckled forehead. "By the way, where are we going?"

"The Registry, downtown."

"Would he still be there?" Gina said, raising one dark eyebrow. Gina's delicate, girlish face was full of mugs and movement, and in this case sympathy. Angie found herself soaking up Gina's warmth. Her friend had a nurturing personality. She was the complete mama to her three youngsters, girl scouts, misfit teens, elderly shut-ins and her husband, a busy gynecologist. The mama in Gina also had a no-nonsense side.

As she turned from a side street onto the Tamiami Trail, Gina said, "If I were you, I'd start thinking setup. The way Anthony ran out

25

doesn't suggest he simply got cold feet. There's this Gulf Stream story. It suggests some kind of scam, Angie. It just has to be. In which case this is no time to be coy. What we need to be worried about is whether it's you who shouldn't be in the emergency room. Suppose you caught something."

Angie's eyes widened. "Of course not. We never went all the way."

"Thank God for small favors," Gina replied.

"Funny, he was pushy in every other way but that," Angie mused.

"Probably impotent," Gina said as she stomped on the accelerator. "So it isn't sex he was after. What was it?"

"A wife who would fit in," Angie said, fastening her seatbelt, as Gina gunned around three cars in the slow lane. "Anthony was totally wrapped up with his powerful family. He thought I just wouldn't cut it with—with his precious Mama Regina."

Gina pulled a long face. "Give yourself a break, Angie. If anything you are too classy—too elegant—for him."

"Thanks for the vote of confidence."

"Listen, sweetheart, he may very well have been after your money," Gina said as she sailed through a yellow light.

Angie laughed. "Money? What money? I could hardly support Anthony's lifestyle. Not with a showroom that's still two years away from turning a profit. I'm still paying off my bank loan, as you well know." Stuck behind a pokey pickup and cut off by a truck on the inside lane, Gina swung to the outside lane and passed both vehicles on the right, flinging Angie into the door panel as she cut back into the middle lane.

"Problem is, the way you do things, Angie, you just look expensive. Besides, you're a Pelham—"

"Which means exactly nothing as far as Anthony is concerned. I have a very small trust fund, that's all. Everything else is tied up in a horrible wrangle that evolved when Daddy died just as he was going public," Angie said, fastening her seatbelt. "Besides, I never mentioned my mother much to Anthony. She never gave two hoops for society. On the other hand, Anthony's mother is a stylish decorator. Regina Abruzzi would consider my mother a frump. Mama owns two pairs of jeans. Orcas mink is dressy to her."

"Orcas mink?" Gina said, jamming on her brakes. She'd been about to run another yellow light and changed her mind when she saw a patrol car at the corner. "Sorry," she said to Angie, who, except for her seatbelt, would have been pitched into the dash.

"It's okay, Gina. You don't have to run every light in town, you know."

"I can't wait to get my hands on that bastard," Gina said, slashing air with the side of her hand.

"Save it, Gina. That cop is watching us."

"Maybe he'd like a smack upside the head," Gina said.

Both women giggled. The funny part was, wiry Gina with her matchstick waist was nobody to mess with. She held a second-degree black belt in karate.

The light changed. Gina eased forward circumspectly. "As I was saying, this Orcas mink is a hand-dyed Indian sweater. Made from natural wool. You never wash them."

Gina laughed. "Just hang on to your sense of humor and you'll make it, hon."

Angie shrugged as she watched the blur of strip shopping centers and palm trees whizzing past on Plaza Boulevard. The charm of DeLeon was in the colorful awnings installed on the front of nearly every shop. At night they were lit up from underneath and from the roadside these awnings blurred together, trailing streaks of glowing color in the dark. Watching the banners of red, green and yellow unfurl on the canvas of the night, Angie felt as if she were locked into some unreal plane, perhaps a time-lapse photo. Or maybe she was sandwiched on some microchip playing out a fictitious life in virtual reality on some vast CD-Rom. At any rate, the unreality of the scene matched the emptiness of her mood.

After a few minutes' silence, Angie said, "Come to think of it, Anthony did seem a little miffed that I didn't say a thing to my mother about the wedding. After all, family seems to be the center of his very existence. You know, I called Mom on the phone. I was going to tell her about him, but her voice was so dead, I just couldn't bring myself to talk about my own happiness. The eerie thing is, Mom knows she's depressed. In her mind, she realizes what the trouble is, but emotionally, she can't respond. Isn't that scary?"

"Is she seeing anyone?"

"She goes to a psychiatrist. She's on tranquilizers, but so far nothing seems to help. Ask her about anything, Island politics, blackberry picking, the summer fest, even Jason, her darling grandson, and she just passes them off."

"Maybe getting ready for a wedding would have picked her up." Gina eased off the Boulevard, following the signs for downtown DeLeon.

"Could be. I don't know. It's just that I had this gut feeling that Anthony would be a little much for her to cope with right now."

"Look at it this way. Maybe it's a blessing," Gina said. "Imagine if your mother were sitting here right now."

"Awful. She'd have been devastated all over again. The shock might have pushed her over the edge."

There was a lapse in the conversation as Gina eased along through jaywalking crowds of teens and students leaving a concert in Founders' Park on the edge of downtown.

Finally, Angie said, "How could Anthony have been after me for money? He did nothing but shower things on me from the moment I met him. I've still got five hundred in cash he gave to me for the plane ride."

"Odd, when plastic is so much safer these days."

"Anthony always had a lot of cash. He handles cases from clients who pay in cash. Some of them didn't sound all that savory, now that I think about it," Angie admitted.

"All the more reason not to carry cash. His clients would be too tempted to recycle their assets."

"He was well aware of that. It's why I let him put cash in my bank account."

There was a long pause as Gina eased up to a stoplight. When the light was red and the big sedan stood still, Gina turned to her, eyes wide in puzzlement. She shook her head: "I hate to say this, Angie, but I definitely don't like the sound of that."

CHAPTER 7

Friday, August 21, 11:30 p.m.

The DeLeon Registry Resort was an opulent establishment with marble floors, Chinese urns, tapestry sofas and tropical art. The night manager was in a white tux. His name was Harl Westwood, a somewhat supercilious young man with killer blond looks punctuated by dimples that he seemed keenly aware of as he checked the computer screen.

"Mr. Abruzzi checked out at two p.m.," he said.

"Did he leave a forwarding address?" Gina said.

"As a matter of fact he didn't," Westwood said, raising one eyebrow. "But if he had, I would not have been at liberty to give it out."

Angie's eyes narrowed and lips pursed as she spoke to Gina. "Anthony checked out even before he dropped me off at the salon."

"Did he say where he was going?" Gina asked.

Across the hall, double doors opened. People in formal wear spilled out the door, women in long gowns of black and white, crimson and gold, the men in tuxes. A bevy of young women in matching royal blue gowns was followed by a bride and groom. Angie gasped as her eyes trailed the newlyweds out the door.

Gina took her arm. "Look at it this way, hon. At least the groom wasn't Anthony."

"Come to think of it, Mr. Abruzzi did mention attending a wedding," Westwood murmured.

"For instance, his own?" Angie snapped. "You're certain when he checked out?"

Westwood betrayed a modicum of tact. He kept his mouth shut, though Angie could practically see curiosity written in neon letters across his forehead.

"Mr. Abruzzi befriended one of our managers. She may know something," Westwood said. "One moment please." He disappeared into his office and returned shortly with a woman in a black uniform trimmed with a white apron, collar and cuffs. "This is our banquet manager, Lucy Sandoze."

Lucy was a very nice Hispanic woman with brown eyes deep as pools. The pools welled with sympathy as Sandoze heard Angie out. She pressed Angie's hand between both of hers as she talked.

"Mrs. Reynolds. This I do not understand. There must be some terrible mistake. Not an accident, I hope? Mr. Abruzzi kept telling everyone who would listen about his wedding plans. He was madly in love with you. He talked about the Park Avenue wedding. He told of the Greek Island honeymoon. We learned how the private plane would come this evening to bear the wedding party to Manhattan. Everybody in the hotel talked of the fairy book wedding, even the other guests."

"That's how they convince you," Gina hissed as they crossed the lobby, weaving their way through the members of the wedding party.

"Who?"

"Con artists, Angie. They are persuasive because they believe their lies themselves."

"How could Anthony be a con artist? He was always spending money on me," Angie said, brightening. "Don't you see what this means? If Anthony wasn't for real, why would he bother to tell perfect strangers such a tale?"

"Maybe to convince himself he was for real?" Gina said.

"I simply can't believe that," Angie said. "I believe something terrible must have happened to Anthony. I think we should go to the police."

"Fine," Gina said. "It's your call."

CHAPTER 8

Friday, August 21, 11:45 p.m.

The calls came all at once: a convenience store robbery, a loud party, a domestic dispute and a mugging. But when intake officer J. Randapolis finally had time to hear Angie's story, she was sympathetic:

"Men!" Randapolis snorted. Her dangling earrings jumped. She leaned over the railing of the dais she sat upon, between her twin oracles, a blinking switchboard and a squawking radio. "Jilting a lady ought to be a lynching offence," said this orange-haired officer in blue. "That's my opinion. However, there's no law 'gainst a man changin' his mind. Now, if your fiancé is missing in action, the law gives him three days to hide. Meanwhile, you got to agonize whether his buddies got him drunk, or whether he's just a louse." Checking over her shoulder to see if anyone was listening, she leaned over the dais and whispered: "If that don't beat all, I don't know what, but that's regs for you. Come back first thing Tuesday morning, and it'll be my pleasure to file a missing person report."

Gina stepped in close and with a hand shielding her mouth said: "What if it's a con job?"

"What makes you think that?" Randapolis said, her brass earrings clicking.

"Funny business at the bank," Gina murmured.

31

The Don Juan Con

"Uh huh." Randapolis peered at Angie over the tops of the harlequin glasses she lowered: "He broke her heart and stole her money? If you ladies will have a seat, I'll see if Lieutenant Vensure is free."

"Gina, let's get out of here. What's the use? They can't help us," Angie pleaded as soon as they were out of earshot. Instead, Gina dragged her to a seat on the perimeter of a Greek revival rotunda where officers came and went, clicking their heels across the city seal laid in mosaic tile, ignoring clusters of dispirited people milling about.

DeLeon was serious about crime—from an architectural standpoint at least, Angie noticed, even while arguing with Gina about the nature of her complaint. "Gina, you must be crazy. I haven't got any bank records with me. And besides, I don't see how Anthony could steal money from me. He kept putting money in my account."

"Face it, honey," Gina said gently, continuing the argument that had started in the car. "You said Anthony also took money out of your account. Suppose he got greedy and helped himself to your money as well as his own?" Gina rummaged through her carryall and brought out a pack of Lifesavers. "Have a lemon, Hon," Gina said.

Angie shoved the Lifesavers away and stood up as a tall, spare man approached them. His rumpled linen jacket flapped from his broad shoulders. "Joe Vensure. Fraud division," he said. He had a high forehead emphasized by a widow's peak, a strong, bony face, and a shock of wiry dark hair cut long. There was something low key about his measured way of speaking and easy stance. Vensure made Angie think *college professor*, not *cop*.

"I'm Angie Reynolds," she said, extending her hand, but wishing she hadn't. "And this is my friend, Gina Goldheim," she said, pulling away, embarrassed by the fact that his plate-sized hands were warm while her fingers were icy.

"Mrs. Goldheim," Vensure said. There was an awkward silence as Gina waited for Angie to speak.

"Fraud?" Angie finally stammered. "Is that what you call the fix I'm in?"

"Whatever fix are you in, Mrs. Reynolds, it must be gnarly," Vensure said softly. "Whenever officer Randapolis can't figure out what's happened, she calls on me to sort things out."

As they approached the dais, Randapolis sounded a buzzer as she answered a phone call. Vensure swung open a paneled gate and they entered a long corridor lined with tiny rooms, all of them occupied with people sitting around small tables. "A busy night we have here," Vensure said. "Must be the lunar influence."

"Is that really true?" Angie said.

"After eight years in this business, I'm convinced something is in our stars," Vensure said. His lopsided grin lifted one corner of a wide, full mouth.

They entered an open bay lined with desks, only one or two of them occupied. A man on the phone wearing a shoulder holster was saying, "Can you tell me again how it happened?"

Vensure led them to one of the few private offices around the perimeter of the room. As they entered, Gina dug Angie in the ribs and nodded to the brass plaque beside the doorway: Chief, fraud division.

As opposed to the stark, institutional setting of the outer offices with metal desks and cubicles, Vensure's office had a decent wooden desk in it and a leather sofa, which he offered the women. He slipped into his own high-backed, upholstered chair and offered them coffee from the spiffy drip pot on the console beside his desk.

"Fresh brewed," Vensure said. "Or would you care for instant cappuccino?"

"No thank you," Gina said.

"Coffee, please," Angie said. "Do you have an aspirin?" she whispered to Gina as Vensure poured coffee into small china mugs.

"Are you feeling all right, Mrs. Reynolds?" Vensure said. "Can I get you some water?"

"I'm holding up under the circumstances," Angie snapped. *Oh God.* Why did she sound like a bad case of PMS? Ignoring her attitude, Vensure produced a bottle of Evian water and poured some into a paper cup.

"Thank you," Angie said, calmed by the civility which Vensure treated her. "I'm very upset. I didn't mean to be rude."

"No problem," Vensure said. He waved a piece of paper in his hand. "I gather from what officer R. said, your fiancé has been missing a few hours."

"It's been eight hours since anyone has actually seen him," Angie said, "But he did call me at seven p.m."

"And?"

"He said the jet he was to meet was delayed."

Vensure shrugged and shifted back in his chair. "Mrs. Reynolds. Your fiancé is a lawyer, or so I understand." Vensure's broad forehead wrinkled as one eyebrow tented up. "You can hardly rely on an attorney to show up in court on time, let alone a social engagement."

"Anthony said he was meeting a Gulf Stream," Angie said heatedly: "There was no jet. I checked it out with the airport."

Vensure tapped his coffee stirrer against his teeth. "So maybe his client lied to him and showed up on a bicycle instead."

"The plane was Anthony's brother's. He's a software publisher. His friends, Nate and Iona Tamblyn were supposed to be aboard. We were all going to fly to Manhattan tonight."

"Tamblyn. The karate guy?" Vensure said, rolling his chair inward, and picking up his pen.

"Yes," Angie said.

"That we can check on. Most of these movie people have private security networks. Vensure jotted down Tamblyn's name. "So far what you are giving me, Mrs. Reynolds, leaves us back at square one. Missing person. As I'm sure officer Randapolis told you, it's too early for us to file a report."

"Well," Angie said, twisting the aspirin tin Gina had handed her, "Gina thinks this is important. As I told her, I let Anthony put some cash in my bank account—for safekeeping," Angie said. "Gina is very suspicious."

"I guess it would depend on whose money it was," Vensure said.

"I assumed it was his," Angie said.

"All right. And so how much money are we talking about?" Vensure said as he doodled on his pad.

"I don't know," Angie said. "He made three or four deposits. Maybe seventy-five hundred altogether."

"What was the biggest deposit?" Vensure said, looking up at her, his hazel eyes gazing at her. It was a neutral gaze, not hostile, from which she discerned that Vensure wasn't condemning her.

"Thirty-five hundred, maybe," Angie said. "To be sure, I'd have to look at the deposit slips."

"Now, Mrs. Reynolds, did you make any withdrawals?" Vensure said softly.

"Anthony did. Why not? It was his money. He'd wire the money to his law firm in New York."

"Do you have the transfer records?"

"No, but I'm sure the bank will. Anthony was very careful to tell me every time he made a withdrawal."

Vensure rocked back in his chair, locking his hands behind his head. "So Abruzzi was free to make deposits to and withdrawals from your bank account?"

"Yes, that's right. After I introduced him to Ned Wadlow at the bank."

Vensure's arms dropped. He stared down at his note pad. "Now,

Mrs. Reynolds, you've known Mr. Abruzzi for how long?"

"Four days," Angie said, her face flushing.

"And you became engaged."

"He was perfectly wonderful to me," Angie said. "He comes from a large, loving family. He—"

"Mrs. Reynolds," Vensure said softly, quieting her with a steady gaze. "Love happens. To the lucky or the unlucky as the case may be. For your sake, let us hope he's a for real guy who got cold feet. No reason to be hard on yourself."

"His mother must have said something," Angie said.

"Maybe you're not Jewish," Vensure suggested.

"Anthony's Italian."

"Okay, so maybe you're not Catholic," Vensure said.

"We went by the Registry, where he was staying. The banquet manager told us that Anthony told everyone in the hotel about our wedding. To me, this means something terrible must have happened to him," Angie said. "He drove a Hertz rental car. Surely you can check that out?" She rummaged in her wallet and pulled out a scrap of school notebook paper with LQT36C scribbled on it.

"How did you get this?" he said.

"My son remembered it. He and a pal were playing a license plate game one day."

"All right, Vensure said. "I can run this down. But while you are here, if I were you, I'd take a peek in my bank account just to be sure everything's tidy."

"What am I supposed to do? Get Ned Wadlow out of bed?"

"Seaboard has an auto teller hotline. Let me get it for you," Gina said. "We bank at the same branch," she said to the detective.

"Impressive," Vensure said as Gina tapped out the number from memory.

"Not really, Gina said sheepishly. "I use a hotline all the time. I never could balance a checkbook."

"Let me check this Hertz number out," Vensure said, leaving the office. "What kind of car?"

"A white Lincoln Continental."

Angie picked up a ceramic figure from Vensure's desk. It was a jar lid in the shape of a head with flap ears serving as handles. The back of the skull was oddly flat, the lips were full and fleshy, the chin was short and under slung, and the eyes were closed. It was probably fifth century Mayan, perhaps from a burial urn? Now what would a police detective be doing with it?

The Don Juan Con

"Angie!" Gina hissed. "Pay attention, can't you please, dear? I'll need your mother's maiden name, the last four digits of your social security number, and the numbers of your checking accounts."

CHAPTER 9

Careful to close his office door behind him, Vensure sat down at an empty desk next to the burly detective in the shoulder holster who was still on the phone. First things first. He logged on and ran a search on Angie Pelham Reynolds.

"Thank you for your help, Ms. Elder," his colleague, Lonnie Barrett, wheezed. Barrett perpetually sounded as if his vocal cords were snagged on a barbed wire fence. "And God bless you, too." As he put down the phone, Barrett stood up, bent his head to one side and slapped the upside ear with the flat of his hand. "Whooeee. That woman like to talked my ear right off."

"Any good news?" Vensure muttered.

"Naw. That poor ole lady ain't got a clue where her skank-ass nephew is."

Vensure shook his head. "Tough," he murmured as he squinted at the screen. Just as he figured, Mrs. Reynolds was clean. Not even a moving violation. Not so much as a parking ticket. This didn't appear to be one of those cases where the woman got mad at her boyfriend and wanted him jailed purely for spite. And obviously, Mrs. Reynolds was stuck on this erstwhile attorney. Despite plain evidence to the contrary, she seemed unwilling to believe her fiancé was anything other than what he claimed to be—a well heeled, well connected and high profile lawyer.

He punched in a few codes and switched to the regional computer bank shared by most of the larger law enforcement agencies on the Gulf. Nothing that seemed pertinent came up. If the boyfriend was a true swindler, he should have seen similar complaints about this Abruzzi. Unless he was just starting his tour of the area. The trouble with these sweetheart swindler cases was, women would let themselves get taken, rather than admit they'd been jilted.

He pushed the escape key and shoved back his chair, his mind on Angie Reynolds. Even with bloodshot eyes and mascara dribbling down her tearstained cheeks, she was a stunner. She had marvelous hair, the deep, milky amber of iced tea in a glass. Skin the color of honey. He could see her square face with the thick, straight brows, the strong nose and lips and gunmetal gray eyes. She was thirty-three years old, looked to be going on twenty-four. Finding dates could not possibly be her problem. Her problem was picking the wrong guy. But why? In what way was Mrs. Reynolds' life out of joint? In his eight years on this beat, he'd run into forty, maybe fifty of these swindler cases. The scam artists came down here to enjoy the sunny winters, just like everyone else. They lavished money on women, promised them the moon, gained access to their bank accounts. A good one could romance several women in a given town over the weekend, and then clear out with their cash before their bankers found out that their so-called deposits were simply bad checks.

It wasn't so much the psyche of the criminal that he found so fascinating. The con artists were simply a kinder, gentler class of psychopath. It was the plight of the victims that intrigued him: how these swindlers had unerring instincts for the vulnerable side of their victims. Just what was out of joint in this gorgeous woman's life? She didn't appear to be one of those self-conscious beauties that couldn't handle good luck. So what was it? As he stretched back in his chair, musing, arms clasped behind his head, he felt Lonnie's breath on the back of his neck.

"What'cha got there in your leather-lined lair? Somebody with fingers in the till down there to the Junior League?"

Grinning, Vensure stood up. He was a full head taller than Lonnie, and he clapped his buddy on the shoulder as he headed back to his office. He'd partnered with Barrett back in their early years on patrol. He loved the guy, in spite of the constant ragging he took from Lonnie when he'd drawn fraud duty, while Lonnie was tapped for the more glamorous narcotics squad. In the beginning, he'd been disappointed. It had rankled him at the time—until Joe realized there were certain advantages to being out in what some of the guys called "La-La Land," and others referred to as the Country Club beat. Regular hours, for one thing. Less chance of being shot. And then there were the victims.

There were merits to meeting them. Cases like this. Perfectly upstanding, decent women, whether cosseted, spoiled, naive, desperate, or whatever, who got themselves into trouble, women who were brought up to expect kid glove treatment and who were going to get it. That was how the new chief, Captain Arnold Damon had put it to him. The chief had actually stuffed a white glove, a badge of Vensure's office, in his breast pocket when he'd given him his promotion. The beat came complete with the leather sofa, a judge's castoff chair, oversized ashtrays, and his own coffee machine.

No doubt Vensure could requisition bonbons if he'd cared to go that far, but that's what the chief wanted. Damon, the first black police chief in the history of DeLeon, had the backing of Mayor Stiles and the blessing of the city council. For this week anyway. Damon owed his job to the first white female police chief, one Miriam Benson, hauled in from Newark. Benson had shaken the good 'ole boys to the core and they'd had to buy her out of her contract at a very hefty and embarrassing sum. By comparison, Captain Damon, with his only slightly blemished record, was within the reach of the city's newly butchered budget.

Vensure headed back to his office, determined to do his best for Mrs. Reynolds, which was in fact, very little, of course. Quite often, victims of these swindlers simply suffered in silence. Angie Reynolds might choose to go away as many of these women did. Mrs. Reynolds was too stunned to know what hit her, much less recognize the implications. These would sink in, soon enough.

CHAPTER 10

Sarasota, FL
Sunday, August 23, p.m.

Tired of a discouraging day, Anthony picked up a half dozen Florida newspapers including the DeLeon Journal and the Miami Herald and went into a deserted bar in the Manatee Mall, just around the corner from the Hilton. The happy hour crowd had gone home to dinner.

His morning jog had yielded no leads. The personals were a dead end. The afternoon happy hour had been a bust. Nothing but paunchy guys bragging about their golf scores. Anthony was depressed. Sundays were terrible. You had to scrounge like hell for a date. As a last resort, when a day yielded no mark, he'd hit the malls, shopping for women, and it was amazing how few of them there were to choose from on a Sunday.

Anthony ordered a mimosa and leafed through the Journal first. Damn. There it was, the lead item in the community news section: Astrologer Found Dead. Thank God, it hadn't made the front page. Whitman, whose clients included politicians, entertainers and financiers, was found in her home late Saturday by a neighbor, the story said.

"Damn," Anthony muttered again, out loud. Supposedly, they were to have been gone on their wedding trip for ten days. That would have saved him. But wouldn't you know? Some buttinsky just had to go over

40

to Maria's hideaway and snoop around. A neighbor's child, selling Girl Scout cookies. Saw the body through a window. Anthony was enraged. The kids people raised these days! This was the last time he'd buy any of their damned mints!

His chest tightened. He began to sweat. Through blurry print, he managed to get "death is still under investigation" out of the next paragraph. He fumbled a nitro pill out of his pocket, plunked it under his tongue and sluiced it with the mimosa. Not the best combination, but this was an emergency.

As the pain receded, he began to think more clearly. Let's see now. The accident happened Thursday night. She was found late Saturday evening. That helped. The coroner would have a hard time establishing a time of death. As for clues, what passed for a police department in Banks would have a very hard time, thanks to his magnifying glass and tweezers routine. He'd rearranged the scene somewhat, creating a scenario of how Maria's accident could have happened. Of course, this was no accident. As Maria would say, there were no coincidences in life. That was the entire meaning of her favorite book, *The Celestine Prophecy*.

No, Maria's death was a sign to Anthony. The truth was, after five years on the road, he had preserved very little of the capital he'd ripped off various women. What with the high overhead involved in the romance business, it was difficult to get ahead. And he also had to admit his gambling habit, fueled by his drinking, hadn't helped.

As the pain in his chest crept back to sleep, he sipped more of the mimosa as his spirits rose. God, he was a genius with women. It was a gift. If only he could go on the stock exchange and sell shares in his racket. He opened the paper to the inside page. As he drained the glass, his enthusiasm for his calling died away. Yes, he was a true journeyman. If Hollywood gave out Oscars for swindling, he'd have a wall full of them by now. But he was sick of the road. He was tired of living out of a suitcase—in his case three of them, each packed with a different identity. Damn, it was tough.

Though nobody would ever guess, he was fifty-six years old. He yearned for the pipe and slippers routine. It was tough to pose as the worldly widower, always the bridegroom and never the groom. He chuckled over his own sardonic joke, drawing a glance from the bartender.

"The Lockhorns always kills me," he said aloud.

He reached in his pocket for cash to settle the tab. Tucked in his billfold was a small Rolodex card. It was Jane Pelham's phone number.

The Don Juan Con

The one he'd copped from Angie's showroom while she was busy with a customer. The Pelhams had relocated to the San Juan Islands, north of Seattle.

In his mind's eye, Anthony saw Jane just as she'd been years ago. She'd stood on the dock, casting off the boat, while the child sat in the co-pilot's seat of the cabin cruiser. Jane with her regal bearing and corn silk hair would have mellowed into a lovely widow by now. There was a mark worth having—for good. Time had come that Anthony settle down. His heart wasn't the healthiest. Angina, the emergency room doctor said, where he'd checked in and then skipped after the hospital pharmacy had filled his prescription.

Yes, it was good to have a goal: the Pelham fortune. Besides that, he had never gotten over the loss of Jane. Never, in all of these years, had he really had feelings for anyone else, including Jane's lovely daughter. He was still angry with Angie that she didn't seem to want her mother at the wedding—never mind the fact that the wedding was a fake. On the other hand, this was a real stroke of luck. If Angie had indeed invited her mother to the wedding, he would never have had the opportunity to start over.

To woo the woman he'd once loved. He'd have to become a different person, of course, a better one. Hackles rose on the back of his neck as Maria Whitman and her dictum came to mind. It was no coincidence that Angie hadn't told her mother about him. It was simply meant to happen. Jane Pelham would be his, and he would love her, cherish her—or a reasonable facsimile of it—and she would honor and obey. Oddly, he'd have to do away with Anthony Abruzzi to make the deal. Once he'd done away with the mobster lawyer, he'd develop a new persona, a man truly worthy of Jane.

He felt better.

All he needed now was the front money to make it happen. He got the notebook out of his breast pocket. The DeLeon trip had been very worthwhile for him. There was the take from Angie. There was the donation from Maria Whitman. He'd had only one loser situation. He'd not done nearly as well as expected on the third one, the much richer widow.

He glanced at his Rolex.

The mall closed in half an hour. If he wasted any more time, he'd wind up working the singles bar scene, which he hated. They were nothing but meat markets, those places. The women all expected you to hop into bed.

He struck up a conversation with a well-dressed but plump young

42

woman in thick glasses at the self-help psychology counter in Barnes & Noble. She acted very jumpy and edged away from him at the first opportunity. Didn't that beat all? A woman lacking even the modicum of self-confidence it took to get ripped off. Maybe that mark should sign up for the Dale Carnegie School of Hard Knocks. Or take private lessons from Angie Pelham Reynolds.

The mall was closing. Security guards were letting people out the main entrance, effectively locking up on a day that had been a complete bust. As he wandered toward his car, he realized his thoughts were back on Angie and her mother. He had to block them out. It was a stupid fantasy. But suppose he *did* develop another identity? One worthy of Jane.

On the other hand, even if he could, then at some point, he'd surely have to pass muster with Angie, and that would be pretty tough to do. Even if Angie never confessed directly to her mother what had happened with the infamous Anthony Abruzzi, she'd bear the scars of their encounter for the rest of her days. And she'd be extremely suspicious of anyone who dared approach her mother.

Then again, there wasn't a good persona on the planet a little research couldn't crack. Of course, there were...*ways*...of taking care of Angie, if she did happen to get in the way. But that wouldn't be nice, now would it? Despite Maria Whitman's unfortunate accident, he didn't care for offing people. The whole idea was way too much. This scheme was becoming an obsession with him, and he knew he had to get off it.

CHAPTER 11

DeLeon, FL
Monday, August 24, 10 a.m.

The gold plaque behind Ned Wadlow's head was a blur. A tom-tom was beating inside Angie's right temple. Her eyes felt like sandpaper. It had taken three shots of Visine to get the red out of her eyes, but the whites were dull and yellow.

Ned buzzed his secretary. He murmured something. Coffee arrived. Angie sipped the caustic black liquid gratefully, though her stomach roiled. Since Friday night she'd lived on coffee—black in the cup, mocha-colored in her favorite coffee yogurt. She'd been able to keep no solid food down. She'd dropped seven pounds.

Angie sat on one side of Ned's pickled oak desk with her personal checkbook open, showing a positive balance, fifteen hundred, and thirty-eight dollars and forty-seven cents. Not much. Most of what she had was in her Southwest Influences account. Or was supposed to be.

On Wadlow's side of the desk was a printout showing in graphic terms what she had learned at the police station Friday night. Both accounts were disasters. Her personal account was overdrawn by forty five hundred dollars. Meanwhile, her business account had a scant seven hundred dollars left in it. This should have been ten thousand, seven hundred. All together, some fourteen thousand dollars was unaccounted for. And then there was all the shopping for the wedding Angie had done on her credit cards. Over the weekend, she and Gina had scrambled to stores, returning as much of the merchandise as they could.

Fortunately, Gina was a personal friend of Shelly Swentz, who owned Glitz in the DeLeon Mall. She took back the Armani Suit, even though Angie had worn it once and had it altered.

"Please Ned," Angie said, waving a fistful of deposit slips. "These were all good faith deposits. Anthony told me they were for cash."

Wadlow's attempted smile was a ghastly death's head grin. "I'm afraid faith doesn't go far in the banking business, Mrs. Reynolds. You may very well have thought that Mr. Abruzzi was making cash deposits. However, except for the very first one, the day you brought him in here, all of his subsequent deposits were personal checks. Bad ones, unfortunately."

"But the withdrawals Anthony made were all for cash?" Angie said. "What about wire transfers?"

"We show no wire transfers at all," Wadlow said. "I've managed to trace a few of the deposits. They came from an account in Banks. Do you know anyone in Banks, Mrs. Reynolds?"

Angie shook her head.

"Well then," Wadlow said, "I'll call the bank manager over there and see if the client will make good on those checks, which all came in NSF. Clearing those would help your position a bit."

Angie stared at Wadlow's lapel pin, a Philly's baseball logo overlaying the wave-shaped logo of the DeLeon Chamber of Commerce. A new stadium was supposed to revitalize DeLeon's economy, even the Palm Square Mall where Angie had her gallery. A few years after the stadium was built, the baseball strike had killed business. But what was the matter with her? Why were her thoughts straying?

"Feeling well, Mrs. Reynolds?" She heard Wadlow's voice dimly, as if from a bad connection at the other end of the country.

"I'm sorry," Angie mumbled. "I haven't slept since Thursday night."

Wadlow nodded, his face stiff. "Now tell me again, Mrs. Reynolds, how Mr. Abruzzi got money out of your account." He folded his hands across the printout in a bankerish gesture that Angie read as dismissive and judgmental, especially as accompanied by Wadlow's formal tone. This morning she's no longer Angie. This morning, when well overdrawn due to the skullduggery of a swindler, she is Mrs. Reynolds.

She spoke. No sound came out. She cleared her throat and tried again. "As I already mentioned," she said in a whispery voice, "I gave the money to Anthony. As far as I knew, I was giving him his own money."

"I see," Wadlow said, stroking his beefy chin.

"He was robbing me," Angie said. "Can't you do something? Aren't you insured?"

Wadlow leaned back in his chair. He wore a solemn expression bespeaking some counterfeit maturity. For the first time in the three years she had known him, Angie noticed his piggy little eyes.

She read the message on Wadlow's tight lips: "I'm afraid the bank can't help you, Mrs. Reynolds. You introduced Mr. Abruzzi to us as your fiancé. In cases like this, the bank trusts the judgment of a valued client. My teller's log shows that last Friday afternoon you gave Hilda Waters verbal permission for Anthony to make withdrawals from your accounts."

"Anthony told me on the phone it was a few hundred dollars," Angie said.

"Our log shows that you gave the okay to do as Mr. Abruzzi suggested, not specifying any amount."

"I don't recall that at all," Angie said. "I was worn out. I was in the middle of a steam treatment at the Salon DeLeon when the call came in. I couldn't hear Hilda very well."

Ned had a smarmy look on his face—sort of curdled sympathy as he leaned across the desk, and his tone softened. "Off the record, I wondered whether this character was good enough for you. Nevertheless, I've always respected your judgment. I assure you I'll do my best to get the examiner to see things your way, but I'm afraid the insurance company will take the position that the bank was not at fault here." He looked at his watch. "You'll have to excuse me, Mrs. Reynolds. I'm late for a loan committee meeting."

Angie took the hint, forcing herself to speak around the lump in her throat. "I had that ten thousand set aside to pay the quarterly installment of my business loan, Ned. As you know, it was due this morning, and if it weren't for this swindler, the note would have been paid."

"Oh. That. I'll get you an extension," Wadlow said. "No problem. Take a week, maybe ten days. Let us know how you want to pay off the loan."

Angie was stunned. "Pay off? Why the balance isn't due for seventeen months."

"That I realize, Mrs. Reynolds. However, the note was written at the bank's discretion. It becomes due at any time without notice. Under ordinary circumstances, the board might choose not to call the note. However, we've just been taken over in a merger as you know. We've been advised to call in all local loans that are not one-hundred percent."

"Ned. You're talking about thirty seven thousand dollars. I can't raise that in just a few days," Angie protested.

Wadlow gave her a strange look. "You must have some other resources, Mrs. Reynolds, perhaps a credit card. After all, you were able to afford a Hermés case and a gold Rolex watch for your fiancé?" He phrased this remark delicately. Nevertheless, to Angie, it sounded sarcastic.

For a moment, Angie, dizzy with shock, could not form a reply. "What?" she stammered. "I never bought Anthony any briefcase, let alone a Rolex, a gold one, no less. Ned, you have to understand something. I'm a Pelham. We're Northwesterners. We take a dim view of status symbols. I had a hard time accepting Anthony's notion that he needed all the props to impress potential clients. He led me to believe these thing count in New York."

Then, registering what she thought Ned must really mean, she sank back in her chair. "Do you suppose he charged a Rolex watch and a Hermés case on one of my credit cards?" She felt clammy and queasy all at once. She clamped her teeth and pinched her lips, sealing her mouth shut. Suppose she barfed right in front of Ned?

Looking alarmed, Wadlow came around the desk. "Mrs. Reynolds, maybe you should see a doctor," he said as he helped her to her feet. Wadlow walked her all the way to her car and then suggested he get George the security guard to drive her home. But Wadlow's sanctimony served mainly to anger Angie. Three years she'd banked with Seaboard. She'd reduced her note faithfully on a quarterly basis. Summarily escorting her out the door was the best they could do?

"How is your mother feeling?" Ned said as he opened the door.

Angie's eyes widened in horror. She had forgotten that Ned had met her mother last time she was down here. "My mother is a sick woman," she blurted. "Hearing about my problems could kill her. As you may know, my father was going public with Sea Escape Designs when he had a heart attack. Now there's a lawsuit. His CEO is suing the board of directors for control of the company. They want to bring in an outsider. All the family assets are tied up. I'm not about to ask my mother to bail me out."

"Yes, of course," Wadlow said unctuously.

By this indirect conversation, Angie and the banker came to an understanding. If Angie were to square her account with Florida

Seaboard, it wouldn't be via her mother's checkbook.

Wadlow attempted to look cheerful as he waved Angie off. In the harsh Florida sunlight, the banker looked pale as an escapee from the underside of a mushroom. A ten-day extension? She had already been to every bank in town to get a loan in the first place. Who would refinance for a woman who had been swindled? Without saying it outright, Wadlow had neatly suggested to Angie that her future as a businesswoman in DeLeon was finished.

CHAPTER 12

Monday, August 24, 9:30 p.m.

He was headed for the perfume counter at Maison Blanche, but spied a tall, attractive woman in her fifties in Parvey & Sons, Jewelers. The store looked right for a scam. It was a tony place fitted out in mahogany paneling, dove gray carpeting and cases lined in royal blue velvet. Here was opportunity. If he didn't make it with the woman, at least he could launder some cash.

His hit was draped over the back of a tall, bentwood stool, swinging one foot, bending the ear of the manager. Obviously, she had nowhere else to go on a lonely Monday night. She was dressed in black culottes and a black vest with Spanish-style piping, Karen Kane, if he was not mistaken. One of those saucy matador hats with a short brim was perched on the side of her head.

All right!

Anthony strolled into the jewelry store. He checked out the woman some more. Her hair was shoe polish black and stylishly bobbed, cut out around the ear to leave spiky sideburns. Her makeup was expertly applied in the most up-to-date fashion. Her lips were carefully outlined in a darker shade of red. Her eyes were shadowed in two shades of bronze but slightly downplayed to her brighter mouth. She wore an emerald solitaire on her left hand, sported a lizard portfolio tucked under her arm and swung pointed cowboy booties on her big feet. As he passed her, Anthony sniffed the spicy perfume she wore. In short, as with so many women, there was an attar of assets all about her.

Come to think of it, the next great perfume could be called just that: *Assets*.

Ignoring the chatting pair, he approached a case of diamond tennis bracelets, studying them carefully. Unable to tear himself away from the gabby woman, the manager left him alone several minutes too long. Anthony raised his arm and cocked his elbow to check his Rolex, which garnered immediate action.

"May I show you something, sir?" the manager said in la-de-dah English, his lips barely moving in the long, patrician face. His watery eyes were cushioned by what looked like mini air bags.

"The middle bracelet," Anthony said.

The manager pulled it out of the case and set it out on a brightly illuminated velvet pad. "Twenty-one diamond chips set in fourteen carat gold."

His closely cropped silvery hair topped off by a bald spot gave him the tonsured look of a monk. Anthony thought of a certain pal of his, Father Barenski, the priest who had once tried to rescue him, but that was in another life. Jeez. He was losing his concentration.

"Twenty one's the wrong number. Knowing my sister as I do, she'll count every diamond and think I'm putting her down," Anthony said. Since the manager looked rather like a butler, he addressed him as one. "What else have you, my good man?"

"One moment, sir," the manager said. He locked the tennis bracelets up and went to fetch a tray from another case. From the corner of his eye, Anthony could see the woman taking an interest.

"Pardon me, but that's a wonderful outfit you are wearing," Anthony said, catching her eye. "You look so much like my sister you could be my sister. Madelina loves the western look."

"I'll be darned," the woman said in a gravelly drawl.

"Texas," Anthony said.

"Galveston."

"Oil?"

"Real estate."

"My business," Anthony said.

"That right?" The woman straightened in her chair.

The store manager brought out several more elaborate bracelets. "Wait a minute. I'm confused. One bracelet looks pretty much like another," he said to the woman.

"Go with the most expensive one," the woman said.

"Now I *know* you are just like my sister," Anthony said. This earned him a chuckle. "Not University of Texas, are you?"

"Nossir."

"Well, neither is Madelina." The woman laughed outright as Anthony introduced himself.

"I'm Nettie French," the woman replied, nodding languidly.

"Well, now Nettie, I really do need your help on this. Sis turns thirty tomorrow and she's down in the dumps. Of course you wouldn't know anything about turning thirty."

Nettie snorted. "Honey, I don't remember turning thirty, and you pack a mean line." Nettie bestirred herself. She slouched off her stool. With unerring instinct or long practice, she plucked the most elaborate bracelet off the velvet tray and dangled it in front of his eyes. "This here's quality. I could have spotted it from across the mall."

"Would you mind trying it on for me, Nettie?" Anthony said.

"Sure? Why not?" Nettie said. She was a big woman, tall enough to meet him eye to eye. He was close enough to see how a thick coating of makeup beneath her lower lids erased a telltale puffiness. Nettie was not nearly as healthy as she looked.

Nettie extended a freckled arm, leaving Anthony to do the honors of removing the heavy, cuff-type bracelet she was wearing. He fumbled around with the safety chain, deliberately keeping a very delicate pressure on her wrist just a shade too long.

"Hey, you're not some guy with a thing for wrists, are you?" Nettie protested.

"Depends what the wrist is perfumed with," Anthony said. "Opium's a favorite of mine."

"Knows his nose, don't he?" Nettie drawled to the store manager, who snorted disapprovingly.

This egged Nettie on. Did she have something going with this stuffy monk? Nettie really got into it. She decided to try all the bracelets. Anthony shifted his feet. She was making him nervous, taking so long, but she had a sense of humor. He liked Nettie. He needed her companionship—not to mention her assets.

After trying three bracelets, Nettie chose the first one. It had small gold tennis rackets with diamonds caught in the filigree strings.

"Notice how each diamond has been incised like a mini tennis ball," the manager said.

"I'll be damned," Anthony exclaimed. "Have you ever seen anything like this, Nettie?"

The Don Juan Con

She gave every single diamond her meticulous scrutiny. "Flawless cutting," she pronounced.

"Nettie, it's so perfect on you that I'd buy you the piece, if only I knew you better," Anthony purred. "Maybe I could buy you a drink?"

Nettie looked at her watch. "A quick one, I suppose. I have a dinner date this evening."

Sure, honey—a date with the comedy reruns and Lean Cuisine, Anthony told himself. He pulled a wad of bills from his pocket and thumbed off a stack of hundreds. "I'll have to have this engraved," he said.

The manager got out the instruction form for the engraving. "Tell you what," Anthony said. "I'd better think about it overnight. I've got to come up with the right phrasing. Maybe Nettie's good at sentiment."

"I'll give it a Texas try," Nettie said.

"You're on, Tex," Anthony said.

The manager handed Anthony his card.

"Lawrence Q. Parvey? My pleasure," Anthony said.

"And mine," Parvey said grudgingly.

Pocketing Parvey's card and the receipt for the cash sale, Anthony took Nettie's arm. As they headed across the fountain court at the center of the mall, Nettie pointed out the real estate office where she worked as a commercial broker.

"Wonderful," Anthony said. "I'm from New York. I'm here to look for some property for one of my RIT clients."

Fortunately, another of his marks in real estate had educated him on all the lingo—as in, Real Estate Investment Trust. That was before he'd hit her for seventeen thousand five hundred, which, unfortunately he'd blown the next week at the greyhound track, or he wouldn't be working right now.

CHAPTER 13

DeLeon, FL
Tuesday, August 25, 10 a.m.

Angie was up on a ladder with hammer and nails, hanging a huge "Prices slashed!" banner across the back of her shop, with the help of her shop manager, Sondra Byrd. The sign was an ugly yellow and black, which clashed with the elegance of Angie's establishment, and most definitely with the elegance of Sondra, holding the banner.

Angie's assistant was a tall, spare woman in a raw silk dress with perfectly coiffed silver hair and a pair of reading glasses hung around her neck. "Angie, I wish you'd wait until my nephew could come help us."

"I can't afford to wait another minute," Angie said. "The jackals are closing in."

Angie was trying to nail the sign into the square pediment on top of a column. It had been Alan's idea to use columns as decorative bays down both sides of the long, narrow shop, suggesting the porch of an old Southern mansion. Some bays were draped with pillows and fabric samples, others displayed arty versions of household objects: vases, pillows, ashtrays, china and silver.

The printer who sold her the horrid banner assured her that in this case, ugly didn't matter. Screaming yellow against black was the most visible combination of all. She tried to focus on the nail between her fingers but she was overcome by dizziness and the nail grew two heads. She was squinting at the nail, trying to figure out which head to hit when she was interrupted by a sonorous voice.

"Allow me."

Angie turned around on the ladder. She found herself eye-to-eye with Lieutenant Vensure. He was dressed in a shiny, sharkskin jacket with the sleeves rolled up over a neon green muscle shirt. A pound of gold chains was draped across his hairless chest.

"Miami Vice?" she said, her eyes narrowing with bemused disapproval.

He grinned. "Pardon the flashy duds. I'm headed for a stakeout of a certain establishment."

"A den of flesh peddlers?"

"That would be vice. I'm just checking out a five-register drinking establishment where the city collects sales tax on only three."

Angie stumbled down the ladder, missing a step. Vensure grabbed her: "Easy now."

He retrieved the nails Angie had dropped on the velvety carpeting, took the hammer, mounted the bottom rung and whacked the nail into place.

"Thank you," Angie said as she watched Vensure move the ladder, take the other end of the banner from Sondra, mount the ladder and tack it into place. "Frankly, I never figured you for a hammer-and-nails type."

"I've driven a nail or two in my time," he replied, handing her the hammer. On the way down, he peered at one of Angie's favorite pieces, a painted metal decoration of koi on lily pads that looked as if they could swim right off the wall. "Nice things you have here."

"You haven't seen anything," Angie said. She led him toward the back of the shop where a series of tall glass cases held collections of hand blown glass: the usual whales, seashells and paper weights, perfect as gems. On shelves positioned in one of the columned bays were bowls, funky and enormous, shaped like huge, squashed hats.

"There's a national renaissance in art glass," Angie said. "Collectors of pieces like these stand to make a fortune on them in the years to come. It took me a year to get distribution from enough artists just to do the displays. There's nothing like this anywhere else on the Gulf."

"I believe it," Vensure said, wincing as he fingered a price tag on a whimsical Tiffany lamp shaped like a toadstool.

"But it's all over. The bank is shutting me down."

"Wouldn't stand behind you, would they?" Vensure said, shaking his head.

"It has nothing to do with me personally. That's what they tried to tell me. It's just that they've been taken over in a merger." Angie said bitterly, "The board called all local loans which don't have perfect records."

"It figures," Vensure said.

Angie noticed they had an audience. Several women had come in. One of them held fabric samples up to the light but it was obvious that the lieutenant was the goods she was inspecting.

"Don't look now," Angie whispered, "But would you like an after-hours job as a shill?"

"Thanks, but I have a day job as a shill."

"Shall we adjourn to the back room?" Angie said, leaving Sondra to mind the showroom.

He followed her.

"Sondra's a wonderful woman. She volunteered to help me out, even though I may not be able to pay her," Angie told the lieutenant as she opened the door to the back room.

The anteroom was crowded with fabric sample books, shelves of lamps, pillows, vases and ashtrays. Angie offered Vensure a seat in an Italian leather chair with a matching ottoman.

"It fits," he said, swiveling side to side, a big grin on his face. "Most chairs are built way too short for me."

"I can offer you a very deep discount on it," Angie said as she poured him coffee.

"Thanks, but I'll have to check with Victoria on the state of my finances," he said.

"Victoria?" Angie said, passing him a delicate cup. "Somehow, I never had the impression you were married."

"Victoria's not a wife, she's a passion," he said.

"Lucky girl." Angie's hand shook as she raised her own cup to her lips, noticing Vensure's concerned stare. "Forgive me," she said, "I'm so wired on coffee that I'm no doubt a danger to myself and others. I ought to be booked and locked up. My life is a shambles. I can't eat. I can't sleep. My attorney has advised me to file for bankruptcy."

"Personal or business?"

"Both."

"Ah," he said, sipping his coffee. "A double hitter."

"The business may survive, if I can raise enough money in this sale to pay my quarterly installment. The judge might give me a break and set aside the bank's foreclosure for the term of the note," Angie said.

"But of course, I have to raise enough extra to pay my attorney first."

"Hey, good luck," he said. "You deserve some. I know you have your troubles, Mrs. Reynolds—"

"Please. Call me Angie."

"My pleasure. I'm Joe."

"Please Joe, I hope you can nail this guy."

"We have nothing so far," Joe said, setting down his cup. "But you can consider yourself lucky on one score."

"What's that?"

"Swindlers of this type are rarely violent. In one of the other cases the department is handling right now, the lady couldn't give evidence on account of her boyfriend shot her through the head."

"Oh God, the poor woman," Angie said. "I suppose I am lucky. I wasn't even raped, except in the head. But look at it from my perspective, if you would. If I were a corpse, you wouldn't make me come back on Monday with better evidence."

On Friday night, he'd told her they couldn't proceed without the bank records. It was noon on Monday before she could get the documents to the police, at which time Joe wrote up a full report, but told her not to expect much. Anthony Abruzzi was, no doubt, hundreds of miles away by then.

He shrugged. "Hey, I happen to agree with you. But the law's the law. We've done what we could. We put out a bulletin on this character. We called Nate Tamblyn's Hollywood agent. The star couldn't have been in Dallas on Friday. He's on location in Japan. We sent out a composite of this Abruzzi, with his silvery hair and hooded eyes. Generally speaking, however, these sweetheart swindlers never stick around too long."

Angie did a double take: "Swindlers plural?"

"Yes, Ma'am. There's a whole class of these smooth-talking flim-flam artists, real Prince Charmings."

Speechless with shock, Angie closed her eyes. Her stomach did a half-gainer. She was just a statistic.

"Angie? Are you all right?" Vensure said.

"Everyone keeps asking me that. So, am I so crazy?" Angie asked, throwing up her hands and shaking her head. "I guess I am. Okay, so? I gave you his license tag number. What did you do about that?"

"The Continental he was driving," Vensure said. "He turned that in at the Hertz rental agency at the airport at six p.m. on Friday evening. Nobody answering his description got on any of the flights. Most likely, he simply rented another car, but there are twenty rental agencies out there and we haven't located it."

"No doubt he headed for Miami," Angie said.

"Or the Keys. Or north on the Trail. Or right up I-75. We just don't know at this point. Of course we were able to get his driver's license number off the rental form. So far, no match on that. Looks like it's a fake."

"What about the address and the phone number I gave you?" Angie said. Four Hundred Park Avenue. Supposedly it was a penthouse in the same building where his parents had an apartment.

"We're still working on that one."

"That leaves his answering service and his mobile phone," Angie said.

"The answering service woman said he paid cash for ten days of service. He gave the same Park Avenue number as his home address. Evidently, she does have a log of his calls, which she said she'd be happy to produce when she sees a court order."

"How long will that take?"

"Awhile. We won't get a warrant for that until we can prove probable cause."

"What about me? I'm not a probable cause? This man has destroyed me. He's ruined my son's life. Jason's friends call him? He won't talk to them. His guidance counselor called me from school. He's a zombie in class. Here's a good student who has simply zoned out. The school wanted to know if we had some family problem they should be aware of." Her eyes filled up and her nose began to run.

Joe handed her a tissue from the box on her desk. "Here we go," he said gently. "Back to our perspective?"

Angie nodded.

"Here's the catch. You gave Abruzzi access to your bank account. It's how these swindlers work. I could have the guy in jail right now, but he'd hire a good attorney—"

"With my money," Angie said.

"With *your* money. He tells the judge he was madly in love with you. He has witnesses."

"So that's why he told everyone he met about the big wedding?"

Joe nodded. "So the judge figures it's just a spat between lovers and tosses us out of court. That's why your case alone goes nowhere. We have to find other victims and show a pattern of behavior."

Angie was too stunned to respond. She grimaced and shook her head.

"Now then. We keep working over what clues we have and hope

for a break. Yesterday, you mentioned a briefcase and a wristwatch."

"A Hermés case and a Rolex Presidential," Angie said, dabbing at her eyes. "I don't think he had them when he arrived. Otherwise, he would have flashed them around. Yet both Ned Wadlow at the bank and his security guard, George Jensen, told me Anthony bragged that his fiancée had bought them. The funny thing is, as far as I can tell, he charged neither one to me."

"Excellent," Joe said. "Somebody around here's going to remember the sales. This we can work on."

"Why would Anthony tell Ned that I bought them?"

Joe rocked back in the chair, which made Angie cringe. He tapped his stubby pencil against his brilliant white teeth. "Could have been telling the truth. Look at it like this. He said his fiancée bought him a Rolex and a Hermés case. He never said *which* fiancée."

Angie slumped in her chair, fingers cradling her face. "My God!"

Joe shifted in his chair, leaning towards her. "You never can tell, Angie. We do know Abruzzi didn't spend all his time here in DeLeon with you. He was gone for long blocks of time, taking depositions, or so he said, which we know for sure he wasn't doing. So we can assume he was doing what he enjoyed the most—romancing girls. It's not uncommon for a sweetheart swindler to have two or three simultaneous weddings heading down the aisle at the same time."

"Look in Banks," Angie murmured.

"Banks?"

"I mean the town. East of here," Angie said. "You remember I said that Anthony made cash deposits in my account? I showed you the entries on my check register?"

"That's right," Joe said. He wrote BANKS into his notebook and underlined it.

"Several of these deposits match up with checks in my account. They didn't clear. My bank sent them back. Ned Wadlow said they came from an account in Banks. That's only fifteen minutes from DeLeon."

"There you go," Joe said. "These swindlers will take checks from one woman and deposit them in the account of the next victim."

"And she's buying him a Rolex and a Hermés, while I'm treating him to a Corneliani blazer," Angie said.

"Right," Joe said. "Now you've got it." He rose, as did Angie. "You take care now. If we do find out more, we'll let you know."

"Wait a minute," Angie said. From the top of her desk drawer, she pulled a manila envelope. She handed it to Joe. "This has handwriting samples from the mushy note he sent me. Would you believe I thought it was the most romantic gesture? Fool that I was."

"Let's not blame the victim for this," Joe said softly.

"You are very kind, Joe," Angie murmured. As she gazed into his eyes, cast green by the light of the muscle shirt, she read compassion. He didn't seem to think she was just a ditzy woman that threw her money away.

"I wrote up a log of our activities as best I could remember, and a profile of his personal habits," she said. "He likes musical theater, jazz performers and Italian expressions. *Capisce*? He loves lawyer jokes."

Joe emptied the stuff on the desk but handled it only with a handkerchief. A gold button rolled across the desktop. He prodded it back into the envelope with the end of his pen.

"That's a souvenir from the new blazer I paid for. Anthony was furious when the sleeve button came off. I was supposed to sew it on but he said the navy thread I had was the wrong shade of navy. Can you believe that?"

"It was a ploy, Angie. His extreme perfectionism was just another way to keep you off balance."

Joe stuck his tiny notebook in the inside pocket of his sleazy jacket, making no move to pick up the envelope or its contents.

"Don't you need the evidence?" Angie said.

"You hang onto it, Angie. Things have a way of getting misplaced in evidence rooms. We can't use any of this unless we find Anthony, and he's got a head start. If we get an indictment, it'll be important, however. If you do elect to prosecute, that is."

After Joe left, Angie spied the florist's card Anthony had sent with roses on their second date. "Now that I've found you, I'd be a fool to let you go," he had written. She was enraged. She rushed out the door after Joe.

She could see the back of his head bobbing over the crowds. He was two doors away by this time.

"What do you mean, `*If*?" she screeched.

Joe neither stopped nor turned around. No doubt he couldn't hear her over the Muzak playing in the mall. Or else he simply didn't care.

CHAPTER 14

Sarasota, FL
Tuesday, August 25

Maybe Nettie's pregnant? Anthony thought. He watched her finish up a pound of prime rib. This was on top of an order of clams casino and three trips to the salad bar. Watching her eat, he lost his appetite.

"I always did have difficulty keeping my weight up," Nettie announced.

The waiter approached. He had black button eyes and enormous ears. A gigantic mouse was waiting on them. Nettie ordered the famous Chart House mud pie from Mickey. Nettie had also ordered the most expensive cabernet on the menu and drank most of it herself. Anthony had a scant glassful but put his hand over his glass as Mickey tried to pour him some more.

"Dessert for you, sir?" Mickey said. The waiter had a deep bass voice.

At least he didn't squeak, Anthony thought as he replied: "I couldn't." He patted his belly. "Unlike my lovely companion, I've never had any difficulty keeping my weight up."

As the rodent left the table, Anthony touched Nettie's arm, exactly the way he'd watched her touch Larry Parvey yesterday. "Let me tell you about what happened to me today," he began, careful to pull back his hand at the end of every sentence, the way he'd seen Nettie do with

Parvey. "Two of my clients are fighting over the same center. I'm bound to represent both to the best of my ability. I have no idea who will wind up with the property. I just hope I don't wind up in cement shoes."

"So? Sell it to the client you like the least. So much commercial property is overvalued these days," Nettie sighed. She stared dreamily at him through her windowpane glasses.

He pressed her arm lightly again; silently blessing the book he'd learned the trick from. Always mimic your contact's body language. He would recommend this technique highly to any con artist. He cocked his head. "The commission on that one sale alone would set me up for the rest of the year."

"Terrific," Nettie breathed as she wolfed down a whopping helping of mile-high mud pie topped with whipped cream that the mouse sidled up with. Watching her made him wonder whether he had packed any bicarbonate.

"Well?" Nettie demanded between mouthfuls. "Did you write an offer?"

Anthony tossed his napkin on the table. "So what happened? I couldn't think straight. I couldn't care less about a shopping center. My thoughts were on you, Nettie, how I'd like to taste your warm, sweet lips." He reached for her arm again. The one holding the spoon, the better to lap up the melted ice cream. It was him or the pie.

"Anthony?" said Nettie, her face warping. "Ya'll are giving me hot flashes, and honey, I mean of the whoop-de-do kind."

Anthony's cellular phone rang. "God. Sometimes I'd like to launch this thing into outer space," he said, releasing Nettie, yanking his flip phone out of his coat pocket. "Abruzzi here." His tone softened: "Oh? Certainly. Put her on."

"My sister," he mouthed to Nettie.

"Thank you, darling. I knew you'd love the bracelet. In fact, I had help from a dear friend of mine picking it out. Her name's Nettie, and you ought to see her. In fact, you will see her if I have anything to say about it. I'm trying to talk her into flying into New York for Mama Regina's anniversary."

Smiling broadly, he watched Nettie's face for a reaction, but something was wrong. Nettie was frowning.

"Ah, I understand, Sis. Bambino calls you. Kiss bambino for uncle. Happy birthday. *Arriverderchi.*"

As he hung up, Nettie was glaring at him through narrowed lids. He reached for her hand. She yanked it away.

The Don Juan Con

"You'll never guess what I did with my afternoon," Nettie said. Her eyes were slits and it looked as if her eyebrows might tie in a knot any minute.

What the hell? he thought.

"My watch stopped again. I had to drop by Larry's store. You'll never guess what bracelet was sitting out there right in plain sight?"

Anthony whacked at his forehead with his open palm. "Is that what this is about! It dawned on me first thing this morning that I couldn't possibly get the bracelet to New York in time for Madelina's birthday. So I called uncle Mort. He's got a big jewelry exchange right on the edge of the diamond district downtown. You know. Where the Hasidic Jews trade their diamonds? It's so colorful to see them in their long black coats, their side curls and fedoras. You must see it, and what a treasure I'm going to find for you! Come with me to New York, Nettie. You simply must."

This explanation mollified Nettie only slightly: "Larry Parvey said you'd heard from your father that your sister's husband got her a tennis bracelet already."

Anthony gave her a sly grin: "This Parvey guy is sweet on you, huh? I can't say that I blame him."

Nettie recoiled. She sank back in the padded upholstery of the horseshoe banquette he'd picked, the better to romance Nettie close range. Now he watched the indignation wash out of her expression, replaced by a pious declaration of innocence. "There's nothing between us. Not since he was still in his twenties and had a big thatch of curly hair. We all called him Nest." Nettie giggled until the tears ran. She was potted. It was clearly time to get her home.

"Let me tell you, honey, the guy is crazy about you," Anthony said. "That's why he doesn't like me so much."

"He said you demanded a refund."

"Honey, Uncle Mort gave me five hundred off on the same bracelet. What was I gonna do? I did fib a little to Parvey, but you gotta help a guy save face. *Capisce?*"

"*Ca-peech*," Nettie said, grinning. She loved learning Italian slang, even if she did pronounce it as if she had the hiccups.

Anthony reached into his pocket and pulled out the check Parvey had given him as a refund. "Now here's my problem. I want us to have the best weekend either of us has ever had. But I was daydreaming over my business today, and you're to blame, Nettie."

Anthony pulled Nettie's hand into his lap and stroked her forearm. "It's all your fault I didn't make it to the bank. You've got me dazzled.

So what I'd like to do is present you this check. Then we'll take out some cash and we'll spend it all on us, down to the last penny."

"*Capisce*," Nettie said, snatching the check.

It was Anthony's turn to laugh. He couldn't help but like old Nettie. There was a little of the con artist in her.

CHAPTER 15

DeLeon, FL
Wednesday, October 21

The ball of light came first. Then the blast. Streams of water stung her skin, sharp as needle pricks. She catapulted through the air and landed in a rain of debris. A whirling pool sucked her down. She was coughing, choking. Lungs bursting, but something pulled her up into an acrid stench. All around her was a sea of flames. She swirled through the slick water, awakened shrieking. She found herself clawing at the white eyelet covering on a canopied bed. Where was she? Sweating and shivering at once, Angie glimpsed a pale, disheveled presence in the mirror on the dressing table.

A knock came on the door. She was awake now. She knew what knocks meant. It meant another creditor to humiliate her, a process server or a certified letter, attesting to the foolishness of her judgment.

Gina Goldheim popped her head around the door. She was dressed in a teal jogging suit with insets of purple and red. A damp sweatband contained the mat of thick curly hair that seemed to want to spring off her head. Gina's flushed face registered anxiousness.

"Angie? Are you all right? Shall I call Len?"

What was she doing in Gina Goldheim's fancy bedroom? Oh that's right. She was penniless, a pauper now. She remembered coming out of the bankruptcy hearing, her lawyer on one side, Gina on the other. Suddenly the midday heat overwhelmed her. The sidewalk heaved.

She had awakened under the bright lights of the emergency room where they'd stretched her out on a gurney. Yes, and Len Goldheim in a white coat mouthed words etched in her mind. "Acute stress. Depression." Syringe in hand, Len had said, "This will make you feel better. You must get some sleep." Depressed was she? God, she was losing it, just like her mother.

"You don't look so good, sweetie," Gina said, tenderly testing the back of her hand on Angie's cheek.

"Only a nightmare, no crackup. Not yet," Angie mumbled. "I used to have that terrible dream all the time. Now it's recurring again, like a disease, some herpes of the mind."

Gina giggled, hugging her. "Atta girl. Come have coffee and bagels. Now that I've tortured myself jogging, I deserve to pig out, and you had better start eating. Len remarked this morning that you are beginning to look like a broomstick with boobs."

Shakily, Angie crept out of bed. She reached for the jeans thrown over a chair. "God, I scared myself in the mirror. I look like some third world refugee."

They settled in Gina's kitchen. It was white and sleek, except for the checkerboard floor and all the fifties kitsch Gina collected. The dining table was chrome and Formica. The plates were garish Fiesta ware. There was even a family portrait of the Goldheims out in the yard, washing their Springer, done in Norman Rockwell style. For the first time in weeks, food had taste. The orange juice was rich, the coffee aromatic.

"Have you see Jason this morning?" Angie asked.

Gina flashed her an odd look. "He's at the hospital. Working. Remember?"

"Oh, yes. I forgot." Len had found Jason a messenger job at the hospital gift shop. It seemed to perk him up a bit. "It's nice to see somebody in the family employed."

"Don't start, Angie," Gina frowned. "I simply can't take you when you start hitting on yourself."

Stung, Angie put down her coffee cup. Though Gina's words hurt, Angie knew her friend meant well. Angie folded her napkin. "Gina, you are entirely right. I've been staring at the wall too long."

After helping Gina clean up the kitchen, she returned her room and unpacked the one battered suitcase she'd allowed herself. She'd sold off her good luggage and everything else she owned. Her Italian, hand painted pine pieces, paintings and furnishings, reminders of a once sumptuous married life, had brought in a scant ten thousand dollars, but it all went out to pay her lawyer and her creditors. She had called every creditor and tried to come to terms. But rather than working with her, they'd turned vicious, forcing her into bankruptcy. Florida law allowed her to keep her condo, but Angie had had to rent it out to make the mortgage payment. She hadn't had time to look for other work. Closing up her business had consumed her energies.

Angie sat on the canopied bed as if sheltered in a tent or a cocoon as she went through her things, sorting out her life. Peace washed over her, even an odd sense of adventure. It was time to unpack, set up, rebuild.

At the bottom of a box full of family albums and pictures, she came across a Moroccan leather passport case her mother had given her when she'd graduated from the Pratt Institute. Why hadn't she sold it? Maybe she could get ten dollars for it? Should she notify the bankruptcy judge that she was holding out?

Inside the case was her husband's death certificate. She snapped it shut. That was why she had avoided it. One day Angie had been married to J. Alan Reynolds, a rising young architect, and the next she was a bemused widow with a child whose husband had choked to death in a French restaurant while dining out with clients.

That was eighteen months ago. Daddy had been there for her then. David Pelham had been going public with his company. Nevertheless, he had helped her keep her sanity through the bad time. Now her father was gone, her mother was pining, and another man had betrayed her. This would never have happened if Daddy were still alive. Angie sat on the bed staring through the French doors at the Goldheims' hibiscus garden. Call Mom today, she reminded herself.

She opened a large manila envelope. What was this? Oh God, the evidence. What was done to her! For a moment, she thought about pitching it out. No way, she decided. Instead, she dumped the contents on the bed. On top were the charge advice notices from the Banks account of a woman named Maria Whitman. That much she'd found out from Joe. He'd told her he'd tried to question Mrs. Whitman, who owned Rising Sign, a New Age bookstore in Banks, but her employees said she was on a trip to Europe. The Park Avenue address hadn't checked out, either. It proved to be a dog-grooming parlor for the wealthy canines of the rich.

"A dog grooming parlor," Angie said aloud. Was that Anthony's cruel joke? Isn't that how he viewed her? As a dog he'd had clipped and dressed at Salon DeLeon while he stripped her of her cash?

She found Joe's number on the back of the envelope. She hadn't heard from him in a month. The officer who answered said the lieutenant wasn't in. She didn't leave her name. What was the use? She slammed down the phone.

No, it was high time she tracked down this Maria Whitman herself. Surely she was back from Europe by now. Maria must be feeling just as rotten about herself as Angie did. Together they could make the police listen to them.

It took Angie less than three minutes to convince Gina that they ought to do lunch in Banks, which had recently been written up in the DeLeon Journal as a colorful cow town of a place twenty minutes east of DeLeon where you could get decent catfish and cornbread.

"Catfish I can do without," Gina said, as she backed the Lexus out of the garage, "But Angie, it's so good to see you doing something, that I'd drive you to Hong Kong for shark's fin soup if that's what you wanted."

"It isn't catfish and cornbread we're going for, it's alfalfa sprouts and insight. We're going to explore the New Age today," Angie said.

CHAPTER 16

Banks, FL
Wednesday October 21

If cowgirls got the blues, they turned to the New Age. Or so Angie quickly surmised. Apart from the ethereal types in sandals and backpacks who usually frequented such stores as Rising Sign, there were numerous Stetsoned lovelies trying on crystal teardrops, buying greeting cards and signing up for sessions with psychics, tarot readers and astrologers.

Gina promptly headed off for the aromatherapy section, where a young woman in a white gauze dress took tinctures from various bottles and dropped them on her wrists: mint, orange, eucalyptus and ylang, whatever that was. Angie watched them for a moment, but quickly lost interest. While she had a fine visual sense, her nose was less discerning. When she began to think everything smelled the same, she knew her senses were dulled and turned away to study the rest of the store.

The cash register rested on an elaborately carved oaken counter with angels carved in it. Angie waited while the clerk wrote up sales of *The Sacred Power in your Name*, *Crystal Balls & Crystal Bowls* and various greeting cards: "Kindred spirits," "For my soul mate," and "We must remember to believe in ourselves and each other."

When she finally had the chance to ask for Maria Whitman, the girl at the register seemed hesitant.

"Are you a client?"

"No," Angie replied, "But we have a mutual acquaintance."

"I think you should talk to our manager, Mr. Wyatt," the clerk said. "If you'd care to wait. He's finishing up a consultation."

While she waited, Angie amused herself running her fingers through baskets of polished stones, opal, amethyst and tourmaline. She inspected readymade Indian medicine pouches and a display of hoops stretched with nets and hung with feathers. Dreamcatchers, these were called.

"Do you have anything to snag nightmares?" Angie said to the girl in gauze.

"For my nine year old, it worked great," the clerk replied.

"I'd try one if I were you, Angie," Gina giggled. "Maybe it'll work on your inner child." Angie glared at her wiseass buddy and put the dreamcatcher back in the basket.

They waited another ten minutes. Finally, a fair and spindly young man made a rattling appearance as the heels of his black, silver-tipped cowboy boots rang across the hand-pegged floor.

"Mrs. Reynolds, I'm Russell Wyatt," he said. He wore a light gray, western-cut suit over a floral vest. His woolly blonde hair was tied in the back with a length of string tie. "I'm glad you've come. As a matter of fact, I had hoped to call on you long before this."

"So, I was right. Mrs. Whitman was hit by Anthony Abruzzi, wasn't she?" Angie blurted.

"Ma'am? Could we discuss this in private?" Wyatt murmured, his dark-eyed gaze boring in on her. "Mrs. Whitman was beloved by her followers. I wouldn't want to upset anyone."

"*Was?*" Angie said, as hackles rose on the back of her neck.

Without a word in response, Wyatt led her through a door to the back of the store, around a corner where a half dozen women in leotards were going through the swaying motions of a t'ai chi exercise class. They wound up in a darkened conference room where waftings of ethereal music mixed with a refreshing scent.

"Mmmm. What is that?" Angie said.

"Star sandalwood. An extremely pure grade."

"Vintage incense?" Angie murmured, biting down an urge to laugh.

Wyatt set a white tea bag into a Japanese cup and poured hot water over it. "This will help you relax," he said, passing her the cup. "It's a tedious drive in from DeLeon, isn't it? The vibrations on the roads are terrible this time of year."

"Vibrations?"

"Yes ma'am, the stray thoughts of people enduring their stressful vacations," he said with a hint of a smile. His eyes were creek-bottom brown, rich agate gems in a rough-cut face. His pitted complexion was rough as sandpaper.

"What is this?" Angie said, taking a sip.

"Ginseng," Wyatt said. As if fishing for trout, his delicate pale fingers played a tea bag through his cup. Here was one cowboy who had neither repaired fences nor punched cows within recent memory.

"How did you know my name?" Angie said, unable to contain her curiosity any longer.

"I managed Rising Sign Enterprises for Mrs. Whitman. Now I'm the executor of her estate."

"She's dead?"

"Mrs. Whitman recently had a very strange accident," Wyatt said. "At least that is what the coroner is trying to call it. I have my doubts."

"I'm so sorry."

"Yes ma'am. Eight weeks ago Sunday she was found, but the accident must have happened several days before that. Long enough that the coroner can't fix the time of death in any sort of helpful time frame. With all the upheaval, the bookkeeping was the last thing any of us thought to attend to. When I did finally find out that some checks of Maria's went into your account, and then didn't clear, I knew this was all wrong. I never in my life knew Maria to overdraw her account. Do you mind if I ask whether ya'll had some business together?"

"Not at all. I'd never heard of Maria Whitman. I got her home number from my bank," Angie said. "I called her two or three times. There was never an answer. Now I understand why. Evidently, we had a mutual acquaintance." She reached for the leather carryall she'd set on the floor but too eagerly. As the room began to spin, she closed her eyes, shaking her head. "I apologize. You must think I'm some dizzy dame."

"No wonder," Wyatt said. "If I may speak frankly?"

Angie stared at him. "Go ahead."

"I see that a number of unsettling events appear to have stirred up some very old, unfinished business. This is troubling you to the degree that you feel overwhelmed. You are drowning in these feelings." Wyatt's tone was soft, his eyes blank.

Angie shivered, folding her arms beneath her breasts and stroking her forearms, trying to warm herself up. "Drowning. Why do you say drowning?"

"If I knew how I know things, my life would be ever so much simpler," Wyatt said, with a sad smile. He peered deeply into her eyes, holding her gaze. Angie dropped her gaze, shutting out his intense stare. Her cheeks seemed to sizzle.

Angie's hands shook as she removed three checks from the manila envelope, one for two-thousand five-hundred dollars, another, for three-thousand dollars, plus a third for five-thousand five-hundred. All of them were stamped "NSF."

"Ahhhh," said Wyatt as he examined the checks. "This explains a good deal."

From a saddle leather portfolio, Wyatt pulled a bank statement, addressed to Maria Whitman. He fanned out a dozen checks and set them down beside the three sent back to Angie.

"Notice anything?" Wyatt said.

"The signatures. They don't look quite right."

"Forgeries," Wyatt said. "Rather good ones, but obvious even to you. Notice, for example, the 't' in Whitman. The way Maria always signed it, the top bar of the 't' was on top of the letter, like a roof, reflecting Maria's lofty attitudes. The bar of the 't' is at half-mast in the forgery. Whoever signed her name certainly isn't to be trusted."

"Tell me about it," Angie said. "Let's match the signatures on the checks with Anthony's handwriting." She pulled out a flowery card he had sent to her the morning after their first date, addressed to "My True Love."

"There," said Wyatt. "The same 't'—the same slant to the letters. Do you have any idea why these checks were deposited in your bank account?"

"I was conned," Angie said, "Taken for at least fourteen thousand dollars. I'm still not sure how much. I suppose he swindled Maria Whitman as well?"

"Yes ma'am. I think he got away with a handsome piece of Maria's change, not to mention her life," Wyatt said, his expression darkening.

"What happened?" Angie said, jolted in her chair by a spasm of fear.

"I believe Maria caught on to this Anthony fellow rather quickly," Wyatt said. His head dropped forward. His voice took on an eerie monotone. "But rather than being angry, she offered to help him," Wyatt murmured, his eyelids drooping as he talked. "She said she'd help him discover why he felt he should steal from her. There were more words. Muffled sounds. Then she screamed, and at that point fell—or was pushed—over her second floor balcony." Wyatt's eyes opened. "Maria has—or *had*—a lovely home on the Banks River, you know."

71

"He was supposed to be taking depositions," Angie said. "Instead, he's killing Maria Whitman?"

"It was days before anyone found her," Wyatt continued. "In the fall, she fractured her head on a marble planter in her foyer. 'Course when she was found, she appeared to have been alone."

Angie was stunned.

"Fact is, Maria was one to keep to herself. She was an astrologer with a national reputation. She did a big volume of telephone consulting. She often handled her most sensitive cases at home and wouldn't come into the store for days at a time. That explains why nobody at the store missed her at first. Then she called in and said she was taking a trip—"

"On a Gulf Stream jet to New York, I suppose," Angie murmured.

"I was in a Tibetan ashram at the time. Sad to say, I didn't even make the funeral. With nothing apparently amiss, the coroner ruled her death an accident."

Wyatt sipped his tea. Only a rattling of the cup and a tremor in his hands betrayed his emotion. "When I did arrive back in Banks and read the autopsy report, it didn't look right to me. The report said Maria appeared to have been drinking heavily. This just doesn't ring true. Granted, Maria had been a bit of a tippler at one point in her life, but that was before she came into her powers. After she turned professional, she never drank at all. Drinking interfered with her psychic energies, she always said. I've known Maria seven years, and she never kept liquor in her house."

"Anthony was a heavy drinker," Angie said. "If he was romancing her, he could well have gotten her started again."

"Could have been," said Wyatt. "I called the coroner about the liquor at the time, but he was unimpressed. Maybe Maria was a closet drinker. That was his explanation. Unfortunately, I never discovered about her missing money until two days ago. It was taken from a reserve business account we use to pay taxes." Wyatt set down his teacup.

"The day before she died, Maria took ten thousand dollars out of that account. So I went back to Maria's place and started looking for the money. All I've come up with so far is this..." Reaching in his jacket pocket, Wyatt pulled out a gold button. "This was on the floor, wedged under the lip of the planter where Maria hit her head."

"Well, that's certainly familiar," Angie said. She shook the envelope of evidence she'd brought over the table and a matching button rolled out. "I believe it's high time we get the police off the dime."

CHAPTER 17

Memphis, TN
Wednesday, October 21

Anthony leaned on the rail, surveying the crowd. The close harmonies of the Legionnaires were as thick in the air as the smoke from the cigar curling over his head. The Legionnaires, for God's sake. Who would have guessed they were still kicking?

And what lucky woman was going to enjoy his company for Fifties Night? He sighed, surveying the crowd aboard the Arkansas Belle Fun Cruise. Lots of grandmotherly types, too deaf for sweet talk over the thumping of the boat engine. A few delectable teens.

A leggy blonde strolled past, her cheeks peeking out beneath raggedy shorts, her calves perfectly formed above her cowboy boots. Anthony felt a pang of remorse. It was a regrettable fact of his line of work. Luscious youngsters were a waste of time. The only assets they could be charmed out of were not of the bankable type. He should be writing a book. Chapter Two of his New York Times Bestseller, Swindler's Bible: Avoid Penniless Kids.

As the paddle wheeler drifted away from the lights of Memphis, Anthony buttoned his jacket against the chill and strolled toward the bow. The sight of two women standing there gave him a start. They were tall and slender, dressed in gauzy dresses that blew against dark legs outlined by the deck lights. Despite the fact that the blonde one held a floppy hat on her head, tendrils of her loosened hair were whipping at her face. The other one's caramel colored hair was a thick, well-mannered shoulder length do. For an instant he saw himself playing with that hair, piling it up, pulling it down, framing the lovely, squared face. They were whooping with laughter, bending over. The younger one put her hand on the other's forearm and whispered in the blonde's ear and they laughed again, their voices drifting toward him. It was the Pelham women. They were laughing at him. His heart jackknifed. He slumped against the railing, gritting his teeth. A steward approached him, his black bow tie etched against a starched shirt front and red jacket.

"Are you all right, sir?"

"Fine," Anthony grunted. "Just getting my sea legs."

"If you need anything, just call."

"No problem." Clinging to the rail, he inched toward the women. The younger one stared at him. Of course it wasn't Angie. Not even close. He scuttled away, clutching the dew-dampened rail. What the hell was the matter with him? Why were the Pelham women breaking into his thoughts? He had to get them out of his mind. A game like his, concentration was everything.

As the Legionnaires soared into melodic harmonies that just didn't exist among the cowboy warblers and the heavy rappers, he realized he was still holding a lit cigar. He took a few puffs waiting for the pain to grind itself away. Finally, he spotted his mark. He tossed his smoke overboard and straightened his tie.

Chapter Three: Follow Your Hunches When Picking Your Hit. This one had a pixie haircut that reminded him of dear old Nettie French. He'd taken Nettie for close to forty large, and it was just too bad he'd had to move on so soon. Nettie had been fun. A real card.

This new edition was about six inches shorter, and not so expensive looking. She wore a blazer over one of those gauzy skirts. From this distance, however, the saddlebag on her shoulder looked to be good leather. The way she clutched the shoulder strap with two hands suggested that she was alone, and very defensive about being that way. Just broken up with her boyfriend, and perhaps out trying it on her own. That was his guess.

Still unsteady on his feet, he managed to weave his way through slow dancing couples. He caught up with her, as she was about to take the companionway stairs.

"Excuse me. Where might I find the casino?"

"B-deck is what I've heard," she replied, "One flight down. Not that

74

I've been there." She had big dark eyes and fine white skin. So what the bulk beneath the jacket suggested she was a bit on the hippy side? She'd do fine.

"Shall we find it together?" he said.

"Well, why not," she said. "This is supposed to be my lucky night."

"Luck be a dark-eyed lady in a pixie cut," Anthony said, treating her to his best leer, still powerful though his knees were weak.

The crush to get into the casino was such that he had to muscle a few old ladies aside to keep up with his mark. When she headed for the roulette table, he pushed in behind her. She stood through several rounds of the wheel, watching the action. Anthony was getting tired of this.

"So how's the lucky lady?" he said. "Have you cashed in yet?"

"I don't know how to play," she moaned. "I'm strictly from slot machines."

"Well, then, you are lucky," Anthony said. He fished a twenty out of his wallet, bought some chips. "They're yours to play as you wish," he said, introducing himself.

She proved to be Kay Larkin, a school librarian from Murfreesboro. When she threw him a dubious glance he told her to pick red or black. Or else go halvsies, which she did for the first round.

Then she doubled her money on black. She was hooked. She got a handful of chips, tried red for one round, then returned to black. As she struck again twice in succession her big black eyes turned shiny with greed and she couldn't seem to play fast enough. Over and over the same combination of numbers. Anthony's twenty bucks soared to three hundred and change. She groped in her big bag for her wallet and cashed in three hundred dollar bills of her own for another stack of chips.

Soon Anthony realized that he was feeling fine and that they'd attracted a circle of fans, who clapped and cheered as Kay won something in every round. They'd been at the table around forty-five minutes when the pot went from twelve to fifteen grand. The crowd was getting thicker and Anthony didn't like it. Suppose the boat started to list? He didn't really like boats very much. They tended to explode and such.

Then he caught a glint in the dealer's eye, or was it a shift in her hip? He couldn't quite pin down just what made him so uneasy, but he did know it was time to walk away. Roulette wheels could be rigged. A shift of a magnet under the table and the greedy gambler was history.

"Okay, Hon," Anthony said. "You've won big. Let's go celebrate over dinner."

Damned idiot woman. She'd won enough to make her worth his time, but he couldn't pry her away while she was ahead. Her string of wins began to falter. She started losing big. Every time he suggested they get out of there, the biddies in the crowd told him to go on and let her play. What was it to them if she was losing? In the end they walked away from the table with about five hundred bucks.

"I've never taken a chance on anything in my life," she chirped. "Those three hundreds are the first support payment from my ex. I waited so long for it that I learned to live without it. When some money finally arrived, it seemed like a gift. So I called the psychic hotline and the psychic said I'd be lucky no matter what I did with the money. Isn't that fantastic?"

"Swell," Anthony said. But for the crowd, he would have belted her. The dumb bitch couldn't distinguish between five C's and fifteen grand. He was thoroughly disgusted.

She offered to split the take with him, but he declined. He invited her for a drink. When they got to the bar he excused himself to go to the men's room, then slipped through a door to the employee lounge.

There was nothing in there but a frayed green sofa and a steward's jacket hung on a clothes tree. Anthony put on the red jacket, then curled face down on the sofa and went to sleep, dreaming of Chapter Three: Profit from Poor Prospects. First you build her up at the gambling table, then you rip her off.

CHAPTER 18

Memphis, TN
Friday, Oct. 22

The blonde in front of Anthony in the teller's line was perfect. She was a big woman with very broad shoulders, a narrow waist and a hard boy bottom. Her hair was pulled back in a fall, which flicked like a horse's tail as she talked.

"Would you happen to know anyone in need of used furniture?" she said to the teller in theatrical tones, as if the setting were not the Volunteer Savings Bank of Memphis on Gayoso and Third, but a repertory stage.

"No ma'am," the teller said, but the blonde went right on talking, "My mother took a spill, was in the hospital and they won't take her back in assisted living. I have to put her into a nursing home.

Though her performance was dramatic enough, nobody waiting behind the velvet rope seemed impressed. Anthony heard murmurs of annoyance, but he liked the girl. He thought she was far more interesting than the soft sculpture canvases on the wall, which were strips of orange tinted fabric meant to look like sunsets, or so he guessed. He'd picked out this institution because of its proximity to the Peabody Hotel, an easy walk north and west on Union. It was a busy bank, too. He'd stood in line for twenty minutes, and there were nearly a dozen people waiting behind him. It never hurt to have a gaggle of irritated customers in line when it came time to do his laundry.

Blondie was dressed in the latest designer country getup and tee-tered on her boots. Flashing oversize turquoise rings on three fingers, including the third on the left hand, she took forever to count her cash and stuff it in her tooled leather wallet. Eventually she finished up and sashayed past him. He took in the silver brads and the fringe on the front of her satin jacket. A hot one. Perfect. He opened his mouth to speak but clamped it shut.

He was in the wrong clothes. This woman was bait for silver-haired Anthony Abruzzi. Today, he was Raymond Tadischi, wearing his bald cap, doing cousin Anthony's errands. All of Anthony's silk boxers were in the hotel's laundry, leaving Raymond crestfallen right down to his Jockey shorts. Then he figured a way out.

"Excuse, Miss? Selling some furniture are you?"

"Oh yes. It's the second time Mama has fallen. The last time she came out of the hospital I thought she'd do fine, but they want her in a nursing home, and I'm so distressed." Her eyes were a fictitious blue, about the shade of his Cool Mint Listerine. He was ecstatic.

"I know how you feel," he said, pulling off his baseball cap, flashing the skin. Domes might not be so hot for romance but they denoted trustworthiness. "My motha is middle stage Alzheimer's. Three times she's wandered off into—"

He felt a tap on his shoulder. "The teller is waiting," hissed the woman behind him with the cane, the four shopping bags and the whiskers on her chin. He stared at the very long hatpin stuck into the floppy felt hat on her grizzled head.

"Please, madam, go on ahead," he said with a gracious sweep of his hand.

"The furniture?" the blonde woman said.

"That I personally couldn't help you on. However, my wife's cousin, Anthony Abruzzi. Also a New Yorker. Also down here for the exact purpose. He's moving his mother into one of the homes here."

"Ohhh," the blonde moaned. "She probably has her own things."

"Well, I wouldn't know. Most of Regina Abruzzi's things are clas-sical. On the grand scale. Anthony offered everything first to my wife. She took a look. It was all so ornate. One sofa would dwarf our whole condo. Sell it with the house. That furniture belongs in a castle. That's what Rosie told him right out.

"Rosie is right," the blonde said.

"Call cousin Anthony," he said. He patted down his coat pocket, took out one of Anthony's business cards and put the Peabody's main number and his room number on the back.

"Thank you, I'll do that," she said. Her eyes went all saucery, swimming in the whites.

"Betta yet," he murmured, "Let me get ya the numba. This man Anthony is always on the phone, always doing depositions. A workaholic let me tell ya."

"I'm Marci Trillin," she said, handing him her card. It showed her in leather and fringe, guitar in hand, sitting on a porch swing. Folk balladeer. Writer. Activist, the card read.

"*The* Marci Trillin?" he said. "Hey. Can I get your autograph?"

By the time the biddy he'd let go in his place had finished her banking, he had a prospect for Anthony. The day was looking up. He had started out in a very foul mood. That librarian on the gambling cruise had killed his average for the week, putting it well under fifteen. He picked up his sample case of class rings and approached the teller's cage.

"Nice lady," he said as he took a white envelope out of the inside pocket of his seedy brown suit and set it down in front of the teller.

"Isn't she?" the teller said as she removed the stack of bills from the envelope he handed her and began to sort and count them. "And she's done so much for her mother."

"Speaking of which, it's Papa Adolph's birthday," he said. "He's ninety-two years old and still the terror of the back nine at the Firestone Country Club. So I'm wiring this cash directly to his bank account in Monterey."

"They've had some awful floods there," the teller said.

"Papa won't be doing much golfing this week," he said.

"Thirty-five hundred," the teller said.

"Wire it to this account at Golden State Bank, Monterey," he said, handing her a slip of paper with his account number on it.

"Adolph Tadeschi?" the clerk said.

He nodded. "Pick out a new golf cart, I tell him. That'll keep him going another six months. That's the main thing. You gotta keep them active."

"I'll agree with you on that, Mr. Tadeschi," the teller said.

CHAPTER 19

Banks, FL
Wednesday, October 21, 4 p.m.

It was a stifling afternoon. Angie, Russell Wyatt and Joe Vensure were on the upper level of Maria Whitman's impressive split level home about eight miles off State Road 29, along the edge of the Banks river. It was a muddy but navigable waterway, engineered in modern times from what had once been a clear, meandering stream. The imposing white stucco house was set in a green pasture dotted with palmetto, saw grass and live oaks along the river's edge. Maria's home was a jewel of a place done in beige and taupe and filled with oriental screens, tapestries and bronzes.

The air conditioning was turned off. Though a live oak tree bearded with moss shaded the house, the interior was sweltering. Angie opened the sliding glass doors, which faced on the river and stood in the doorway of the upper level, lifting her hair off her damp neck. Odd, she thought, how a matching pair of gold buttons had finally taken the fancy of the police lieutenant.

Vensure had stripped off his linen blazer and tossed it over the back of a plum-colored leather sectional. He'd loosened the paisley tie of his denim work shirt. In this light, she noticed, there was something wolfish about the detective's sculpted face with its beveled, dimple-tipped nose. His knotty cheekbones were bastions for a pair of changeful eyes—now a deep, gunmetal gray—that served to illuminate Vensure's moods. Or was it simply that those interesting eyes of his took their cue from their surroundings? Angie couldn't say. She didn't know him well enough.

At any rate, his strong, bony chin was emphasized by a deep cleft, and his pointed eyebrows arched in skepticism as he heard out Russell's story. Then he asked the very question Angie had wondered about when Russell had told her the same tale.

"Maria Whitman, standing right about here, confronts someone— maybe this Anthony," Vensure said. He had a soft, unhurried way of speaking, and a predatory way of pacing while he talked. "She offers to help him. She's going to help him find out why he does what he does. She asks him how come he wants to clip her, and then take off with her ten thousand bucks. There's some arguing back and forth, but you never hear what Anthony says—"

"No sir," Russell replied as he idly turned his Stetson around by the brim. Also sans jacket, Wyatt stood shoulder to shoulder with the detective, looking slender and boyish beside the broad but gaunt Vensure

"Then there's a scream. Maria falls over the balcony, and bashes her head on the planter below us," Vensure said, brushing back an unruly wisp of soot black hair.

Angie left the deck and approached the balcony. Warily, she peered over the low wall, into the open lower level. The sight left her queasy. The lower level centered on an atrium-like rock garden, lighted by a bubble dome in a cupola over her head. At the far end of the adjoining study, there was a computer and printer on a rosewood desk and a seating group beyond that, big comfortable sofas covered in white duck, red lacquered Chinese tables, and an extensive library, with everything neatly shelved. Though she hated looking there, Angie could see, directly below, an ominously stained area in the porous coral tile with the outline of a body chalked around it.

"Okay," Joe said. "Tell me where you were, Mr. Wyatt, when you heard what Maria said."

Russell's boots clattered as he strolled over the tile floor to the step-down bay at the center of the upper level. It was filled with an amber Chinese rug decorated with peacock blue and rose red dragons. The rug was bordered on three sides by plum sectionals

"I was sitting exactly here," said Russell, sinking into the center seat, "It was close to midnight, Sunday."

"Wait a minute," said Vensure, crossing his arms. "Maria Whitman's been dead well over a month."

"Nearly eight weeks, sir," said Russell calmly. "Some of us who were friends and clients of Maria's were holding a memorial séance. The remarks I repeated to you were channeled through me from Maria herself."

One of Vensure's brows shot up. Sauntering over to Russell, Vensure crowded his space. "Give me that again?"

"Channeled. I was in a trance, a deep hypnotic state. In fact I didn't really hear Maria talking at all. I was the earthly conduit through which she spoke." Joe folded his arms, continuing to stare, until Russell added: "I'm merely repeating what a half dozen witnesses will tell you."

"Uh huh. And do you think a jury'll buy that?"

"No sir. I just thought that if you had some idea how Maria's death happened, it might be easier for you to look for the party involved."

"And if you know so much, you just might turn out to be the party involved," Vensure said.

"I was not involved," said Russell, fingering the Stetson gently, as if stroking a pet. "I was in a Tibetan ashram that entire time."

"I presume you can prove that," Vensure challenged.

"With no doubt whatever."

Vensure's mobile eyes raked over to Angie. "Mrs. Reynolds? What do you think of all this?"

"I think that if we can locate Anthony, there'll be two buttons missing from a blazer we bought in Fort Lauderdale. The purchase shows up on one of my credit cards."

"So you believe Anthony was two-timing you with Mrs. Whitman?"

Angie flushed. "It looks that way. Particularly since checks which she didn't sign showed up in my bank account."

Joe approached Angie, crowding her. He was close enough that she noticed a knot of bone in the middle of the curving bridge of his nose and his full, sculpted lips. "Tell me, Mrs. Reynolds, did you sign the credit card charge for this blazer?" Though his tones were soft, his voice was menacing.

"Yes I did. Anthony was crazy about the Italian men's wear designers like Canali and Gianfranco Ferre. When he saw this new Corneliani Blazer, slightly fitted with side vents, with six buttons at the cuffs?" Angie shrugged, "I intended for him to have it as a wedding gift."

"Uh huh. And on the last day that you saw Anthony, he was flashing around a Rolex watch and a Hermés briefcase you had bought him."

"Joe," Angie said, frowning. "I personally never set eyes on either item. As you know, he made a point of showing the Rolex and the briefcase to Ned Wadlow, my banker. I haven't a clue where he got them. Neither of the purchases showed up on any of my charge cards, thank God for that."

"But you did let Anthony make deposits to your bank account."

"We've gone through that. I thought they were cash, as I've said." What has gotten into this man? she wondered.

"And did your fiancé move in with you, Angie?"

"Not at all. And as far as I'm concerned, you can save the cross examination." She was furious. Up to now he'd seemed the soul of consideration. Why was he being so nasty?

Joe grinned slightly, stepping back. He picked up his jacket and slung it over his shoulder. "Call it a mild introduction to what you'd face on a witness stand."

Angie stalked for the balcony door to close the sliders, but Joe motioned her still and closed and locked the doors himself. She was seething. Why had he been so mean to her?

"Let's say this Anthony slips up somehow. Maybe we get lucky and find him," Joe said, back to his easy self. Just what was the deal?

They took the stairs down to the entry hall and Joe opened the foyer door for her. "Then we put you on the witness stand, Angie. Anthony's lawyer goes on about how you were his intended. And you couldn't dispute that."

"I've never hidden the fact that I was a complete fool," Angie said through clenched teeth. They were out on the landing. She trotted down the stairs, wanting to escape Joe and his needling, but the long-legged Vensure was right on her heels. "And you gave him money, and you bought him gifts," he said softly.

Angie stopped. She turned around, facing him, staring up into his face. Seeing an amused glint in his eye got her dander up. "Gift. Singular," she snarled. "One blazer. I did not give Anthony any money that I thought wasn't his. I think we have gone over this ad nauseum."

But Joe kept on prodding: "Even so, Mrs. Reynolds, the deposit slips you show as evidence don't say Anthony's money here and Angie's money there, do they?"

"No," Angie whispered hoarsely.

Beside her, Vensure took Angie's elbow, leading her gently along the walk as Russell trailed behind. "So what'll Anthony say? He'll say he never had any money and was spending yours, Mrs. Reynolds," Vensure said.

Close to tears, Angie said, "But it wasn't that way at all. I thought you believed me."

His expression changed. She watched his eyes soften, as they seemed to absorb the blue right out of the daylight. "Of course I believe you, Angie. It's just that some time has elapsed here, and I wondered whether you are still interested in pursuing this."

Angie laughed sarcastically. "Am I interested? I tracked down Maria Whitman. You didn't."

Joe grinned. "Nice work, certainly. But I just wanted to refresh your memory about what it would be like to go through the humiliation of a trial."

They had reached Joe's car. She hurled her handbag in through the rolled-down window. It landed with a satisfying thud. Joe helped her into the nondescript, government-issue sedan and closed the door. Russell got into the back seat.

Leaning into the open window, and addressing both of them, Joe said to Russell. "As I've already explained to Angie, these swindler cases are very hard to prosecute. It's the heart of the scam that a romance was involved. The swindler gets on the stand and says that the victim gave him money of her own free will, which in a sense she did."

Joe held up his hand as Angie started to protest. "Now then, maybe it's different this time. Maybe we'll get what we need, more than one victim. Thanks to the efforts of both of you, we can probably get the coroner to reconsider the suspicious circumstances surrounding Mrs. Whitman's death. After all, we've got Anthony buttoned to the scene." Joe paused. He was waiting for them to laugh over his little pun, but she was so angry that she made a face instead.

"So, we have probable cause to indict him," Vensure said. "However, poor Mrs. Whitman can't tell us anything—except through her spiritual mouthpiece here. Unfortunately, Russell, the court will consider your séance nothing more than hearsay. But what if some other woman besides Mrs. Reynolds or Mrs. Whitman bought him the Rolex and the briefcase?"

Startled, Angie leaned forward in the seat to stare up at him. "You *did* find her. There's another victim. She bought the Rolex and the briefcase. You have been working on this. Why didn't you say so?"

One corner of Vensure's mouth lifted. "I rather doubt the party involved will come forward." He walked around the car, climbed in and turned on the ignition.

"Let me talk to her," Angie said as they sped down Maria Whitman's circular driveway. "Let me tell her about Maria Whitman lying in her grave. Let me explain how I'm bankrupt, and how Anthony put me in the hospital, how I've lost my livelihood, and how I can't take proper care of my son. And what's happened to this third woman? Do you think she'll ever trust a man again? Maybe if I agree to prosecute, she'll testify."

Vensure said nothing as he turned onto the narrow country road squeezed between groves of fat orange trees and the levee of the Banks River.

"Anyway, I no longer care about humiliation," Angie said, folding her arms. "I faced that in bankruptcy court. I assure you, I'll catch this Anthony Abruzzi if I have to do it all by myself. And I'll prosecute when I find him."

"I too intend to pursue this," said Russell from the back seat. "Maria was a dear friend."

Vensure stared at Russell and back at Angie again. A certain gleam seemed to backlight his eyes, now a moody gray. "All right, you're on."

CHAPTER 20

Thursday, October 22, 5 p.m.

Angie and Joe turned off Royal Palm Boulevard, lined with the stately trees the street was named for. On Key Lime Lane, they headed west toward the Gulf. The street ended in a cul-de-sac dominated by a Spanish-style mansion of cream-colored stucco protected from the gulf by a massive seawall. Joe pulled into a brick-lined drive shaded by live oaks.

"Why are we stopping here? This is Suzi Islamorada's house," Angie said.

Vensure turned to her, raised his brows, and opened his hands.

"No!" Angie said. "Not Suzi. My God! Why didn't you tell me?"

"You know her?"

"I did this entire home."

It was true. Top to bottom. It took them six months. They had had such a good time. They were so close. Suzi was just as adventurous in her tastes as Angie. They shopped not only flea markets and estate sales, but also the Carolina furniture marts, and the design studios of New York. Suzi was Angie's last major client before Alan died. Then Angie got busy with the opening of Southern Influences, and Suzi was busy raising the last two million dollars DeLeon needed to open the Islamorada Centre for the Performing Arts, to be named for Suzi's late husband.

86

"The poor darling," Angie said. "What did Anthony hit her for?"

"One Rolex and one Hermés case," Vensure said. "When things started getting heavy, Suzi arranged for Abruzzi to meet her lawyer, who asked him for his financial statement, and that was the last she ever saw of him."

"That's a relief. Was she any help to you?"

"Her description corroborates yours. I'm afraid she won't file charges, however."

"Let me talk to her," Angie said.

"I'll head back to my office and return a few phone calls. I'll pick you up in an hour or so."

Trembling with rage, Angie dashed up the worn steps of the broad verandah. How *dare* he? Suzi Islamorada was a beloved figure in DeLeon. She was the wheel horse behind dozens of civic projects. Stray cats. Orphans. Unwed mothers. The down and out. It didn't matter who or what. Suzi helped scores of people, without ever making a big deal out of it.

Behind the iron hinged door, Angie heard the chimes ring and the familiar foghorn voice of Suzi's massive maid, Cotilde, who opened the door tentatively, then threw it wide when she saw who it was.

"Miss Angie, honey. Miz Suzi's been a missin' you. Where you been keeping yourself?"

"It's been too long, for sure," Angie said, submitting to Cotilde's crushing embrace. As she stepped into the entry hall facing the staircase she noticed that the porous, unfilled travertine they'd chosen for the entry hall was not showing traffic wear as she had feared it might.

"Well don't you be no stranger no more. I'm on the phone to the grocer. You go on ahead. Miss Suzi's out on the screen porch, just a waiting for to hear from you."

Angie crossed the long parlor, taking pleasure once again in the medley of fabrics taken from antique patterns she'd special ordered from Brunschwig & Fils in New York. The screened porch at the back of the house was a different matter. Angie had made it into a working office, done in rattan pieces upholstered in shades of green. She'd filled it with Suzi's beloved African Violets and her fern collection, so that Suzi's twin passions, gardening and fund-raising, could come together in one room.

Suzi was stretched out regally on the chaise lounge Angie had had filled with squishy, down pillows, talking on the cellular phone Angie had recommended. Suzie was in her mid-seventies, had endured three back surgeries, and sitting at a desk wasn't the thing for her. She blew a kiss to Angie as she talked.

Cotilde arrived with a tray of freshly baked banana bread, a brick of cream cheese on a silver dish, cut glass bowls of her wonderful home-made preserves and a pot of the English tea that Suzi preferred over coffee. It was not possible that anyone should set foot in Suzi's home lest the tray and the tidbits arrived. Both Suzi and Cotilde were throwbacks to a more gracious era. Being around these two had made Angie realize just how much civility women had sacrificed when they'd abandoned the hearth for the workplace.

"Founding members will be honored on the special wall of bronze plaques in the sculpture garden," Suzie was saying. "I can't think of a higher tribute to your grandmother, Andrea. After all, Cecile was a wonderful cellist. If she hadn't chosen family life with your grandfather, we'd have seen her in Carnegie Hall. Of that I have no doubt." Grinning, Angie shook her head. Crafty Suzi had wheedled millions out of people in this town by flattering the amateur artistic talents of the well-heeled.

"Let's see. Cecile's birthday is next month. Eighty-three isn't it? Ninety-two? I don't believe a word of it. Subscribe now, my dear and we'll have just enough time to have the plaque engraved and mounted. Oh, thank you, sweetheart. *Ciao.*" Suzi hung up the phone and slipped her tortoise shell reading glasses off her nose. "Angie, darling. It has been far too long. I've thought of you so often. It was so clever of you to turn my tired old sun porch into a little old office."

"A little old office that's turned over millions," Angie said, kissing Suzi's cheek. Her skin was fragile as tissue paper, crisscrossed by lines that bespoke a face that had done a great deal of smiling.

Suzi motioned Angie into a rattan loveseat beside the chaise. Her businesslike expression was replaced by a tender look of love and concern. "Now, dear. What's this Joe Vensure tells me?"

"It's true. Anthony Abruzzi took me good, Suzi. He ruined me—ran my business into bankruptcy, sent me to the hospital, humiliated my child..." As Angie's eyes began to fill, Suzi handed her a freshly ironed hankie of the type rarely seen since the advent of Kleenex.

"Angie Reynolds, I just don't understand why you didn't come to me. I could have lent you something to tide you over."

"That's very kind of you, Suzi. Frankly, I've been so upset, it just never occurred to me to ask."

"And here you are a well-brought up girl—a Pelham?" Suzi raised her eyebrows.

"Oh yes, the Pelham label," Angie said bitterly. "When Daddy was alive, I wouldn't have hesitated to ask him for help, but he's been gone six months. His estate is tied up in a lawsuit, and Mama still isn't herself. Last time I talked to her, she told me she's impoverished and living on oatmeal. She always did pinch every nickel, you know. The Kenners—that was her maiden name—could live on what other people threw away. That's Mama's credo. Scrimping is how her family acquired their wealth in the first place. So I just couldn't bear to tell her about what happened. She'd just write me off as irresponsible."

"Well, darling, maybe there's a way. Let me speak to my lawyer. The question is, what's to be done now? Let me help you reestablish, dear. Goodness knows, stodgy old DeLeon can certainly use your talents."

Angie shook her head. "It isn't right. I'd be taking your money. I'm not into beautiful rooms right now. I'm going to do a couple jobs for Gina's friends, and put my main effort into catching Anthony."

"Do you think really that's wise?" Suzi said as she poured tea and handed a cup to Angie.

"Suzi, there are all kinds of these swindlers out there preying on women. We're a cottage industry for cons. We allow ourselves to be victimized because we won't prosecute even when the police do catch them."

"What a lot of pluck you have. Good luck to you on it. I mean that." Suzi squinted. Her mouth turned down at the corners. "But Angie dear, you can't expect anyone as old as I am to testify. Why, I'd be the death of your case." Suzi scrunched herself down into the turtleneck of the cotton shirt she wore beneath her denim work shirt. The gesture made an old woman out of her. Wily Suzi was playing the part of the old lady she certainly wasn't, but Angie knew better than to protest. Suzi Islamorada was not one to be pushed into anything.

"We're lucky, Suzi," Angie said. "Anthony cost you a couple of baubles. I lost my business. But that's nothing. There's some evidence that he was involved in the death of a well-known psychic in Banks."

"Dreadful," Suzi said, her chin trembling. "Why I'm such a lucky old fool, I have no idea."

"Suzi, you've done so much for everyone, you deserve your own personal angel."

Suzi's eyes shone. She never mentioned her help to individuals, but she loved it when her public beneficence was recognized. Then the animation left her face. "It was humiliating enough to admit to my own lawyer that I'd been taken in by a pseudo suitor. A younger man, too, which made it even worse. That's why I don't dare go to court. The newspaper would have a field day, and suppose my children find out? They'd have me committed—and rightly so. I must be getting senile!"

Angie put down her cup, sat on the arm of Suzi's chair, hugged her shoulders and brushed a kiss across her cheek. "If you're senile, Suzi, then they'd better commit me right along with you. Maybe we can share beds in the same ward."

Suzi giggled over that, patting Angie's hand. "Do you really think you could catch up with that scum?"

"Now that poor Maria Whitman is dead," Angie said, "The police are finally beginning to pay attention to me."

"Well, there is one thing I can do," Suzi said. "I can raise funds for the effort."

Angie squeezed Suzi's shoulders. "I couldn't take money for that," she said softly.

"You just get back my Rolex and that briefcase and I'll be way ahead," Suzi said, writing out a check. "Now, keep track of expenses, won't you? Otherwise, I'll be in hot water with my accountant."

The doorbell rang. "That must be Joe Vensure coming to get me," Angie said. "He's the case supervisor on this. It took some persuading, but he's finally taking a personal interest in this."

"Well, he ought to," Suzi said, "With a fine-looking girl like you."

"Suzi! That *isn't* what I meant," Angie said, flushing.

"Well, it *is* what I meant. That boy has been Lee Bingham's despair for as long as I can remember," Suzi murmured, her arm clamped around Angie's elbow.

Angie helped Suzi stand up. Suzi had arthritic knees and walked with difficulty. As they made their way past the dining room, Angie glanced at the floor beneath the mahogany table. She'd had the wood refinished in black lacquer, the way floors were originally done in old Southern mansions. She was gratified to see that the finish still gleamed like a pair of brand new patent leather shoes.

Cotilde held the door open, pushed back the screen and invited Joe into the hall.

"Joey," Suzi said, taking his big hand in both of hers. "Are you still giving your mother a hard time?"

"Miz Suzi," he replied kissing her cheek. "No man who has a welder for a mother ever gives her a hard time."

"Welder?" Angie said. "You must be talking about Manda Bingham."

"Amanda Lee Bingham, that's right," Suzi said. "She didn't take up Manda until she became notable for her art."

"Mom works under her maiden name," Joe said. "That was after Dad made a few cracks about her original work."

"Manda Bingham is a wonderful sculptor," Angie said. In fact, I commissioned your mother to do the fountain at The Cockatoo Club on Sanibel. It won all sorts of prizes."

"You restored the Cockatoo Club?" he said.

"With a little help—from a few dozen people," Angie said.

He looked down at his watch. "Fortunately, my shift has just ended. Come on. I want to show you something."

Joe hugged Suzi, then ushered Angie down the steps. Joe had turned in his unmarked sedan in favor of a red pickup truck. As he helped her into the front seat, Angie caught a glimpse of Suzi standing at the top of her steps, propped on Cotilde's arm. Suzi had a sly grin on her face.

CHAPTER 21

Three blocks away, Vensure pulled up in front of a dilapidated Victorian home on Jacaranda Drive. It was a monster of a place, Angie noticed, grandiose but a bit unbalanced as these nineteenth century edifices often were. This home, a peeling mustard yellow, enjoyed the twin hallmarks of the era: a hexagonal tower topped off with a witch's hat roof, paired with an equally steep gable.

"Angie, meet Victoria," Joe said proudly.

"Why, Lieutenant Vensure. You've been holding out on me," Angie said wryly. "She's...she's a real Victorian, isn't she?"

They started on a tour through the downstairs. First stop was the powder bath installed in what had once been a closet beneath the entry hall stairs. It was finished, right down to an oaken water closet with a high, wall-hung tank and a pull-chain handle. The wainscoting was sleek as mink to the touch.

"Did you do this finish work?" Angie asked. "It's really impressive."

Joe nodded. "The subcontractor who is helping me thinks I'm a nut case. Nobody does finish work one room at a time."

"Not on commercial jobs," Angie said. "For therapy, where's the harm?"

92

"I completed the bath just to see some finished results. I had to prove to myself I could really do it."

The rest of the house was rubble. The ceiling in the dining room had caved in. The room stank of mildew. The wretched green linoleum on the kitchen floor was worn through to the flooring in several places and the cabinets had rotted out.

"The upstairs is just as bad," Joe said. "Would you like to see it?"

"Of course," Angie said.

They were headed up the creaking stairway to the second floor when the tour was interrupted by a beep on the pager Joe wore clipped to his belt. He excused himself and went downstairs to use the phone. Angie was on her knees examining the bottom of the claw foot bathtub when he returned.

"I don't think the rust deposits will come out," she said. "It would be better to refinish it."

"How do I do that?"

"I'll give you the name of someone," she said as he helped her to her feet. "Of course it might cost more than a stock replacement."

"I knew there'd be a catch," he said, rolling his eyes and changing the subject. "Now then. The office called to say the autopsy report has finally come in on the Whitman case. I think I'll take a run over to Banks and walk through the crime scene again. Would you like to come along?"

"Crime scene?" Angie said as she stepped into the entry hall. "You mean you now admit a crime has been committed?"

Joe crowded her in the narrow, dimly lit hallway. She could barely make out the outlines of his face, but his eyes had taken on a golden cast. His big hand lingered lightly on her shoulder for just a moment as he leaned in close to murmur, "Lady? You are some piece of work."

Jolted by his touch, Angie shrank away.

"Sorry," Joe said, dropping his hand. "I didn't mean to frighten you."

"I'm not frightened," Angie said. This was all wrong. She was way too attracted to this man and a liar on top of that. She wasn't merely frightened. She was scared to death.

CHAPTER 22

Banks, FL
Friday October 23

Thank God for bromeliads. The ragged orange shafts in the atrium of Maria Whitman's home drew Angie's eye away from the outline of her body chalked on the floor.

The front door was open. A breeze crept along the backs of her arms, sending a shiver of pleasure through her, followed by pangs of remorse and sadness that dragged at her gut. Poor Maria. Never again would she feel the breezes tumble through the house, never again watch the flame creep up the stalks of these faux cactuses as they crept into bloom. But try to distract herself as she might, Angie couldn't help overhear what the men were saying.

"It's not in the toxicology report," Joe said. "Despite the fact that Scotch was spilled down the front of her caftan and her fingerprints were on the bottle, she never drank a drop."

"That's more like it," Wyatt said mildly. "That would be consistent with the Maria I know."

"Here's something else." Joe began reading sections he'd high-lighted in yellow. "Her spike heel was caught in the hem of her caftan, suggesting she'd tripped and fallen. The trouble is, the heel is caught way to the side of the skirt, not in back as you'd expect."

"The caftan bothers me," Russell said. The floor pinged as he shifted around in his silver-toed cowboy boots. "Maria wasn't one for fancy stuff. She was the original red flannel country girl."

Red flannel? Angie's stomach churned. "Would it be all right if I go upstairs and poke around in her closet?" she said.

"Go ahead," Joe said, "Just remember the gloves, okay?"

As they had entered the house, Vensure had passed out surgical gloves to her and Russell, and stuffed a pair for himself in his jacket pocket.

Possibly this was simply a dodge, her way to avoid hearing any more grisly details from that awful report, but as Angie mounted the stairs, there was still no escape. Joe's next words drifted after her: "There was a broken glass on the credenza, but no sign of blood, no cuts anywhere on Maria's body. There's nothing under her nails, suggesting she might have fought off her attacker. In fact, there aren't any fingerprints or fibers left anywhere. It suggests the place was cleaned up."

"Didn't you say something about bruising?"

"Her right ear was bruised, all along the rim," Joe said. "Possibly she was struck by a flat object, but there's nothing to suggest she was bludgeoned or punched."

The air upstairs was cloying and stale. Angie opened the sliders to the breeze, noticing how the greenish brown river went silver as it rounded a bend away from the house. She passed between the credenza and the plum sofas, found the light to Maria's closet and switched it on.

Yes, Russell was right. Maria was not exactly a clotheshorse. There were a few nondescript suits and blouses and several pairs of slacks in neutral colors, a few tops, a basic black cocktail dress, and a couple of coats. The rest of the spacious closet was taken up with boxes of books and papers.

Angie was about to leave when she noticed a separate section of the closet, behind the door. There the story was entirely different. There was a whole section of brand new dresses and suits, expensive items from good designers, all very sophisticated in their cut and detailing: Lily Pulitzer, Anne Taylor, Versace and Dior. All of these were winter things, too heavy for Florida. The hangtags were still on the garments. From Saks, Jacobson's, Improv, and Bleeker & Wyman. The very same upscale places Anthony had taken her.

On the floor were the new shoes to go with the outfits: two pairs of Ferragamos, still in boxes. In a Manolo Blahnik box, she pulled out a mouth-watering pair of ankle boots in stretch satin that were the color of glazed chestnuts. Beside the shoes was a whole shopping bag filled with the trimmings: belts, scarves, and stockings. A Sax Fifth Avenue bag was filled with exquisite lingerie from big name designers: Lily of France, Olga, Guess, Calvin Klein. There was also a Victoria's Secret bag. With a feeling of dread she pulled out three charmeuse lace peignoir sets, the same type of frilly gowns Anthony insisted he wanted to see her in on their honeymoon.

Suppose she'd bumped into Maria right in the aisle of one of these ritzy stores as they frantically shopped for their forthcoming weddings to the same man?

"God help me, Maria. I'll find that bastard if it's the last thing I ever do," Angie whispered as tears welled in her eyes.

Downstairs, she found Joe standing behind Russell as he read Maria Whitman's computer files. "It's the same system we have at the office. There's a daybook built right into the program." He swirled the cursor arrow around on the screen and clicked the mouse button.

"Where to start?" he muttered.

"Try August seventeenth," Angie said. "That was the day I met Anthony. My lucky day."

Russell pulled the date up on the screen.

"Okay," Joe said, clapping Russell on the back.

"A dozen roses arrived this morning from the attorney, Anthony Abruzzi. A most sensitive, spiritual man," Vensure read.

"He met her before he met me," Angie said, her hands darting to her face, cradling her flaming cheeks. She might as well have been slapped. Here was the ultimate humiliation. She wasn't anything at all special to Anthony.

"I should have thought of the computer sooner," Russell said, half to himself. "Too often we psychics have our sights set on messages from the beyond. We overlook the obvious."

"Can we get copies of these?" Joe said.

"No problem," Russell replied.

As the printer screeched away, Angie read the details:

> A very interesting man stopped by the Rising Sign this afternoon, Anthony Abruzzi, an attorney from New York. His family knew Edgar Cayce, who had healed his sickly grand aunt. After that the family worshipped him. Cayce spent most of his summers with the Abruzzi family in their cottage in upstate New York. Anthony is also fond of my books. He quoted one of my favorite passages from New Age, New Spirit. We are to have dinner together tonight.

As the next pages came up on the printer, Angie's heart sank. "Would you look at this?" she moaned, "It's exactly the same kind of schedule Anthony had me make out."

August 20

8 p.m. Gulf Stream in from LA. Meet Leon Abruzzi, publisher, Bio-Med Software. Wife's name: Sylvie. Two children, Bud, 7 and Sissie, 5.

"Sylvie!" Angie said. "Yes! That was what he said his sister-in-law's name was."

11 p.m. Arrive LaGuardia.
12:30 p.m. Arrive 400 Park Avenue.

"Headed straight for the kennel," Vensure said.

August 21

11 a.m. UAL flight 207 to Glasgow
Arrive Glasgow, 5 p.m.
Arrive Findhorn 7:30 p.m.

"Findhorn?" Angie said.

"It's a spiritual community in Scotland," Russell said. "It was Maria's fondest dream to read *The Book of Miracles* with believers from all around the world."

The printer was silent. On the computer screen, Russell clicked onto the next entry. "Wednesday, August 19. She's very down. Anthony has had her running all day, looking for clothes. She's so tired she can't concentrate. She's trying to do a chart for Anthony, but everything is mishmash."

At the bottom, in bold letters:

CHECK ANTHONY'S BIRTHDATES.

"It's the last entry," Russell said, "Right here in the hard drive."
"Hard evidence," Joe said.

CHAPTER 23

Memphis, TN
Friday October 23, 11 a.m.

The collective sigh of relief was nearly audible as Dr. Joyce Brothers told a lecture hall full of aging Baby Boomers what they wanted to hear: they were still young women. They should take advantage of the fact that they had other lives left.

"Advances in medical science, diet and exercise mean that what we used to think of as age fifty is now forty, the sixty year olds are fifty and so on," Brothers said. The efficient Brothers in her pale pink suit with gold buttons and her cream silk blouse had neatly lopped a decade off every life in the Excelsior Room of the Old Hickory Armory in downtown Memphis by the time the waiters in the chocolate uniforms arrived with trays of Napoleons, Danish, and mini bagels.

"Let's take a break, shall we?" Brothers announced, "We'll reconvene in twenty minutes or so, and I'll take questions from the floor."

In the third row center, Anthony sneezed as a woman brushed past him wearing enough of some musty smelling perfume to make his eyes leak. What *is* that stuff? Lethal Injection? He watched the ash blonde Brothers take a sip of water and turn to the panel moderator as the crowd began to break up.

Dr. Brothers. A widow. Well, well. Now there was a woman who

98

might enjoy the diversion of a little romance. After all, the newspaper story about her which accompanied her appearance in Memphis noted that Brothers herself said she was such a busy woman she'd had little time to develop close friendships.

Anthony headed to the back of the room, picked up two or three copies of Brothers' books. Yes, the good doctor herself was a worthy prospect for the future, but what with the high overhead involved in running a scam in the Big Apple, he'd have to put off a New York run until he had a bigger bankroll.

Meanwhile, he was careful to introduce himself to anyone wearing a badge that said she was from the Zonta organization, sponsors of the event. Businesswomen were very good about handing out their cards. Every one of them was an outstanding prospect. By the time he made it to the coffee urn, there weren't many candidates left. His attention focused on a woman right in front of him. She wore a dazed expression as she looked back over the audience. Maybe she'd forgotten her glasses?

He said to her, "Since Dr. Brothers has just removed a decade from our lives, I guess we can relax now and have the sweet rolls."

"An inspiration isn't she?" the woman replied. She had short, pert features and the freckle-splotched and wrinkled skin of the tennis playing, horse-riding, outdoorsy type. She wore a navy blazer and a preppie pleated skirt, a bit on the short side. Her hair was meticulously died in one of the more unreal shades of copper, and the amount of jewelry she had on marked her as an excellent prospect. The zippered case under her arm gave him the opener he needed.

"Are you perhaps a lawyer?" he said with a nod toward the case.

"Why? Do you need one?" she shot back.

Anthony laughed. This was a spunky one. Maybe she'd be some fun. "I'm here to take depositions and I'm in need of some assistance."

"Sorry, I can't help you," she said, "And I don't believe anyone else in the club could, either. I should think you could find someone through the local bar association."

"Oh, definitely," Abruzzi nodded, "It's just that Mama Regina's a Zonta chapter president. She always said you won't find higher caliber people."

"Always take Mama's advice," the woman said, beaming. Her face lost its diffuse look. She seemed present. Focused.

"Are you in real estate?" he said.

"Ready to wear," she said, "But I retired last year."

"How exciting for you," Anthony said.

The woman looked around the room. The two of them were among the few who hadn't yet gone back to their seats. She murmured, "I don't believe I can recall where I was sitting,"

"Allow me to help you," Abruzzi said, taking her arm. "Now that I've met you, I don't recall where I was sitting, either."

Dr. Brothers' lecture inspired him to review his life. She asked everyone to write down a five-year plan. His career, though lucrative, involved too much travel. It was time to find a wife and settle down. Goal: Marriage, he wrote in prominent letters on the Zonta pads everyone had been given, tapping it on his knee, so that his new companion might take note of it.

But then the pad stopped moving of its own volition and he felt the compulsion to write "Jane," next to the matrimonial word. A pain knifed up through his jaw. It was his damned heart acting up again. He willed the P-word away. Why couldn't he escape the Pelhams? He had to concentrate on the woman beside him. She was perfect.

As the lecture broke up, he followed Navy Blazer up the aisle. At the doorway, she seemed disoriented. "You know, I can't remember whether I drove my car here or not," she said. "Silly me."

"I have to confess," Anthony said, "I travel so much and work so hard that I sometimes can't even remember what it is that I'm driving."

The woman giggled. "What a pair of losers."

"I wouldn't say that. Not at all," Anthony replied. "You do know your own name, don't you?"

Blazer frowned, her forehead wrinkling in puzzlement, until she realized he was teasing. "I'm Jenny Sawyer," she said, her bright look back.

"Jenny? I'm Anthony Abruzzi," he replied, raising his wrist, flashing his Rolex. "Tell you what. I have to be in chambers by two, which means I've got to find the nearest restaurant quickly. Won't you please join me—if two such forgetful people can find a restaurant, that is?"

Laughing, Jenny rolled her eyes. "Cattleman's is the only thing around here. That I do remember."

"Let's go," Anthony smiled.

CHAPTER 24

DeLeon, FL
Monday, October 23

The noon hour rush was on, and the Chili's on the edge of the campus was crowded with students in cutoffs and sneakers, with a few more formally dressed faculty types in seedy jackets and fashionably unfashionable ties. Angie gave the hostess her name, and asked for a secluded corner table if one came available, then sat down to wait on a padded bench in the foyer. On one side, a longhaired young man in sandals hummed a very off key version of The Doors' "mysticated wine" song into her ear. On the other side of her a trio of coeds, with their hair dyed a cotton candy blonde, giggled like nine year olds. The odor of mesquite wafted into the lobby as a waitress passed by with a platter of burgers and steaks, distracting Angie momentarily from the list of names she studied.

In all, she had collected eleven names and phone numbers. These were the sweetheart swindler cases that she'd found on Friday afternoon in the public records at the courthouse. She'd narrowed these down from a startling thirty-five complaints over the past three years. Joe had told her that flimflam artists followed regular routes around the country and would hit the same places time and again.

The eleven cases she was most interested in obviously involved Anthony. He'd been coming to DeLeon late in the summer for the last

101

three years. Angie had contacted all of the victims she could find, which turned out to be only five. The other six had moved away. Two had left forwarding addresses and phone numbers, but neither of these could be located beyond their second moves. Her appointment for lunch was Melissa Lopez-Baer, who worked for the University. Angie had talked to her for nearly an hour before Melissa had agreed to meet her. This poor woman had lost far more money than anyone else, some forty thousand dollars. Angie needed her desperately. How best to approach her?

"Angie?" said a soft, lilting voice.

Angie jumped up, stuffing her notes into her leather carryall. "Melissa?"

Angie found herself eye to eye with a tall, delicately built young woman with a tumble of curly dark hair falling down her back, and an angular face made all the more interesting by a long sculpted nose. Melissa's narrow eyes were a lively, toffee brown. She was dressed head to toe in an oyster business suit, looking immaculately fresh in the steaming heat. She greeted Angie with a warm smile and a hug.

"I'm so glad we could meet," Angie said, after they were seated in a small, dark booth near the swinging door to the kitchen. Perfect, Angie thought. Nobody would notice them, much less overhear their conversation.

"I have a business meeting in one hour," Melissa said, "I hope you don't mind if we order right away?"

Heart sinking, Angie nodded her head. They both ordered the cheese and broccoli soup and house salad and chatted until their salads came. They were both single mothers raising sons, who were about the same age.

"My son, Roy, he is a good boy. He helps his mother all he can," Melissa said.

"How did he react when you had your...*problem* with Anthony?" Angie asked.

Melissa's eyes found her plate. "Thank God, he was only eight at the time. He never really understood quite what happened, how it is we are still living with my parents." Melissa picked up the pile of the coasters Chili's was famous for, and began sorting them, methodically turning the logos face up.

"Well, this man dragged my son right into his plot," Angie said bitterly. "Jason went into a depression. Did you know that kids can be depressed?"

Melissa shook her head. "Unbelievable," she said, shuffling the rearranged coasters through her fingers.

"You are just one of eleven victims that Anthony hit right here in DeLeon over the last three years. I'm one of three this season. One of them is dead. Anthony made it look like an accident, but I know in my heart it wasn't. It might have been either one of us."

"My God," Melissa said, crossing herself.

Patiently, Angie explained exactly why she needed Melissa's help. How victims had to testify as a group so they could show a pattern in Anthony's behavior. "I've lined up two other witnesses," Angie said, trying to keep her tone bright and casual.

"There's Katie Byers. She runs a cleaning business. Anthony took her for ten thousand dollars about eighteen months ago. It had taken her eight years to save that money. This was money Katie desperately needed for special schooling for her autistic son.

"Then there's Sylvia Jackson. Anthony got twenty-five hundred out of her salon. She lost her lease and the six women working for her lost their jobs. It has taken Sylvia three years to reestablish herself."

"And these women will go to court?" Melissa said.

"Yes, absolutely. And so will I, but we really need your help."

Melissa set down the coasters in a neat, precise stack. She unrolled the bundle of flatware and distributed it beside her plate, lining up fork, knife and spoon just so.

"My grandfather was a shrimper. No education. But he was a good man—a hard worker, and grandmother, too. They raised six children in a tiny shack on the Back Bay. When we went to high school, kids from more prosperous families snubbed us. The boys fished and crabbed with grandpa and the girls had jobs washing down boats. Sometimes they shook crabs. Even so, in my generation we all went to college. How? Because grandpa went without luxuries to buy land. When his estate was settled, a handsome legacy came to each of the children, grandchildren, and us. And that was what Anthony Abruzzi stole from me," Melissa said, eyes blazing, "my family heritage. Fortunately, I was finishing my master's degree when this happened. It was my son Anthony took from."

"So? You'll help us?" Angie said.

"That was three years ago," Melissa continued. "I took a part time job at the University, in administration. I worked very hard, eventually went full time, and then became a supervisor. I wrote a grant for a new program. Technology—education for minorities. It has just come through. I will manage a staff of six. My budget is three hundred fifty thousand dollars. I'd like very much to help you, Angie, but you see, I am afraid. If the story came to light, it might reflect badly on my ability to handle money."

Angie had a lump in her throat. She had a hard time saying it, but she forced herself to sound cheerful. "I understand, Melissa. But let's leave it this way. If we do catch up with Anthony, I will call you again. Maybe you'll change your mind."

Melissa tilted her head. The sympathy in her eyes was evident. "Angie," she said softly. "When this happened to me, I felt just the way you did. I was infuriated when I got so little help from the police. I dreamed of catching up with Anthony and doing evil to him in return. Then I accepted what happened. I determined that I'd make a better life for Roy and myself than I'd had before. I haven't succeeded yet, but I'm well on my way. Don't waste your life on revenge. You must save your effort for your son."

CHAPTER 25

"Joe?" Angie called as she peered into dingy rooms through a brand new screen door. Beyond it an impressive front door with leaded glass panels stood wide open. These had been installed since she had last visited. She was pleased to see that Joe had picked one of the three doors she had recommended, the most elegant and expensive of the lot, with the beveled glass panels, deep carving and a satin finish. Front doors were first impressions and it paid to buy good ones.

"I'm in the kitchen. Come on in," he said.

Carrying her briefcase and a roll of building plans, she passed through the empty foyer with its hideous flocked wallpaper and bare bulb hanging down on a twined cord. She passed through the adjoining parlor with high, spacious ceilings and a hexagonal window bay that offered good lighting. The rotting wood in the window bay would have to be torn out and rebuilt. With some work—quite a lot, unfortunately—this could be a delightful room. The adjacent dining room was well proportioned, and had a bay window as well. It had good wainscoting that could probably be salvaged. The front rooms would have to wait until something could be done about the decrepit kitchen. Angie propped the roll of building plans against the wall that separated the dining room from the kitchen. It was obvious that Joe was too busy to look at them. He was on a Kneesy pad, scraping linoleum off the floor.

"Is this a proper activity for a police detective on a Monday afternoon?" she asked.

With a hoot of triumph, he yanked up a whole section of grimy flooring and tossed it into a garbage can, stripping off his gloves as he stood up. "After thirty-six hours straight, it was time for somebody else to uphold the law. So I figured I'd come home and kill my knees." He wiped his dripping forehead on the sleeve of his denim shirt. His eyes were bloodshot.

"The sting?" she said.

He nodded.

"Did you get them?"

"I can't discuss details, madam," he said. "But I think the cop reporter has the story."

"So I'll see you on the six o'clock news?"

"Let's hope not," he said. "There's nothing more useless than an undercover cop with his mug on TV. And how did it go for you, Ms. Investigator?"

"Just what you told me to expect," she sighed. "I just had lunch with Melissa Lopez-Baer. She lost forty thousand dollars and won't help me."

"Typical," he said, opening a cooler and handing her a Bud. They stood in the bare kitchen, leaning against the rotting counters as they drank. Dust motes drifted on shafts of light coming through the grimy windows. The room smelled rank with decay. Angie wiped her sweaty face with chilled fingers. Today would be another sauna.

"Melissa said she's afraid for her job. I'm running out of leads. Early this afternoon I reached the last two possibilities. Same thing with a psychiatric nurse and a physical therapist I talked to. These women are scared to death."

"Welcome to Fraud 101," Joe said.

"I did get the woman with the autistic son who owns a cleaning business, and the one who owns a hair salon. They'll definitely help me. But I was hoping to get one of the really heavy losers in terms of sheer dollars and cents. Melissa would have been perfect." Angie lifted her hair and set the beer can against the back of her neck.

"The more they lose, the less they'll talk," Joe said.

"I don't think it's the money," Angie said. "It's the emotional investment. The victims blame themselves. They know there is such a thing as true love, but they think they are unworthy of it because it didn't turn out right for them."

He gazed at her, started to say something, but held it back. She dropped her eyes. There was a long silence broken by a tiny lizard, chirping on the sill.

"So?" he said, folding his arms as he turned away from her. "You got a sense of what we're up against."

"On the way over here, I had an inspiration," Angie said. "Why don't we try a frontal approach?" She paced in the long space in the big, old-fashioned kitchen. It was long and boxy, with narrow cupboards. She passed a rickety table piled with building plans near the back door and the refrigerator with the rounded corners, a Norge, now an antique. She turned to face him.

"Frontal approach?" Joe said, arching his one expressive eyebrow. He put his empty beer can in a paper bag under the kitchen sink.

Angie wheeled around and started back. "That's right. We know he goes after small business owners, and hangs out at charity events. So we send out fliers to these groups, asking them to look out for him."

"Advance notice of his arrival to potential victims," Joe said, rubbing his bony chin. "Might help us pinpoint where he's working. On the other hand it might just scare him off."

"Can't we try it?" Angie stood directly in front of Joe now, arms crossed. "I spoke to Russell Wyatt about it. He could get a mailing list of New Age bookstores around the country. I could get ones for real estate and design."

"The New Age uses the post office and not telepathy?" he said. "I'm crushed."

"What do you think?" Angie said.

"You could try it, I suppose."

"I'm seeing Russell on Monday. He's moving Rising Sign Enterprises into a renovated sugar mill on the Banks River. I'm designing the store for him," Angie said as she fetched the tube from the dining room, then spread the blueprints out on the peeling table. "I brought back your drawings for the kitchen.

"It's a good layout," Angie said. "The island's nice. It makes use of all the space you have in here. You might want to move it about eighteen inches to the left. That will leave room for the breakfast nook here. The pantry can go behind it on the outside wall. Then we can tear out the old pantry, put in a window on the side wall, and you've got the den you said you really wanted."

"An excellent idea," Joe said. "I hadn't thought of that."

"And you might consider putting a sink in the island. That way, you'll have two work stations."

"Do I need two?" he said. She was very aware of the spicy, sweaty odor of him as he crowded her space. His proximity had a galvanizing effect on her. She felt the hackles rise on her arms.

"Well," she said, "A lot of couples like to cook together these days."

"Couples," he said, gazing down at her. "Which reminds me. I haven't had any real food in three days."

"It can't be true that the entire justice system is fueled on coffee and doughnuts," Angie said. She sidled away. Get a grip, she told herself. You can't handle this.

"That's a terrible exaggeration." Those capricious eyes of his were filled with mischief and mirth.

"I'm relieved," Angie said. She rolled up the plans and stuffed them in the tube.

"Justice is more often served over pizza," Joe said. "So what say to a steak?"

"I just had a salad but thanks anyway." She picked up her shoulder bag and started for the front door.

"Hey, don't run off," Joe said, following her.

"I've got to go. I promised I'd drop off some wallpaper books for one of Gina's friends, and she's meeting with her builder at three."

"Tonight," Joe said as he escorted her to her car. "My place. Around seven."

"I don't know," Angie stammered, once she was behind the wheel of the van the Goldheims lent her. "Please don't be offended, Joe, but I don't feel very social these days."

"Social?" he said, leaning into the window. "This is all business. I want to see why two people in one kitchen need separate work stations. Since you insist on being all proper and stuffy about the deal, you can bring the steak."

CHAPTER 26

Angie's hands were full of lettuce. She was headed for the fridge to return what she didn't plan to put into the salad. Joe was on the way from the spice cupboard to the counter beside the stove with the blackener he intended to smear on the steak. While trying to pass each other in his postage stamp kitchen they danced a duet instead, each stepping forward on the right foot, then the left, until they were face to face, and laughing about it.

"Shall we?" Joe said. He raised Angie's left wrist, bypassing her hand, which clutched the damp romaine. He rocked her around to the big beat of the weird music on his CD player. She felt the spice can he held etch a square lightly into her back.

Their steps were long but necessarily few, due to the constraints of the impromptu dance floor. The bass throbbed underfoot. Riffs of primitive and unearthly sound rose over the howling of dogs.

"What is that?" Angie said.

"UFOrb. Like it?" He released her with a flourish and headed for the steak.

"It's distinctive, I'll say that."

"Techno," Joe said. "Synthesizer stuff. My musician friends hate it, particularly the vocalists. Afraid it might cost them their jobs."

"Tell them not to worry just yet," Angie said as she opened the refrigerator and deposited the lettuce.

"So now you see what I mean about a second work station in the kitchen," Angie said. "That way, two people can work without tripping over each other."

"But would there be dancing?"

"I hadn't thought of that," Angie said with a smile and a tilt of her head.

Joe slashed the edges of the thick sirloin with a knife, rubbed in the seasoning on the top side, flipped over the meat, then stopped short. He said, "I've made a terrible assumption."

Angie looked at him.

"That you like meat that bites back."

"Will it do anything for bad sinuses?"

"It's guaranteed to cauterize every pipe you've got."

Angie grimaced. "I'll take the cure."

"I always knew you were a gutsy girl."

She stopped what she was doing. "Because I want to prosecute?"

"Well yes," he said, after a lengthy pause. "But if you don't mind, let's not talk business. Except for one thing."

"Yes?"

"We've found someone Anthony hit. In Sarasota. In a psychiatric hospital. Would you like to meet her?"

"Oh, Joe," Angie said, tearing up. "Thank you, and thank God, and yes, definitely."

"We can go tomorrow afternoon. Unless something else breaks."

"Fine. No more business?"

"None," Joe said.

"So I won't ask you how you got to be a cop."

"Fair enough," Joe said. He sprinkled more of the spices onto the meat. "You've heard of candy and liquor," he said, "But nothing fells them faster than blackened steak."

Angie glared. "Not sexist, are you?"

Joe's brows shot up in feigned innocence. "Me? I'm no sexist. I'm a frustrated chef. Now, we'll need a platter. It's in that cupboard behind you, just over your head."

Angie turned around to look for it.

"Never mind. I'll find it." He brushed against her back as he reached over her head. As she stepped aside, she read a question in his eyes. She looked away, stepped out of the magnetic field he seemed to create. It was clear he was eager to start something, but she just couldn't. She liked Joe. Sure, she was attracted to him. But she was out of whack, drained, exhausted, and not capable of any entanglements. Her emotional wiring had shorted out.

Joe lived in the Coral Villas apartments off Summerlin Road not far from the Sanibel Causeway. Built in the fifties in the Spanish Colonial style, with lots of cupolas and curving balconies, the complex of six and eight-unit detached buildings were clustered around a network of canals. Angie followed Joe off his screened porch. A snazzy two-seater with a cutty cabin bobbed at the dock.

"Is that your boat?"

"Joy Ride? Yes ma'am." Joe lifted the lid on the barbeque grill and set the steak on the rack above the coals he'd lit earlier. "I thought after we'd burned out your windpipe on the steak, we'd cool you off with a spin on the river. We could stop by The Bridge for a nightcap. Friend of mine's the jazz pianist there."

"Great," Angie said.

Joe look bewildered. "Really?"

"Why not?"

"Most of the women I know won't set foot on a boat."

"I was brought up on them," Angie said.

"Where was this?"

"In the San Juan Islands."

"Puerto Rico?"

"Wrong ocean. Washington State, the part where the corner's cut out, there's a scattering of islands that straddles the Canadian border, south of Vancouver Island. Daddy had a boat works on Orcas Island. He built day sailors mostly."

"Well then," Joe said, "You can run the boat and I'll have a nap."

"Let me do something," Angie said after they had returned to the apartment with the steak, striped with charred lines, sizzling on the platter.

"Everything's ready, but since UFOrb didn't thrill you, it's your turn to pick out some music."

There was a vast assortment to choose from: classical, jazz, rock, pop. A good deal of the jazz was stuff that Angie had never heard of. She wanted something upbeat and uncomplicated and finally settled on some Norman Brown.

As the strains of "Just Between Us" filled the room, Angie strolled around the small apartment while Joe tossed the salad. It was laid out railroad style, with the small living area just beyond the kitchen and the dining area. It was furnished with a couple of chunky sofas covered with denim slipcovers. The modular coffee table proved to be a half dozen apple crates painted red, white and blue and clustered together. There were no end tables, only a pair of lamps, the el cheapo kind, from Home Depot. However, Joe's vast music collection and enormous CD player were housed in a bank of wall-hung cabinets done in rosewood and glass. Angie ran a finger along the polished surface. The work was excellent.

"Who did your wall units?" she asked.

"Yours truly."

"Nice."

The dining set was a plastic patio table and chairs. Joe pulled out a chair to seat her. "You'll notice my classic taste in furnishings," he said.

"Really, this is a clever idea," Angie said. "These plastic sets are well designed. It's a good way to start out."

"Poverty is the mother of invention," Joe said as he passed the plate of sliced steak.

The first bite of the steak threw Angie into a coughing fit. Joe handed her a glass of water, then scraped off the blackened stuff, leaving a delicious portion that she wolfed down. He'd fixed artichokes in drawn butter and baked potatoes. A homemade vinaigrette accompanied the salad.

"You must give me the recipe for this," Angie said, waving her fork.

"It's Nora Ephron's."

"Really?"

"In *Crazy Salad*. Nora figured her husband might walk for another woman, but he'd never abandon a good vinaigrette."

"But it didn't work for her," Angie said.

"Even vinaigrette isn't binding," Joe said with a grin. "Nothing sticks."

"Didn't work for you, either?" Angie said.

"Nope."

"What happened?"

"Heather? She was a free spirit. I was too square for her."

"And?"

"She took off for Guatemala with a horn player. The guy is an ex friend of mine."

Angie winced. "That must have hurt."

He nodded. "So much it took me three years to admit it. She had two nice little kids, too. Nathan and Bonnie. We did all the right stuff. Trips to the zoo, Disney World. It took awhile, but I'd managed to build a decent relationship with them. Then they were out of my life. Just like that." He picked up the plates.

"Let me do that," Angie said, reaching for a plate.

"Hey," Joe said. "You're bleeding." He handed her a napkin. "This calls for ice."

Angie stared at the thin cut on her index finger. What had she done?

Joe came back with an ice pack and a hand towel. He daubed the blood off Angie's finger, checked the cut, applied the ice and wrapped her hand in the towel.

"I think I'll live," Angie said with a grin.

Joe set a snifter of brandy in front of her. "An early day pain remedy," he said, taking a seat beside her.

"It doesn't hurt," Angie said. "I can't figure out how I did it."

"I'm relieved," Joe said. "I thought my cooking drove you to a suicide attempt."

"Joe, your cooking is wonderful," Angie said. "I'm impressed. As for your dinette set...frankly, I think I cut myself on the side of the chair."

"Wonderful," Joe said. "I invite a lady to dinner and seat her on a lethal weapon."

He moved her to the sofa, then went back and upended the chair. "You're right. There's a sharp ridge right along the bottom. I suppose we could sue the manufacturer."

"I don't think that will be necessary," Angie said.

"Coffee?" he said.

"Why not?" her finger was beginning to throb, very lightly, nothing much, and the wine and the brandy had softened the edges of her consciousness. She wanted the coffee to bring her back into focus. She was having such a good time with Joe that she wanted the night to go on and on.

It was after nine by the time the Joy Ride left the dock. They eased down the narrow canals, careful to leave no wake. An enormous pale moon threw molten silver shards across the blackened waters.

Joe gunned the engine and the nose of the boat rose, settling Angie back into her seat. The breezes furled through her hair.

"It's lovely out here," Angie shouted, "but how do you know where you're going?"

"Don't worry. I know where every sandbar is." Moonlight glinted off his teeth as he added the punch line: "I've been stuck on every one of them."

"That's comforting," Angie said.

They rode along in a companionable silence, Angie stealing glimpses now and then of Joe's strong profile. He could build a house. He liked music and art. He was attractive, had a sense of humor, and could protect her. She felt safe with him. She was drawn to him. She felt all the right vibes. But what did that count for anything? She had been so wrong before.

CHAPTER 27

Memphis, TN
Monday, October 25, 11 a.m.

A breast rounded and bloomed on a scarred chest wall. Grotesquely oversized bosoms shrank before Anthony's eyes. Noses thinned, bellies flattened, saddlebag thighs turned pencil thin. Anthony sat in awe watching a promotional video in Dr. Frederick Rossellini's office.

"It's a little racy for a waiting room," Jenny Sawyer whispered.

"The score is tacky," Anthony said. "A little Beethoven, or maybe some Vivaldi would be better."

"What about Stravinsky?" Jenny said, giggling. "The Rite of Spring. Ta-ta-ta." She jerked in her chair, emphasizing the pounding beat of the symphony she imagined in her head.

"Jenny," he said, gazing into her eyes. "You are my springtime. You've made me bloom," he said, stilling her with a pat to the back of her hand, "Now pay attention, my dear. Notice what we don't see here—no swelling, bruising or bleeding. This man is pretending metamorphosis can be had without a moment's discomfort."

"I know that, dearest, but isn't it wonderful? And I am going through with it. After all, Dr. Brothers said to go for it. I'm giving myself permission," Jenny said pouting.

"Mrs. Sawyer? Dr. Rossellini can see you now," a nurse announced.

115

The Don Juan Con

They were escorted into a palatial office, filled with cherry paneling, leather sofas and silk flowers. Despite the staid setting, Rossellini proved to be a kid sporting a moustache, which looked as though it had been pasted on his face.

In the past three days, Anthony had escorted Jenny to every plastic surgeon in Memphis, and they came in all types. The dashing Chilean with dark Latino looks, the blond, Germanic type who had been brought up in South Africa, the Jewish prince in the bow tie, and the art collector with the booming voice, complete with Adonis statues all over his office and tasteful nudes on the wall. Not the usual sort of shopping trip his lady friends enjoyed, but so what? Anthony was getting a complete education here. These doctors had made him aware that with judicial applications of money, he could easily make Anthony Abruzzi completely disappear, and soon it would be time for the dashing lawyer to vanish.

By now, Anthony was accomplished at his role in the proceedings. He got out the tiny spiral notebook Jenny wanted kept. Her memory wasn't what it used to be. She couldn't keep the various prices, procedures and practitioners straight in her head.

He had to repeat them to her over and over again, even over the expensive dinners he lavished on her, but so what? Jenny was having the time of her life, and he didn't even have to promise to marry her. With Jenny, he played the role of the son she had but who had never taken any interest in her.

Dutifully they reported what Rossellini needed to hear: Yes, Jenny was in good general health, and no she didn't smoke, and of course she could supply her medical records from her family physician. What Rossellini proposed to do was pretty much standard fare: first a phenol peel to burn off the sun damaged skin, which would probably eliminate about seventy percent of her wrinkles. This would be the messiest and most painful procedure. The deeper wrinkles could be dealt with by Botox injections. The face-lift, cheek implants, and the eye and nose job could all be done at once. With that much surgery, he encouraged a hospital stay, rather than an outpatient procedure, and, depending on the bruising, which they couldn't predict, she'd probably need a month to six weeks to recuperate.

"Why, I could have everything done while you are trying your case, and I'd be all ready for Italy in the fall," Jenny said, beaming at him.

Folding his hands, the doctor looked at Anthony. It was quite obvious the doc was fishing for an explanation of what he was doing there.

"Jenny's a dear friend," he explained. "She's agreed to accompany

116

my mother and sister on a junket to the old country later in the year. And she wants to look perfect for the trip."

"If we start next week," Rossellini said, visibly relieved at Anthony's explanation, "That should give Mrs. Sawyer ample time to recuperate."

When they were safely in the elevator outside Rossellini's office, Jenny nuzzled up to him.

"I haven't a clue which doctor to choose," she said. "I can't even remember how many I've seen. And how many more are we scheduled to interview?"

The elevator door opened, letting them out into the parking garage. "We've just enough time to do a leisurely lunch at that French place you mentioned," Anthony said. "Then we'll just have to part. I'm tied up in depositions all evening."

"Oh, pooh," Jenny pouted. "You'll miss the country club dinner. I'm dying to show you off."

There was a card with a single red rose for Jenny on the cushioned seat of the Lincoln. It said, *You are perfectly beautiful, just the way you are.*

"Now Anthony, we've been all through this," Jenny said, her eyes tearing as they pulled out into the street.

"Yes, my darling, I know. Far be it for me to tangle with that precious woman's psyche. And Joan told me herself that this sort of thing is really a morale booster."

"I'd love to meet her," Jenny said.

"She lives like a Russian duchess, you know," Anthony replied. "Her people were white Russians. That nosy neighbor she plays in her comedy act is all a put on."

"I think I'll go with that young Rossellini. Usually they say the more experienced person is the best, but he told me he's trained in that new method. What do you call it? My mind is a sieve."

"The SMAS," Anthony said, "Now that you've convinced me you really are serious about this, why don't you let me talk to Mama Regina? Haroldson did her, you know, and everyone insists, much to her delight, that mama and I are brother and sister. Haroldson owes us one. After Mama did up his dingy offices, he always said his patients seemed to heal more quickly, and his practice increased by twenty five percent. As a personal favor, he might work you in."

"Haroldson?" Jenny said.

"He does most of the Broadway people. Naturally, he's excellent. Expensive as hell, but I've heard Joan say he's worth every penny and you know she knows only the best."

CHAPTER 28

Sarasota, FL
Wednesday, October 28, 3 p.m.

Deputy Phillip Lowry was built like a side of beef. His hulking presence menaced the raspberry pink ambience of The Cloisters, a tony psychiatric hospital in the heart of establishment Sarasota. It was just off University Boulevard, a short walk to the Asolo Theater and the Ringling Museum of Art. The tapestry sofas in its waiting room would do nicely in the lobby of a five star resort. Angie and Joe settled down on the peony sectional. Russell Wyatt was enthroned in a Chinese peacock chair, while Lowry squirmed on a claw-footed bench upholstered in an oriental tapestry. He looked as content as a circus bear at a tea party as he talked about his sister, Nettie French.

"Never did see Nettie like this. Nossir." For all his bulk, Angie noticed, Lowry had a delicate chin, which wobbled with emotion as he talked.

"When did it happen?" Joe said.

"Sunday night. I got to worrying," Lowry replied. He removed his peaked felt hat, set it beside him on the bench and nervously swiped back his spiky crew cut with a beefy hand. "Sis answered the phone, but it didn't sound at all like her. She does go on a bender now and then, so I hustled right over, thank God. Nettie is one tough gal. I've knowed my big sister to throw off some awful big disappointments without it bothering her a bit. But this time something snapped."

118

The deputy took a folded square of canary paper out of the flap pocket of his uniform shirt and passed it to Joe. "I found Nettie on the floor with this in her hand."

Angie threw Russell a rueful glance, but he was studying the silver conches threaded into the leather hatband of his Stetson. The flier was one of a thousand she and Russell had printed and mailed.

"Didn't pay it no mind at the time," Lowry said as Joe studied the yellow notice. "Too busy getting pills and booze pumped out of her stomach. Later, I found out ya'll had sent these to real estate offices hereabouts." The deputy handed Angie a manila envelope he took from a zippered portfolio propped beside the bench. "Is that your fella?"

Angie's hands were trembling so that she could barely open the envelope. She slid out a sepia toned eight by ten inch photo in a silver filigree frame. "What do you know, but I took one look at the flier, and later I saw the dude all framed up on my sister's grand piana," Lowry said. In the photo, Anthony was standing in front of a fountain, one foot up on the rim, a hand extended.

"Anthony in his glory," Angie said with a grimace. "Can't you just hear him belting out Three Coins in a Fountain?"

Joe inspected the photo. "Slick," he murmured and handed it to Russell.

"He looks so trustworthy," Russell said. "He reminds me of that Barney Miller character who used to be on TV."

"Well, guess what? Show's canceled," Joe murmured.

"But he wasn't slick to talk to," Angie said. "He was earnest to the point of earthiness, and so disarming."

"So what did he disarm your sister for?" Joe said to Lowry.

"Forty-seven five. It was the first sale Nettie had made for months. Claimed to be in real estate just like her. Nettie told him how she'd had this long dry spell, and how her bills had piled up and she was going to pay everything off with this hefty commission check."

"Did he deposit any money in her bank account?"

"Oh yeah. He gave her ten thousand in deposit slips over three days time. All bogus, except the first, which was a refund check from a local jeweler, Larry Parvey. The jeweler's a friend of the family, by the way. He can identify this character."

"How did Anthony get away with Nettie's money?" Joe said.

"He rode right along with Nettie when she deposited her big check. He ran around the bank like a nut case, bragging to every customer in there what a great saleswoman she was." Lowry shifted on the bench, brushing back his thin crew cut with both hands, obviously uncomfortable in the role of someone being questioned. "Then they went over to Renaldi's for a fancy lunch. It's one of them places with a bunch of potted palms and a good view of the yacht harbor. Nettie's broker and her best friend from the office went along. Anthony played it up big. He ordered a magnum of Dom Perignon. They had a good start on it when Anthony gets this call on his cellular. He tells Nettie his partner needs the ten thousand right away. Supposedly, this was money he had stashed in Nettie's bank account for safekeeping."

"No need to interrupt the party. He'll go to the bank, wire the money, then rejoin them. He makes a show of getting Nettie to call ahead and authorize him to get his money," Lowry said, shaking his head. "Setting up his alibi, see? Then he drives right down to Nettie's bank and cleans her out while she and her friends did some serious damage to the champagne. Anthony never made it back to the party, but he did leave five-hundred dollars under his plate. I guess so's Nettie wouldn't be completely destitute," Lowry said, settling back on the bench, crossing his arms.

"But this all took place three months ago," Joe said. "He hit Nettie just after he took Angie. He probably wooed some other Sarasota belles at the same time."

"No doubt," the deputy said. "But nobody complained to us. And as you know, when I began to look into it, the driver's license he used was a fake."

"At this point we still haven't a clue who Anthony Abruzzi really is," Joe said.

"Nossir," the deputy said. "I filed a report and all, but we got zero response. Deputy prosecutor's a friend of mine. Said that even if we found the guy, a good lawyer would cut Nettie up bad in court. Then how would she look? She's a well-known commercial broker with a reputation to maintain. I took sis out, bought her a few stiff drinks, and told her that for her own sake we'd best forget about this. Nettie held up. I tell you, she's a real trooper. She put in fifteen-hour days to make up her losses. Her broker helped her out.

A nurse appeared. "You may see Ms. French now," she said.

The deputy rose and picked up his hat. "And now this. What this is, the doctor thinks, is a delayed stress reaction brought on by Nettie working herself to the bone. Then Anthony pops up in her face again, right on your little ole wanted poster."

"I'm so sorry. I feel terrible for her. I never would have sent those out if I thought they would upset the victims," Angie said. "May I see her?"

CHAPTER 29

Angie tiptoed into Nettie's room where lavish bouquets of carnations and roses were wilting on the nightstand. The sour odor of floral decay had set in. A pile of get-well cards lay unopened on Nettie's lunch tray. One bite had been taken out of a turkey sandwich. The accompanying trimmings, coleslaw with bits of red pepper in it, and a round of jellied cranberries, went untouched. The face was still on the pillow. Nettie's mouth turned down. Black, puffy rings hung under her eyes, which were open but unfocused. The sheets and bedclothes, as well as Nettie's hair were disheveled. It was obvious that her current exhaustion had to do with a struggle that had taken place on the previous lengthy night.

"Nettie? I'm Angie Reynolds. May I talk to you?" she murmured. "When I sent out the fliers, I was just trying to...I didn't mean to..."

Nettie, sallow and wan, seemed not to have heard. Angie found herself staring at Nettie's ear, peeking out from a fashionable haircut grown shaggy. If she didn't know that Nettie French was a successful commercial real estate broker, Angie might have mistaken her for some refugee whose hair had been tortured with tin snips.

Angie dropped into the chair next to Nettie's bed and poured out an elaborate apology. "It never occurred to me for a minute that my flier would upset a victim. Believe me, if I ever guessed any such thing, I would never have sent it out. And here you are in this hospital, Nettie. I know the feeling. When Anthony ran me into bankruptcy I just couldn't cope. I collapsed right after the hearing, and wound up in the emergency room. On top of that, my son was traumatized. Then I found out there are a lot of us out there, and we're kissed off by the police because we won't fight back. So I put out the flier to get the jump on Anthony. But I just can't tell you how terrible I feel when I look at you, Nettie. I know exactly what you are going through." Angie saw a tremor in Nettie's tanned arm, now a faded yellow except where it was banded at the wrist by a broad white patch.

Angie reached across the bed and took Nettie's hand. Her fingers were icy. Angie rubbed warmth into them. "What do you want, Nettie? How can I help?"

"Where's the controller for the damned bed?" Nettie rumbled, her voice thick from disuse. Angie found it for her and guided it into her palm. Nettie sat up. She blinked. Her head turned, dispelling her dulled expression. "Would you get my purse darlin'?"

Angie found Nettie's purse in the closet.

"Now, you should find a little mirror there in the side pocket." Nettie took the mirror and sat examining herself, pulling at the loose skin along her jaw line. "My skin fits me like a baggy suit, don't it? Hell, looking like this, I couldn't sell St. Armand's Circle for two cents to Donald Trump."

Nettie tossed the mirror on the bed. Shifting the covers, she pulled her knees in close to her body and wrapped her elbows around them, rocking in place, as if she were trying to calm some wounded infant deep inside herself.

"I'll never again trust any of those walking pricks, never! I'm so stupid, I couldn't even get exclusively swindled. I was just the newest pledge to Delta Fucked Upsilon, Sorority with the World's Highest Dues." Nettie's face darkened. Her brows drew together. Her forehead scrunched up and her teeth were clenched. Tears of frustration leaked from her narrowed eyes.

Fighting for control, Angie choked back her own sobs. She heard Joe's gentle knock. Joe and Russell moved toward Nettie's bedside, but Angie shook her head. "Give us some time here," she snapped. Then she realized she was taking out her anger on them. Her tone softened. "I'm sorry. I don't mean to pick on you guys, but why don't you go have some damned doughnuts."

Daylight was leaching out of the sky by the time Russell and Joe called again at the door of Nettie's room. They found the two women laughing about the identical cards they'd gotten from Anthony, pledging his undying love.

"You take care now," Angie said, patting Nettie's hand. "I'm sorry we had to meet under such awful circumstances, but you're a survivor. You'll put this behind you."

Nettie said nothing, but she at least tried to smile. Half making it, she squeezed Angie's hand so hard her fingers felt numb.

"Nettie isn't sure she's going to help us," Angie murmured to Russell. "I told her about Maria Whitman. Maybe you can help me convince her to testify." She introduced Russell to Nettie, and then took Joe's arm. "Let's give them some private time."

As they hovered outside the door, they heard Russell's gentle murmuring. At one point, Nettie moaned in horror. Then a nurse quickly went in with a syringe and Russell came out.

"Visiting hours are over," he said.

The three of them stood in front of the elevator.

"My feeling is, Nettie wants to help us," Russell finally said as they watched the overhead numbers descend. "I expect we'll hear from her tomorrow." Then he turned to Joe, "I believe there's an important link in this case to a certain bracelet Nettie always wore. Her arm's all white and bare where it used to be. When I happened to touch that white place on her arm, a strong feeling came over me. Nettie said she gave the bracelet to her brother. I would urge you ask deputy Lowry to have it dusted for fingerprints."

CHAPTER 30

Memphis, TN
Wednesday October 28

Jenny Sawyer paused in front of the people mover conveyor. Passengers dodged around them in the busy Memphis airport.

"I know you love showing off your new Valentino, my dear, but this isn't that kind of runway," Anthony said.

Giggling, Jenny stroked the wide velvet collar of the fitted houndstooth coatdress. It was a little too warm for a humid afternoon in Memphis but perfect for the plane ride where cabins tended to be cold, and exactly right for late night dining in Manhattan, Anthony had told her.

"I caught a shoelace in an escalator when I was four. It dragged me down the stairs," Jenny said. "I've never trusted any conveyor since."

"Scarred for life, you poor dear. It's a good thing I'm here to take care of you," he said. He shifted his flight bag to the opposite shoulder, slipped his arm around her waist and urged her forward. She stepped onto the conveyor and grabbed the handrail. While other passengers strolled right along, Jenny clutched the rubber railing in one hand and his briefcase in the other and refused to budge.

"What time will we get to New York?" Jenny said. She fanned her sweaty face with a pair of first class tickets as the conveyor moved along.

"Certainly in time for dinner at The Four Seasons. I invited Mama to join us. I hope you won't mind."

"Mind? Why should I?" Jenny said. "I feel as if I know that grand woman already. "What was her name again?"

"Regina, my dear."

"Anthony, I'm so terrible. I know you told me your mother's name before. Do you suppose they have plastic surgery for brains?"

"My dear Jenny. Never lose that wonderful sense of humor," he said, pecking her cheek.

It took them nearly fifteen minutes to reach South Concourse. At the gate, a flight attendant had already announced first class was boarding.

They passed a long line of Japanese students in sweatshirts, jeans and backpacks, and caught up with what few first class passengers there were: an elderly couple in golf togs and matching tams, and a cluster of businessmen in western cut suits.

He settled Jenny in the window seat and handed her his briefcase. "Now, my dear, put that under the seat in front of you and make sure we don't forget it when we get off the plane."

"Why would a surgeon like Haroldson need cash?" Jenny said.

"Shhhhh," Anthony said, leaning close to whisper in her ear. "The IRS. He doesn't dare show another penny in income this year. I have the same problem. The government is trying to bankrupt the working professional."

"You know, I'm so tired," she murmured.

"I kept you out too late, dear," Anthony murmured.

"Oh, but it was so much fun," Jenny said. "Wait'll I tell everyone at the garden club we gambled in three casinos, danced in Overton Square, did Beale Street from one end to the other and closed up B.B. King's?" Behind Jenny's bright smile were the pinched and weary face and the yellowed eye whites that signaled exhaustion. Jenny definitely needed to catch some sleep.

A stewardess came around with blankets, magazines, complimentary headsets and playing cards and an engraved menu listing the beverages available. Anthony ordered a split of champagne. The phone beeped in his pocket. He had to unbutton the Novecento jacket he wore. It was loosely woven but tightly fitted. This gift from Jenny knocked him out.

"Damn. Wouldn't you know," he hissed as he unfolded the phone. "Abruzzi," he barked. His face broke into a broad smile as the caller identified himself.

The Don Juan Con

"Mr. Rombino." His tone was pure bootlick. "How's the don today? How can I help you?" his eyes widened in alarm. "What? An indictment?" A passenger across the aisle stared at him. He lowered his voice and hunkered down in his seat. "Those bastards. The D.A. himself promised me they wouldn't do such a thing. I'll take care of it, as soon as I get to New York. What? Handcuffs? I don't believe it..." He held the phone away from his ear, making a face for Jenny's benefit. She laughed. After a long pause, he put the receiver back. "Yessir. I'll be there in fifteen minutes."

"Miss, hold the plane," he shouted to a stewardess who was drawing a curtain across the back of the section.

"Jenny, sweetheart," he said. "I'm so sorry. A client has just been taken into custody. They've got him in the Memphis jail right now, waiting to grill him. I have to go." He opened the overhead bin and got down his flight bag.

"Why, it's all right. We can take a later flight," Jenny said, reaching for the sleek case under the seat in front of her.

"Mama Regina will be so disappointed," he said. "I tell you what. You go on. I'll call ahead and have her meet your flight. I wouldn't want you to miss The Four Seasons. Reservations are so hard to get. Now, if you happen to meet Eddie Bronfman, whose family owns the Seagram Building—where the Four Seasons is?—you have to ask him to do a bar or two of the new song he wrote for Barbra. She hasn't recorded it yet. I'm going to try to wrap up this Rombino thing in the next hour. I'll follow on the six o'clock shuttle and meet you girls at the restaurant. "If Jenny is a good girl and sleeps all the way to New York, Anthony promises he'll take her out to the disco this evening. *Arrividerchi*, doll," he said, kissing her cheek.

He peeled five hundred dollar bills from a thick roll in his pocket and pressed them into her hand.

"What's that for?" she said.

"Cab fare, a new outfit. Whatever." he said. He closed in on her face with a soulful glance, "Don't let that case out of your sight," then dashed down the aisle. Then he came back. "Oh. And would you do me a very great favor and wear that Carolina Herrera with the oversize cuffs this evening? You are so witty in it."

"Land, Anthony, I don't know where you get your energy," Jenny called to his retreating back.

The plane was overbooked. In the business section, puzzled people were standing in the aisles while flight attendants tried to find seats for them. He handed a twenty-dollar bill to the male flight attendant who was reopening the side door of the plane to let him off. "Take care of my lady. *Capisce?*"

He hurried up the boarding tunnel, checking his inside coat pocket for the key to the briefcase that was under Jenny's seat. No way would she discover, any time soon, that the case she had was a ringer he'd switched in the parking lot. Her twenty-five thou was now in the twin briefcase in the trunk of his car.

He recapped his week as he stepped on the people mover for the main terminal. With Jenny's twenty five, plus the fifteen he'd have from Marci Trillin tonight, added to the seventy-five hundred from that mousy little secretary that should be ready to hit by Friday, Memphis was looking good. Memphis was a winner. It was time to do another laundry and move on.

He checked his Rolex. He had to hurry. It was three ten already. Twenty-two minutes to get out of the airport, twenty-five minutes to Marci's ranch. This afternoon he and Marci were shopping for her trousseau, and Marci had a show to do tonight. He couldn't believe Marci wouldn't set foot in any of the designer salons he'd tried out on her yesterday. She insisted on that corny cowboy stuff from The Hayloft. She'd bought him cowboy boots. These he'd ship to Adolph Tadeschi out in Monterey.

As he strode along in the fast lane on the people mover, he smiled mirthlessly. For once it wouldn't be acting when it came time to hate everything Marci tried on. She'd be so tired and frustrated that she'd be secretly pleased if he had trouble with the arrest of the don, Mr. Rombino, and couldn't take her home after her show.

He winced and his stomach roiled at the thought of taking the secretary out for barbeque after he dropped Marci off at the stage door, but duty called.

As he rode the people mover, he fixed his next immediate destination in his mind: the parking lot, section F, aisle twelve, row twenty-three. With his subconscious programmed to hone on his next move, he was free to get back to romance. He pulled out his flip phone, punched in the first number and glanced at his Rolex. He would allow seven and a half minutes of love talk to each of his sweethearts.

CHAPTER 31

Sanibel Island, FL
Friday, October 30

The awnings of the Mucky Duck restaurant ruffled in the breeze. The waves piling in wore scallops of foam. It was perfect parasailing weather along the golden beaches of Captiva Island. Angie squinted so hard her eyes teared. Her smile spread to its limits with pride and delight as she watched Jason zip and tack along.

Jason had spent the whole day trying to master this new sport, and it was evident that if the adults let him have his way, he'd be out in the Gulf until midnight. A pod of dolphins dipped and bobbed through the waves. Jason trimmed the sail closer to the wind and the board shot ahead as he tried to follow them.

"Uh oh," Angie said. "How soon do you think he'll spill?"

"I'd give him about two minutes," Joe said.

They'd spent a lazy day snorkeling and shelling on the apron of beach near Lighthouse Point on the southern tip of Sanibel Island. Angie, sand covered and a bit sunburned, was relaxed to the point of laziness. When Joe had suggested they drive north to Captiva, take in the sunset and have dinner, she was only too happy to comply.

As Jason caught a puff of wind, the sail bellied out. His body canted over the waves as the board sliced through the water. "Beautiful," Angie murmured, glancing at her watch. Then the sail flapped and sagged,

128

the board slowed and Jason peeled off with a resounding slap. "Ouch." Her face squinted up.

Joe smiled, "He'll be all right. So how'd he do?"

Angie glanced at her watch. "Seventy five seconds. Official lapsed time."

"Not bad."

"Thanks for inviting him. He seems to be coming around a bit."

"He needs time."

"Don't we all?"

"Not all of us," Joe said softly, leaning into her space, fixing her with his changeable eyes. Today they were silvery disks in a darkly tanned face. "I'm ready to move ahead."

Angie stared into her Mai Tai, stabbing at it with her swizzle stick. Oh God. Why was she always saying the wrong thing? It would be so easy to start something with him. His need was there. Joe was such a good man. He cared for both of them. Jason adored Joe. But Angie was knocked out. Anesthetized. Numb to the core.

"Angie," he said softly, his expression tender. "I get the feeling you want me to be in the picture, so long as you can leave me dangling from the edge of the frame."

"I'm sorry," Angie said, dropping her eyes. "I'm not ready for a relationship." Her face was propped on one hand as she toyed with her drink. "After Alan died, I couldn't face it. I denied how much he hurt me. I tried to pick up and go on. I never gave myself time to heal, and that's where I got in trouble with Anthony. He offered me a chance to escape from myself. Now I'm really messed up." Where this was heading? She had to avoid it. Why had she agreed to have dinner with him? Because he has something to show me, that's why. Not because he fixes me splat like a bug on a slide with those beautiful eyes.

Joe's jaw worked. His expression darkened. "That's the victim talking, Angie. How long can you punish yourself?"

"What's that supposed to mean?"

"Nothing," Joe said, lifting his shoulders, looking away from her.

Angie picked up the eight by ten inch glossy photo he'd brought her. At first glance it looked like some arty shot of the rings on a tree stump.

"Russell Wyatt may be a wacko. I have no idea why he picked up on the idea that Anthony might have left a print on Nettie French's bracelet, but there it is," Joe said.

"Which finger is it?" she said.

"Right thumbprint. You tell by the elongation of it, and the direction of the shape."

"It's so clear."

"Oh, yes, indeed." He lolled in his deck chair, legs sprawled out. For a while, they said nothing at all, simply soaked up the salt air. Angie studied Joe as he gazed into the horizon where a line of flattened clouds battened a ball of sun heading for a splashdown.

As his bony fingers worried a spoon, Angie watched the mesmerizing cartwheel: bowl to handle. Bowl to handle. Weren't the two of them just like that? Wheeling along at the opposite ends of a fulcrum?

She clamped her hand over his to stop the motion. "Busy fingers, busy mind. So tell me. What's gnawing at you?"

He looked down at her hand placed over his, then gave her a sidelong glance. The corner of his mouth lifted in a grin. Angie flushed and withdrew her hand. Joe shook his head, picked up the spoon, and tapped it on the edge of his plate, "Here's the trouble. We get a perfect print off Nettie's bracelet. We should have had a computer match like that." He snapped his fingers. "Instead, we draw another blank. So who the hell *is* this guy?"

"What's so strange? You've always said police rarely catch these swindlers," Angie was irritated with herself. She hated to admit it, but she was miffed that he'd let her get them back to the business at hand. Obviously, he wasn't so taken with their relationship. But then why had he said what he said? And didn't the annoyance she was feeling prove what she'd just thought, that they were always at opposite places at any given moment?

"We do catch them—but not for swindling. We get them for petty stuff. Loitering. Traffic tickets. Jaywalking. Drunk and disorderly. Parole violations. We just can't put them away. As active as this guy is? It's impossible he hasn't taken a fall somewhere."

"Fall," Angie murmured, with a shudder. "God. Here I am in this beautiful spot, right in broad daylight, but in my mind's eye I just saw Maria Whitman going over those stairs."

"That's another thing. The Whitman incident is entirely out of character. Sweetheart swindlers are nice guys," Joe said, pulling at his bony chin. "They aren't rapists. They aren't vicious. They are very careful not to rough women up. They take the money and run." He shifted his chair, squaring it with the table, and shrugged his jacket straight.

"Are you trying to say he didn't kill Maria?"

"Of course he killed her, but I doubt very much that he planned to. I haven't a clue how Russell figured it out, but I believe he's right about how it happened."

"It's still murder, right?"

"Yes, ma'am. Maria Whitman's death happened during Anthony's attempt to defraud. What bothers me is, the scene at Maria's was just too clean, too professional."

Angie leaned forward on her elbows. "He didn't plan for it to happen, but he knew what to do when it did. Doesn't this mean he makes a habit of doing in his victims?"

Joe shook his head. "If that were the case, we wouldn't have so many victims still alive who've recognized him. Nettie French, you, and all those cases you've identified in our old police files. There has to be some other reason why the pieces won't come together. Maybe this Anthony is more than a flimflam artist."

"So what do we do next?" Angie said.

"Consult the Feds," Joe said, picking up his menu. "Fortunately, I've got a good contact."

CHAPTER 32

Memphis, TN
Saturday, October 31, 3 p.m.

The Witches' Brew was right down Main off Union Avenue where the concierge at the Peabody Hotel said it was. It proved to be an elaborate costume shop complete with birdbaths running red with fake blood, a rogue's gallery of rubber masks of the recent U.S. presidents, and racks of costumes which took up two floors of the shop.

Anthony enjoyed the heavy pirate coats with big brass buttons but couldn't find a proper fit. There were also screaming orange prison jumpsuits, which made him nervous. He finally settled on a Dracula cape because he enjoyed the feel of the velvet it was made from and the flow of it when he walked, which suggested he might cut quite a figure on the dance floor. Besides, he could wear it over his white dinner jacket with a red bow tie. He bought some white theatrical paint for his face, enough charcoal mascara to make dark circles under the eyes, a set of plastic vampire teeth and enough fake blood to dribble on his chin.

At the cash register, the manager wore a turban and an Osama bin Laden mask. There was a bloody glove dropping out of the pocket of his sweatsuit. He put the magazines Anthony had picked up at The Peabody newsstand into the shopping bag with the costume. He asked, "So Count Dracula reads *Bon Appétit?*"

132

"For how to make the blood pooding," Anthony whispered, working to capture the understated menace of monster meisters like Peter Lorre and Vincent Price.

The costume shop was located in the center of an airy, brick-lined plaza, closed to traffic, and lined with small shops. Next door was an old-fashioned nut house, where he watched small boxcars of nuts traveling through roasters and salting machines. For some reason, his thoughts strayed to Marci Trillin, whose money was now on the way to Monterey, right along with Jenny Sawyer's handsome contribution to his retirement fund.

He should have been long gone from Memphis by now. But with Jenny Sawyer and her notoriously bad memory off in New York, he had little to fear. Jenny would probably forget he'd existed, long before someone took pity on her and put her on a plane for home.

As for Marci, thanks to a blank check he had borrowed from a lovely lady in Mobile, Alabama, his ersatz deposit wouldn't show up as bogus in the singer's bank account for another five to seven days. Since he was having such a good time, there was no point in rushing off.

He tossed the peanuts in a trash can, eyed the hotdogs roasting on a wagon outside Witches' Brew, and decided to take in air instead of more fat. In the fictitious end of the legal profession, the waistline counted for more than with bona fide members of the bar.

He'd started past the next shop, a bookstore, except that a trailing whiff of incense caught his attention and prompted him to turn back. Crystal prisms and teardrops hung in the window. When he peered in, he saw that the shelves were marked off: Tarot. Paranormal. Astral Projection. He noticed the name of the place on a brass plate beside the door: The Aura. As Maria Whitman would say, this was definitely a sign that he was to check the place out—especially the willowy blonde in horn rimmed-glasses at the cash register.

"May I help you?" She said in a high-pitched voice that was a dead giveaway.

"Toronto, eh?"

"Montreal, eh?" she replied. They burst into simultaneous laughter at the trademark Canuk locution.

"So what brings a Canadian lovely to Memphis?"

"A blues singer boyfriend." She smiled showing beautiful teeth.

"Do you know Marci Trillin?"

"She's more in the folk tradition, but my boyfriend was in the group that backed her last album."

"Well," Anthony said, waving the shopping bag from Witches'

Brew, "Ms. Trillin's my life's blood tonight."

Bitter smile. "Ahh. The costume party on Beale Street?"

"Fright Night. Will we scare you there?"

She shook her head. "Mark has a gig."

"Blues and New Age. That must make for interesting conversation,"

"Or none at all," the blonde replied, laughing.

"You have a lovely laugh, very musical," Anthony said. "He must love you for your voice."

"And not my luscious body?" she struck a hipshot pose, head tilted back, and ran her fingers through her flighty hair.

"Lovely, lovely," he said. "Your Mark is a lucky guy."

But the woman straightened her shoulders and folded her arms over the counter. The flirtation was over. "What can I do for you, sir?"

"I'm looking for whatever you have on Edgar Cayce. He was worshipped in my family. He cured my great aunt of what today would probably be considered depression."

"How interesting," the blonde said, trilling on the words. Anthony was fascinated. He could listen to this woman talk all day. "It does seem to me there is something new on Cayce," she said, muttering to herself. "But the question is: Do we have it in yet?" She pecked away at her computer keyboard.

"Yes. You're in luck, Mr.—"

"Abruzzi. Anthony Abruzzi. I'm on a lesser plane of the field of justice," he said, handing her his card.

"An attorney?" she said.

"Yes, but true justice is eternal, as my old friend, Maria Whitman once said."

Behind her glasses, Anthony watched faint crow's feet squint in surprise. "Did you know Maria Whitman?"

"Through her books. Only her books," Anthony said.

"We have her collected works in a new edition," the woman replied, her expression turning somber. "You of course know she's dead?"

"Mrs. Whitman?" He widened his eyes in feigned surprise and covered his mouth with his hand. "A terrible loss. However, I feel certain she's alive in another dimension."

"Right." The blonde smiled nervously. She punched at her keyboard some more, a little jerkily, Anthony thought. "Come to think of it, the Whitman is still in the back. The Cayce's over there in the prognostication section, if you'd care to browse through it, while I go back and have a look."

"Thanks. I'm dying to see whether the author got the account from my family," he said.

The Canadian beamed. "Wouldn't that be exciting?" Her hair swung to one side as she dodged around the counter and headed for the back.

Anthony looked through all the Cayce books, and had read four pages from the most recent biography, when he checked his Rolex. Fifteen minutes. What could be keeping blondie? And why hadn't he nailed down her name? He really was slipping. He went to the rear of the store through swinging doors. On the left was a room that reeked with the earthy smells of roots and incense. On the right was a small, unoccupied office. He walked toward the desk. Right on top of the blotter was a canary flier with a bad drawing of him on it.

"Wanted for questioning in the death of astrologer Maria Whitman. Known to frequent New Age stores," he read, grimacing as his heart went into seizure mode.

He wadded up the flier and flung it to the wall. The damned drawing made him look like a common criminal. As he darted out, he grabbed the shopping bag he'd left on the counter and strolled toward the front door, but a uniform in a badge was on the way in. He wheeled around and lunged for the root room in the back, wiping his forehead with his elbow. His face was dripping. His body, pumping adrenaline, jerked and twitched. His nose began to run. The smell in that cramped place was unbearable. He had to get out of there before he started to sneeze.

He emerged from the root room so dizzy he had to inch along the wall of the hall for support. He crept toward the back exit. He tried several doors as he heard approaching voices.

"Stop!" the Canadian woman shrieked as he finally found the right door and bolted. The daylight blinded him. He couldn't see a ready escape route, so he opted for diversion.

He picked up a rock and hurled it against the side of a rusty dumpster streaked with yellow paint about thirty feet from the door. As the rock pinged against metal, the officer poked his head out the back. Anthony stepped behind a pile of packing boxes as the cop rushed the container, opening the lid. The dumpster was chest high on him and big enough to hold ten men.

"Put you hands on your head and come out of there," the cop shouted, drawing his gun. Anthony crept away in the opposite direction, and then realized he was trapped in a cul-de-sac.

The Don Juan Con

Damn. He'd distracted the cop into blocking his own exit. Holding the container lid above his head, the officer shifted cardboard boxes inside with the barrel of his gun. Anthony made a dash for it.

Hearing him coming, the cop turned his head.

Wham!

Anthony smashed the container lid down on the uniform's skull. Groaning, the officer slumped, his eyes glazed. A trail of drool marked his slide down the side. The cop landed on his face, unarmed. He'd dropped his Glock into the trash.

"Officer!" the blonde woman yelled as she emerged from the back of her store. "Are you all right?"

"The damn fool. Must be a rookie," Anthony muttered. He saw blondie hunker down beside the cop as he staggered away, sliding his back along the alley walls. His breathing was ragged, his legs watery. He couldn't keep going and was desperate to hide. As the din of distant sirens grew louder, he tried the next several doors. Then he heard barking. If dogs picked up his scent, he was cooked. What he wouldn't give for a little aromatherapy right now.

A back door opened. An unseen hand thrust a big box out, propping the door open. Anthony crept up beside the crack in the door and listened. No way did he need a run-in with the occupant. His chest was grinding on him. He had to get off his feet.

He heard the phone ringing inside, then a voice answering it. "Witches' Brew," a deep voice said.

The costume place. What luck. He slipped in the back door. He found himself inside a crowded storage room crammed with rows of shelving and cardboard boxes. Fortunately, whoever had set the packing case outside the back door had left. The door from the storage room to the sales room was ajar. The manager was on the telephone with his back to the door. Carrying the Witches' Brew shopping bag, he walked right past the manager, eased around the counter and worked his way upstairs to the balcony, stopping every few steps to rest. Nobody noticed his sweaty face and shaking hands except for a staring toddler being led downstairs on the hand of his mother. The kid took one look at him and shrieked, creating another diversion.

Upstairs, he slumped behind a rack of orange and black T-shirts with batwing logos advertising Beale Street Fright Night. He was gasping for breath. No way could he handle any more of this. His legs were gone.

He crawled to a dark corner and lay down, using the shopping bag as a pillow. He rested a few minutes then heard someone come up the

136

stairs. It was a pair of little girls with tiny breasts imprinting on their thin T-shirts—rape meat for sure, these two. What could their mamas be thinking?

"I'm going as Cinderella," said the plump, dark haired one. "What are you going to be, Sue?"

"A ho," said the taller one, sticking out her chest.

"You wish!" said the dark one, followed by peels of giggles.

They opened a can of green hair dye and shot it off. They ripped open some neon paint and glitter. Giggling, the girls chased each other around, shooting blots of colored foam at each other. The shorter one backed the tall one right into Anthony's corner. She stomped him in the ribs with her witchy, pointed shoes.

"Hey! There's a body in here," she screeched.

Anthony lunged at them, baring the vampire's teeth from the costume. "Yeaaaah!" Girls want to play? He could play too.

Screaming, the girls tumbled down the stairs.

Anthony grabbed the green paint and sprayed it on his wig, then shuffled after them in his vampire cape and snaggle incisors.

The manager, his bin Laden mask down around his neck, confronted him at the base of the stairs. He had curly hair, sideburns and a good-natured but frowning face. "What's going on? Where'd you come from?"

"Count Dracula *Bon Appétit*," he panted. He tried to raise the shopping bag but couldn't lift his arm. He waggled it beside his knee, instead.

"Oh yeah. I thought you'd be long gone." A half dozen people were crowding the counter. Clearly, the manager was going to drop the matter. He was elated.

"Hey mister," the manager called after him.

Anthony stopped. He didn't turn around. He couldn't, not without falling down. He merely cocked his head toward the voice.

"You are one sick-looking Dracula."

Waving weakly, he headed out the door, not looking back. A patrolman and a dog were working the other side of the street.

He managed to reach a pretzel vendor's bench before falling down. With a shaking hand, he bought a hot pretzel, then struggled to a table. His heart was forcing the air out of his lungs. He was seeing spots in front of his eyes. Sweat ran freely down his forehead by the time he felt a cold nose push into his hand.

"Nice pup," he said. His hands shook as he fed the pretzel to the dog.

The Don Juan Con

"Hey, man. Nice outfit. You truly do look like death," a voice said.

Through his blurring vision, Anthony saw a pudgy pink face floating over a row of brass buttons. The cop stooped down beside him, feeling his damp forehead. "Bitten by another vampire, were you?"

"This silver-haired guy jumped me," Anthony wheezed. "Knocked me down. My heart."

"Stay quiet, sir." The cop got on his radio and called for an ambulance. Then he called his dispatcher. "Brady here." I'm in front of the costume shop. A guy here is having a heart attack. Says Abruzzi knocked him down. Seems to be heading south. Would you put out a call to seal all exits?"

CHAPTER 33

DeLeon, FL
Saturday, October 31, 6 p.m.

The chain saw sputtered and stopped.

"Try again," Joe said.

Jason, down on one knee in the Goldheims' back yard, yanked at the pull chain. The chain saw sputtered and stopped.

Angie heard the phone ring inside the house. Clutching a can of mosquito repellent, she raced in, grabbed the cellular phone and returned to the screened porch to watch over her son.

"Hello, Angie," her mother said.

"Mom! How are you?" Angie beamed. She cradled the phone on her shoulder, sprayed out some repellent and slathered the stuff on her arms as they talked. Her mother was initiating a phone call? This was new.

"I'm doing well. And you, dear?" Her mother's buttery voice was back. She sounded like her old self.

"I wish you could see Jason, this minute," Angie said. She shoved open the screen door with one shoulder and headed toward the guys. "He's got this part in a Halloween show. He's going to be—a chain... Well, he's doing the special effects," Angie murmured. What was she thinking? Her mother would have a fit. She plugged her right ear as the chain saw roared, sending up a cloud of blue smoke. Joe leaned over

Jason, talking into his ear.

"Halloween has gotten to be such a production. Hasn't it?" Jane Pelham said. "I just finished making six dozen raised doughnuts for the elementary school Halloween party."

"Doughnuts?" Angie stammered. Her mouth watered. Her mother's superb doughnuts were formerly a staple of every community event. Her mother would stand for hours in front of the vats of boiling dough, face flushed, wisps of her pale hair falling out of her hastily tied bun as she fished fat doughnuts out of the oil with a long fork. Angie's job had been to dust the hot doughnuts with a shaker of sugar and pack them into waxed cartons.

"The biggest fright here is the state of my kitchen," her mother said, laughing.

"I can imagine. It's wonderful, you doing this." A pang of remorse swept over her. How long had it been since they had done anything together? Indeed, how long had it been since her mother had done anything at all? "Six dozen is a lot of work, Mom. I hope you aren't overdoing it."

"I am a little tired," her mother said. "But I do have help. Three women from the garden club are scrubbing down the kitchen. They put me out on the porch and told me not to bother them."

"Well," Angie said, and paused. She was so overcome with joy and relief she found it hard to make her mouth shape the words, "You sound so much better."

"I was just thinking, Angie. You haven't been up to the island in months. Why not come up this summer?"

"Why yes," Angie said. "Maybe we could work that out. We'd both love to see you."

"Can you get Sondra Byrd to handle your shop?"

"Oh," Angie said as she sank into a lawn chair, "The shop. Didn't I tell you? I had difficulty with the landlord," Angie said. She couldn't go on. There was a long pause.

"What about the landlord?" her mother said.

"He wanted to raise the rent. I couldn't see it. It takes awhile to establish a place, you know?" Angie's voice cracked as she lied.

"Well," her mother said, her voice harsh. "So you dumped the shop. As I think I may have mentioned..." Angie held her breath and closed her eyes, steeling herself against the expected tirade.

But her mother checked herself. "It can be so tough to start out, and I admire you for trying."

"A temporary setback," Angie said, stretching her mouth into a put-on smile and trying to sound confident. "Until I find a better space."

"It will come, dear. Hang in there."

Angie pulled the phone away from her ear and stared at it. Was this her very own mother, the redoubtable Jane Pelham speaking?

"Is everything all right?" her mother said.

"Just fine, Mom." Angie's mouth was out to here as she blathered away. "Hold on. Let me get Jason." She punched the hold button and carried the phone down the steps. She hailed Jason through a thick cloud of blue smoke as he revved the chain saw from idle to high and back.

"I think he's got it," Joe shouted, grinning broadly. Jason had the job of providing the chain saw sound effects from underneath DeLeon's famous Haunted Boardwalk, built west of town, over the city's renowned wilderness area, Cypress Slough.

She was sure he'd be bitten by snakes or mosquitoes or cut his fingers off, but Joe had taken her aside and told her to lighten up. He'd been supervising the show for five years, and every single spook had survived. She stuffed the phone under her arm and did a referee's time out signal in front of Jason's nose.

"Talk to your grandmother," she shouted, waving the phone. Jason cut the chain saw off and took the receiver.

"How is she?" Joe said as he watched Angie wipe tears out of her eyes with the back of her hand.

"I'm so relieved," Angie said. "She's beginning to sound like her old self again. Correction. She sounds like someone else entirely. Someone I think I'm going to like."

She teared up and sobbed openly.

"Hey," Joe said, pulling her close.

He was damp and sweaty and smelled of gasoline and bug spray but the stroke of his fingers on the back of her neck was mesmerizing. "I told her about the shop. For once she tried not to say I told you so."

"The wonders of modern therapy," Joe murmured. He released her, kissed her forehead, then wrapped his arms around her again.

Angie felt safe enough to confess, "I fibbed. In fact, I lied outright. I just couldn't bring myself to tell her about Anthony."

"So?" Joe said. "That's a hard thing to do on the phone. Maybe you sensed the time wasn't right."

"Or maybe I'm a coward," Angie said, forcing herself to break his embrace and look him in the eye. She saw neither pity nor impatience in his expression, only compassion.

"If you are going to punish yourself, why don't I loan you the chain saw and you can cut out the bad part?" he said. He released her with a final little pat. He picked up the saw, carried it over to the trunk of Angie's car and set it on the pavement beside the gas can.

"The key?" he said.

Angie got her keys out of the ignition and opened the trunk for him. "Mom invited Jason and me up to see her this summer."

Joe started to say something, stopped, ran his hand through his wiry hair. "My decorator? Leaving? In the middle of a project?"

"Nice try," Angie said, sidling up to him. She put an arm around his waist. "You know, I think I'll drive. That way, Jason will get to see the country. I might be able to line up a few more witnesses."

His expression was lost in the gathering dark, but his weary sigh betrayed his impatience with her. "Angie," he said, flinging an arm around her shoulder. He hugged her hard, then released her. "Face it. It's been ninety days now. You have to accept the fact that maybe we aren't going to catch up with this Anthony."

Angie flung his arm off, and swung around to face him square on. "Don't say that to me, Lieutenant Vensure. I'm not your average victim that the police can kiss off."

By the porch lights she could see the deep lines of irritation reading out across Joe's high forehead. "Kiss off the victims? Is that what you think we do?"

"Well?" Angie shouted, realizing she was unreasonable, but yelling anyway. "What have you done for Maria Whitman? What about Nettie French? And what about another dozen women he must have hit since then?"

"I'm still making inquiries," Joe said lamely.

"Inquiries? Where? Nobody cares. There's no hotline for victims. The National Center for Crime Statistics doesn't even keep any stats on sweetheart swindlers."

"Get a life, Angie."

"Oh sure," Angie hissed. "Murderers, rapists and serial killers—that's all well and good. But is our society so sick that we have nothing to offer women who have been raped of their capacity to trust, robbed of their faith in the human race?"

His face went slack. "Is that it?"

Angie turned away from him, starting toward the house.

Joe caught up with her. He took her by the elbow and turned her around. "Angie, do you hear yourself? Do you understand the implications of what you just said?"

"Do you?" Angie snarled.

"I'm afraid so," Joe said softly. "The bottom line is, you've just admitted you can't trust me because of what happened with him."

She twisted away from him. "I have to get Jason to his party," Angie said. "Are you coming?"

"Coming?" Joe said. "I'm running the thing."

"Tell Grandma goodbye, Jason. We're due at the boardwalk in fifteen minutes."

"We'll take two cars," Joe said. "Once the show is over, I'm outta here."

"Are you on duty tonight?" Angie's tone took on the hollowness she felt. Oh, God. Why was she pushing him away?

"Nope," Joe said. Light shining from the porch caught his jaw knotting up. "I just think both of us could use a little space."

CHAPTER 34

Memphis, TN
Tuesday, November 3

He was dozing in and out over a mid-morning talk show when Juanita shook his shoulder. "Time for you lunch, Mr. Tadischi." He bolted upright, brushed his hand across his bald head and pulled up his covers. Juanita arranged his tray on a rolling stand and wheeled it right to his lap.

"Juanita, how are you today? And how's your little boy?"

"Aye," she said, rolling her dark eyes upward. "Gregory? He saw his daddy with a hammer—and the next thing I know?—he's climbed up on the tool bench, got down the hammer, smashed up my clay pots."

"A hammer? Already? Hey, I bet you got an architect on your hands," Raymond said. He wasn't half as interested in Juanita's two year old as he was in Juanita, and the way her skin glowed when she talked about the kid.

"Enjoy your lunch, Mr. Tadischi," Juanita said.

"Wait, honey. Aren't you going to stick around to whet my appetite?"

She switched to the noon news and handed him the remote. "Not when you got the hots for that anchor woman."

He'd finished the little cup of coleslaw and was squeezing mustard out of a blister pack when he happened to glance up at the TV screen. The pretty anchorwoman with the thick dark hair and the dimpled chin said something about a missing heiress. There was a mug shot of Jenny Sawyer. A ten years younger Jenny Sawyer, but you couldn't miss that fifties primness about her, Donna Reed and June Allyson rolled into one.

He turned up the volume: "Jenny Reid Sawyer, widow of Memphis philanthropist Burton Sawyer, has been reported missing by her son. Mrs. Sawyer was last seen a week ago in the company of this man." Raymond shot mustard all over himself as that disgusting poster of cousin Anthony appeared on the screen.

"Friends say Mrs. Sawyer was planning to visit the family of this man, posing as New York attorney Anthony Abruzzi. Mrs. Sawyer's son, Price, alerted authorities when he had not heard from Mrs. Sawyer in several days. The New York phone number and address where she was to stay did not check out.

"Abruzzi, who is not listed as a member of the New York bar, is wanted for questioning in the death of astrologer Maria Whitman of Banks, Florida. He was seen on Union Court Plaza Saturday. He was chased by police, who failed to apprehend him."

The screen dissolved to a photo of a sandy-haired young man with Jenny's same apple pie face standing in front of a red brick mansion. "My mother is in the early stages of Alzheimer's disease. She may not remember how to contact her family. We are appealing to anyone who may have seen Mrs. Sawyer or Anthony Abruzzi."

"Kee-reist," Raymond exclaimed, punching away at the call button. "Juanita?"

"Something the matter, Uncle Raymond?" A pale head peeked around the doorway. It was the kid again: Bradley, the twelve-year old with the hole in his heart. They'd met one boring afternoon while waiting three hours for their cardiologist to show up.

He'd entertained little Bradley with napkin tricks. Brad's favorite was the one where you fold the napkin in two peaks and dance them around on your chest.

"Bradley, son. Hand me that pitcher of ice water, will you? I splattered mustard all over myself."

"How'd you do that, Uncle Raymond?" the boy said as he passed the pitcher along.

"Practicing my mustard trick,"

"You promised you'd play gin rummy," the kid said. He went right for the deck of cards he kept in the nightstand.

The Don Juan Con

"So I did," Raymond said, wiping himself with the towel. He felt his heart going haywire again and swiped the terry cloth across his sweating face for good measure. No point in upsetting himself. Anthony Abruzzi was officially DOA. Yes sir, and his cousin and good buddy, Raymond Tadischi, was now recuperating in the hospital from a nasty bout of the disease the two men shared, angina. Damn but he hated to lose Anthony. The guy had it made. He dressed well, lived high and he managed to convey just the right combination of charm and menace. Women fell all over him. How could simple Ray Tadischi compare with Anthony Abruzzi, esquire?

In his clumsy way, Bradley dealt the cards, his lips moving as he counted them out. The kid was strictly from a horror show. He looked as if he'd been assembled from pipe cleaners. His skin was a ghastly skim milk blue. His arms were purple from all the shots he'd had and his hair was shaved off in a buzz cut, which only emphasized his ungainly proportions: a tall, narrow forehead combined with low-slung, scoop shovel ears. Make those ears into lug bolts and you could put him in a starring role on The Munsters. His mama was a hotel chambermaid who lived three counties away and came in only on weekends. His father had long since skipped out.

"I don't know if I can afford to play with you, Brad," he said, tossing a nickel into the ashtray they used as a kitty. "Last time you cleaned me out."

Bradley grinned and his big, rabbit teeth stuck out. At that moment, Raymond Tadischi was smitten. He had to admit the kid aroused stirrings of feelings he'd forgotten, denied or repressed. This was scary. Emotional baggage he didn't need. Yet, Bradley had the better of him. He himself had had big, ugly, spreading teeth, a struggling mama and a strikeout in the father department.

"After I won two offa you, Uncle Ray, I won five dollars off that doctor's kid," Bradley said proudly.

"Didn't cheat, did you?" Anthony said.

"Hell no."

"Try that again," he said, glaring.

"No sir, I didn't." Then Bradley grinned, his lopsided grin. "Well, maybe a little. But so what? He can afford it."

"*Brad*-ley," he warned. "You gotta be straight up, kid. You want to wind up in detention?"

"So what?" Bradley said. "They don't do nothing to you, and besides you get to eat three meals and lay around and watch TV."

"Wrong," Raymond said, smacking the table. "The food is slop and

146

the TV never works, but that's minor inconvenience. The thugs in there are so mean they're gonna make a girlie outta you." He stuck his face in Bradley's: "Understand?"

"Yes sir," Bradley said.

"Be a good kid, Bradley. You don't disappoint Uncle Raymond, or I'll never play gin rummy with you again."

"Nossir, I won't."

"That's better," he said, "Now shut up and draw."

CHAPTER 35

Banks, FL
Thursday, November 5

Angie set her briefcase on the floor next to a painter's ladder and strolled around the cavernous lower floor of the old sugar mill on the Banks River. Rising Sign was one of the fifteen shops going into the project. The upper level would be converted to office space.

The building was a gem. The proportions were wonderful. Directly in front of her, tall paned windows faced the Banks River. If the frames were still good, they could be sanded down and painted in some bright color for a wonderful effect. She noticed a step-down bay to the left, which would be perfect for the coffee bar. To her right was a long narrow alcove where the books could be shelved. The floors were pine and made a delicious creaking sound underfoot as she crossed them. It would be silly to do anything to the library area but sand and refinish the original flooring.

Lighting, ventilation, flooring, access. All the issues whirled around in her mind, but she felt emptiness in her belly as she shook off all the practical considerations. Her thoughts drifted back to Alan, and how he would have loved this. Together they'd have paced off the room, then hailed each other across it like two kids. Angie stopped dead center in the room, listening for a moment. She heard only the tapping of a hammer off in the distance.

"Alan? Alan? Hello!" she shouted to the ceiling. As a "lo" echoed back, she grinned. "I know you'll always be there for me," she murmured, eyes tearing over.

Oddly, as she began to talk to Alan, she felt a great sense of release. Nobody was around to hear her, so she spoke out loud. "Wouldn't it be great to hang some huge banners with Tarot card motifs from the ceiling in the main space? The gift shop could rest in a pool of royal blue carpet, as if floating on a river of its own. The library area ought to be restful and intimate. We could paint the ceilings a soothing eggplant purple. We might suspend some Tiffany shades low over the tables, creating pools of cozy light."

As a vision of the entire project passed through her mind's eye, Angie laughed aloud, then looked around guiltily. What if someone should hear her? They would think that she was crazy. So? Maybe she was a little tetched.

"Alan," she murmured as she moved toward the bank of tall windows and stroked the frames, checking for dry rot. "I really couldn't face up to the loss of you. I thought if I just stayed on my feet and kept moving, I'd be okay. I tried to outrun my grief, but inside, I had to pay. I kept doing these totally stupid things. It's as if I wanted to lie down in the middle of I-75, shut my eyes, and let a truck roll right over me."

She crossed the empty space, where cobwebs draped the piping overhead, forced a rusty latch and pushed one of the windows open. A salty breeze from the river washed over her face

"I couldn't accept the fact that business didn't go well for me because you were no longer a part of it. You were always my creative wellspring. I couldn't admit to myself just how my own creativity fed off yours. Now I realize there's nothing to fear. I'd already internalized your energy—your way of doing things. It's been a part of me all along," Angie whispered. "Then I let that monster Anthony test my denial. He was the devil incarnate, feeding on my vulnerability. Of course he succeeded in wrecking my life. That was because it was all false...what I was doing, all a sham."

Angie drew her initials in the dust on the windowsill.

"And people sensed what was happening. Gina knew I was out of my depth. She tried to warn me, but I wouldn't listen. I went right on pretending, acting as if it were more noble to declare bankruptcy than to depend on anyone else. It was simply more stupid—another destructive excuse, another failure to face up to facts. I was like some drowning woman too panicked to save herself, even when the life ring is right in front of her."

The Don Juan Con

A splashing in the river interrupted Angie's reverie. For the first time she noticed the wide deck the building sat on. A pair of peeling doors off the central bay led out to the deck. Her own footsteps echoed in her ears as she crossed the room, then shoved against the doors with her shoulder, managing to force one of them open. She found herself on what must have once been a loading dock. About fifty feet from the dock, something was thrashing in the water. A dark, lumpish shape rose now and then, but it wasn't exactly a fin.

As Angie struggled to make sense of this commotion, she heard the thump of Russell's boots on the planks as he arrived.

"What is it?" Angie said.

"Manatees. Sea cows, probably a couple of them," Russell said. "So ugly they're cute. I heard from an old fella who worked out here that you can count on them here every season. These two are really early. We won't see whole pods of them until December or so."

"What a drawing card," Angie said. "This is simply a wonderful space, Russell. We'll have to have tables and chairs out here. I'd put them under a striped awning. We could set out big pots of impatiens for color and add some lighting along the face of the building. You may have seen those white metallic lamps with the fluted shades and the big globes shaped like Christmas lights? They give the right utilitarian touch. We need to preserve as much of the original character of the building as we possibly can."

"To me it's a space," Russell said with a shrug, "Frankly, space frightens me. Making it wonderful is your department." He slapped a roll of architectural plans against the palm of his hand and an awkward silence fell between them. He murmured, "I'm doing this for Maria, you know."

"Oh?"

"She loved this old building," he said. "She'd have wanted to be a part of it. It's a shame she can't be here. All I can hope for now is, we have Anthony in the slammer by the time we dedicate the new store."

Angie gaped at Russell. "You've heard something?"

Russell stared at her. "Didn't you get a call from Joe this morning?"

"He may have tried me, but I was on the road by six thirty."

"Why ma'am," he said, grinning broadly, "Allow me to do the honors. We are now in a whole different league."

CHAPTER 36

Russell slipped an arm around Angie's shoulders, leading her back inside. "In spite of how it hurt Nettie French, we did right to send out those fliers. Anthony tried to hit a New Age bookstore in Memphis. The manager recognized him right off and called the police."

"All right!" Angie raised a clenched fist in triumph. "He's in jail, I hope?"

The echo of her voice reverberated back to her: "JAIL...ail...ail." Startled by the expansion of their conversation in the vast hollow chamber Russell and Angie burst out laughing.

"That's the tough part," Russell said, after they'd settled down. He propped the roll of plans in a corner, removed his Stetson and fanned his face, exposing his hardscrabble complexion and wild hair. The morning light teemed with motes of dust Angie had raised in her earlier explorations. "He managed to get away from the first officer on the scene. The police sealed off the mall, but evidently it was too late."

"We'll get him next time," Angie said.

"Damn right," Russell said. "Even bigger news is: the case is going on Crimestop. Joe is elated."

"The national TV show?"

"Right. It seems that Anthony hit on a prominent Memphis

woman. He dumped her on a plane to New York. Twenty-five thousand dollars of her money is missing. The woman is in the early stages of Alzheimer's. She couldn't find her way home. She evidently wandered onto a subway platform and was mugged by street thugs. Jenny Sawyer, her name is. The story's been page one in Memphis for a week. A Memphis newspaper reporter found her in a charity hospital in New York. She's still in a coma, but a half dozen witnesses linked her disappearance to Anthony."

"Horrible as it is for Jenny, we can definitely use the coverage," Angie said. She closed the window she'd opened earlier, latching it tight. "God. I sound like some sort of monster." She turned back to Russell.

"You're just being realistic, Angie." He put on his hat, closed the doors to the deck and dusted his hands. He noticed the squiggles of Angie's initials in the sill and smiled at her, shaking his head. "Incidentally, another victim turned up. A Memphis folk singer. Anthony was romancing her at the same time he was squiring Jenny Sawyer around."

"A folk singer?" Angie said. "It just goes to show, Anthony appealed to all types."

"A woman named Marci Trillin. He took her for fifteen thousand. Joe said Marci was already on TV in Memphis this morning, so she won't be bashful when we see Anthony in court."

Angie gnashed her teeth and let out a frustrated sigh. "If I could get my hands on that man, I'd claw his eyes out." She picked up her briefcase, held it in both hands in front of her.

"You may get your chance to be a TV star," Russell said. He picked up the roll of plans and escorted her out into the hall where an enormous skylight sent broad shafts of light splashing across a grimy floor, tiled in what had once been elegant scrolled patterns worked in terrazzo. "Joe told the Crimestop producer that it was your idea to do the flier. I know he wants to talk to you."

"I can't be on TV," Angie blurted.

Russell's eyes narrowed. "Angie," he said. "You swore you'd do anything to get Anthony. You can't back out now."

"Yes, but I never told my mother," she said. "If I go on a national show, she's sure to find out."

Russell put a hand on her shoulder as his agate eyes bore into her. "You're drowning in your old emotions. Some old business. I see such turmoil."

Angie turned away from him. "You've said that before, Russell, but

152

can't you be more specific? I don't understand what you are talking about."

When he didn't respond, Angie turned back to him. His face seemed vacant and his eyelids drooped. "I see Anthony climb into a boat with a struggling child in his arms."

Angie's skin crawled. "No!" she shouted. "Not Jason. He was never near Jason on any water. Never."

Russell twitched; animation returned to his face, his expression changed. Watching him, Angie shuddered. Russell had been somewhere else, in some other dimension. Now he was back to business, just like that.

"Okay, what have we got?" he said. "We want to open in ninety days. When do I get an estimate?"

"Russell," Angie said, straining to smile when she felt like fleeing: "You've got a winner here. This is a wonderful location. The space itself is a natural for your purposes. Let me get right back to you with a story board, so you can see how it will all come together."

"Thank you, Angie," he said, tapping his leg with the tube of plans he'd picked up. "It'll be a great relief to me. I want something that personifies Maria. She was attuned to the way our spaces enhance our energy, but I'm not into this Feng Shui."

"You?" Angie said with a laugh. "With all of your—what? Sensitivity, shall we say?"

Russell shrugged. "People tell me I see things in their lives, and I guess I do," he murmured, "but to me it's all blackouts and lapses. You can't imagine how often I wish I knew what the hell I'd just said."

CHAPTER 37

Akron, OH
Friday, November 6

His fingers drummed on the powder blue steering wheel of his rented Town Car. Though the air conditioner was running, he was feeling the heat and the smell of road dust filled his nostrils. He stared at the awning on a building just off Market Street that reminded him of a dollhouse at Christmas. He was engaged in a heated phone conversation with Buffy Albion, owner of Buffy's Best Cleaning Service. Her pink Cadillac was parked in its designated space.

"Marry Charlie?" he was saying. "But Buffy, honey. I thought we had something going."

"That we did, darlin'. It's been real nice on the telephone, but you got to understand Charlie and I go way back."

"Sweetie, you told me at least half a dozen times how that was exactly the problem." With the phone squeezed between ear and shoulder, he riffled through his address book, even as he pleaded. It was getting on toward sunset. He was meeting Melinda for drinks at six and could easily work Buffy in for dining and dancing. "Babe, I've driven over twenty-five hundred miles just to meet you in person."

"Well, I do feel bad about that," Buffy said in her whiskey voice, "But you got to understand. I never in the world thought you really would get your butt on down here."

"Just name your party, Buff. Give me a chance to change your mind."

"Well, let me tell you, honey. Charlie did commit himself. Oh yeah, big time. Three one-carat diamonds in an old European setting, and Raymond? Could you be that bald guy out in the parking lot in the Lincoln?"

He laughed. "Say, girl. I like your spunk."

"Well, I like your initiative, Raymond, truly I do, but I have to admit, I like a guy with hair on top. Charlie's strands may be iron gray, but he's still got them."

"Good luck to you, Buffy," Raymond said.

"You too, darlin." He hung up and peeled the Lincoln out of the parking lot. He turned down Market, heading downtown. Damn but there was one lucky bitch. Jilted again. And he must have spent fifty bucks wooing her long distance. It was going to be a meat market night for him.

The singles' bar scene was much rougher going for Raymond Tadischi than it had been for Anthony Abruzzi. His average take in the last three weeks was down a good five grand. Underneath the suit was the very same guy with the same pitches and lines. The exception was outward appearances. Ray Tadischi was a bald salesman and Anthony Abruzzi was a hirsute attorney. He was a walking test of his own theory. The women didn't care about the man. They just wanted the image. They were all gold diggers out to hook a rich attorney. The true love stuff was all a crock, and every broad he'd hit deserved to be taken.

He'd chosen the Fairlawn Hilton due to its outstanding proximity to Akron's best hunting grounds. It was right on Market, next door to the Summit Day's Inn, across the street from Mountain Jack's, a popular watering hole.

He passed a huge silk flower arrangement in the Hilton lobby and veered into the lounge, where everything was upholstered in paisley print, except, of course, the massive horseshoe bar. Raymond felt a pang of remorse. The place looked like something out of a Ralph Lauren catalog. It was definitely an Anthony Abruzzi kind of place.

Then he told himself to cut it out. What good would it do to have Raymond jealous of Anthony? After all, it was Abruzzi who had gotten him into trouble in the first place. Look what Anthony had done to Maria Whitman. And the trick he pulled on poor Jenny Sawyer? Frankly, cousin Anthony wasn't all that nice, and nice had to count for something.

He sneaked a mini roast beef sandwich off an appetizer tray. The women wouldn't show for another hour. Sandwich in hand, he headed for the elevator. He had time to go back to his room and shower.

As he lathered up with the complimentary soap, he figured his bank balance in his head. He'd had some notable lapses, but over three years he'd curbed his gambling habit enough to salt away two hundred grand in his other cousin, Adolph's, bank account in Monterey. Take in another twenty, it would be time to go in for an overhaul. There was no point struggling along like this. He set the soap in the dish and pinched himself under the chin. Jenny Sawyer wasn't the only candidate for plastic surgery around. He could well afford to get himself rebuilt in some body shop. After a good rest and retooling, it would then be time to begin his pursuit of the top of the line in well-heeled broads.

He was out of the shower, toweling off, when he stared in the mirror at his baldhead. "Ray?" he said. "Even a swindler can have an identity crisis. You are the living proof."

CHAPTER 38

DeLeon, FL
Friday, November 6

Joe sat in the corner of Joy Ride with his long legs stretched up under the bow. Angie sat with her neck resting on the top of the seat, her feet on the dash. The dock they were tied to pulsed with the highly amplified riffs of Jeff Purdy, the blues guitarist they had come to hear. Purdy was closing in on the end of his first set at The Hatchcover, DeLeon's new nightspot just downriver from the city's yacht basin.

"More champagne?" Joe said.

"Definitely," Angie said. Maybe she'd regret this tomorrow, but every foamy sip she'd drunk thus far had failed to quench her thirst for a higher high. Crimestop? She couldn't believe it. At last they were getting the break they needed.

"I talked to the producer today," Joe said. "You're safe. You won't be going on air. They're focusing on the Memphis case. Otherwise the show wouldn't hang together."

"Really? That's wonderful," Angie said, hugging her knees. "Russell was really upset with me when I said I didn't want to be on any national TV show."

"Now you see why victims cop out."

"I do. I also see that I'm a coward."

"You'd have done it if you'd been called to, I know it. As it is, they

157

want you to be a technical advisor."

"I can't believe this," Angie said. She was beaming. She took another sip of champagne.

"Your job is to see that the makeup looks authentic and that the actor playing Anthony does him right. The Crimestop producer told me they make every effort to be authentic. It seems that an arrest of a featured criminal makes their ratings shoot up."

"Yes!" Angie shouted, waving her glass. Sated on the grouper The Hatchcover was famous for, they'd returned to the boat to have champagne and listen to the music. Purdy was to join them down on the boat between sets.

"How did you meet Jeff?" Angie said.

"I heard him play one night. Some hole in the wall. I may have been staking the place out. All I remember was how fantastic he was. I'd catch his shows wherever he played and promote him to clubs where I knew the owners. Then we got to having a drink or two between sets, and I've been invited to a couple of his openings."

The set ended. The crowd whistled, stomped and roared. The emcee announced that Purdy would return shortly. The boat jostled to life as various couples came out to stroll past the boats. Then a dumpy shape in a hooded sweatshirt hustled toward them. Joe extended a hand and swung Purdy into the backseat.

"Jeffrey, you are in form," Joe said as he introduced his friend to Angie.

"Hell, yes," the guitarist replied. "I had back to back closings today. Keep me in guitar picks for three weeks!"

"You sell real estate?" Angie said.

Jeffrey nodded. "I couldn't feed my daughter on the bupkas the Hatchcover pays me. I do these gigs to nourish a starving ego."

"Jeffrey found Victoria for me," Joe said.

"She's a beauty," Angie said.

"The seller was ready to have her hauled off. He thought the lot would sell better without her. He was probably right," Jeffrey said.

"No doubt about it," Angie blurted.

Joe stared at her. "What? I thought you loved Vic."

"I do now."

The three of them drank more champagne and laughed over Jeffrey's scandalous stories of the harrowing life of the road musician he'd once been. "One time, we're playing these waterholes in Texas where there's eight straight hours of sagebrush between every gig and we pulled into this club in this border town and we were far down the list on the entertainment. The featured acts were the fights.

"I was so sick of the music business by then. It ain't no way for a man to live. Finally, it's close to two a.m. I stagger up to my room. We've got to be on the road in less than six hours. I'm dying for sleep. I open my closet to hang up the last shirt I've got to perform in and out jumps this great big gal in her cowboy hat and that was all, and I could tell that sleep was the last thing she had on her mind. Hell, she was ready to start something with me? They sure were desperate out there."

Angie laughed with this gnome of a man with his curtain of longish hair rounding his bald spot and his round eyes bugging out of his square face. A sex symbol he wasn't.

"So what happened?" Angie said.

"I told her the party was cranking up in my buddy's room on the floor below and that I'd be right on down. Then I handed her duds to her, shut and locked the door behind her, and then collapsed flat out on the bed. I was in a coma, man."

"Jeffrey! You didn't push that poor woman out in the hall with no clothes on?"

"God, I hope not," Jeffrey said. "Hell. Maybe I shoved her in a closet. For all I know, she's still in there. I was wasted."

After Jeffrey left and his second set started, Joe cast off and cranked up the outboards. "I thought we were going to hear his next set," Angie said.

"Of course we are," Joe replied.

The channel was paved silver by a glaring moon hanging white in the sky, glowing pure as a huge communion wafer. He dropped anchor in the shadow of a bushy atoll, thick with mangroves. Jeffrey's melodies drifted across the water to them.

"Well, here we are," he said. "No phone. No pager. No Jason. No Russell."

"And no Anthony. Not yet, anyway," Angie said.

"Spoiler," Joe said. He touched his fingers to her lips, then brushed her throat with the back of his fingers.

"Joe? I…" Angie protested.

"Shhh. Listen." He nipped at her lip, a tentative kiss, followed by a deeper one. Angie couldn't help herself. She kissed back and felt her body melting.

She let him lay her across his knees and clung to him as he kissed her. His mouth was a broad, soft pillow and every stroke of his lips thrilled her down to her toes. When he slipped her sweater off her head, she was too weak with desire to protest. He released the catch in her

159

The Don Juan Con

bra, stroked her nipples gently, then squeezed them lightly between his teeth and ran his tongue over them. She moaned as she felt an itch between her legs, her juices began to run and his hand slipped down over her navel, loosened her jeans, found the button, then the zipper, opening it, sliding her from the tight denim shell like some oyster shucked from its shell and his hand found and parted her, then stroked the dormant coil hidden there and she was gone.

While torrents of his friend's guitar music seemed to leap around the boat like so many minnows, she was Joe's instrument. He played her shamelessly, first with his fingers, then his tongue until she reached for the rest of him, taking him fully in her hands, her fingers demanding that he enter her and he sat her up long enough to kick away his own clothing.

He stretched her across the damp, cool seat in the stern and she moaned as he entered her. His thrusts sent the vessel rocking on the water. She was pinned between the man and the river. She felt open to him as she could recall no other time and her own being was swept away in the tide. She dissolved into something as elemental in nature as the simple shell animals with their spiky antennae that parade their glorious housings along the sandy beaches at dawn.

When it was over, they dozed through the dying away of the music. Finally, they were awakened by the buzz of a motorboat approaching.

"How do you feel?" he said.

"Reborn," she replied.

He kissed her gently in response, a little nip. The Joy Ride, tugging at her anchor, drifted into the path of the moon. She sat quietly, watching his dark eyes as he stroked her.

"You are absolutely beautiful," he said. "I never was good enough to paint what I see, but what I see is a Greek goddess in an old wooden vessel, her alabaster skin much too fine and delicate to be real."

As the other boat approached, Angie reached for her sweater. They scrambled into their clothes and Joe hauled anchor. As they sped away, the surface of her skin dappled with the chill as the breeze furled her hair, and her belly was full of delight mixed with dread.

She sensed that Joe loved her or else it might come to that, and here she was, this mass of dread. Soon they would have Anthony in hand and then Joe would lay claim to her, left naked, devoid of excuses. What then? How could she ever heal enough to be anything to anyone at all, let alone to a lover so deserving?

160

CHAPTER 39

Memphis, TN
Saturday, December 1

Angie presented her security pass at the gate and drove along a paved drive to a multi-gabled mansion in the heart of the once fashionable, now venerable Old Downtown Memphis, not far off Union Avenue. Owls hooted back and forth in the Magnolia trees. A squirrel chucked in indignation as shadowy figures scurried around boxy production trailers in the predawn light. Angie followed a trail of thick cables up the front steps to the broad veranda where huge white wicker pieces skulked in columned shadows. She banged the brass knocker on the deeply carved door.

"I'm Angie Reynolds," she said to an attractive young black woman who answered.

"Nelda Wallace, said the willowy woman, with cornrows in her hair and huge hoop earrings.

"You're the Crimestop producer?"

Nelda smiled. "That's right. Come on in. Join the party."

Angie followed her into a hallway hung with a wonderful Federal period mirror. A gilt eagle spread its wings over a garland of olive branches. A triple candelabra was affixed to the bottom. This was a highly practical gadget for its day. The convex mirror multiplied the points of candlelight and beamed them all around the room.

The Don Juan Con

Nelda turned to supervise the move of an antique sofa to the opposite end of a long parlor, where numerous end tables, chairs and coffee tables had been pushed together.

Angie gasped, "Tell them to please be careful. That's Hepplewhite."

"I know," Nelda said. "Too bad we had to shuffle the furniture, but we couldn't get the right light any other way. We'll be ready for you shortly, as soon as the makeup lady finishes up with Jenny Sawyer."

"She's here?" Angie said.

Nelda shook her head. "The actress doing the part of Jenny, I mean. Jenny is still in New York. Barely conscious. The doctor said she might come around in a few days. We'll try to tape her statement when we get back to New York. Meanwhile, her son, Price, is here. We're shooting his plea to find this Anthony, in case the footage with Jenny herself doesn't work out."

A ginger-haired, middle-aged man with a broad, friendly face spattered with freckles approached them.

"Angie Reynolds, meet Price Sawyer," Nelda said.

"Mrs. Reynolds," he drawled. "I'm so pleased you agreed to come. You have a clear notion what this Anthony looks like. Except for the one photo and the police composite, the rest of us are at sea."

"And how is your mother?" Angie said.

"We think she recognizes family members. She can communicate 'yes' or 'no' by a squeeze of the hand." His controlled tone was tinged with resignation and anger.

"Did the folk singer come?" Angie said.

"Marci Trillin? She's out on the back porch. KMEM TV is doing a morning talk show about Crimestop coming to Memphis," Price Sawyer said. "Do we have a minute to watch that taping?" he asked Nelda.

"Sure. I'll find you when makeup is ready," she said to Angie.

Marci Trillin was rocking in a porch swing flooded in light, strumming her guitar. "I loved you honey, but you loved my money, and it ain't funny," she sang.

She launched into a verse about how Anthony had promised her the moon and a half-acre of heaven and Angie found herself nodding her head and tapping her foot. As she watched Marci, her pulse quickened. She felt both vindication and relief. Here was this beautiful, talented woman, taken in by Anthony. If Marci Trillin had also misjudged him, perhaps Angie wasn't such a fool, after all.

As Marci wound up the song, everyone clapped but Angie, who was too stunned to move. The sense of vindication was followed by a terrible revelation. Was her search for other victims just another way to

162

seek out the truth about herself?

The hostess of the KMEM show was a dark, sleek woman whose makeup looked like freshly applied enamel under the glare of the TV lights. She smiled and applauded. "What one thing did Anthony do which made him so convincing?" she asked Marci.

"He was so open. So eager to talk about us to everyone. The maitre d', the people dining at the next table," Marci said. "You somehow think a con artist would be sneaky or furtive."

"Exactly," Angie murmured, as someone touched her arm. It was Nelda. "Time to meet Anthony—our version."

CHAPTER 40

Salmon, Idaho
Tuesday, March 31

Panes of ice cracked under his mare's feet as he trotted her into position. With three other drovers, Adolph Tadeschi was to guard the perimeter of an Idaho meadow. Several other cowboys drove a herd of whiteface cows and their new calves into a holding pen, where they were to be trucked to better pasture, farther down the mountainside.

With a loud bellow, a blocky calf broke from the herd and barreled straight for Adolph's mount. He reined the side of Chica's neck. His quarter horse dodged the hurtling calf, then wheeled around and gave chase.

With the burst of speed, Chica overtook the calf in twenty yards. Adolph looped out his lariat, whirled it over his head and dropped it around the calf's neck. As he hanked the rope around his saddle horn, Chica backed up. Adolph slid back in the saddle and dug in his heels to stay mounted as his horse sank on her haunches, digging in her hooves. The calf bellowed as its feet flew out from under it. The square body made a splatting noise when it landed with a hollow thud on the frozen ground.

Owing to persuasion supplied by a tightened noose around his neck, the baby bull scrambled to his feet and trotted along behind Chica, docile as you please. Once they entered the corral, mama quickly found him. Adolph released the lariat. Cow and calf nuzzled in reunion. The drovers all whooped and whistled as Chica, without a shred of direction from Adolph, took her place again in the outside of the circle. Tadeschi buttoned up his sheepskin jacket and patted his sweaty chestnut's neck as Chica snuffled through her velvety nose.

This was his proudest moment in his two-month stay at the Circle R Bar Ranch and Spa, where he'd gone to recover from his surgery. Early on, while learning to ride, he'd taken a nasty spill in an icy stream. But he loved the feeling of union with the animal. He'd faithfully practiced his roping and riding skills since day one in the saddle.

The ranch was nestled in the foothills of the Bitterroot Range north of Ketchum. Guests were kept so busy swimming in the indoor pool, hiking, riding or fishing that they went to bed early. In this peaceful backwater with its piney air, there wasn't much of a crime problem. People paid little attention to tabloid TV shows such as Crimestop. Fortunately for Adolph, he was still in bandages in the Santa Monica hospital recovering from plastic surgery when he happened to catch that miserable piece of so-called journalism about cousin Anthony on TV. As much as he missed the charming attorney, his death in Memphis had proved most timely.

Each and every morning as Adolph watched his new face emerge, the possibility that anyone would recognize Anthony Abruzzi grew more remote. He'd stayed in his room the first two weeks after surgery, but once he was on the mend, he'd never hidden the fact that he'd had reconstructive surgery, supposedly to rebuild a face bashed up in a bad traffic accident on the Los Angeles freeway. And while he was recuperating, this third generation vintner's son was reading scripts for a production company he intended to launch.

Tadeschi now had a thin, straight nose, a stronger jaw line, a full upper lip and round eyes, thanks to the fact that he'd had his lids tucked up. He now had a head full of short, dark hair and a much higher forehead than cousin Anthony had enjoyed. And better yet, Adolph's hair was real. A speech therapist had taught him to use the lower range of his vocal register and cleansed his speech of any of the grosser New York locutions. Tadeschi now spoke softly with the clarity and the regionless inflection of a television commentator.

Yes, Adolph Tadeschi had altered his entire persona as well. He'd erased the flamboyant and gabby Abruzzi persona with a classic, closed-mouth Clint Eastwood type. Tadeschi emerged as a suave man of droll words and pungent observations, which other guests hung on and swapped over dinner. Typical was the remark Tadeschi made to head drover, Wayne Staunton, who rode over on his gray stallion.

"Hey, Adolph. Nice work. Real professional. Keep that up and the Circle R Bar will have to stop taking your money and start paying you."

"Thanks Wayne," Adolph replied. "I find I much prefer punching cows to chasing women."

CHAPTER 41

Salmon, Idaho
Tuesday, March 31

After a buffet lunch with the other guests, Tadeschi collected his mail, several more movie scripts, a few resumes from hopeful actors, and several newspapers. He headed upstairs to do his homework. He parked his Stetson on a hook behind his door, threw the scripts on the pile collecting on the second bed, and pulled off his boots, once a gift from one of his cousin Anthony's ex-lovers, folk singer Marci Trillin. He plopped himself in an easy chair with a three-day old copy of the *Wall Street Journal*. He turned to the section for island properties. A new listing caught his eye right away.

"Stunt man's fantasy," it read. He got out his Atlas and checked to be sure, and yes. The farm in question was on Orcas Island, which was nearest to tiny Puffin Island, Jane Pelham's home base. Tadeschi was elated. He would visit the San Juan Islands in pursuit of property, whereupon he'd have the perfect opportunity to run into Jane Pelham purely by chance.

As he got on the phone and asked the switchboard to put through a call to the real estate office in Eastsound Washington, he sucked on the pipe he'd just taken up. Though he gazed out at the pasture where his beloved Chica and Wayne Staunton's roan were nuzzling one another, his attention was not on the horses. His thoughts were fixed on his old obsession.

Odd how the death of cousin Anthony had failed to extinguish his interest in Jane Pelham. On the contrary, his fantasy of a real life occupied his dreams. He could see Jane, watch himself stroking her back or taming her unruly hair. Adolph Tadeschi was free to do what Abruzzi never dared. The false bravado and fake arrogance put on by the ersatz attorney had given way to the out-and-out confidence enjoyed by Adolph Tadeschi, a man of genuine competence. A man with family backing, cash in the bank and deals in the works.

Abruzzi, that insufferable loudmouth, had nothing on the strong, silent Tadeschi as a ladies' man. Tadeschi needn't bother to chase after Jane Pelham. She would come to him. After all, it was David Pelham's quiet demeanor, wry observant wit and air of competence that Adolph had adopted as his own. Jane would fall for him, hard. And if Angie dared get in the way? Too bad, but there were ways of taking care of her. The cowardly Abruzzi had some compunctions where Angie was concerned. Tadeschi had absolutely none.

CHAPTER 42

DeLeon, FL
Friday, April 3

She was finished. Well, the downstairs, at least, and Victoria was a beauty. Angie was able to gage her successes by Gina Goldheim's curiosity. She and Joe had walked Gina through the house and they wound up in the kitchen.

"Herb drawers?" Gina said, pulling open one of the six little doors running along the bottom edge of the knotty pine cabinets in the kitchen. "And I love the distressed wood and the paneled glass doors."

"We splurged on the kitchen," Angie said. "There's this new place in Coral Gables that models the cabinetry on the English manor style."

"So then you put down broken tile in the powder room?" Gina said. "Leave it to Angie."

"She promised me we could do the guest bath for next to nothing if only I'd spring for the high priced cabinets," Joe said. "Talk about distressed? That was me. No, wait. I was *depressed*. The tile got off pretty easy. It was merely busted."

They passed through the dining room, painted with a mural of eighteen fifties Ft. DeLeon. The wainscoting and wooden shutters were a sea foam green taken from the background. Simple Queen Anne chairs and a refectory table completed the room. Or at least started it. A sideboard or corner cupboards could be added later.

169

"Did you do the mural?" Gina said.

"Joe's mother. That woman can do anything," Angie said.

"And the stenciling in the living room?"

Angie nodded. "Once we steamed off the wallpaper, I found about three feet of this charming stencil design on the wall next to the fireplace. I fell in love with it. I tried to duplicate it in a wallpaper pattern, but it just wasn't out there. So I asked Joe's mom if she could cut the patterns for us if I brought her a tracing."

"Stencil," Joe snorted. "Those aren't curlicues up there on the wall. They're sweat stains."

"I'll never tell," Gina said, beaming at Joe. She adored the man and never missed a chance to sing his praises to Angie.

"I love it, love, it," Gina said as she kissed each of them goodbye. "I never realized how much charm there is in these old places. Listen, I've got to run. The milk and cookie set gets out of school in fifteen minutes. Bye guys."

"You've done it now, Angie. Once Gina puts out the word to those doctors' wives, you'll be swamped with business," Joe said as they stood on the porch watching Gina get into her car and drive off.

"I wish," Angie said, sinking into one of the weathered rattan chairs that had yet to be repainted

But Joe wasn't going to let her rest. "Come on, Angie, I've been thinking about how to do the upstairs." He attempted to pull her to her feet.

"I plead exhaustion," Angie said. I just don't think I could face any more water stains and mildew."

He sat down on the broad chair arm and made a production out of feeling her forehead. "Our Miss Intrepid must be ill. This will only take a minute, I promise. Then we'll rustle up some eats."

"We can't use the kitchen. The grout has to set on the counters."

"So, we'll go out," Joe said. "Now come on."

Angie extended a hand. Joe pulled her up. At the top of the landing, he flicked on the old-fashioned switch plates. The hall filled with a telltale electric smell.

"You've got to get the upstairs rewired. One of these days you are going to burn the house done."

"Hey, it's Preston and Weeters, signed, sealed and done by code."

"Of 1947," Angie said, and they laughed over the proud designation Angie had found, engraved on the ancient service panel.

They stood at the top of the stair landing, looking down a narrow hall with two sets of doors leading off it on both sides.

"Take a look at this," he said, handing her a big white envelope with a drawing roughed out on the back. "Now this isn't all neat, the way you'd do one of these," he said, "But just consider the idea. What we have up here is four postage stamp bedrooms. But I've checked it out and there's no reason why we couldn't just knock out the walls between them and then we get this."

Angie took the envelope and studied Joe's rough sketch. There were two big rooms. The oversized bathroom had been cut down into two smaller ones.

"And what's this?" Angie said, looking at an alcove adjoining the larger one.

"It's that old storage room. We make it into a sleeping alcove for Jason. I see it with a skylight over it."

Angie winced. "Too modern. Dormers would be better."

"Purist," Joe said. "So...we do dormers. More work and expense, but I'm used to that. Anyway, he has a bed at one end and a desk at the other. It's tiny, I admit, but kids that age all want their little nest."

His astute observation startled her. "You know, you are absolutely right," Angie said. "Jason would sleep in a broom closet, if I'd let him."

"The rest of his space becomes a big Rec room. He could sleep twenty-nine on an all-nighter. He could have his own pool table. So what do you think?"

"It's very good design," Angie said, "But really, I don't..."

"Damn right, it is." Joe hauled her into the big square shaped bathroom. "Now take a look. We divide this into two baths using a back-to-back shower."

"Fantastic idea—"

"The drawback is, you don't get a tub," he said leering, "So when you want a soak you have dibs on mine."

"Okay," Angie added. "And corner windows for ventilation—"

"And for once I can afford the renovation. Now that I've got old Victoria up to snuff, downstairs at least, I can finance a construction loan, and have a contractor finish off the entire upstairs before you and Jason get back from Grandma's."

"Joe, it's a good floor plan, but you can't count on us. It's, well, it's more than...it's just too much." Angie fled the bathroom and started down the stairs. She had to get him away from there. It wasn't the right place to say what she had to. Once downstairs, she grabbed her jacket, shoulder bag and briefcase and turned to face him. "Joe, I hope you understand, but I just can't commit myself to—"

"You don't have to commit yourself to a thing," he cut her off, following her out onto the porch. "Hey, you don't like the lighting? You can't stand the neighborhood? Just move out."

"It wouldn't be that easy, and you know it," Angie said as she headed for the curb. "Sure the layout is wonderful, but a move in? I'm not sure I'm ready."

"Look, you're still obsessed with this swindler. I accept that. I can't force you to let it go," he said, trailing her down the sidewalk.

"I can't stop now. Look at all the women who called in from Crimestop. We now have warrants out for the man in twenty four states," she said as she reached his pickup.

He opened the door for her and walked around to his side of the truck. He climbed in, rolled down the window and backed out the driveway before he said another word.

"Take your trip, Angie. Visit every one of Abruzzi's victims. See all twenty-four of those states, but Hon, do me one favor. Just don't expect to find this guy."

"I really can't understand your negative attitude," she cried. "Look at the national coverage."

They were at the end of the driveway. Joe put his foot on the brakes, a little too hard, jerking Angie in her seat. As he turned to her, Angie read the exasperation on his face in the lifted brows and wrinkled forehead. "We got no fresh leads, Angie. Nothing at all past Memphis. Not one sighting from anywhere. A guy that works by being the life of the party? It doesn't wash. I was very disappointed. He should have been spotted somewhere."

"So?" Angie said, her tone challenging.

"When the police nearly trapped him in the mall, he read the warning signs and finished up with Abruzzi in Memphis. For all I know, he watched the Crimestop show. Smart crooks will do that," Joe said. "The guy's got himself a new act, one that we don't recognize at all. I wouldn't be surprised if he isn't on tour with it already."

CHAPTER 43

Orcas Island, WA
April 1

The canvas was raked with violent slashes of black and white. The painting dominated the landing of the upper level of the ranch house—the ranch house Adolph Tadeschi knew he was going to buy. He had to step back a few feet before he could see the pattern that the slashes formed. A pack of wolves was attacking a band of wild horses. He studied it for a while, then said, "The world isn't all dog-eat-dog. Sometimes it's wolf-eat-horseflesh."

"Mr. Tadeschi. You are the most ironic man," Jennifer Jackson gushed. She was the real estate agent. "This is Charles Russell in a savage mood. It gives me the willies every time I show this house."

They descended a split log stairway coated in a gleaming finish and strolled through the main floor of the log house, hewn from hand-adzed hemlock: the kitchen with its massive wood stove; the sprawling living room graced by the egg shapes of the river stone fireplace and hung with a Sioux beaded shirt; the bay window seat where a stuffed owl was suspended in flight with the tiger striping of its wings in full display; the dining room hung with an antler chandelier; the solarium with its spur collection and a saddle mounted on a sawhorse. All the rooms were furnished in leather sofas and Native American Indian rugs. Paintings by prominent Indian artists lined the walls. He stopped in front of the console table in the entry hall, a half hexagon with three center drawers with brand marks incised in them and a pair of matching doors carved with Indian teepees.

"This is a Molesworth piece. It's worth a bundle," Jennifer said. "He was a forties era furniture designer who did western motifs for clients like the Rockefellers and the Coca-Cola tycoon. I'm told Dwight Eisenhower had one of his pieces."

"Let me guess: A peace pipe crossed with a golf club on a field of wampum?" Tadeschi murmured.

"There you go," Jennifer said, smiling big.

He strolled out on the deck to survey the pond where a flock of ducks was swimming, beyond which stood the red stock barn and equipment shed, the barrel riding and roping rings side by side, the horse pasture next to it and the herd of Black Angus cattle grazing on the hillside orchards in the distance.

"How many acres did you say?"

"One hundred forty eight."

"And the owner was a Hollywood stunt man?"

"Clint McCall worked on about fifty westerns. He rode and roped for the best: Gene Autrey, Roy Rogers, the Lone Ranger, you name it."

Tadeschi smiled thinly. When dickering it was essential to suppress excitement. "They want nine hundred? Offer them eight seventy, all furnishings and memorabilia included."

"A cash offer?" Jennifer said. She was a big, freckled redhead with pale lashes, whose natural beauty could have stood a touch of mascara. She let it be known she was a top producer in her office. Prime for the plucking. Lucky for her, the time was long gone when he'd be interested in such a minnow.

"Twenty thousand with the offer, fifty thousand on acceptance, the balance in cash in thirty days. I'm rolling over proceeds from the sale of one of the smaller vineyards, and if I don't structure a simultaneous closing, my accountant would be very unhappy with me."

"No problem," she said. "I'll have the offer ready for you to sign this afternoon. I can meet you at Rosario around four. Oh, and I will need the twenty thousand, which I can hold in un-cashed form until the sellers accept."

"Not a problem," Anthony said, patting his breast pocket. "I have a cashier's check with me. I was resting at a dude ranch in Idaho when I read about this property in the Wall Street Journal. Even then I had the feeling it might merit looking into." Their feet crunched on the gravel in the drive. He sucked in the nippy air: "The air here is so pure and this

174

island is so lovely."

"I hope we can keep it that way now that Californians have discovered it," she said.

"You have my word that this Californian will do his part to preserve the McCall spread exactly as Clint would have wanted it. We're in the same business, you know."

"Are you an actor?" she said.

"Producer," he said. "I'm a new kid in the business, but I do have three great properties under option."

"Wonderful. As for the farm, I'm so delighted you don't intend to subdivide."

"Please ask for immediate possession upon closing," he said.

"I don't think that will be a problem. The property has been on the market for six months and the family is anxious to settle the estate."

"Here's my cellular number." He handed her his card. "I intend to spend the rest of the day prowling around this lovely island," he said as he helped her into her Jeep Cherokee.

"In that case, there's a new exhibit of island memorabilia at the museum in Eastsound. Some news clippings about Clint McCall are included."

"Wonderful. I'll take a look at it."

He climbed into his rented Mercedes convertible and followed Jennifer's Jeep up the long drive that wound through a woodlot of fir, bordered with madrona trees with their red, peeling bark. The road climbed out of the Crow Valley hollow where the McCall ranch lay. At the top, he pulled off on the shoulder of the Horseshoe Highway to look back at his acquisition.

The log house was barely visible from the road, hidden by an orchard full of snowy apple trees in full bloom. It was the perfect plaything for the Hollywood mogul. As soon as the offer was accepted he'd have to get some film and have Jennifer take pictures of him riding around on his ranch. As he turned right, heading for Eastsound, the waves of exhilaration he felt were punctuated with twinges of dread.

He'd made the down payment on a real life. He could really settle down and be something, provided he could find some wonderful lady to finance the balance of the purchase.

At the Outlook Inn in Eastsound, he ordered a sandwich at the bar. He took a call on his cell phone and talked just loudly enough that the bartender might catch part of it: "Dwight Bigelow? Whose agent? I thought she was with Orowitz. Okay, put him on." He sat silently, receiver to ear. "Okay, she might work. Could be she's too young and

175

sexy. This is a classic part, more for a mature woman, Shirley, maybe. Possibly Barbra, but if you say so, I'll send her a script and we'll have her read, but do me a favor, dude. Don't call me up here. I just bought Clint McCall's wonderful little ranch in the San Juan Islands, and I need time to bond with my Anguses. Clint? He was a famous stunt man in the fifties. That's the trouble with this business. It has no sense of history. *Ciao*."

CHAPTER 44

The Orcas Island Historical Museum was a tiny log building a bit to the west and around the corner from the Outlook Inn. He signed the register, gave the Beverly Hills Hotel, Hollywood, as his address, paid his donation and went inside.

He didn't see any newspaper clippings about the stuntman in evidence, but took in the photographs of apple orchards and a primitive packing operation. The captions said that at the turn of the century, Orcas Island was a major exporter of apples and plums in the days before commercial pesticides were developed. This was because island-grown fruit was free of worms.

"May I help you?" the docent asked. The musical voice gave him a start. As he turned around, there she was, her blonde hair a bit faded but as unruly as ever, falling out of the bun in which she perpetually tried to contain it. She'd become a classic beauty in her maturity, her skin still taut over the cheekbones, and her eyes, a gemstone blue, dazzled as sharply as ever from her face. The thick, straight brows that Angie had inherited. The fact that she was as casual as ever in one of those Indian sweaters and a pair of faded jeans brought a smile of recognition to his face, which he quickly realized he had to find some other explanation for.

The Don Juan Con

"I've just bought a ranch here, and was told by my real estate agent that I might find some history about the owner. Now I see why there are orchards on the property."

Jane Pelham beamed. "Certain varieties of apples here are found nowhere else in the country."

"Is that so?" he said.

"If you'll tell me what property it is, I'll be happy to go through our files," she said.

"It's a ranch in Crow Valley, once owned by a Hollywood stunt man, Clint McCall.

Her face lit up. "Really? That's a wonderful spread."

"I think so," he said. "You seem to know it."

"Clint was a dear friend, active until the end. One week I saw him on the ferry. He told me he had a spot of cancer, nothing to worry over. Three months later he was dead."

"Our days dwindle away," Tadeschi said. "I shall count my precious few, here on the island."

She smiled an acknowledgment of this theatrical turn of phrase. "Clint's Anguses are known around the state. To top that off, there are morel mushrooms on that property."

"Not poisonous, I hope?"

She laughed. "They are most delicious, impossible to cultivate. They look like pine cones nestled in the ground. If you pick them carefully, they'll come up year after year."

"How will I find them?"

"I'll have to drop by and show you where to look. It's late in the season, but there may be a few left."

"A wonderful idea," he said. "Let me call you as soon as the earnest money is signed. It could even be this afternoon. I'm Adolph Tadeschi, by the way."

"Jane Pelham," she said, extending her long-fingered hand. He hurried out quickly, his heart paining him, but not much. Since his angioplasty, his heart was much stronger. This was no doubt due to the excitement. What he had so long hoped for and imagined was coming true. After all, it was she who suggested visiting him. She was attracted to him, he was certain. Morel mushrooms were simply an excuse.

CHAPTER 45

DeLeon, FL
Saturday, June 6

The rhythmic pounding of men driving nails came from the second story. The front door stood wide open. Angie called through the screen but couldn't make herself heard over the clamor.

"Maybe they can hear us if we go around back," Angie said.

"Come on, Mom," Jason said, opening the screen door. "Do you think Joe will arrest us for trespassing?" Leaving Angie at the bottom of the stairs, he bounded up the landing. Some of the hammering stopped.

Over the pounding and a radio playing, Angie couldn't make out exactly what was being said. She did hear the breathless exclamation of her son's delight: "It rules!"

Joe was taking his time showing Jason around. That was obvious from the fact that neither of them seemed to miss her. Finally, there was total silence. The carpenters took a break, and Jason came down with a puzzled expression on his face. "What are you doing down here, Mom? Come on up. You have got to see what's going down."

"Do you mean going up?"

"Get a life, will you, Mom?" Jason said.

"It's only polite to wait to be invited," Angie said.

Joe, descending the stairs behind Jason, rolled his eyes and said to Jason, "Now that ya'll are leaving us to swelter through the summer, your mom's going stuffy on us."

"He's making a way cool place up there," Jason said, "And we need a place to live!"

"We have a place to live," Angie said.

"With the Goldheims? It's all little kids," Jason whined. "Over here I could have a pool table."

Angie cast a glacial look at Joe.

"Pool table?" Joe said with a pious look. "Now there's a good idea." He handed Jason a rule from his tool belt. "Would you do me a favor and measure that big room on the right? If a pool table is going in there, it would be easier to move in before the wall is finished."

Like an overgrown eight year old, Jason skipped across the landing and bounded up the stairs.

"You promised me you wouldn't put any ideas in his head," Angie said.

"Now sweetie," Joe said, pulling her close, "That kid doesn't need anyone to put ideas in his head. He's perfectly capable of coming up with them on his own."

"I didn't realize you were going ahead with the upstairs," Angie said, pushing away from him. She tried to sound neutral, but knew she sounded hurt. They had stopped seeing each other over the last two months. Once the decorating project was finished, there was no natural reason for them to be together all the time, except the most natural reason of all. Joe had accepted her demurral over moving upstairs in good grace, and simply stopped calling her. It stung her that he hadn't consulted her about the upstairs project, and she was doing her best not to show it.

Joe stepped back, lifted her chin, his gaze locking on hers, "I'm moving on ahead, Angie. You are, too, but maybe just a little more slowly." He kissed her forehead and ruffled her hair. "But that's okay. You'll catch up."

Angie wiped her eyes and her tongue loosened, "I'll miss you. *We've* missed you," she blurted. "Why don't you come up to the island, once we get settled up there?"

"And leave sweltering Florida in the dog days of August?" Joe said, running a hand through his hair. "I do admit, I thought you'd never ask."

Angie grinned. "I've got to go. I'm meeting Nettie French in Sarasota for lunch. This evening I'm seeing the two women in Gainesville Anthony hit after her."

Joe sighed. "Be sure you track down every last victim," he said.

"You need to do this right."

"Absolutely," Angie said. "I'm on the man's tail. I'm going to break him. I know it."

Jason came clumping down the stairs. "There's room for three pool tables in there," he said to Joe, handing back the rule.

They piled into the van Gina Goldheim had insisted on lending Angie for the long trip north. Jason had stocked the fridge, and loaded in his tape player and his Xbox.

"Plush rig," Joe said.

"Suzi Islamorada advanced me expense money," Angie said. "She has absolute confidence in me."

"And so do I," Joe said. "If you nose around Memphis a bit, you may pick up Anthony's trail, but don't get anywhere near him. Understand?"

"I'm trailing the victims, Joe," Angie said wearily. "The police are supposed to be trailing Anthony."

"See that that's the way it stays," Joe said, ignoring the sarcasm in Angie's tone. "We still haven't a clue who this guy really is."

"Nothing from the FBI?"

He shook his head. "I've bugged my contact three times. This makes me very suspicious. I should have had a yea, or a nay, long before this."

CHAPTER 46

Carmel, California
Saturday, June 13

Adolph was seated on the thick Aubusson carpet in Thalia Markham's sunken living room, awaiting the show. He rested his back on the front of her curved sectional, his legs stretched out to one side of the coffee table.

Sooki, one of Markham's fifteen greyhounds, was dozing in his lap. The script of Thalia's forthcoming movie, *The Greening*, lay open on the coffee table before him, along with the remains of an elegant dinner. He had read the script three times and knew the story by heart and he sat here, miserably uncomfortable, waiting for the action to begin.

After two weeks of nightclubs, dinners, luncheons, suppers, and various animal rights benefits, they had decided to dine in. For the evening's entertainment, Thalia was doing her final scene just for him, with the help of her houseboy-cum-actor, Stephan James.

Stephan was her nephew. Or so she said. Adolph had his suspicions about their true relationship. Stephan was one of those razor jawed, glowering types with a mop of hair, a day's growth of beard, and overly-developed abs who appear in print advertising for various jeans makers in magazines like Vanity Fair and Harper's Bazaar.

While Thalia went to dress, Adolph surreptitiously rubbed his aching back and shifted his legs, so as not to disturb the drowsy dog. Two other dogs were dozing on the sectional, one of them snoring in his ear. Only the dogs Thalia rescued from extinction after careers on dog tracks were allowed to occupy the sofas and chairs. Thalia preferred to sit on the floor and insisted that he join her. She was a devotee of yoga, as limber as a pretzel. Frequently she took up some position resembling one.

Though he hated being ordered around by this kooky woman, she fit perfectly into his plans, which were rolling along quite smoothly. After building a bank account via long distance for more than five years, Adolph Tadeschi had one day materialized on the fiduciary scene. He'd walked into the Golden State Bank and introduced himself to banker Ned Carver, whom he had dealt with solely by correspondence and wire transfers. He told Carver he was tired of wineries and interested in the movie business. Carver arranged his immediate introduction to another depositor, Thalia, a reclusive and aging actress who lived in her walled, Spanish-style hacienda in Carmel. Thalia had starred in twenty-seven films, none of them within recent memory.

Stephan, playing the butler, minced out of the kitchen, carrying a tea tray, which he set on a small table beside the hearth. He wore a poet shirt with balloon sleeves and scandalously tight pants. His swishy gestures amused Adolph. The kid really was quite an actor. Stephan had put his own spin on the part of the pompous butler. He plumped up pillows in a wing chair and stirred the coals in the hearth.

As he watched Stephan playing the fussy retainer, his thoughts drifted elsewhere. Adolph fervently wished for this romance to end. He'd paid his dues. He'd spent a fortune at the dog track, after all. His lavish support of the patron saint of greyhounds ought to have earned him a ticket or two the next time he hit the track. However, he didn't care to make a lifestyle of this. In Thalia's household, his was not a dog's life, but something less.

Thalia swept into the room in a magnificent white lace dressing gown, which revealed her remarkable cleavage. She was delicate and small boned, but her commanding, bosomy presence seemed to dominate space, as she ordered Stephan to get out of her boudoir and leave her to her despair. She was playing legendary screen actress Myrna Winters, who awakens from her cryogenic chamber in Southern California in the year twenty fifty, only to find that she and a few other technologically resurrected souls are among the last true humans on earth. Everyone else has been transformed into a race of plantlike humans who live by photosynthesis. Her beloved California is in a shambles, except for Disneyland, where the last true humans are assembled in a zoo-like environment, kept as curiosities by the new race.

In this scene, Myrna discovers that the love of her life, Orson Bacon, has become one of them.

"I slept my celestial sleep, soaring through the spheres, only to be awakened into a nightmare," she said, pacing in front of the fireplace. "Where is there anything human? Nothing remains of the pleasures of the flesh. All there is to encounter are these shuffling, shimmering, shapeless, creatures dithering along in their leafy beings. Oh yes, they tell me. It's nothing at all to become one of them. A simple transformation, and mortal fear shall leave me once and for all, and I'll taste the simple freedom of tumbleweeds blowing in the wind.

"What is it to them I relinquish this face I've spent a fortune preserving? What do they know of art, of literature, of acting? There's only a freakish curiosity I see in their grim, green little eyes." She moved away from the fireplace and in a few pantomimed gestures made it seem as if she were opening a window. "And where is the precious valley I remember? All gone now, the vineyards and the pastures, the homes and the gardens, all gone to ruin, left untended by these unruly, no account weeds."

Winters turned away from the space that represented the window, while Stephan appeared behind it. Anthony was amazed. These two really were good. He could visualize the window that they pantomimed.

Stephan slithered in through the very space that represented the window. He wore a shredded green blanket and his long hair obscured his face. His arms trembled as if palsied. He brushed his trembling hands on Winter's throat.

She cringed and shouted, "I cannot seek a breath of air but one of them comes after me. Get away from me you wretched creature." She shrank to the back of the room. Stephan advanced, all tics and tremors.

"Myrna, Myrna, my love, don't you know me?"

"What is it I hear but the wind moaning," Winters replied.

"Myrna, darling, it's me, your Orson."

"Orson. I can't believe it?"

"Myrna, come with me. I want to show you another life."

Sobbing, Winters rushed to embrace the trembling Orson, "Oh Orson, how could you have done this?" she sobbed. Real tears flowed down her face. Anthony was impressed. "What am I to do with this living flesh that burns to hold you once again?"

As the two actors held their pose, Adolph got to his feet, clapping. "Bravo, my darling. And Stephan. Excellent work." He shook the miserable young man's hand. He saw a glint of pleasure where he usually read sullen hatred.

He lifted Thalia off her feet, twirled her around, then set her down again and waltzed her in front of the fireplace. A passel of greyhounds swarmed around them, no doubt let loose by Stephan as he slammed out of the room.

So much for Stephan's pleasure. It was obvious to Adolph, if not to Thalia, that Stephan resented him, but Stephan was in a terrible fix. He didn't dare ruin his chances with a possible benefactor.

Thalia, sweaty with exertion, was beaming. "What do you think? Will they let me come back? Adolph? I've been out of work for the last nine years, you know."

"Let you come back? Why, they'll be crawling to you."

"I...I haven't been on screen for so long," she said. "Are you *sure*?"

"Sure enough to produce this myself," he said. "Frankly, my dear, it's not you I'm worried about. What bothers me is: who are we going to get to do the Orson part? Stephan has great promise, of course, and we'll see that he has a strong supporting role. But you need a mature actor for the Orson character."

Thalia flung her arms around his neck. "Adolph, you are the dearest man, and I love you truly." Maybe her glow had faded, but Thalia still had her limpid dark eyes and piles of thick dark hair. "Yes, it is true, what they said at the Bette Ford Clinic. Once you kick the habit, the high is real life. It truly is most amazing and beautiful."

CHAPTER 47

Memphis, TN
Sunday, June 14

Marci Trillin was dazzling in the spotlight. The white satin gown with the fringe dripping down the front was a cowboy-style wedding dress. Feather trimmed earrings and chunks of turquoise jewelry completed her outfit.

"Thank ya'll for turning out on Beale Street, this here drizzling overcast Memphis afternoon," she said. "Now I want ya'll here who are married to a good man—*or*—woman to show your appreciation..." she said, as whoops and catcalls flooded her out. "...in a tasteful manner, I mean. What ya'll do later on at home ain't none of my business...so long as it's nice..." she said, to giggles, "...and consensual." More bursts of laughter.

"Reason I'm sayin' all this, is there's some of us just ain't lucky in love. We find ourselves in love with the likes of Bill Bailey, or maybe some tormented soul like Billie Joe. Then there's my own case where I met this charmin' man. Named Anthony Abruzzi.

She strummed her inlaid-mother of pearl guitar, setting up an ominous rhythm and the crowd moaned.

"Now this Anthony was a real nice guy, minded his manners; didn't even come on to me."

The women cheered. Men groaned.

186

"He took me all around and whispered sweet nothins' in my ear. So what am I doin' here in my weddin' dress? Why, I'm dedicating this song to a little ole' sorority of sisters right here with us tonight. Women who loved Anthony with all their hearts, but it did them no good, caused them untold grief and pain. Why? 'Cause Anthony didn't love none of us. All he loved was our bank accounts."

Swaying, her tooled boots tapping, her pale sleek hair bunching on her shoulders, Marci launched into her song:

> *My trip to heaven was lined in debt,*
> *I loved you honey but I ain't paid for it yet,*
> *It's plain to see it just ain't funny,*
> *When the man you love, just loves your money.*

"Nuuuh Uhhhhh." In her wheelchair, Jenny Sawyer beamed.

"What did I tell you?" Price Sawyer said with a triumphant smile. "She understands. I know she does. It's just that she can't say anything."

"At least not yet," Angie said, squeezing Jenny's hand. "But you keep working on it, Jenny. It'll come back."

Jenny's face moved, at least on one side. Her mouth raised in a crooked smile.

Maybe Jenny would recover. And maybe they would catch Anthony. Angie still had to hold out hope, though the trip wasn't going so well. She definitely had Nettie French, the real estate broker, in her corner. Two other Sarasota women he had hit at the same time were doubtful, however.

Here in Memphis, she had her star witness in Marci. Poor Jenny, the most damaged by Anthony, could say nothing when it came to trial. If Price would let her attempt to talk on the witness stand, well, that would be the most powerful testimony of all. But Angie checked herself, and she realized with terrible remorse what Joe had tried to tell her from the beginning. Sometimes the cost of revenge came at too high a price. How could she even think of asking Jenny for her help? She did have some hearsay evidence in the form of two women from the Zonta Club who could place Jenny in Anthony's company at a lecture by Dr. Joyce Brothers. Two flight attendants for Northwest airlines had identified Anthony from a photo and were willing to testify. The Canadian woman who managed a New Age bookstore in the Memphis Mall could testify that Anthony had committed battery on a police officer. She was willing to swear that Anthony had given her the same Cayce

187

story that he had used on Maria Whitman.

Last night, after they'd returned from their obligatory visit to Graceland, Angie had called Joe. He'd dampened her spirits. He'd gone to the district attorney to plead for an indictment for murder in the Whitman case. Yes, they had the button on his coat and the Canadian woman's testimony was interesting, and they had Maria's log from her computer, but the judge might rule out much of this as hearsay. There were no witnesses and no other physical evidence. Finally, the prosecutor agreed to convene a grand jury on the Whitman case. Since Nettie French would testify, an indictment in Angie's case was also a possibility, but the prosecutor's office wanted more local witnesses, since the judge might rule the Memphis witnesses weren't germane to her case.

Price Sawyer rose as the lights came up. "Angie, if Jenny could talk, I know she'd be plugging for you. I personally admire you for your grit," he said. "However, it's time to get Mother home. This outing has been wonderful for her, but the doctor warned me not to tire her out."

Onstage, Marci took her final bows. The audience roared its approval. As Marci had instructed her beforehand, Angie slipped through an unmarked door beside the stage, which led through a dingy hallway to the dressing rooms. She knocked on the third door from the end of the hallway.

"That you, Angie?" Marci drawled.

"Yes, it's me." The door opened a crack.

"Come on in and be sure to lock it behind you. Some of the fans?" Marci said, rolling her eyes.

Angie found herself in what appeared to be a motel bedroom with a burnt orange shag carpet that was at least three decades out of date. The tiny room was dominated by a big mirror and dressing table. There were flower arrangements and cards piled on every surface. Marci certainly did have a following. Angie unzipped Marci's white gown and helped her step out of it, careful to avoid smearing makeup on it.

"This is a wonderful dress," Angie said as she draped it over a padded hanger. "You have exquisite taste."

"Anthony has exquisite taste, you mean," Marci said, her face darkening.

"Oh no!" Angie said, realizing what had happened. "They wouldn't take the dress back?"

"I'd already had it altered. Three grand right down the drain. I'm still making payments on it. With interest. Frankly, that dress gives me the willies every time I put it on, but then again it helps me get into the song."

In her bra and panties, Marci was an enviable sight. She had a knockout figure. She was a big boned and full-breasted woman, with not a trace of cellulite on her firm and rounded thighs.

"Were you really in love with him?" Angie asked.

Marci, slathering cold cream on her face, bugged her eyes at Angie. "Honey, I was infatuated, big-time. How can you love somebody you only knew for three days?"

"I guess you're right," Angie said.

"What I was in love with, I now realize, is he told me how wonderful and talented I was. He said he had a big-time client in the record business, and implied he'd make me a star. I believed all his guff, of course, because I wanted to believe it. That's where I'm vulnerable. Career-wise, I am just too ambitious for my own good. Or *was*. I think I've learned my lesson." Marci slipped on her jeans and a sweater, uncorked a bottle of champagne sent backstage by the management and poured a glass for Angie.

They clicked glasses in a sarcastic toast to Anthony.

"I have to admit, that bastard did me one favor," Marci said. "I'd never recorded any of my own songs, and here, look at this one. It's number fifteen right here in town, and starting to catch on in Nashville."

"Wonderful," Angie said. "I hope you sell a million copies." She raised her glass to Marci and drank more champagne. But when she lowered it, she found Marci staring at her.

"What?" Angie said.

"You don't suppose, if I get a hit, I'll have to pay that bastard royalties?" The two women had a good laugh over the possibility.

"So what about you, Hon?" Marci said.

"What about me?" Angie said, feeling uncomfortable.

"Come on, girl. You know what I mean," Marci said.

"I wasn't really in love with Anthony," she stammered. "I remember now that I had doubts from the beginning. But I didn't care, you know? I'd just lost my husband Alan, and I didn't really expect to love anyone else that way, ever again. I realize now that what Anthony offered me was a way to escape from DeLeon. It wasn't working out, trying to stay there, and work with Alan's old colleagues. Too much had changed," Angie said, her voice cracking. "I was completely numb where work was concerned. I was so used to working with Alan that I couldn't seem to do anything on my own.

"Of course, I could have gone home to my mother, but she'd just lost Daddy, you see. I was a plain coward. I hadn't faced up to Alan's death, and I suppose some part of me thought that if I just stayed out of the Pacific Northwest, it meant Daddy would somehow still be there. I just couldn't face up to so much grief all at once."

"Hey," Marci said. "Who could?"

Angie took another sip of the champagne. "It wasn't just that, of course. I guess I was afraid of being smothered and fussed over. My mother always seemed to feel she had to run interference for me. Daddy had always served as a buffer between us, and I was afraid I just couldn't handle being with her without him being around."

"That's hard for me to imagine," Marci said. "I always got on with my mama. Which is a good thing, since my dad run out on us when I turned thirteen."

"I have this new friend. He's—well…he's the lead investigator on the case, and he's telling me that at this point we can't expect to find this Anthony, and that I've got to get on with my life."

"Hey," Marci said. "You've lost everybody. You need time.

Angie nodded. "That's what I keep telling him."

CHAPTER 48

Big Sur, CA
Sunday, June 21

The pounding rollers shook the spongy sand they strolled in bare feet. Adolph was in an ebullient mood. He'd spent close to three weeks in the steady company of Thalia Markham. Though it would soon be time to move on, he was enjoying the novelty of romancing one woman at a time. What a joy it was not to have to dash through these romances and head on to the next date. There was something to be said for fidelity.

Beside him, Thalia, in her helmet of dark hair, looked wonderful in the gauzy white gown she wore over her black maillot. She truly was a regal woman, and fun to be around. Long term it was not, however. Maybe if he hadn't already seen Jane Pelham in the flesh? Maybe if he hadn't met Markham under false pretenses? And then there was the matter of the dogs. One greyhound he could handle. Fifteen, with two more on the way? Never. He had absolutely nothing at all against dogs. He loved greyhounds, particularly as they ran around the track. It was just that he refused to become a part of Markham's kennel.

"Redford?" she said.

"Clint. Clint McCall." He replied.

"Clint McCall?" Thalia shouted above the roar of the surf. "Who is he? I don't want to risk going with an unknown," she said with a frown.

"Adolph. You have to realize that I am the unknown quantity here."

Adolph started. God. He'd let himself think ahead to his farm. Where in hell was his concentration? Had he caught the Alzheimer's bug from Jenny Sawyer?

"Redford," Adolph said, smiling. "No, my darling, he won't do."

"And why not?" Thalia said. "He does beautifully in romantic roles."

"Think of Robert Redford covered entirely in leaves, my dear," Adolph said. "And there's the problem."

"So? We offer the part to the Jolly Green Giant," Thalia said, and they both laughed.

Adolph kissed her, pulled her in close, until he felt their heat mingle along the seam where their bodies joined, closing out the chilly sting of the surf. So the woman was a kook. She was a nice kook, anyway. Thalia went limp in his arms. "Adolph, I feel a scene *From Here to Eternity* coming on right now." She grabbed at his trunks and he eased away from her.

"Not yet, my darling," he whispered. "I want you for eternity. But it shouldn't be like this."

Thalia pushed him away. "Adolph, if you have some sort of problem, baby, tell me," she said, sticking her tongue in his ear, swirling it around. The hackles rose on the back of his neck.

Then she pushed him back and stalked away up the berm, her body stiff as a toy soldier's. It was watching her walk away that did it for him. For the first time in months, he felt himself stirring. He dashed after her.

"Problem?" he said as he caught up to her, swung her around and ground himself into her. "Yes, yes, yes," he panted, "I'm in absolute agony. I need you desperately."

Moaning, Thalia pulled one of her yoga numbers. She flung one leg around him, digging her heel into the small of his back. He staggered backwards into the dunes, pulling Thalia with him.

"Darling. My leg," she said.

He rolled sideways, freeing her limb, then grappled with her tangle of gauze and Spandex, but Thalia had the advantage. She reached right up his trunks and squeezed his balls. Her strong fingers collared his shaft. Desperately trying to hold back, he groaned. When her yoga-trained hand closed around the head of his penis, his control was gone and he shot off in her hand. Like a shock wave, the heat of release coursed through his body. He was hot from scalp to toes.

"Thalia! What you do to me," he gasped.

"Well now," she said. "So the strong silent man is putty in my hand," she said, her face one big sloppy grin. Triumphantly, she mounted him and rode him hard, raking his flaccid cock with her rapier pubis as she groaned in delight. She bucked and pounded, on and on, driving him into the sand. Finally, she tensed, gave a little shriek, then flung herself down beside him. They dozed in a spent, sandy heap, their slumber broken only by the boom and hiss of the surf. Eventually, he was aware that beside him Thalia was stirring. She sat up, stretched, then shook him.

"God," she said. "Some people are coming. We have to go. I can't get caught like this. I'll wind up in *The National Enquirer*.

Adolph grinned. With an extended hand he motioned the headline into the air in front of them: "Lover Tells All: He's Never Had It Better with Sex Goddess, 67."

"Adolph, darling. That's the nicest, most touching thing you've ever said to me," she said, her limpid black eyes emitting sparks of love.

"Never forget that I said it. I'm not the most expressive guy, you know."

"Of course," Thalia giggled. "Mr. Silence and Mystique. Now we know where you store your emotions," she said, squeezing between his legs.

A pair of surfers, boards glimmering in the sun, approached them up the beach. "Sorry, dear. Those boys are not a mirage," she said.

"We ought to go. I want to check out three more locations this afternoon," he said, failing to add that he had to return the Bentley he'd rented by eight o'clock or face an additional charge.

"Slave driver," Thalia said as she stood up and shook the sand out of her dress.

"Now what we have to have in a leading man," Adolph explained, as they strolled up the beach, "is a commanding voice, and bedroom eyes. Nothing else matters."

"Sean!" Thalia said.

"Yes," Adolph said. "Exactly."

"But do you think he'd play a plant?" she wondered.

CHAPTER 49

Memphis, TN
Monday, June 22

Jenny Sawyer's physical therapist was waiting at the hospital entrance when Angie drove up. "How's our beautiful lady today?" said Rosie Alberts, as she opened the car door.

"Jenny's had one busy week," Angie said from behind the wheel.

Angie found herself staring. Rosie Alberts was the biggest woman she had ever seen. Well over six feet tall. Her thighs were like tree trunks. Very solid tree trunks. This woman worked out. But where on earth would she buy panty hose? Angie wondered.

"Outings are great for her. As long as she doesn't tire herself. Come back by noon," Rosie said, her square face cheerful as she settled Jenny into a hospital wheel chair. "I'll guarantee we'll have whipped up Jenny's appetite." Angie was ashamed of herself. What did Jenny's therapist's panty hose have to do with anything? Particularly since Rosie was such a concerned woman.

Angie got out of the car and followed the wheelchair inside the hospital. "Could you tell me where the admissions office is?" she said. "I'm tracking down the man who did this to Jenny. I found out from the police department that another person had a run-in with him. He was evidently the last to see Anthony and as a result, he checked into the hospital with a heart attack."

194

"South wing," Rosie said, turning her wheelchair in the opposite direction. "The supervisor is Helen Mandel, a good friend of mine. She knows all about Jenny's case, which is no surprise, of course. All of Memphis knows about it. I'm sure she can help you."

Angie was directed to a small waiting room outside the administrative offices of the hospital. It was done up in green and mauve. What was it with public buildings? Angie wondered. Was it some national ordinance that all institutions around the country were required to use the same color scheme? While Angie waited for Mandel to get out of a meeting, she got out her small black binder and pored over her current list of Abruzzi victims in the Memphis area. Sad to say, Marci Trillin and Jenny Sawyer weren't Anthony's only hits in Memphis.

There was Annette Newbridge, a podiatrist's wife, who was of no help at all. She had just separated from her husband when Anthony hit her for seventeen thousand, which she needed to pay off a second mortgage on her house. Newbridge had turned to her religion for solace. She was certain God would not want her seeking vengeance against Anthony. Angie drew a line through her name.

There was Carmen Rames, owner of a nail salon, who was thinking about it. She'd come close to losing her business when Anthony bilked her, but Carmen had a new boyfriend who knew nothing about Anthony, and she wasn't certain how he would take it if he found out. Angie put a question mark beside her name.

The next woman, Sherry Knowland, had told her: "I'd like to do a nice little nail job on that man. With a pair of pliers, if you know what I mean. Just kidding, Hon, but call me when you catch him, and I'll get on the next plane." Angie smiled as she put a star beside Knowland's name.

Her next listing was Kay Larkin, a librarian from Murfreesboro. Larkin had called Crimestop to tell the producers they must have the wrong man. Angie had met her over coffee at the Peabody in Memphis, but Larkin wouldn't budge. "All I can say is, the man was perfectly polite to me, taught me how to play roulette and left me all the winnings."

"Let me guess. He left you with five hundred dollars," Angie murmured.

"That's right," Larkin said. "How did you know?"

"That's what he left me. It's what he left Jenny Sawyer when he abandoned her on a plane to New York," Angie said, but Larkin didn't seem to get the point and there was no use messing with a hostile witness. Angie drew a wavy line through Larkin's name.

"Mrs. Reynolds?" Angie glanced up. A tall, spare woman with an angular face and the alabaster skin of a Madonna was smiling down at her. Angie stuffed her list in her purse and stood up.

"Hello. Jenny Sawyer's physical therapist thought you could help me," Angie said, "It occurred to me to ask about a patient you had last Halloween. I'm tracking down the fellow who put Jenny in the hospital. The police believe your patient was injured by this same man."

"Oh, yes. I remember," Mandel said, her eyes beaming behind her wire-rimmed glasses. "Raymond Tadischi. Some sort of heart condition. Angina, I believe."

"I'm crossing the country, lining up witnesses," Angie said. "Perhaps Mr. Tadischi could tell us something."

Mandel's desk was immaculate, Angie noticed as they settled into her office. Mandel poured Angie a cup of coffee and opened her computer file with some difficulty.

"We've just changed our record keeping system, and I fear the hospital will be bankrupt by the time we all get the hang of it," she sighed. "Now, let me call one of the nurses who took care of Mr. Tadischi. She adored him."

"Brenda? It's Helen," Mandel said on the phone. " If you could spare Juanita Diego for a minute, could you have her come down, please? Thanks."

Mandel turned to her computer screen. She pecked at the keyboard. "Ahhh yes. Here it is. I was afraid of that. Mr. Tadischi gave us two thousand dollars in cash after three days of admission and an insurance card. At the moment he still owes us over twenty thousand dollars."

"What address did he give, by any chance?"

"I probably shouldn't tell you this, but I'm sure Mr. Tadischi wouldn't mind. He was so well thought of by the staff, and he did so much for young Bradley...Yes, here it is...The Beverly Hills Hotel, Hollywood. Mr. Tadischi does stay there periodically, but he seems to do a good deal of traveling. I called the hotel myself."

"You mentioned a Bradley?" Angie said.

"Yes," Mandel said, stirring her coffee. "They had the same cardiologist. That's how they met. Brad was twelve, pathetically thin, and so lonely. He'd already had several operations by the time he came to us."

"A child with a heart condition?" Angie said.

"It was congenital," Mandel said.

There was a diffident knock on her door.

"Yes?" Mandel said.

A nurse poked her head through the door. "You called me, Mrs. Mandel?"

"Yes, Juanita. Come in. This is Mrs. Reynolds. She's looking for that Abruzzi fellow, the one who put Mr. Tadischi in the hospital. She wanted to talk to Raymond."

"Aye?" Juanita said. She was a lovely Hispanic girl with golden skin, an ample mouth and bedroom eyes. "Bradley is gone. It will break his heart, but I have something to give him, if you can find him," Juanita said.

"Tell me," Angie said. "What did Mr. Tadischi look like?"

"Not too tall, about average height, ball, *gordo*," Juanita said, brushing a hand back across her head.

"Bald?" Angie said. "Fat?"

"A little heavy, yes? And completely ball, but for dark hair on the sides, yes?"

"And do you know what he did for a living?"

"Class rings," Juanita said, brightening. "He gave one to Bradley. He tell Bradley he's in a class by himself. His mother tell me they bury him with it."

"And what did Bradley leave Mr. Tadischi? If it isn't too personal to ask."

"No problem," Juanita said. "A fine deck of playing cards that Mr. Tadischi had once given to him."

CHAPTER 50

Carmel, CA
Wednesday, June 24

Adolph was stretched on a lounge chair on the terrace, allowing the sun to dry the water on his back. He'd gradually built up his strength at the Idaho spa and was determined to keep up with his exercise regimen. He'd done fifty laps in Thalia's pool, in anticipation of a wonderful lunch that Stephan was preparing. Thalia was winding up her yoga exercises with a headstand. The cellular phone beside his lounge chair began to ring, but he ignored it. Here was one call where he needed Thalia's attention.

"Anthony, darling, could you pick that up? It's ruining my concentration," Thalia said on the tenth ring.

"Uhhhh?" Anthony grunted, sitting up. "Yes, of course, sweetheart. Forgive me. I must have dozed off." He reached for a towel and sponged off the back of his neck, letting the phone ring twice more for good measure. "Tadeschi.... Counselor. How are you? How was the weekend? Wonderful. Couldn't be better. Yes, we must do dinner. I have someone very special I'd like you to meet. So? What's up? What? No, no, no. I don't like this at all." As he talked on the phone, he watched Thalia's legs fold down, then stretch out straight on her mat. She looked like a triangular piece in a wire puzzle.

198

"Morty," he said, dragging out the name. "You assured me the closing would take place on the first. I have four other deals pending. I have to renegotiate anything, I'll pay through the nose. You just tell them the deal is off." There was a long pause. He spoke again: "Contingency? I don't remember any such contingency. I want this deal done now." He pitched the phone on the lounge and put on his shirt.

"Is anything wrong?" Thalia said.

"Damned lawyers," Adolph said. "They are all alike. At least the ones that are licensed, that is." He smiled at her. "Not to worry, it's just business."

"You lie right down," Thalia said, perching on the edge of the lounge. "I hate to see you get so tense." She kneaded the ridge of his shoulders. "Now tell Thalia all about it."

"The buyer is stalling on the sale of one of my vineyards. Morty said the Mondavis have an automatic, thirty-day extension. Meanwhile, I'm trying to close a deal I have going up on this charming retreat in the San Juan Islands, north of Seattle."

"Have I heard about that one?" Thalia said.

"I meant it as a surprise," he said. "A ranch. Clint McCall the stunt man used to own it."

"McCall? So that's what you were thinking about on the beach."

He nodded, amazed that she remembered his slip. Thalia missed nothing. "I've known the McCall family for years. They are anxious to settle the estate. The price is right. This is a wonderful property. It used to be a working cattle ranch." He turned, took her hand, licked her palm. "I knew you'd hate hearing that."

"Clever boy," she said. She'd worked over his back and began to pound it with the sides of her hands.

"I see it as a horse farm," he said. "Or perhaps a kennel?"

"What did you have to pay for it?"

"One point five," he said, "an absolute steal."

"Whew!" Thalia said.

"It's close to five hundred acres," he said.

Her fingers worked up his neck, playing his spinal column like an instrument. Moaning, he closed his eyes and listened to the chirping of the birds in the canopy of trees overhead and the burbling of the fountain spilling into the pool.

"Feel better?" she said, releasing him.

"Wonderful," he said, sitting up. "You have such fantastic hands."

Thalia moved off the lounge and commenced to set out place mats and silverware on the umbrella table beside the lounge. "Stephan will be here with lunch, any minute. How about a martini?"

"Iced tea," he said. "Dammit, sweetie. I may have to go spend the rest of the day on the phone, and you know where I'd hoped we'd be." He treated her to his lady-killer leer.

"Whatever the universe has to send your way will be yours," Thalia said as she poured the iced tea into goblets and squeezed in his prescribed three drops of lemon.

"I hope so, Thalia, but I haven't told you the worst part."

She set down the pitcher. "You have a wife and six children waiting for you up there on that farm."

He laughed, seized her arm, and dragged her down into his lap. "Silly bitch. If that were the problem, I'd just have to ditch them all. You've got me dazzled."

"So what is it?" Thalia said.

"The seed money for *The Greening* is wrapped up in this deal."

Thalia's face scrunched up. "I don't get it."

"Our banker friend, Ned Carver, is lending me one five in seed money up front."

"So he told me."

"But since I'm a new producer, with no track record, he wanted real estate as collateral."

Thalia brightened. "We could use my home as collateral. It's worth at least two and a half."

"Sweetie," he said. "You are a doll to offer. But I couldn't let you do that. At any rate, when the winery went into escrow, he agreed to accept the McCall property as collateral. If my winery sale doesn't close, I can't sew up the McCall property, which means we can't lay hands on the funds we need to produce the movie."

"The McCalls will wait for their money," Thalia said.

"I hope so. Problem is, the week after the McCalls signed with me, a much better offer came in from a land developer, three and a half." It's in escrow already as a backup."

Stephan set out crab salad with big chunks of avocado and tomato, Thalia's face brightened. "Stephan. Aren't you just the stitch? You are saving our day here," she said.

Adolph took two bites, raved over the food, then set down his fork.

"Yes, I'm quite wonderful as a chef," Stephan said sarcastically and stalked away. He was barely speaking to either of them; ever since he found out they were not casting him for the male lead in *The Greening*.

"Darling," Thalia said, ignoring Stephan's pique. "I can't bear to see you so unhappy. Neither can I bear to have my picture held up any longer. Now let me get this straight. You don't need the whole one point five to close on the McCall farm."

"Not at all. A measly nine sixty will do. The sellers agreed to take back a mortgage for the balance."

"Right after luncheon, you'll bring me all the paperwork on it, and I'll help you."

"Thalia, I do appreciate the offer, but really. I doubt Ned would approve."

"You let me handle him," Thalia said. "Don't you worry, sweetie, little Thalia can take care of herself. We'll get this Morty of yours to draw up a promissory note to me, with interest, just to cover the down. I'll take a lien on the McCall property. You don't mind, darling? It's just business."

"Thalia," he said, pulling her into his lap. "I love the way you take care of yourself. But Morty shouldn't do this. You need to use your own attorney," Adolph said, not mentioning that the real reason was, his attorney, the so-called Morty, did not exist.

"Fine. I'll call him this afternoon," Thalia said.

CHAPTER 51

Yosemite Valley, CA
Tuesday, June 30

The helicopter swooped down toward the lake so that they could catch a better glimpse of Yosemite Falls.

The rotors thumped rhythmically against the roar of the spume. Transfixed, Angie stared down at the bottom of the spillway, seeing not beauty but an old maelstrom: *a ball of light, a blast, plumes of water rising up, missiles of debris raining down on her. She was sucked under water, the breath forced out of her lungs, she was gasping and fighting...*

"Mom!" Jason shouted, shaking her. "Mom, what's wrong?"

Through her headphones, she heard the pilot telling Jason to hold on. That they were heading in. His voice was tinny, like something out of a can. Angie was conscious and sitting up in her seat by the time the pilot landed the chopper on the roof of their hotel.

"I'm really fine," she pleaded. "Please, can't we finish the tour? Jason will be so disappointed."

The pilot grinned. "No problem. Be here at one thirty tomorrow and we'll do it all over again. On one condition."

"What's that?" Angie said.

"You don't pass out again, Mrs. Reynolds. I'll take it personal—as a reflection on my flying."

"I don't know what happened," Angie said. "Somehow, when we

202

flew over the falls, it sent me right into my old childhood nightmare."

"Well then," the pilot said, "We'd better leave Yosemite Falls off the agenda for tomorrow. Right, Jason?"

"Right," the boy said.

"I'm so sorry, Hon," Angie said as Jason helped her down the stairs. "I can't figure out what got into me."

They got back to their room. It was rustic, a log cabin, warmed up by nature prints and patchwork quilts. Angie sat out on the deck in a big Adirondack chair hewn from redwood.

Jason poured them each a soda. "You know what, Mom?" he said. "Joe is right. You need a break from this manhunt."

"I suppose you're right," Angie murmured.

"After Memphis, we didn't develop a single fresh lead," Jason said.

Angie laughed. "You sound just like Joe."

"He's the pro, Mom. Listen to what he's telling you."

"What's our score so far?" Angie said.

"We talked to thirty victims. Less than half of them agreed to help us. If they don't care, why should we?"

"They are embarrassed and scared," Angie said. "That doesn't mean it doesn't hurt them just as much." She stood up and stared out over the lush grounds of the Redwood Regency.

A party of hikers were getting into a van. Several parties teed off in what looked to be slow motion on the golf course. The sound of a motor drifted toward her. Somewhere a gardener was manicuring the grounds of this place. It was a posh resort Suzi Islamorada knew about. Some tie-in with her husband's corporation. Nothing she and Jason could have afforded on their own. Her hand trembling, Angie fought back tears. There was no way to tell Jason what was eating her. It was Carmen Rames. A suicide. She was the Memphis woman who had nearly lost her nail salon when Anthony cleaned her out. She was on Angie's "maybe" list to testify. Now she was dead. She'd found out when she'd called Marci Trillin to find out if Marci had called back this wavering victim. Rames' fear had been that her new boyfriend would find out about Anthony. She was afraid he'd leave her, Marci had said in a hushed phone conversation that took place after Jason had gone to bed.

Something had happened.

Marci didn't know all the details. She'd read about Rames in the paper. Rames had overdosed on her own tranquilizers, the story said. Marci had gone to the funeral, spoken to Carmen's mother. Carmen's new boyfriend was a jealous man, was all the mother had said. Angie

203

hadn't slept last night. Carmen's boyfriend must have found out about Anthony. *I'm responsible for this. Anthony doesn't have to kill off his victims. I'm doing it for him.*

"Mom," Jason said, breaking into her reverie. She hastily wiped the tears out of her eyes. "You promised this trip would be some fun. So far it's been pretty boring."

"Hey. You made it to Graceland," Angie said, forcing herself to smile through a blur of tears. "You saw the Pueblo villages in New Mexico. We took in the Grand Canyon. We've hiked all around Yosemite."

"So?"

"So, tomorrow we'll head for Los Angeles. We'll do some studio tours. We'll stop in the Beverly Hills Hotel one afternoon and see if we can't locate this guy Raymond Tadischi."

Jason rolled his eyes. "Mom! You promised."

"I did. This will only take a few minutes. If he isn't there we won't push it, but I promised that nurse, Juanita, in Memphis that I'd get in touch with Mr. Tadischi about that poor little Bradley, the boy who died. Besides," Angie said, sipping her coke, "Raymond Tadischi is the very last person ever to encounter Anthony Abruzzi, as far as I know. Maybe he can tell us something."

CHAPTER 52

DeLeon, FL
Tuesday, June 30

Joe picked up one bronze, then the other. "They sure do look identical," he murmured. Twin birds of prey, wings outstretched. "Used to be known as fish eagles. Found on nearly every continent. Exist entirely on fish. Never got much sympathy until the fish turned toxic. Then they acquire their own conservancy to save them, and now, by golly they are osprey and they are art," he said.

"Of course. To me, too," Bette Steinhausen nodded in agreement. "Tree-hunnert tousand dollar each, what vee pay. Our appraiser spotted the copy. This one," she said, picking up the hawk on the left. What we want is, the gallery owner to take this one beck. Otherwise, vee press charges." Joe winced when he saw which gallery they were talking about.

"Jake Waller? In Sago Square?" he said.

"Yes, why not?" Bette Steinhausen said. She held her lighted cigarette pointing straight up, like a spear. It was obvious she intended to do battle.

"Jake Waller has been an art dealer for thirty years. He's on the DeLeon city council. Did you talk to him about this?"

"Oh yes," Mrs. Steinhausen said, lifting her chin. She was blonde and pretty, despite her bulk. Her husband was thin, doleful and dark and had little to say.

"What did he say?"

"He say both pieces are good, as far as he knows."

"I'll personally go see Mr. Waller this afternoon," he said.

"Ven ve hear from you?" Mrs. Steinhousen said, handing him her card. The address, Twelve Compass Rose Harbour, was in one of the poshest enclaves on the Gulf.

"I'll call you this evening," he said.

Lordy, lordy, Joe thought as he escorted them out. Moneyed Europeans were moving here by the hundreds. So what if word was passed around in jet set circles that a DeLeon city councilman had ripped one of them for a third of a million bucks? Surely this was just a mistake.

He escorted the Steinhausens all the way out to the street. Their car proved to be a perfectly restored, nineteen fifty-seven Ford Thunderbird. Joe whistled.

Manny Steinhausen's gray eyes lighted up. "Only seven thousand miles on it," he said.

"Now there's a piece of art," Vensure said. "Another piece of art," he added hastily. Quite frankly, he wasn't wild about the Steinhausen's choice of osprey with fish in their claws, even if they were now politically correct and supposed to have been done by Gutzam Borglund, the carver of Mt. Rushmore.

Jenny Randapolis flagged him down as he passed her command post. "Where you been? I got the FBI on hold for you," she said.

He took the call on the spot. "Vensure."

"Joe, boy." The whiny wheeze was unmistakable, like the squawking of a rusty hinge in a high wind.

"Well, Satch. I thought you'd forgotten me," Joe said.

"Sorry, it took so long, buddy. Your boy Abruzzi must have heavy connections somewhere. I was trotted down every blind alley we've got on this one. Frankly, I discovered a few snarls I didn't know we had. Finally, I hear from a District Attorney in New Jersey. Abruzzi's real name is Johnny Octave. He was a precocious kid. Started out running numbers at age eleven. Then became a mafia bagman. His rap sheet's a mile long. He did time in a federal hotel for mail fraud, forgery, and theft. There's some evidence he was also a hit man. He was linked to two unsolved hits on New York chieftains. Then he was set up to do one of the mafia chiefs in Trenton, but turned evidence and got into witness protection. Equipped with a new identity, he moved to Ann Arbor, married the daughter of a college professor. That lasted about eighteen months. Then he took off and has been unheard of, until you made the connection. Congratulations."

"Thanks," Joe said. He wanted to puke.

"Say, buddy, when are we going pig hunting?"

"I thought we just did."

"I mean for the boars."

"I know what you mean, Satch," he said. "Hey buddy? I owe you one hell of a hunt. Get yourself a week off, give me a month's notice and I'll put in a reservation on Judge Fowler's hunting camp out in the Glades. All expenses. Personally. On me. In fact, if you want to do an African safari or a snipe hunt on the moon I'll borrow us a rocket, but at the moment I gotta take care of some friends who are out hunting Octave."

"Good luck, buddy," Satch said.

His hands were shaking when he pulled the scrap of paper from his wallet, the one with Angie's Yosemite number on it. He'd spoken to them late last night. Angie had sounded weary, tired of the chase. Something was bothering her but she wouldn't say what it was. As the phone rang, he grimaced inwardly. Dear Lord God, how could I be so stupid as to let Angie and Jason run around the country on the trail of a mafia hit man?

When the hotel operator answered, he gave her their room number. The phone rang some more.

"No answer," the operator said, breaking in.

"Please have them paged." Joe said. "This is urgent."

CHAPTER 53

San Juan Islands, WA
July 3

Gulls swooped in, plucking pieces of bread from the young woman's hand as her boyfriend snapped pictures. It was a silly thing to do. Inside one of the cavernous saloons of *The Kaleetan*, a triple-decker ferry, Adolph sat sipping a latte, idly watching other passengers react to the couple out on the deck. Some were amused by the antics of the young couple; others were offended.

Adolph didn't much care what they did. Three seats ahead of him another couple necked. Across from him a woman napped, her jeans-clad snatch hung out in the aisle. Now that was a little much.

Forewarned that the holiday traffic would be terrible, he'd waited in line for an hour for the earliest of the afternoon ferries to Orcas Island, but still the crowd was enormous. Scores of bicyclers with backpacks, vans, campers, pickups and trailers had been shoehorned aboard the vessel, and then there was Adolph with his Mercedes coupe, top down, cool, unhurried. He patted his breast pocket. It held a certified check for eight hundred seventy thousand dollars, the entire balance owing on his farm. Thalia had very generously financed the entire purchase. Plus he pocketed ninety thousand on the transaction.

His farm. The very thought made him swell with pride. He really owned something outright. No longer was there any need to run. Of

208

course Thalia Markham would be peeved if she ever found out he'd inflated the sales price just a tad. She'd begged to come up with him, and he'd reluctantly agreed.

Unfortunately, her precious Sooki somehow got into the box of chocolates he'd bought for Thalia. The dog lay in grave danger in a veterinary hospital back in L.A. He sighed. Perhaps he shouldn't have been so careless with the chocolates. Perhaps he should have paraded Thalia around on Orcas Island. She still had a recognizable name in certain circles, after all. Would an open link to Thalia Markham have made him more of a catch in Jane Pelham's eyes?

Thalia had given him the cash only on the condition that it was secured by the property, which meant in effect that she was the true owner. If she ever cared to come after him in court. But so what? Once he was married to Jane, he could deed the property to Markham if it came to that.

He bought a copy of The Sounder, the Orcas Island newspaper, and read the classifieds. The McCalls had shipped out the last crop of Black Angus steers to a feedlot and auctioned off all of Clint's champion quarter horses. He had enough money left to buy a couple of presentable horses and some livestock. For once he wasn't going to play the part, He was going to do real stuff. As he watched troops of healthy kids preparing to head off for cycling trips or hikes in the island, he had an inspiration. What if he used the McCall property as a ranch for kids like Bradley? Sick kids that couldn't keep up with their peers. But so what? They could sit on a horse if you propped them up.

And what about those tough kids, the juveniles that had no chance in life? He could offer his ranch to the church. After all, he owed something to Father Barenski, who had once tried to straighten him out. It was not the good father's fault that he had failed.

He circled the livestock ads and those for hay and feed, finished his latte, and went for a stroll on the deck. It was a magnificent day. To the west, the skyline was filled with the crystalline peaks of the Cascade range, hovering like a mirage above a groundswell of clouds. To the northeast, the vast gleaming mound of the Mt. Baker volcano hulked on the skyline. He felt the pulse of the diesels underfoot, and the ferry heaved a time or two, sending him into a weaving stagger. He'd nearly reached the big swinging saloon doors to the deck when he saw her. She sat alone in her Indian sweater, her grayish blonde hair endearingly messy. She sat in one of the booths, making notes from a book. The reading glasses she wore kept slipping down her nose.

"Mrs. Pelham," he said. "You seem to be working hard for such a lovely day."

"Oh," she said, clutching her chest. "You startled me."

"I'm sorry," he said, removing his new Stetson.

"Why, I don't..." she said, obviously puzzled at first. "Oh, yes. Mr. Tadeschi. Of course. You bought the McCall place."

"As a matter of fact, I'm closing on it this afternoon," he said. "I've got the check for the balance in my pocket. The family has a backup offer for twice what I paid, and my broker advised me that time was of the essence."

"Congratulations," she said.

He showed her the folded newspaper, the circled classifieds. "This is a new sort of farming for me," he said. "We Tadeschis are old country vintners. We're used to pruning and spraying, picking and stomping."

Jane laughed, "My husband and I kept a few head of livestock. Cows and sheep were his department, but I'm an old pruner and sprayer from way back."

He hesitated.

"Won't you sit down?" she asked.

He slid in to her side of the booth. "You were kind enough to show me where the morels were to be found in my orchards. Perhaps there will be more."

Smiling, she shook her head. "It's too late for morels, I'm afraid. But you will have wonderful blackberries along the fence lines. They're early this year. You just have to avoid being raked over by the brambles when you pick them."

"I tell you what," he said. "If you'll come by and help me pick some for dessert, I'll grill some steaks. Not only that, but I brought along a case of estate bottled wine, just for such occasions."

"Well," she demurred. "This is a terrible weekend. I'm in charge of the children's division floats for our parade tomorrow. It starts at eleven a.m., right in Eastsound. I suppose I could stop by at your place on my way back to Deer Harbor."

"Why don't I come to the parade and meet up with you afterward?" he suggested.

"Now don't expect the Rose Bowl," she said.

"My dear lady, I'm moving out of California to get away from the Rose Bowl. I should have escaped years ago, the way Clint McCall did."

CHAPTER 54

Beverly Hills, CA
July 6

The renovation of the historic Beverly Hills Hotel was extraordinary. Back on the scene was the twelve-acre tropical enclave with private bungalows where movie stars had trysts and producers made deals. Colorado oil baron Marvin Davis had flipped the famous but decrepit property to an Arab sultan for ten times what he'd paid. The sultan spent two years and a hundred million dollars giving the place a facelift. Perhaps the mysterious owner would now pay a visit?

Angie had followed the story of the renovation with interest. Though expanded in her imagination by the glowing reports in the press, in reality, as she strolled through the lobby, she found it very well done. It retained the intimacy and character of the residential hotel it was meant to be back when both the century and the nation were young and innocent. Innocent? Well, maybe not.

"Now here's a project I'd have liked to have had," Angie said as they crossed the mossy green floral carpeting and passed beneath a massive chandelier, shaped vaguely like the lower half of a hot air balloon, giving the impression that this crystal vision was about to take off through the ceiling. Deep columns, tall banana plants and a forest of tochere lamps, their bowls balanced on their heads, lent a final touch of tropical exotica.

"Mom," Jason whispered, "Check out the gold piano, will you?" he nodded toward the elevated lounge filled with velvet upholstery.

"That's what they call the Tea Lounge," Angie murmured. "It's where you go to sit and be seen. That would be why the designers raised it up."

"Cool," Jason said. "Why don't we check in?"

"Because rooms here start at two hundred seventy five a night," Angie said. She considered herself lucky to have found them a fifty seven dollar room in a motor lodge which had one redeeming feature: it was situated nearby on Beverly Boulevard.

At the reservation desk, she waited while a family in elegant sports clothes checked in with their two seemingly well-mannered children. Yuppies, Angie thought. Moneyed professionals. They looked the way She and Alan and Jason had once looked.

"Mr. Tadeschi has checked out," the reservation clerk said when her turn came at the desk.

Angie sighed. Why did she have such terrible luck? "Do you know whether he's planning to return? I have something for him."

"Ma'am, I am not allowed to give out any information. If it's about the picture, check with Mr. Flowers, our concierge."

Flowers was a deeply tanned man whose thin hair had faded to the color of straw. He was having a grand time helping a couple of nubile young girls plan an afternoon tour.

"But I don't care where Clark Gable used to live," one of them whined, the one with deep purple hair, evidently dyed to match her mohair sweater. "What about Johnny Depp?"

"Depp, I don't know about, except he owns the Viper Room, which hasn't had such a hot name since that boy River Phoenix expired, and you two girls are under age for going there. Now Graumann's Chinese Theater is right here," he said, unfolding a map.

The other girl, the one in the apple green vinyl boots and ragged jeans wasn't interested in the map. She turned around and looked Jason up and down, while her companion took down the directions.

"Hey, who needs Johnny Depp," Boots said, leering at Jason.

"Okay, I think I've got it," her companion said, stuffing her notes in her purse. "Come on, Mindy. Let's get a drink out by the pool. Who knows? Maybe we'll get discovered."

"Bye, honey," Boots murmured, casting Jason a sidelong glance as she swayed out.

Angie looked at her son. He was beet red from the top of his hairline to the bottom of his neck. She whispered, "Well, you are getting to

212

be a handsome guy."

"The girls these days?" Flowers said, rolling his eyes and Angie smiled.

"The desk said you might know when Mr. Tadischi will return."

"Auditions are scheduled for the twenty third. By invitation only. What part you reading for?"

"Part?" Angie said. "Are we talking about a movie?"

"*The Greening*," he said. "Readings were announced in Variety this morning."

"Oh," Angie said. "Maybe I've got the wrong Tadischi." She rummaged through her bag and came up with the deck of cards in an envelope marked with the words. Flowers looked at it, *Raymond Tadischi,* and shook his head.

"Wrong Tadeschi? Right Tadischi? Maybe you've got the right Tadischi and I've got the wrong Tadeschi. Who knows," he said, letting his eyes roll around in his head as he stuck a finger down his collar. Jason laughed.

"Hey kid, you appreciate talent. You wanna be my agent?"

Jason laughed again.

Angie smiled. "Raymond Tadischi is a traveling salesman," Angie said.

"So is Adolph Tadeschi." Flowers asked, "So what does your Tadischi sell?"

"Class rings, I think," Angie said.

"For sure, it's a different guy. Adolph Tadeschi peddles movies."

"To video stores?" Jason said.

"If his movie isn't any good, that's where it'll wind up. No, he's a producer." He leaned toward Angie and lowered his voice conspiratorially, "Mr. Tadeschi is going to bring back Thalia Markham, or so I hear."

"Who is Thalia Markham?" Jason said.

"Kid, you put your finger on the problem. In my opinion, he ought to cast Angela Lansbury or Anjelica Huston, but the word on the street is, Markham has a lock on the script."

"And this Raymond Tadischi never stays here?"

"I couldn't say that," Flowers said. "All I can say is, Raymond Tadischi has got an 'i' in the middle of his name. But Adolph Tadeschi has an 'e'."

"Oh...right. Well, thank you," Angie said. She and Jason trailed back to the reservation desk, and asked for Raymond Tadischi, spelled with an 'i'.

"Mr. Tadischi, spelled with an 'i', is not registered," the clerk said.

"But does he stay here sometimes?" Angie said.

"Ma'am, I cannot give out that information."

"So what's next, Mom?" Jason said, as they strolled toward the exit.

"Fun and games," Angie said. "I promised. While we're here, we'll look for something for Grandma on Rodeo Drive. This evening, we'll take in the fireworks on the pier. Tomorrow we start with the studio tours, maybe head out for Zuma Beach. Want to see the LaBrea Tar Pits? We'll do whatever you want. We can play tourists until we meet your grandmother in Seattle. Right now, we'll have something at the Polo Lounge."

"First, let's check out the pool," Jason said.

It wasn't lost on Angie, that he was leading her in the direction taken by Boots and her companion.

As soon as they were seated under the elegant canvas awnings with the polished wood frames, Angie got out her notebook. "Before we decide what to do first, I want you to remind me to call Joe." They had left Yosemite a day early and it was possible he had tried to get in touch with them.

CHAPTER 55

San Juan Islands, WA
July 14

Angie was seated in front of the flagstone hearth, brandishing a long match. On the grate lay a layer of wadded newspaper piled with drift-wood, white as bleached bone.

"Now watch the fireworks, Jason," Angie said to her son, who sat cross-legged in her father's big leather chair scratching behind the long, floppy ears of Towzer, one of his grandmother's bird dogs. Towzer's mate, Ox, dozed by the fireplace.

Earlier, they had gathered on the wide deck to watch the sunset blaze a fiery path across the placid waters, but the bite of a moderate evening in the Pacific Northwest was too much for the newly arrived Floridians. Angie, no longer acclimated to her native land, was shivering, eager to take off the evening's chill by the fire.

The fireplace dominated one of the octagonal walls that formed The Roost, as Angie's father had christened their home, shortly after they moved in. It was a tri-level cedar and glass home that seemed to tumble down a series of mossy cliffs on the one promontory on Puffin Island, one of a score of private islands that dotted the archipelago. Puffin was a speck on the charts, which lay southwest of the Deer Harbor Marina on Orcas Island between Fawn and Crane Islands.

Their earliest days on Puffin had been spent in the old farmhouse set in the orchards on the other end of the island, which eventually became Dad's office and guest quarters. Angie was eleven when her parents announced plans for a new home on her birthday, and the whole family had spent the next several years working on the project. The Roost is where Angie's love of buildings and their shape and function had begun.

The main rooms, midway down the cliffs, were a pair of octagonal modules, a vast, open living area with a smaller dining room and open kitchen attached. There were spectacular views from every angle and the rooms, which rose into spoke-like central cupolas, seemed to spin around them. The furnishings were a blend of mission, shaker and Scandinavian, which shared clean lines and fine craftsmanship. There were also gaily-painted chests and accent pieces that Jane had painted and refinished. Framed nautical charts of the islands dominated the walls, and her father's collection of model ships were in the glass cases that divided the dining area from the living room. Except for a few tiny sails that seemed to float like down in the darkening room, these details were lost in the gathering dark, and it was the gleaming bonelike driftwood set against the fire-blackened walls of the hearth that drew the eye away from the dying light framed in the plate glass windows.

"Wait a minute, Mom. I want to light it," Jason said, pushing Towzer aside.

"Towzer is so happy," Jane Pelham said. "He really misses having a man around the house to wrestle around with."

Angie got up, handed the long match and the box to Jason, who got down on his knees, made a few magician like gestures and struck the match with a flourish: "Ta dum."

The paper disappeared as a charred black line consumed it and the first pieces of driftwood sizzled and crackled, sending off sparks of bright orange, teal and magenta.

"Fantastic," Jason said.

"It's a chemical reaction of the sea salts in the wood," Angie said. "When we go out on the boat at night, we'll see the same colors flashing in the waves."

Jason picked up one of the fire irons and poked at the flames, sending the colorful sparks flying. As the fire began to die down, he got up, brushed off his knees and reclaimed his chair.

"Can I ask you something, Grandma?" he said.

"Ask away," Jane Pelham said.

"I mean, it's cool that you have your own private island and all, but you have to go everywhere by boat."

"It beats driving any day," his grandmother said. "You have to remember, Jason, Puffin Island is less than twenty minutes away from Deer Harbor Marina. We lie in one of the most protected sounds in the entire San Juan group. Look here, Jason," Jane, said, getting up to show him on a chart on the wall. "Here we are."

"Here?" Jason said.

"No. That's Fawn Island. It's closer to the marina. We're this speck to the south of Fawn. This is us."

"Hey Grandma, Puffin hardly exists."

"That's right, Jason. Puffin is very tiny, as islands go. We're small but rugged and very sheltered. Deer Harbor is sheltered from the northeast by the spiny ridge of Orcas Island. We're sheltered from the northwest by Spiden Island and then Stuart. To the south, there's Crane Island, then Shaw, and to the west, San Juan Island. It's quite a cozy spot.

"Whoa," Jason said. "San Juan is way bigger."

"Way bigger," Jane said. Now look, we just hop in our boat and go down the San Juan Channel. We can get to Friday Harbor on San Juan Island in our own launch faster than we could go from Orcas Landing on the ferry."

"But there aren't any people around."

"No malls. Is that what you mean?" she said with a smile.

"No kids. No other people at all."

"Just the dogs and me and a few deer," she said, "It's so quiet and peaceful."

"But don't you ever get lonely?"

"Son," she said, snapping her fingers at Towzer, "Not with these hairy nuisances around. Besides, I talk to the coast guard station on the radio every day."

"It isn't scary?"

"Yes, sometimes, I have to admit. Did I ever tell you about someone out on the deck, making a racket?" Jane said.

Angie's eyes widened. "Out here? I'd have been terrified."

"Oh, I was. Why, the second night it happened, I got the shotgun out of the closet."

"Did you shoot them?" Jason said.

"Nope, I just stayed in my bed and shook," his grandmother said.

"Did you find out who it was?"

"The third night, I got angry. Cowering in my bed like a fool. I was determined I'd catch whoever it was. So I got out Grandpa's big spotter flashlight, and when I heard the noise again, I jumped out the front door and turned the light right on them."

"Mother, you didn't," Angie gasped.

"I did," her mother said.

"Who was it?" Jason said. "Juveniles?"

"Juveniles? Why yes, come to think of it, that's what they were. Juvenile otters, playing tag."

"It took guts to go out there like that," Angie said, after their laughter had died down.

"Sometimes you just have to face things head on," Jane Pelham said. "Your father taught me that."

As the fire died down, Towzer stirred. He picked up his ragged tennis ball and stood right in front of Jason, staring and wagging his tail.

"All right, all right. We'll go out and play catch on the beach," he said.

"You might want your windbreaker," Angie said.

"Ahhhh, Mom," Jason moaned. He left the room, shoulders hunched, feet dragging, the picture of the hen-pecked male.

"It tickles me to hear you say that, Angie," her mother said with a smile, as soon as Jason was out of the room. "You were always peeling off your sweaters and throwing them in a heap. I was sure you would die of pneumonia before you turned ten."

Absent boy and dogs, the fire crackled peacefully and the room seemed devoid of energy. The women sat silent for a while, lost in their thoughts. The room was quiet, except for the lapping of the surf and the ticking of the grandfather clock in the hall.

"Jason does have a point, Mom. You must get lonely."

"Of course, I do. Some nights I ache for Daddy until it hurts; but that won't bring him back." Then she brightened. "Oddly enough, a very interesting man has appeared on the horizon. In many respects, he reminds me of David. I guess that's why I like him."

Angie felt her throat constrict. "Oh?" She set down her glass.

"He bought the McCall place. I gather he intends to spend much of his time here."

"Does this guy want to marry you, Mom?" Angie blurted.

"Why Angie, we've only had dinner a few times."

"Did you have him out here?" Angie hissed, leaning forward.

"Well darling, he wanted advice on what to plant. I showed him around the island, yes. Where's the harm?"

"Harm?" Angie said with a scornful laugh. "Maybe there is none. Then again?" She shook her head. She moved to the edge of her seat, her eyes narrowed, her voice hard, her hands clamped between her knees, as if locked in a vice: "He hasn't said he's madly in love with you and must marry you the next minute?"

Jane sat back in her chair, arms folded: "Would I be silly enough to do something so rash?"

"Mom, you are a wealthy widow. There's a whole class of men who pretend they are in love with you, but what they really love is your bank account. They take your money and run."

Her mother laughed as she stood up. "And where would my friend run to? Eastsound? I hardly think a man who bought the McCall ranch for cash could possibly need any money of mine."

"You do know for a fact that he does own the ranch?"

"Angie, sweetie," Jane said. "Whatever could have put such ideas in your head?"

CHAPTER 56

Orcas Island, WA
July 17

They had a grand lunch at Bilbo's Festivo in Eastsound, renowned for its Mexican food. They'd loaded the battered pickup truck that her mother kept parked at Deer Harbor with enough to supplies to fill the launch. Deer Harbor, their point of embarkation to Puffin Island, was about twenty- five minutes west of Eastsound on the Horseshoe Highway, a road aptly named for the general shape of the island itself. On the way back to Deer Harbor, they stopped at Island Hardware, a local Mecca, where the local ranchers and summer people stocked up on gardening supplies and feed for whatever livestock they maintained, whether wild or domestic.

"I'm going to look over the bedding plants," Jane said. "I'll only be a few minutes."

"Of gardening time?" Angie teased.

There was a sad twist to Jane's brave smile. "I haven't heard that expression since." She seemed to bite off the thought. Then she brightened, turning to Jason, hugging him around the shoulders. "They keep the popcorn machine running here, and it's free. Let's go get you some."

Angie stood in the aisle, watching her mother and Jason strolling off, arm and arm. It was so amazing how her mother had recovered.

She seemed so calm and uncritical. But was it the therapy or this new boyfriend?

"Can I help you?" said the woman at the counter. The clerk was wearing a western cut shirt with pearl buttons. A black cowboy hat set off her curly blonde hair, framing a short-featured doll's face.

"I need some sealer for decking and some paint to redo four wooden deck chairs. The big Adirondack type," Angie said. The chairs were a deep teal blue. Angie had chosen the color herself, years ago. It was the trim color of the outside windows. She had learned in an art class that the Mediterraneans believed the color warded off evil, and so they had selected it, failing to realize how quickly the blue faded. Angie sighed. Nowadays she tried to steer clients away from blue houses, but here she was, bowing to force of habit. After all, if Daddy were still alive, he'd insist on the Mediterranean blue.

Angie followed the clerk down one of the crowded aisles across from the counter, where two women were stocking up on cartons of farm eggs. They were dressed alike, in faded denims and plaid shirts and each wore a patina of soil that could only have come straight from a garden or barnyard.

"These here eggs is the real McCoy," one of them said. "The shells on store eggs are thin as tissue."

"And it's a cinch a hen that scratches around after bugs is happier," the other woman replied.

"Better eggs from scratch, ladies," said the man who had just arrived, sending the two women into self-conscious giggles.

"Why if it ain't Mr. Tadeschi," said one of the women to her companion. "Ethel, I'd like you to meet a new neighbor. This is the fella that bought the McCall place."

Angie dropped the can of paint she had in her hand. Fortunately, it was well sealed. The clerk picked it up for her.

"I'm sorry," she stammered. "Here I am trying to shake it up before I've even paid for it."

"Will that be everything?" the clerk said.

"I'd better take a scraper," Angie said, her voice barely a whisper. "I'm not sure Mom has one at home."

As Angie emerged from the aisle, she saw Jane coming toward the group assembled in front of the counter. Tadeschi stepped forward to kiss her on the cheek. Jason, behind her with a flat of marigolds, stared at the floor.

"Jane, darling," Tadeschi murmured. "How wonderful to see you."

"Adolph," she replied. "I see you have already figured out where

Islanders come to spend their money. Here. I want you to meet my family. This is my grandson, Jason."

"Nice meeting you, son. Let me help you with that." Tadeschi took the flat of plants from Jason and set them down on the counter.

"Jason, have you seen your mother?" Jane said. "Oh, here she is. Angie, this is Adolph Tadeschi. He bought Clint McCall's ranch."

"Ah, the lady who slings paint around," Tadeschi replied, getting a laugh. Reassured, Angie smiled at this suave man, trim and dapper in stonewashed denim, hand-tooled cowboy boots and a blanket vest over a twill shirt. In contrast to the two island women, his clothes looked as if they just came out of the box. He had chiseled features, short, thick dark hair flecked with gray, hazel eyes and the aura of command her father had. No wonder her mother was interested.

"Do you make movies?" Jason said.

Tadeschi's eyes widened. "Movie," he said, his glance broadened to include the women. "I'm as green at movies as I am at ranching."

"What movie?" Jane said. "Is that what you meant when you said you were in the entertainment business?"

Tadeschi nodded. "It's just a side venture, my dear, quite risky. To tell you the truth, I'm not sure I'd be doing this if it weren't to help out an actress friend whose connection with the family goes way back." Then he looked at Jason. "In fact, I'm such an obscure producer that I'm surprised a young guy would know anything about it."

"This is all a weird coincidence," Angie blurted. "We heard about you while looking for another man—Raymond Tadischi. He also gave the Beverly Hills Hotel as his address."

"Yes?" Tadeschi said with a look of surprise.

"The other Tadischi and I have mutual acquaintances in Memphis," Angie said. "So when we toured Hollywood we stopped off at the hotel to deliver a package."

"Yes, of course," Adolph said. "I can't say I've ever met the fellow, but occasionally our messages do get mixed up. He's some sort of traveling salesman, I believe."

"He's not a relative?" Angie said.

Tadeschi shook his head. "If we are related at all it's probably from before our ancestors got on the boat. As I recall, our last names don't have the same spelling."

"Well, that explains it," Angie said.

"So nice to meet you," he said to Angie. "A pleasure, champ," he said to Jason. "Perhaps you three will come for dinner one night? I might be a miserable rancher and a novice movie producer, but I do happen to be a fair cook."

"David's nice, isn't he?" Jane said once they were seated in the truck.

Angie looked at her, shocked. "Mother!"

Jane's eyes went round. "Oh, my goodness. Adolph, I mean. Well, there you have it. I have to admit I was thinking that Adolph has that very nice, self-deprecating quality that so many successful men have. It makes others want to reach out to them. It was a quality I much admired in your father."

Angie said nothing. Merely shook her head.

"Angie, darling, I'm sorry," Jane said. "You seemed so upset when you met Adolph."

"It's just that we chased—uh, were looking for someone with nearly the same name in the same hotel. It's odd."

"Strange things do happen," Jane said.

CHAPTER 57

Orcas Island, WA
July 17

As the calves galloped down the loading chute, Adolph decided they'd be better off in the small corral until they'd gotten used to their new home. He rushed to close the gate, but the calves had other ideas.

Three of the bigger ones hurtled right for him, like a flying wedge. They sheared the gate right off the hinges. Adolph was bowled off his feet and pinned under the fallen gate. Three-dozen blocky, Black Angus calves dashed right over the top of him. Fortunately thick boards protected his body.

"Heeeyah," a voice shouted, somewhere above him. "Git!"

The gate was lifted off of him. The huskier of the cowhands, the younger one, pulled him up. "Sorry about that, Mr. Tadeschi. Them calves are real skittish, especially when they've spent all morning crammed in a truck."

"Thanks," he grunted.

"You okay?" said the older one, a stooped and wizened old man missing his front teeth. Adolph, in a daze, couldn't remember their names.

"Just let me sit a minute," he said. He could barely breathe. His heart was tearing at his ribs.

The two men picked up the broken gate and set it against the log fence of the corral.

"Don't you worry about that," Adolph wheezed. "I'll take care of it."

The older man produced a battered tobacco can from his flap pocket, pulled some papers out of it and ceremoniously unfolded them. "We send this into the state, nice and legal. There's a head tax on live-stock," he said. "At the end of the year, you have to account for what you done with every last dogie, so's Uncle gets his cut when you sell."

"I'll do that," Tadeschi panted. He wiped sweat out of his eyes onto the sleeve of what had started out as a crisp new cowboy shirt.

"We'll be going now. Got to make the two thirty ferry, or we'll shore enough be sleeping on this island," the stooped one said, tipping his hat.

As the drovers' ancient truck pinged its way up the steep drive, Adolph limped toward the house. He felt a sharp pain in the hip that had taken the impact.

"Call me Black Butt," he muttered to himself.

Eventually he reached the orchard at the foot of the lawn and paused to look back. A cloud of dust trailed over the lower pasture where the calves lowed and frolicked like so many rolling lumps of coal.

Adolph smiled, mirthlessly. What should have been the high point of his stay, the arrival of the stock, now meant nothing. Hell, the cattle might as well be made out of cardboard. Getting stomped by his own feeders was merely symbolic of the way his new life had already shat-tered. He lifted the latch of the tall wire fence that sheltered the orchard from marauding deer, letting the spring on the gate slap it back into place as he passed through. He felt blah. Punctured like a balloon.

How could he have made such a dumb mistake?

His wretched heart had done it. In his delirious state back at the Memphis hospital he must have given Raymond Tadischi, who was supposed to live in Salinas, his own—or at least Adolph Tadeschi's—prestigious Beverly Hills address. Screw up one essential detail of the brew and spoil the whole batch, as his uncle used to say.

And then, the crowning blow: Angie Reynolds makes up with her mother. Never would he have predicted such a thing. And how much had she told Jane about her brush with Anthony Abruzzi? If she hadn't said something yet, it would come up soon. Even if she hadn't said a thing, she was sure to pressure her mother into having him investigated if he continued to pursue her. And that could only lead back to Thalia Markham. Hell. Her name would show up as a lien on the ranch in the next title search.

The Don Juan Con

In the kitchen, he tossed his hat on the table and shuffled for the liquor cabinet. He got out the good Chivas, fumbled around to get the seal off the bottle and poured himself a shot. He'd been on the wagon ever since he'd recuperated from surgery at that spa in Idaho, but what the hell? He might as well sit here and drink himself into a stupor. As the liquid seared his gullet, he asked himself the main question: If he were Angie Reynolds, would she accept the connection of Tadeschi and Tadischi as pure coincidence?

Would he?

He was on his third shot when Maria Whitman popped into his mind. "To you, my dear Maria," he said, pouring the liquid down. "Here's a chance event with deeper meaning."

First off, Angie Reynolds had no business in Memphis. The fact that she'd been there at all meant that she probably knew about Jenny Sawyer. If she knew about Jenny Sawyer, she probably knew about the Crimestop show and the folk singer. What was her name? Trillin? It was also quite possible that she knew about that Sarasota real estate woman. God. He could see her face with that smart little haircut, but who was she? Oh yes, Nettie French. Now there was a good time, and such a good hit. And what about Suzi Islamorada? Suzi and Angie were right in that same little Florida town. And if Angie was aware of all of these women, she was also quite likely to have heard about Maria Whitman and her unfortunate accident over in Banks. In short, Angie Reynolds knew way too much for her own health.

"How sad life is," Adolph said aloud as he poured yet another shot.

Dammit, he didn't like doing people. It made him sick. It was why he got out of the business in the first place. It was, however, a fact of life that accidents do happen to the nicest people, as Maria Whitman so regrettably found out.

CHAPTER 58

As she waited on the line for Jenny Randapolis to track down Joe, she sat curled in the window seat of her old room, cradling the phone on her shoulder. The striped ticking she had chosen for her first redecorating project when she was fourteen had long since faded to a warmish gray. On the beach below, she saw her mother and Jason out gathering driftwood for tonight's fire. Thank God. They wouldn't have a clue what was going on.

"Oh, Joe, please be there," Angie whispered, her eyes squeezed shut.

"Angie?"

"Joe! Thank God."

"What's up?"

"This may be nothing, but it really bothers me," Angie said. "My mother has this new boyfriend."

"And he's dying to marry her?" he said.

"I think she's dying to marry him," Angie said.

"So?"

"His name is Adolph Tadeschi," Angie said.

"Tadeschi...wait a minute. Like the guy that Abruzzi put in the hospital in Memphis."

"Exactly," Angie said, "It's spelled a little differently, that's all." She paused to peer out the window. Jason and her mother took turns tossing the tennis ball to Towzer. Ox, who was too old to play catch, was wagging his tail and barking his head off.

"The fellow she is interested in is supposed to be Adolph Tadeschi. Spelled with an 'e'. He's a California vintner who is making a movie."

"And you think he's a fake?"

"I don't know," Angie said. "I do know he paid cash for the ranch he bought here. This movie, he's making, The Greening, was written up in Variety."

"Maybe he's for real," Joe said.

"Maybe so. I met him today. He's not at all like Anthony was. He's much thinner, almost wiry, taller. He has a much higher forehead, a full head of dark hair, and he doesn't have the hooded eyes. No New York accent, either. He's perfectly charming but in a very different way. Anthony was sort of a braggart. Adolph puts himself down. He's very self-deprecating and low key. My dad was also that way, as Mom was quick to point out."

"Angie, honey, maybe you can't face up to the fact that your mom needs someone in her life. You hate to think this Adolph will take the place of your dad."

"That's not it at all," Angie snapped. "What bothers me is, they have the same address, the Beverly Hills Hotel. A little upscale for a class ring salesman, wouldn't you think? That's what Raymond Tadischi did for a living. Class rings. When I stopped in at the hotel, the concierge thought I was looking for Adolph. A fledgling movie producer. Then, this same Adolph just happens to show up in the rather obscure San Juan Islands, and winds up dating my mother. Just too convenient, wouldn't you say?"

"So I'll run a check on both these guys."

"Joe, I'd feel so much better, and please, if you should happen to talk to Mother, don't let on that you talked to me about this Adolph. Okay?"

"No problem. Now, to bring you up to speed on our featured act."

"Johnny Octave? You mean you've found something more?"

"I got another call from my friend with the feds. After Octave had done some time in the East as a young man, he relocated to Seattle and got into the boat business. The company was called Bellweather Boats. Octave was sent to prison for embezzling and insurance fraud."

"When was this?" Angie said.

"The mid-sixties."

"That would have been back when my dad was just starting out in the boat business. I would have been three or four. I'll ask Mom if she recalls anything about Bellweather Boats, but it doesn't mean a thing to me."

CHAPTER 59

McCall Farm
Orcas Island, WA
July 18

Adolph rocked in the swing on his front porch, sipping iced tea while he watched Milo Binder work. Milo was an artist—far and away the best stump man on the island, when he was sober, or so Adolph had been informed at the hardware store. Problem was, Milo was an independent guy. There was never any telling when he'd show up to do the work. But then nobody had ever promised the toothless old dude twice his usual fee for busting his butt to get on over here.

Through field glasses, Adolph watched Binder meticulously dig around the stump, tamp the dynamite into place with a long probe, string the wire for the fuses, take shelter behind some firs at the edge of the meadow and plaster himself to the tree when he set off the charge.

The blast rattled the porch and sent the Anguses running for the creek at the foot of the pasture. The ice cubes jumped in the glass. Adolph had finished his drink by the time the old fellow ambled up.

"That's the first of them, Mr. Tadeschi," Binder said as he chewed on the white end of a shaft of ice cream weed. "Truth is, I must of blasted my brains right out of my skull. I sure nuff thought I had the dynamite and the caps to do them other stumps right here on the truck, but no. I'm getting awful forgetful. I'll go back and pick them up."

230

You know, I'm really not sure I'll have the other stumps done," Adolph said, rising. "They are a little close to the orchard. I don't want to disturb any of the apple trees."

"Nossir."

"But listen, Milo. I do appreciate the very great favor you did me. I just couldn't stand that stump being so close to the pond. It was ruining my view." Adolph peeled two hundred dollars cash off a roll of bills.

"Let me get you an invoice on it," Binder said.

"Forget it. A little transaction like this isn't worth the bookkeeping. If you don't tell Uncle, I won't," Adolph winked. "And Milo, you've been so prompt, I've got something special for you. Come on in."

Once they were in the kitchen, he opened the liquor cabinet and got out a fifth of Chivas, still in the box. "It's been sitting here so long, it's a bit dusty," Adolph said. He grabbed a kitchen towel, wiped the box clean, then handed it to Binder, careful to handle it through the towel.

"You'll spoil a man," Milo said. He cradled the bottle in his arm as if it were a precious infant.

"Now Milo, don't you abuse good Scotch," Adolph said. "I have to admit I love this stuff so much I misbehaved rather badly a few days ago. My gut still feels like it was put through a blender. I've gotta get off the sauce for awhile, and I've heard you are a man who appreciates a drink now and then."

"I do sir," Binder said, drawing himself up. The delight in his grin was nearly salacious.

Adolph stood back from the cab of Milo's truck with his arms folded as Binder got in, and remained standing in the driveway as the truck whined up the grade behind his house. He waited until the truck had disappeared around the bend toward Eastsound before he opened the trunk of the Mercedes.

Yes, there they were, a box of dynamite and the blasting caps he'd pinched off Milo's truck while the old fellow was digging away. Hard as they might try, there was no way the cops could ever trace anything to him. Give Milo a few hours with the Chivas and he'd no doubt forget he'd ever lost them.

CHAPTER 60

Friday Harbor, WA
July 19

Jason jumped from the launch to the dock and hanked the bow line around a cleat.

"Nice work," Angie called, smiling big, trying to sound cheerful, though her temples pounded and her stomach was so acidic it felt as she'd lived on pepperoni pizza for a week.

"Jason looks like he's been handling boats all his life," his grandmother said.

"It has to be that Pelham blood," Angie said, punching out her words with a false gaiety she hoped her mother wouldn't detect.

They walked up the dock toward the sleek, cedar and concrete structure housing the University of Washington's marine labs. At the desk, Angie signed Jason up for a three-day course. Dozens of other youngsters in jeans and windbreakers milled around in the lobby. With the same disinterested expression all the other kids wore, Jason faded into the pack. Obviously the appeal of the marine sciences wasn't the drawing card here, Angie realized. It was a kid's simple desire to mix with other kids.

"I'll be here at three. If I'm not, meet me at the public library. It's near the courthouse," Angie said. "I'm sure that somebody here can give you directions."

"No problem," Jason said.

"Got your lunch?"

Jason sighed. "I told you three times already, Mom. It's in my backpack."

Angie untied the launch and jumped aboard as Jane fired up the twin engines. "We'll tie up at the public dock. It'll cut at least a mile off our walk," Jane said as she drove the boat up the channel.

It was eight thirty a.m. by the time they had tied up. The sun was breaking through a light fog as the women trudged up the rise that took them away from the boat harbor and toward the center of town. A whole new complex of shops had been built on what used to be a ramshackle dock at the edge of the harbor. "Things seem to be picking up in the islands," Angie said.

"It's good for the economy, I guess," Jane said, "but to tell you the truth, Angie, I loved those days back when there were only a handful of winter residents and a couple of thousand tourists the whole summer."

The simple, barn-like style of Northwest building was everywhere in Friday Harbor, giving it the look of a village comprised of fishing shacks all painted in various earthy grays and browns. These were very witty and sophisticated shacks, however, judging by a jewel palette of colors employed on the doors, mullions, porch rails and trim, and the scores of flower boxes set out everywhere, bursting with riotous color. By the time they'd passed shops selling Indian artifacts, gifts, sporting goods and a tavern or two, the sweat was dripping off Angie's brow.

"Here's my first stop," Jane said, ducking into a hardware store. "I understand they have some dwarf rhododendrons."

"I want to dig around in the library, Mom," Angie said, with a brightness she didn't feel. "So why don't we split up and meet back at the harbor for lunch?"

"How about eleven thirty?" Jane said. "That should give me enough time."

"Fine," Angie said, rushing off. Yesterday evening she had casually brought up Bellweather Boats while her mother was dropping dough for dumplings onto the stew that had simmered all day. Her mother had calmly said the name didn't mean a thing to her, but within five minutes she'd pled a migraine, gone to her room and left Angie and Jason to dine alone. When Adolph Tadeschi called to set up a dinner date, Jane asked Angie to take a message. Acid burned in Angie's throat. Something was definitely wrong. She could feel it.

But what was it?

The library was a misty gray structure defined by brick red trim. Inside, fir flooring and teak reading tables gave it the look of a sturdy ship. There was no card catalog to be found. The computer had control even here in the far-flung islands. Angie sat down at a terminal and typed in "Bellweather Boats."

She grimaced as a lengthy digest of articles appeared. "Explosion in boat works threatens Ballard," read one. Then came the follow-up stories. "Arson suspected in boat works fires," and "Company owners charged in boat fires."

All in all, there must have been ten articles in the Seattle dailies. Several references also listed the smaller, island papers. Angie pushed the print button and got a printout of the references, which were all on microfiche. In drawers lined with envelopes about the size of index cards, Angie found the packets of the films she wanted. Then she located a bay full of film machines, which instructed her to ask for help setting up.

A woman with a mop of long frizzy hair parted in the middle and braided at the sides came to her rescue. "You slide the film between these two glass plates, and crank this dial, which brings up the magnification. If the story is still fuzzy, use this knob to get it right for your eye."

"Like this?" Angie said.

"Right," the woman said, checking the viewer. "Ah, the Bellweather story. There's been a lot of interest in that one lately."

"Oh?" Angie said.

"I helped a researcher for *Fortune* magazine on it a few months ago," the librarian said.

Angie's throat closed up. It was all she could do to spit out her next question: "Why would such a big magazine be interested in an old boat fire?"

"It was about the time one of our biggest yacht builders, David Pelham, was going public with Sea Escape Designs. After he died, there was some sort of lawsuit. Bellweather Boats was David Pelham's original company."

Angie stared at the woman. Not a word came out of her mouth, but the librarian must have read her expression as a sign of interest. "*Fortune* hasn't published anything. I suppose the story got tabled after Mr. Pelham died so unexpectedly."

"Could? I mean, do you think the Bellweather story could have had anything to do with Mr. Pelham's heart attack?" Angie stammered.

"I doubt it," the librarian said, "At least not from a business standpoint, but you never know. After Bellweather failed, Mr. Pelham rebuilt. He had a sterling reputation, from what I understand. But the personal side must have taken its toll. Memories of his daughter's kidnapping could have come flooding back. Now, if you'll excuse me," the librarian said, "I've got to get back to the desk."

A kidnapping? Angie sank into the chair in front of the machine, clutching the edge of the table.

"Miss? Could you help me find this reference," said an elderly man. "I'm looking for an obituary for Reverend Samuel Cameron, who died in nineteen twenty six."

"I'll be right with you," the librarian said. She turned back to Angie. "Do you have it now?"

"What?" Angie said.

"Can you work the machine by yourself?" the librarian said, spacing her words as if speaking to a child.

"Oh, yes. I'm sorry. Don't worry about me," Angie muttered.

Heart pumping, hands jerky, Angie cranked her way through the files. On March second, nineteen sixty-six, fifteen new power yachts were destroyed in an early morning blaze that put two firemen in the hospital. Within a week, investigators hinted that the fire was of suspicious origin. Company owners David Pelham and Johnny Octave were arrested. My father was a partner of Johnny Octave? Angie thought, shaking her head.

How could this have happened?

The next story said the fire started in the plant, six weeks to the day that the pair bought a million dollar insurance policy. An audit of the company's books showed a quarter of a million dollars missing from the business. The trial, six months later, was front-page news in The Seattle Times. There was a shot of Daddy embracing Mama, his dark chiseled profile mixed with her Norse goddess looks. Angie had forgotten what a beautiful couple they were. The story said Pelham was able to prove that he was on a sales promotion tour in the months preceding the fire. But Octave had control of the money, and was embezzling it to cover gambling debts. He'd forged David's signature on the insurance policy. Octave was sentenced to prison. David Pelham, though exonerated, declared bankruptcy before the trial.

But there was more to the story, Angie realized. She was only halfway through the references. In June, Octave got out on appeal, pending a new trial. He followed the Pelhams to Friday Harbor, where David Pelham had relocated. Tears running down her face, Angie sobbed silently as she read how she had been kidnapped at gunpoint by Octave, trying to flee to Canada.

The Don Juan Con

Angie felt dizzy. Jogged by the headlines, she saw what she had never seen in her dreams, how the fire started. They were surrounded by patrol vessels. A man with a bullhorn was shouting for Johnny to come on deck with his hands up.

"I'll never let them take me alive," he cackled. He shot a hole in the propane tank for the galley stove. A fireball appeared before her eyes. Angie, in a life jacket, was sprawled on the deck. Johnny scooped her up and tossed her overboard.

"Swim for it, babe," he shouted. By the light of the fire his eyes were wild. She tried to paddle away from the burning vessel but was dragged under when the hull went down. Her throat closed up as she felt the water invade her lungs. Then the sea roiled and she bobbed to the surface. She was screaming and crying. Searchlights from patrol vessels beamed across the water, blinding her.

"Hang on, kid," someone shouted as a rubber boat approached. Angie rose up from the slick water. Strong hands carried her high in the air. Her throat burned as she gagged on grease and fumes.

Another trial, more headlines: Death penalty waived in kidnapping. A brief story said that at the request of the Pelham family, prosecutors had agreed not to seek the death penalty. Jane Pelham had pleaded for Octave's life. He had saved her daughter by tossing her overboard.

For the next hour, Angie read and reread all the stories. Then she noticed a sidebar she had missed in a story covering the Octave trial and found exactly what she was looking for, Octave's history. He was born in Ithaca, New York but was orphaned at age three when his parents were killed in an auto accident. His maternal uncle, vintner Adolph Tadeschi and his wife, Renata, brought him up in Napa Valley. Tadeschi suffered a fatal heart attack after he had bailed Anthony out of jail before his trial.

There it was: Abruzzi was Octave, and Octave was Tadeschi. Angie was shaking. Her thoughts were confused. She couldn't decide what to do first. Her mother was walking the streets of Friday Harbor completely unprotected. Jason was at a marine biology class, unaware that he was in mortal danger.

"Excuse me, Miss? Do you have change for a quarter," the old man said.

"What?" Angie blurted.

"Change? I want to print out a copy of the Reverend Campbell's obituary. He's my great grandfather. My wife will be so excited. We enjoy genealogy, you see."

"Copies?" Angie murmured.

"You put in a quarter, press the green button and you get a legible copy, if you are lucky," the old man said. His too perfect smile widened above his grizzled chin.

With shaking hands, Angie opened her change purse. "Here," she said, handing him a fistful of change. Then she stuck another quarter in the machine and printed out the story linking Octave and Tadeschi. It was proof, right in her hands.

The copy was still warm from the printer when she shoved it into her bag and started off.

"Miss? Miss?" the old man shouted after her. "Here's your change..."

"I'll be right back," Angie said, darting for a bank of telephones by the checkout stand. She placed a collect call to Joe. Her hands were shaking so that she had a hard time dialing the operator. She recognized Jenny Randapolis' voice telling the operator that Joe wasn't in.

"Tell her it's a break in the Abruzzi case," Angie said to the operator.

"Party accepts the charges. Go ahead," the operator said.

"Jenny, I've located Johnny Octave, also known as Adolph Tadeschi and Anthony Abruzzi. Or I should say, he's located us. I've got to speak to Joe right away."

"Honey, he won't be in for at least an hour. He's at a news conference with the mayor. Jake Waller has been indicted on an art forgery charge."

"The city councilman?" Angie said. "I can't believe it."

"Honey, you ain't the only one," Randapolis said. "Where can the Lieutenant call you back?" Angie drew a blank. She had no idea where she would be in an hour.

"Tell him I'm at the library in Friday Harbor, Washington. I'll... I'll call back," she said, looking around the room. Then she spied a fax machine on a librarian's desk. "Give me your fax number there," she said.

Sensing her distress, the mop-haired librarian loaned Angie her own typewriter. Angie typed a cover sheet, then the message: "Adolph Tadeschi, a real sweetheart, has come to call on us."

"What do I owe you?" Angie said as she watched the transmission wind through the machine.

"That will be a dollar fifty," the librarian said.

Angie handed her what she had, a five, and left. "Miss? You forgot your change," the librarian called after her, "And your fax." But Angie was gone.

237

CHAPTER 61

Adolph cut the engine on the motorboat he'd picked off the dock of a weekend resident of Spring Point, a community of homes hidden in the craggy recesses of the granite walls that lined the western shore of Deer Harbor. Nobody would give a second thought to a man in a motorboat approaching the backside of Puffin Island. He made sure no other boats were in view as he drifted behind the float that David Pelham had once used as a bird-watching blind. Jane had shown it to him on one of the lazy afternoons they had spent exploring her island.

He tied up the dinghy, then carried off the box of dynamite and the blasting caps, teetering along the rickety chain of floats that connected the blind to the island. Oh, yes, and a fine mess of blackberries swung in a plastic grocery bag looped over his arm. Blackberries and blasting caps. Now there's a bang-up breakfast.

Breathing hard, he hit the trail over the turtleback rise that sheltered the house, a path overgrown from disuse. Weeds wrapped around the top of his boots. Cobwebs masked his face in their soft, horrific grasp and branches swatted at him. He wore hospital booties to disguise his tracks, but they absorbed mud and slowed him and so he kicked them off. His meticulous planning sometimes slowed the action and in such cases, action ruled.

Adolph tramped along, stoking his rage on the wrongs and slights done to him by Angie and Jane. He could feel betrayal through a telephone wire. He knew something was terribly wrong when he'd called last night to invite the women to dinner. Angie had answered the phone, doing her best to sound nonchalant. Jane was down with a migraine. Or so she said. This was a direct insult to him. Never before had Jane refused to talk to him. So he'd offered to drop off a big plate of blackberries for their breakfast, and Angie hemmed and hawed and made excuses. She'd said they were going to Friday Harbor, first thing, to enroll Jason in the marine institute day camp. Neither of them would guess that he'd accept this fact as an open invitation to visit.

He was out of breath by the time he'd carried the box on his shoulder to the top of the small knoll. His heart was beginning to grind. The damned angioplasty he had actually paid for with real cash wasn't worth a shit. He had a few nitro pills with him, but he had to save them for later. Best to rest now, pace himself. His hands were a little unsteady, he noticed, as he raised his field glasses. This might have had to do with the fifth of Scotch he'd killed last night. His stomach was sour and his throat burned, but soon, as he willed his fury to a fine edge, his body would bend to the task.

He trained his field glasses on the boat dock. Sure enough, Jane's red launch was gone. He checked his watch. Eleven forty five. Wonderful. He'd have lots of time to get everything set. He'd called the camp and found the sessions would not end until three. That meant they would be unlikely to return before four.

A half hour later as he approached the front gate to the main house, he heard nothing but the crickets buzzing in the grass. In the channel, the eastbound ferry for Anacortes loomed in a silvery wake, looking entirely out of scale in a landscape dotted with tiny atolls, some of which were smaller than the ferries that churned past them. A robin chirped in a tree overhead. He used a handkerchief to open the gate latch, rousing the two dogs dozing on the porch.

"Hey fellas, remember me?" he said, keeping his tone calm and friendly. But Towzer advanced, stiff in his front legs, his fur standing up. The decrepit Ox sat on his fat haunches and bayed.

"Shut up!" he bellowed, which made the dogs howl all the more. At least nobody came to the door. He had to do something about this awful racket. Obviously these mutts weren't going to cooperate.

"Hey guys," he said heading for the barn, where he knew Jane kept the dog food. "Let's have lunch. On Uncle Adolph."

CHAPTER 62

Angie had paced the circumference of the vest pocket park at the foot of Friday Harbor's main street not once but three times. Finally, she saw her mother, arms laden with parcels, lurching toward her in an awkward downhill stride. She bolted the short, iron railing bordering the park and rushed toward Jane.

"Thank God, you're here. Let me take some of those."

"I can't be late," Jane said, smiling. "I worked so hard to avoid any accusations that I'm running on gardener's time."

"It isn't you, Mom. It's us. We're in trouble." Angie steered her mother down a steep ramp to the city dock.

"I thought we were having lunch," Jane said. "I'm famished."

"Mom. Listen to me. Please, don't get upset with me, but do you remember when I asked you last night about Bellweather Boats?" Angie said, striding down the dock, her mother rushing to catch up.

"Oh, that." Jane halted. She took off her hat and fanned herself with the brim. "It's over and done with. Long ago. I'm sorry I didn't tell you at some point, Angie. I meant to. It just caused us all so much pain."

"I understand that," Angie said. They had reached the launch. Angie stowed her mother's packages in one of the dockside hatches. "Our problem is Johnny Octave. He's come back."

240

Her mother's entire body sagged. "How did he get out of prison?"

"I have no idea. He may have escaped years ago. At one point the government made him a protected witness in a mafia case."

"He *did* have mafia connections. We found that out years ago. After it was too late, of course."

"So guess who Johnny's posing as this time?" From her bag, Angie pulled the clipping she'd photographed in the library. "The Adolph Tadeschi Johnny claims to be was his uncle, who is long since dead."

"Adolph?" Jane said, her eyes misting. Her hands flew up to her head. "How could it be?" Without seeming to realize what she was doing, Jane pulled loose the clip that held the roll of her faded blonde hair. It tumbled in disarray down her back.

"He was madly in love with me," Jane said. "He wanted me to run away from David."

"Mother!" Angie cried, "You didn't—"

"Never," Jane said, "David was the only man in the world, as far as I was concerned. But when Octave made advances, my real crime was, I didn't tell David early on. The men were partners. I didn't want to be the cause of a breakup of the business. Johnny tormented me. He managed to get hold of some of my personal…things. He said that if I told my husband, he'd ruin me…our life. Though I said nothing, he ruined us anyway—or tried to, and nearly killed you." Jane's eyes squeezed shut, but still the tears ran freely down her face. "What are we going to do?"

"We'll get in the launch, pick up Jason, and make a run for Anacortes. I've got a call in to Joe. He'll take care of putting Tadeschi behind bars."

Nodding, Jane climbed into the driver's seat. "I'll drive the boat. I know these channels better than you do."

"Okay Mom," Angie said as she cast off.

When they got to the end of the dock, however, her mother nosed the boat north and west away from the main channel.

"Mother?" Angie cried. "What on earth are you doing?"

"We'll run by Puffin and pick up Towzer and Ox."

"Are you forgetting Jason?" Angie said.

Jane shook her head. "Jason will be perfectly safe where he is. We'll be back inside an hour. We could be gone for several days and I refuse to go dashing off and leave my darling dogs. They were such a comfort to David. He'd sit by the hour stroking those dogs when he was too weak to lift a finger to do anything else. It would be criminal to abandon them now."

CHAPTER 63

Nothing had moved on Puffin Island since they left, except for the tide, which was high. A ripple of waves lapped at the belly of the dock as Jane expertly pulled the launch alongside. Angie glanced at her watch. It was just after noon. They'd made the trip in an impressive twenty minutes. Her mom had pulled out both throttles and sent trails of spume planing across the swells as they'd made a mad dash for home.

"We'd better refuel," Jane said as she jumped out of the boat while Angie secured the mooring lines. "I tell you what. I'm going to pack a few things."

"Don't forget your pills," Angie said. "I'll be right up."

Angie had topped off one of the fuel tanks and was putting the hose into the other, when she happened to notice her mother returning from the front gate, a puzzled expression on her face.

"Have you seen the dogs?" she called to Angie. "They aren't on the deck."

"I thought we locked the front gate," Angie said.

"I could have left it unlatched," Jane said. "Damn. Now I suppose we'll have to chase after them."

"I'll look in a minute," Angie said, "You go ahead, Mom."

"I'll make that little phone call," Jane said.

"Take a deep breath and smile when you talk," Angie said.

Since Adolph had called last night, they had decided that the best way to allay his suspicions was to tell him they were running down to Seattle for a night or two, and arrange to have dinner with him on Friday night.

Angie knew she was nervous when it took her three tries to hang the hose back on the gas pump. She tightened both caps on the fuel tanks, trotted up the dock, then turned around and rechecked both gas caps again.

At the foot of the garden, she looked at the gate. The latch was loose, and Towzer was a smart dog. He could have jiggled it open.

"Towzer? Ox? Here doggy dogs, let's go for a ride," she shouted, but not a bark returned her call. Instead, she watched a seaplane drift up the channel, sending a roiling roar across the little island, blissfully silent until then but for the caw of a stray gull and a light breeze setting up a rustle in the tall sea grasses along the shore.

Then she heard a yelp.

She thought it came from the barn. Sure enough, the sliding door was rolled back a crack, she saw as she hurried for the barn. Jason must have left it open when he fed the dogs this morning. Angie stepped from bright sunlight into shadows redolent with the musty smell of old hay. Pinholes of light blinked like stars through loose shingles in the roof. Towzer came rushing at her out of the shadows.

"There you are, bad doggie. I hope you haven't gotten into the chow. You'll be sick," she said, stroking his ear. It was damp, slick.

"Towzer? What'sa matter, baby? Did you tear your ear on some nasty barbed wire?" Angie said as she dropped on one knee.

"As a matter of fact, Towzer took a nasty crack in the head."

Angie leaped to her feet, her heart in her throat. "Adolph!" she stammered, trying to sound casual. Her own words came back to her: Take a deep breath and smile while you talk. "You startled me. How did you get here? I didn't see your boat. We were just going to call you about dinner plans for..."

"Were you?" he said. "Or were you going to run?"

"Why no," Angie said. "Actually, I read about this, ah, design show in Seattle, that I wanted to..." but her voice trailed off when she realized it was no use. Her eyes had adjusted to the light. She saw that he had a gun.

"Where's Ox?" she said.

"Dear old Ox has had an accident," Adolph said. "I'm sorry, my dear, but he wouldn't stop yowling. His racket made it impossible for me to concentrate on my plans."

"What plans?"

"For our little boat trip," he said. "I want to thank you for topping off the fuel tanks. That just makes it easier for me."

"What shall we call you? Adolph, Anthony or Raymond?" Angie said, "Or shall we go back to basics and settle on Johnny?"

He laughed. "Honey, that depends entirely on what day it is."

"It doesn't really matter to me who you are," she said, soothingly. "Today, I read in some old newspapers how you once saved my life. I want to thank you for that."

He nodded. "Oh yes ma-am, I'm quite the hero."

"I know you've been in trouble, Johnny, but underneath there is good in you," she said. "I know it. Bradley thought so, too."

"Who the hell is..." then he paused. "Oh. The kid in the hospital."

"Unfortunately, he died," Angie said, very softly, "But to everybody in that hospital back in Memphis, Raymond Tadischi is a good, kindly man."

"I'm touched," he said sarcastically.

"Bradley left a little package for you. Wouldn't you like to see it?"

"Stow it!" he said, waving the gun. In the distance, they could hear her mother calling. "Cut the crap," he said, waving the pistol at her. "We'll table the discussion of my tender side for another day. For now, Angie, you shut up and do what I say, and perhaps you'll live to tell me what a kindly man I am." He stepped toward her, close enough that his stale, alcohol-tinged breath on her neck set her body convulsing in fear. "Don't you hear your mama calling you? Now I want you to answer her, nice and calm."

CHAPTER 64

Memphis Airport
July 18

As the call to headquarters in DeLeon was going through, Joe listened to the drawl of a woman paging passengers. Her Tennessee accent was neither southern, nor western. Tennesseeans had their own unique cadence, soothing as the patter of rain on a tin roof, and he was in desperate need of some soothing.

"DeLeon Police Department. Randapolis speaking."

"Officer Jenny. How are you?" He made a special effort to sound relaxed, cheerful, and totally certain of what he was doing.

"Joe Vensure? Where you at?" Jenny growled. From her tone, he could read the expression on her face, jaw set, brows knitted in a glare.

"I'm in Memphis. Changing planes for Seattle."

"You were 'sposed to be at a press conference one hour ago. Don't tell me you didn't know about it. I reminded you last night. The chief's put out a purple alert for you." The old man turned purple before he stripped officers of their rank or put people out on suspension. A purple alert was something it was best to dodge, if at all possible.

"Jeez," Vensure said. "Tell him I'm following up on a hot lead on a murder case. I'll take time off to do it. I've got some leave coming." Forget the fact that there was a warrant out for Abruzzi. No chief in his right mind would send a man five thousand miles to make the arrest when he could ask the other jurisdiction to handle it.

"Abruzzi?" Jenny said. "I told the chief I thought that was it."

"How did you know?" Joe said.

"Miz Reynolds called here first thing this morning."

"Hell." Joe said. "Why didn't you say so?"

"She said to tell you Abruzzi is up there with her."

"Up where?"

"Oregon. Or wherever it is. Alaska? She even sent a fax, 'cept it wasn't about Abruzzi, but some other Eye-talian sounding gentleman."

"Tadeschi?"

"Hold on, let me find it. Yes, here it is. Yeah, that's right. 'Adolph Tadeschi, a real sweetheart, has come to call on us.' That's what it says."

"Can you tell where the call came from?"

"Hold on a minute, I got to take another call." Jenny was off the line so long that his flight was re-boarding.

He was exactly fifteen seconds from hanging up before she came back.

"Sorry," she said. "That was a call from a grade school. A kid takes a pistol to show and tell. Can you believe that? Okay, here it is. "The Library, Friday Harbor."

"Thanks Jenny," he said, hanging up.

The pancake plain just outside the Memphis city limits served as a hub of the nation's shipping business. Northwest Airlines Flight Forty Seven rolled past the impressive fleets of United Parcel and Federal Express, then shuddered into the sky and circled the treeless tundra below.

A stewardess came by and plunked a package of peanuts and a cocktail napkin on his tray table. Waiting out the announcement that it was okay to use the telephone located in the seatback in front of him, he put the napkin into service, jotting on it all of Octave's aliases: Anthony Abruzzi, Raymond Tadischi, and now Adolph Tadeschi. The sweetheart. Yes, Angie's fax had linked Octave to Tadeschi, and since Abruzzi was also Octave, there it was: Angie had solved the case. QED.

The word that sweetheart swindler complaints had been filed against Raymond Tadischi had turned up late last night. He'd attempted to reach Angie with this news, but the phone was off the hook.

He looked again at the dates of the complaints, filed in Akron, Ohio and Denver, Colorado. So far the only known complaints against Raymond were filed after Anthony Abruzzi dropped out of sight in Memphis. Though their physical descriptions didn't match by any stretch of the imagination, Angie had somehow found the link.

"Will you have something to drink before lunch?" the stewardess said.

"I'd love to have a martini and forget the whole afternoon," he said. "Unfortunately, I'd better stick with iced tea."

"Whatever you say," the stewardess said, giving him the eye.

Watching her sashay up the aisle only made him long for Angie. Obviously, Her library research had paid off. Surely she would have sense enough to get out of those islands as fast as she could and let the authorities collar the dude. But what if she had not had a chance to get to the police?

He was on the phone the second the stewardess announced that use of electronic devices was now allowed. He got the operator on the line and put in a call to the San Juan County sheriff's department in Friday Harbor. He sipped his tea as the call was going through. Damn but he'd love to collar Tadeschi himself, but there was no point in taking chances. Let them take him if they could. Meanwhile he'd have to beg some protection for Angie from a department that had to be just like his: notoriously short on funding and staff.

CHAPTER 65

"Angie?" Jane said, poking her head around the open doorway.

The salty, sweaty clamp that was Johnny's hand loosened over Angie's mouth. "Call her," he hissed, jamming the pistol into her throat. Her skin shriveled at the touch of cold metal. Her body felt strangely detached from her consciousness.

"Julia Jane?" Angie said, hoping that the use of her mother's full name would warn her off. Her mother hated nothing so much as her first name, which she considered stuffy and formal. Nevertheless, Jane stepped further into the dark.

"Where are you, darling?" I can't see a thing," Jane said.

Johnny wrestled Angie into the light, shifting the gun to her temple. "Here we are, babe, just one happy family."

Jane stepped forward. "Johnny Octave, you let go of her," she cried. "Or Adolph. Or Anthony."

"Whatever name you prefer, my dear," he said, his tone full of menace, a mockery of a lover's tone. "Here we are. Together again after all these years."

"What are you planning to do to us?" Jane said.

"I think for the time being, I'll put you in there," he said, nodding toward the door of the storage annex where the farm tools were kept. Jane didn't move. She simply stared at them.

"Well, Janey, are you going to move, or do you want me to blow your daughter's head off?"

Jane sidled into the small room. Johnny shoved Angie along behind her. Angie watched Jane's fingers fly to her mouth, stifling a gasp. Two of the plastic chairs that usually sat by the back porch had been aligned back to back. A roll of duct tape sat on the counter. Beside it lay a boning knife from the kitchen. Towzer, sensing the danger, rubbed against Angie's bare legs, whimpering.

"All right, Janey, you do the honors. Cut me about eight strips of tape, each a foot long," he said. "What a shame, Jane, dear. I had high hopes you and I could cut the cake. Instead, we cut the tape."

"And Mrs. Reynolds, a lady I once jilted," he said, waving the gun in a mock salute. "I felt rather badly about leaving you. You weren't the typical gold digger out to rip off a rich attorney."

"Angie?" her mother gasped. "You?"

"That's right," Angie said softly, "I also remember kindnesses. I owe you my life, Johnny. So just let us go, and I guarantee I won't prosecute."

"Shut up," he ordered. "One more word from you, Mom's gone."

Towzer raised his ears and began yapping softly.

"What is it boy?" he muttered. He ordered Jane to sit down and Angie to bind Jane's legs to separate legs of the chair. Then he had Angie tape Jane's hands together behind her back. He himself positioned tape across Jane's mouth, patting her cheek when he was finished.

"I see that the tape isn't tight?" he said to Angie, "I blow you both away."

He ordered Angie to sit down. He put the gun on the tool table and began to bind her up, but Angie saw her chance. As Johnny stood in front of her she kicked him in the groin.

Octave doubled over, howling in agony, Angie lunged for the gun. But Johnny rolled into her knees, sending the weapon flying out of her hands. Angie fell across Octave's back. He rose, dumping her to the floor. She was flat on her back. He climbed astride her and proceeded to slap her across the face, punctuating every word with a blow: "You! Do! That! Again! You! Are! One! Dead! Babe!"

He stopped hitting Angie only when his own rage was spent and he was himself gasping for breath. He had to rest awhile before he managed to drag her limp figure to the chair. He quickly taped her arms and legs. He ran his hand over every limb to be sure the tape was tight.

"You bastard!" Angie managed to croak through swollen lips. He cut another strip of tape and slapped it over her mouth.

"Now, Towzer, let's go see who has come to call." he said, shoving the pistol in his pocket and grabbing a spade as he lurched out.

CHAPTER 66

Someone was coming. They had a chance. Angie squirmed in her chair and made grunting noises through the tape, trying to reassure her mother. She had to get loose, but how?

Of course. The chair. One of those plastic chairs like the one she'd cut herself on in Joe's apartment. She ran her fingers along the outer edges of the chair arm. It was sleek and smooth. Damn!

She glanced down at it, looking for a way. But wait. She hadn't checked the inner edge. The inside of it, close to her body, looked sharper. She ran her thumb along the inner top edge of the chair arm, a few inches in each direction. Sure enough, there was a sharp, rough place underneath. She checked the left arm. For some reason, it was sharper yet.

She tugged on the tape around her left wrist, working her wrist and forearm arm back and forth until the tape gave a little. Angie made room where she could use her thumb and forefinger to draw the edge of the tape across the sharp ridge under the chair arm. She pulled and sawed on the tape until her whole body was slick with sweat. Finally she worked a very small tear in the tough tape.

Towzer was making a racket, down on the dock. She heard a boat arriving. She had to hurry, before Johnny sent them away. The tape gave way. Then, miraculously, one arm was free.

CHAPTER 67

Johnny Octave stood in the shade of the barn and viewed the approaching boat through his field glasses. It was a sheriff's patrol vessel. Though he willed himself to stay calm, the little tussle he'd had with Angie had taken a toll. That bitch was a lot stronger than she looked.

He felt the pains begin to clamp at his chest. He checked the boat again. Oddly, there seemed to be only one guy aboard. He watched as long as he dared, expecting to see another figure emerging from the cabin, but he finally gave up and headed toward the dock. He had to draw attention away from the barn.

Towzer raced ahead, rushing down the dock, barking at the approaching vessel. Johnny shuffled along the footpath in the direction of the boat, using the shovel he'd brought from the barn as a cane. He made sure he wasn't on the dock as the boat came alongside.

Instead, he made a show of turning up a little dirt in the planting beds just outside the front gate. He didn't rush to help the officer tie up. That way, if there was anyone else on the boat, he was sure to emerge. When no one else appeared on deck, he sauntered down to take the dog by the collar.

"Sit, Towzer," he commanded. "Don't you know to respect the law?"

The Don Juan Con

The officer wrapped a stern line over a cleat and maneuvered the boat alongside the dock. "Afternoon, sir," said a lanky, sharp-featured young man, who lifted his cap long enough to reveal a blond buzz cut.

"Afternoon," Johnny said, "What can I do you for, officer?"

"I'm Ed Byers of the San Juan County Sheriff's office. We're looking for a Mrs. Pelham and her daughter, Angie Reynolds, and her grandson, Jason Reynolds." In the stern, the officer put one foot up on the hatches. From the cabin, the marine radio crackled.

"Right," Johnny said, scratching his head. "They all took off for Friday Harbor early this mornin'." he drawled. "Miz Pelham left me behind to catch up on the yard, but the day shore got away from me."

"Is this your boat?" the officer said, indicating the launch.

"It's Mrs. Pelham's boat. She had me drop them off. She wanted me to do some maintenance on the vessel. I got the filters changed and she runs good as new. I got to go get them, soon's she calls."

"Are you Mr. Pelham?"

"Oh, no. Mr. Pelham passed away is my understandin' on that. Meantime, the place was getting away from Mrs. Pelham, so she hired me to do some mowin' and such."

"You are new around here, then?"

"I'm sort of new, the family isn't. I'm Jim McCall, a cousin to Clint McCall, up visiting from Salinas?"

"McCall?" said the young man, frowning suspiciously.

"Yessir, my dad is one of Clint's brothers. I rode him up here to see Clint before he died."

This story set the officer's mind at ease. "Clint was a fine old guy," he said. "Used to go fishin' with my dad. But somewhere I heard the family sold the ranch?"

He shook his head. "Dad was agin' it, but there was some cousins that wanted money out of it."

"Sold to a Hollywood producer, I heard," the officer said, looking up at him from the corner of his eyes.

"That I wouldn't know about," he said. "Say. You must be real thirsty. Come on, you can wait for the ladies in the kitchen. Mrs. Pelham's bound to call soon. I'm shore she wouldn't mind."

"Thank you, don't mind if I do," the officer said, climbing out of the boat.

CHAPTER 68

The stench of old hay filled Angie's nostrils as she poked her head into the loft. She sneezed and made her way up the ladder, then helped her mother up onto the small platform. There was barely enough room for the two women to turn around.

"I can't see a thing," Jane said.

"My eyes have adjusted," Angie said, helping her mother to a seat on a rotting bale of hay. "Just wait here. Don't move, okay?"

"I still think we should have run, while we had the chance," Jane said.

"We don't know who's come, Mom. It could be somebody to help Johnny, for all we know."

"Or Anthony. Or Adolph," Jane said bitterly.

"Or even Raymond Tadischi, with an 'i'," Angie murmured as she edged away from Jane, heading for the peak of the barn and the small window just beneath it. The window offered the best view of the porch, yard and dock. It was a place Angie had come as a child to watch the passing boats and sort out her thoughts.

The window, a two-foot square, was covered with a hatch, dogged into place by rectangles of wood. Angie moved one of the dogs. It came off in her hands. Unfortunately, the others were swollen with age. She had to beat at them with the broken dog.

"I hope he doesn't hear you," Jane said.

At that moment the hatch fell out of the window and clattered to Angie's feet, though the noise was somewhat baffled by the hay on the floor.

Angie poked her head through the window. Johnny Octave was talking to a sheriff's deputy who was standing in his boat, the engine running. They hadn't been noticed.

"There's only one man on the boat, Mom. We can't show ourselves. It's too risky. Johnny is armed. He'd shoot the deputy and then where would we be?"

"We'll have to hide in the woods," Jane said.

"I'm afraid Towzer would lead him right to us," Angie said. "Wait. The deputy is shutting off his outboards. He's getting out of the boat. He's tying up. It looks as if they are going to go into the house."

"What should we do?" Jane said.

"Wait for an opportunity," Angie said.

CHAPTER 69

It was a long, slow trip to the house. Deputy Byers had to help the old codger up the stairs to the deck. He was sweating like a pig.

"Are you sure you are all right?" Byers asked.

"I shore ain't much good with a shovel," Johnny said. He gritted his teeth and sank forward, over his knees.

"Maybe I should take you to a doctor," Byers said.

"Naw. I'll be all right. I got to take them pills is all," he said as they entered the house. "Hep yourself to a beer."

Byers declined a beer, accepted a glass of iced tea, then asked to use the bathroom, which, Johnny knew, gave the deputy an excuse to poke around in the house. He'd taken a terrible risk, asking the cop in, but if it worked, the deputy would report back to headquarters that Angie and her mother were nowhere to be seen.

With trembling hands he took one of the nitro pills. He was at the sink, washing off a bunch of blackberries he had earlier stashed in the fridge when the officer came downstairs again.

"Found these this mornin', right along the road," he said, holding them up.

"Excellent," the officer said.

"Tell you what, son, take some along with you. Miz Pelham would be glad to let you have them," he said, dumping most of the berries into a paper sack he retrieved from under the sink.

"Thanks," the officer said. "Glad you're feeling better."

The pair ambled back to the dock. Johnny courteously helped him out with his bowline. The young man sped off, smartly sending white trails of spume combing through the glassy swells. Johnny could see him pick his microphone, reporting in. Luckily, Byers never looked back to Puffin Island, or toward the barn, at the sight that gave Johnny an awful start. A white flag was waving from the small window in the peak.

CHAPTER 70

Angie blinked back tears as the deputy's cruiser picked up speed. She handed Jane her white shirt, what they had used as a flag. Jane scrambled back into the garment, but her hands trembled so that she could not button it. She left it gaping open like a robe. Angie caught a glimpse of Johnny heading toward them, straight for the barn, using the shovel as a crutch to steady his crabbed gait.

"On to plan B," Angie said.

Jane scrambled down the ladder. There was a sickening, splintering sound. Jane dropped to the floor. "The rungs, Angie," she hissed.

Angie was on the ladder herself, a few steps above Jane. "Go for it, Mom. Run." Then she had to negotiate the rung-less section of the ladder. She lost sight of Jane, who was headed for the annex and the door out the back of the barn. They would take the old trail to the bird blind. It was the only other place on craggy Puffin Island where anyone could land a boat without a monumental effort.

Johnny had to have come over by boat. His boat must be tied up at the blind, since it wasn't on the dock. Their agreement was: if they became separated for more than five minutes, the first of them to reach the boat was to run for Deer Harbor for help. It wasn't far.

Angie's foot stretched to find the next rung. It was out. Then the next. Then she realized the problem. Two rungs were gone. Possibly three. She leaped off the ladder, just as Jane had done, flinging her body outward, trying for a mound of hay that would break her fall. She landed in a sprawl.

She had just caught her breath, gotten up on her arms when she took the hit. She was flattened. All the lights went on in her cranium, then off. She was sucked into a sickening, whirling vortex. Had her brain exploded? By some instinct she managed to get up on one elbow, to turn her head, to look, only to see a blurry vision of two hands clenched overhead, pulling something downward.

She dove behind the ladder. The blade of the shovel glanced off a riser, thunking harmlessly into moldy hay. Johnny bellowed in his outrage, taking it out on the damaged ladder, which lost its legs, then its shape. In a few strokes, Johnny's shovel reduced the ladder to a pile of splintered shards.

His feckless fury gave her the time she needed to scuttle into a dark corner, behind some bales of hay. She'd managed to retrieve a splintered section of the ladder, dragging it with her. Calmly, she waited, willing out her pain, balancing the weight of the smoothed, peeled pole in widespread hands. She took courage from the dry, woody scent. That and the fact that the cured timber was light in her hands. She would not go down without a fight.

"Angie?" he purred. He was calling to her, but she couldn't make out what he was saying above the torrential roar of her own ragged breathing.

Calling to her softly, he worked his way along the wall, creeping toward her. Then she realized he was employing the old endearments of his former self, her ex lover, Anthony Abruzzi. She sobbed silently, biting down tears. She had lost her self to this man.

Was she to lose her life as well?

When she failed to respond to his cajoling, he came bellowing after her, a black tower of rage, shovel upraised. Somehow he'd seen her, perhaps made her out from her shadow on the wall. On one knee, like a supplicant, she offered the broad side of the pole to the falling shovel, deflecting the blow, though the weight of the blade nearly tore her own weapon from her hands.

For an instant, as the shovel glanced away, he was off balance. Though the pole now felt heavy and her arms were quivering and weak, she managed with exquisite will to squeeze a tight grip and took merciless aim. She drove the ragged spear through Johnny's middle, tearing at his flesh. And again. And again. She stabbed him with deadly and deliberate precision. The makeshift spear grew slippery with his blood.

Johnny fell to his knees, a whimpering mass. Her own rage now had her in its grip. She went for his head, pounding him. She never wanted to stop hitting him. He sprawled flat, covering his head with his hands and was still.

Appalled, Angie threw the weapon away. Sobbing, swallowing down the urge to retch, she knelt beside him, touched the bloody pulp that had been his ear. She bolted for the barn door, for the streaming light, for the promise of salvation from the nightmare.

Oh God, how could I have become equally so evil?

Then the sting of the slug seared past her ear, even before the sound of the shot reached her ears. He ordered her to halt, but there was no need. Angie lay flat, hugging the ground, weary, accepting, praying that her death, now upon her, come quickly, praying, God forgive me my attempt to murder.

CHAPTER 71

The six-seat commuter plane rolled to a stop on the landing strip that comprised the San Juan County Airport. Joe sped through the mini terminal building in six strides. A green and white patrol car barreled through the entrance gate and screeched to a stop. Joe leaped in.

"Joe Vensure, I presume? I'm Larry Whiting," the driver said with a nod.

"Thanks for helping us out," Joe said as he sized up Whiting, liking what he saw in this square-jawed, chubby-faced fellow. Whiting had taken his call from the plane, listened hard, asked the right questions and assured him of their department's full cooperation.

"Did our warrant come in?" Joe said.

"Yessir. God bless the NCIC." Whiting said.

"So you fellas are online?" Joe said, impressed. There were a lot of local law enforcement agencies that didn't have computer access to the national hookup that helped immeasurably in cases like this.

"Oh, we've got the hardware," Whiting said. "No staff and a building falling down around our ears, but the terminal we do have. I think the fathers on the county commission believe that terminal's going to walk right out of the office and make the arrests."

"So? Where are we?"

"A deputy on Orcas swung by the McCall ranch. Found nothing there but a bunch of fine-looking Anguses and a pair of dandy quarter horses. No sign of Tadeschi—or his Mercedes. He doesn't seem to have gone on the ferry. Nobody recalls loading a fancy car like that this morning. We pulled in two relief deputies to help him out, but that leaves only three men to comb fifty square miles of a densely forested island."

"What about the women?" Joe said. "Surely they've turned up?"

Frowning, Whiting chewed his lower lip. "The last person who saw Angie was a librarian. Here in Friday Harbor. Said Mrs. Reynolds acted real funny. After she sent the same fax that your department faxed us, she rushed off. So far, all I've got custody of is the three dollars and change that Mrs. Reynolds left behind at the library."

"Has anyone checked out Puffin Island?"

"We sent out one of the boys in a Whaler. We should hear back from him any minute. Don't expect much. If there was trouble out there, Jane Pelham would have been on the marine band in a minute."

The sheriff's department was less than a mile from the airport, down a two-lane blacktop highway. Whiting swung onto a gravel side road beside a horse pasture and drove up a slight incline.

The San Juan County Sheriff's department was the most benign-looking law agency he had ever seen. It was a long gray building set behind a split-rail fence, sheltered under a canopy of firs.

"Are you sure this isn't a forestry camp?" Joe asked.

Whiting grinned. "I was a green kid in L.A. metro. Came up here to visit relatives. First time I saw this gem, took me ten minutes to apply for the next available opening. Never could stand smog."

Whiting screeched around to the rear entrance of the building and slammed on his brakes. Joe hauled his portfolio and overnighter out of the back of the patrol car and the men sped into the building, past a cord of wood stacked on the back porch.

"You have a fireplace?" Joe panted.

"We supervise a scout troop," Whiting said. "The boys cut firewood for shut-ins."

They entered through the back door. Whiting led him down a narrow hall, into a cubbyhole of an office. "What should I put in your cup?" Whiting said.

"Anything high test," Joe replied, as he hung his overnighter on the back of the door in Whiting's cramped office. He followed Whiting down a narrow corridor, hoping to work the lead out of his legs. After being cooped up for five hours on the flight out of Memphis and another forty minutes on San Juan airlines' commuter flight from SEATAC, south of Seattle, he felt stiff, sluggish and disoriented.

As he passed by the dispatcher's desk, he was startled to see a familiar thatch of umber colored hair on the figure slumped in the waiting area. "Jason," he said, "What are you doing here?"

"I was supposed to meet Mom at the library," Jason said. "The librarian said she went off in a big hurry this morning. She even left this on the desk."

Jason handed Joe the copy of the fax that Angie had left behind. He glanced at it and gave it back to Jason. It was the same one Jenny Randapolis had read him on the phone.

"I checked the whole city dock. Grandma's launch isn't there. I called Grandma's. There's no answer," Jason said.

Just then another officer joined them. "We have a report just in from Deputy Byers. We sent him by to check on your grandmother's house, son. He said your grandma's launch is at the dock. The gardener said he's to pick up your mom and your grandma later this afternoon here in Friday Harbor."

"We brought the launch over to Friday Harbor this morning ourselves," Jason said, frowning. "And I don't know what gardener he's talking about. Grandma doesn't have one."

"Dammit," Joe said. "It's Tadeschi. He's holding them on Puffin Island. We've got to get out there."

"I know Puffin," Whiting said, slamming down the two cups of coffee he'd just poured. "Get us a patrol boat at the harbor," he shouted to the dispatcher as they rushed for the door, where Whiting paused.

"What about an air search?" Joe said.

"We don't have our own chopper. Can't get support from the Marine Patrol. They strictly do narcotics stuff, and man-overboards."

"Hell," Joe said. "There have to be choppers around here. I saw a couple of them at the airport."

"They do sightseeing tours," Whiting said.

"Wait a minute. Get one of them on the phone. I'll send Jason out to do a little sightseeing by chopper," Joe said.

"We'll swing by the airport on the way to the harbor," Whiting said.

"All right!" Jason said, brightening.

"What's the time to Puffin?" Joe said.

"Thirty minutes," Whiting said.

Joe shook his head. Thirty minutes? An eternity.

CHAPTER 72

Angie's legs buckled under her. She sagged across Johnny's shoulders. He staggered.

"To tell you the truth, Angie," he said, "I hate to get physical with you girls. I really do respect women, you know? Without ladies like you, how would I have gotten where I am today?"

Through a searing pain in her skull, she fought to remain conscious. What had happened? Oh yes, the chair. Fraying the tape. Crawling into the loft. The deputy leaving. The ladder smashed. Her mother, gone for help. The shot. She was down. Johnny dragging her. Why? He seemed to know she wasn't dead. Why hadn't he simply killed her? And where was her mother? Surely she was on her way with deputies by now.

She felt her body shifting. Johnny was moving her. He'd lifted her arm from across his shoulder. He was setting her down. Her head lolled on her chest.

"Now put your back against this beam, my dear," she heard him say through the fog in her brain. She settled against the post gratefully, arms flopping at her side. She felt warm liquid trickling down her face. Tasting it with her tongue, her own blood.

Oh God, Joe, where are you? Surely he had her message. By now, he would be arranging their rescue. If only she could hold on.

The Don Juan Con

"I have to blame you for this, Angie," Johnny wheezed. "If you hadn't butted in, your mama and I, we'd have been enjoying our wedded bliss by now. I'd have gone right ahead and run my little ranch, and your mama might even have helped out on my movie production and our philanthropic projects. Adolph Tadeschi was a real guy."

Angie tried to lift her head, wanted to mumble a response, then thought better of it.

Rest now. Still have a chance.

"So what am I going to do? Go back to prison? No way. With my heart condition? Never."

Angie squinted, letting her head loll on her chest. Heart condition? That was it! It was Abruzzi who had a heart attack in Memphis, and now she understood. He had hidden out in the hospital as the heroic Raymond Tadischi, friend to the poignant child, Bradley. No wonder there was no trace of Abruzzi after Memphis.

"So what do I do, Angie? You kept me from going straight. So? You got your revenge. I'm sick of running. I'm a sick man. I might as well end it and take you and Janey with me. We can be wed in hell," he panted.

Angie's hopes sank as she heard her mother's name. Had she failed to reach Deer Harbor?

Slowly, clumsily, he got to his feet. She felt herself being hoisted up, over his shoulders. She let her body drag, doing her best to weaken him.

Lurching along, he hauled her out of the barn. She felt the salty breeze and sensed the light on her face. One eye wouldn't open. Through the other, she could make out the path beneath her feet. Grass and stones swayed by. The sky hung upside down.

When they got to the dock, he laid her on it, face down. Warm, silvery boards, dried to a leathery softness through years of use, were a comfort to her throbbing face. Through the corner of her eye, she could see the gleaming red hull of the launch.

Then she heard a moan. It was her mother! She was in the boat and still alive. Angie lay perfectly still, roused by a surge of hope. It was late afternoon now. Jason would have the police looking for them. And Joe would be coming.

With a grunt, Johnny picked her up and dumped her into the launch. She landed on the padded hatches, letting her legs fall slack. The boat swayed as he jumped aboard. Then he propped her up.

"Sit up now, Angie," he said, shaking her.

She opened her one good eye in response.

"There's a girl. You'll feel better when we get underway."

She let her head loll back, taking in the entire cockpit. Her mother was propped in the opposite corner, one arm posed across the back of the stern. God, what a mess she was. Both eyes were black. There was a dark, bloody patch in her hairline. Her lips were swollen. Her chest was rising and falling. There was a rasping noise in her throat. Her mother was having trouble breathing, but at least she was alive.

Johnny started the powerful outboards, climbed up on the starboard rail, released the bowline, then pulled in the stern line. Angie lurched at the roll of the vessel as it slid away from the dock.

And I topped off the fuel tanks for this, she thought. For a few minutes, the boat moved along at a smooth, gentle pace. Through her narrowed gaze she saw him pull past the last marker, guiding them out of the shallow channel in front of the island.

"Off we go, into the fiery red yonder," Johnny bellowed as the vessel picked up speed. Angie's body slid toward the stern as she felt the bow rise. He'd opened the throttle all the way. He was going too fast. They were planing.

She heard the angry wail of a boat horn as they swerved to miss an oncoming vessel. After a few minutes the launch began to veer out of control. Angie opened her eye. What was happening?

There was nobody on the wheel. She looked over the stern to see a dark shape, frantically swimming away from them. Johnny had jumped overboard? Why?

Then the hairs stood up on her arms. She felt an electric charge crackle through her hair, and she understood everything. She had been here before: that was the message of her dream. She knew what was coming.

"Mom!" she shrieked, "Jump! Now!"

CHAPTER 73

Jason, strapped into a seat behind the pilot and co-pilot, spotted the red launch. "There it is," he shouted, "Just past the last channel marker to Puffin Island."

The pilot bore down on the launch. The co-pilot turned around in his seat. Jason pointed out the spot. The co-pilot looked through his binoculars. "They sure are in one hell of a hurry."

Jason saw the boat begin to veer back on itself. "Hey! Nobody's at the wheel," he said. Then there was a flash of light, a fireball, flames, a shower of water and a rain of debris.

The chopper hurtled upward and yawed sideways. "Hang on," the pilot shouted.

"*Moooom!*" Jason screamed, but all the breath left him and his stomach headed for the sky as the chopper whipsawed, flinging him against his seatbelt.

By the time the chopper was stabilized and swooped around for a look at the wreckage, the launch was heeled completely over on its side.

Below them, the patrol vessel with Whiting and Joe aboard was approaching, siren wailing.

"Do you see any survivors?" Through the headset he was wearing, Jason heard Joe asking the pilot, on the radio.

"Not yet," the pilot replied, "but it's too early for anything to have surfaced. We gotta give this some time."

Jason sobbed hysterically

"Stow it son," the pilot growled. "We've gotta keep our heads, here."

Jason choked down his tears. Chest heaving, he scanned the water. "There!" he shouted. "It's my mom."

"Woman overboard, about ten degrees starboard of the wreckage," the pilot said to the vessel. "Easy, easy. Now!"

Jason, his hands clamped over his mouth, watched the rescue boat slide toward her. As the chopper hovered above, he could see his mother's hair washing across the back of her head like so much sea-weed. Her navy and white striped tee shirt ballooned off her back.

Joe dove off the boat and rolled her body over. Whiting tossed him a life ring. The shadows of the rotors on the water seemed to make the life ring spin. It was a wheel in motion. Prickles of water raised by the chopper snapped angrily, all around his mother. Jason glimpsed her battered face, her mouth hanging open, as the men pulled her aboard. Her body was limp. Like those crash dummies he'd seen on TV. Then she was in the bottom of the patrol boat. All Jason could see was Joe's powerful shoulders pumping rhythmically as he straddled her back, squeezing water out of her lungs.

"Dear God," he muttered, "I know I haven't been too good, but please, please don't take Mom," he whispered.

"Chopper? Have you spotted Mrs. Pelham?" Whiting said.

"Hold on, skipper, we're looking around here."

"There's something," the co-pilot said as the chopper swung around. "Let's looksee in all that debris, due east, maybe a hundred yards."

In the water, Jason could see a hatch cover, a shiny piece of the rail-ing, a fishing rod, and the cooler Grandma liked to keep on the deck. It was half submerged, with the top open. Then a cushion floated past.

"Hold it," the pilot said, "I think I see…Yes. Her face! She can see us."

Jason unbuckled his seatbelt and slipped into the seat behind the pilot. Almost directly below him was his grandmother's face, her eyes wide with terror. She was treading water, but seemed unable to do any-thing with her arms.

"Jason? You fastened in good?" The copilot said, as he opened the side door of the chopper. They lowered a life ring to his grandmother.

"It missed her," Jason said. "Try again."

Though the life ring went close by her on the next pass, his grandmother made no move to reach for it.

"She can't lift her arms," Jason said.

"We can't set the chopper down. We'll swamp her," the pilot said. "Woman overboard," he said to Whiting below, in the rescue boat. "Due east of you, approximately seventy yards."

"Roger," Whiting said as the patrol boat sped forward.

"Skipper?" the co-pilot said. "Shall I call the Coast Guard for a rescue chopper?"

"Yo," the pilot said. "We did the search. Let them do the rescue."

Jason watched as the boat neared his grandmother. Joe dove off the stern, swam up beside her and eased her head onto his shoulder. Then he shouted something to Whiting who relayed the message to the chopper.

"She seems to be paralyzed on one side. Okay, he's shifted to the other side. She's got an arm over his shoulder. Whiting's tossing out a life ring," the co-pilot said.

Joe caught the life ring and slid it over Jane's head. He stabilized her body as Whiting began to haul her in.

"I want to go down there," Jason said. "I can help them."

"Son, if I get close enough for you to swim to the vessel, these props would cut up the water. They'd shake up Joe and your grandma pretty bad," the pilot said. "Another rescue at sea is something we don't need right now."

But he was talking to air. Jason was gone.

"The damn kid cannonballed right outta the bird," the copilot yelled. "There he goes. I hope he don't break his fool neck."

Jason rolled into the water the way he'd been taught in diving class, head tucked under, his shoulders taking the wrenching cold like so many knives jabbed in his neck. He went down so long he thought he was never going to surface. Then he was rising, through the deep, dark green murk, his lungs aching for air.

Once he broke the surface, it wasn't hard to find Joe and swim fast. It was too cold to do anything else. He swam up beside the boat.

"Jason," Joe said, extending his hand, "Thanks for dropping in." He pulled Jason aboard.

"Grandma," he said, shocked. Her whole face was one big bruise. "I'll help get you out of here."

"Can you drive a boat, son?" Whiting shouted.

"Yessir."

"Then I need you to get aboard and hold the boat steady, while I

268

help Joe hoist your grandma aboard."

Fortunately there was a gate in the transom, which meant they didn't have to carry her up the ladder. Joe shifted her around so that she lay across his arms. Whiting opened the gate, got down on his haunches, and took her into the boat. He laid her down on the padded stern, then took the wheel from Jason.

"Nice goin' son," Whiting said, "But I don't want to catch you jumping out of any helicopters. Unless you absolutely have to," he said with a grin.

All in, Joe sat in the stern wrapped in a blanket Whiting had tossed over him. His skin was an awful grayish blue. His teeth were chattering. His gaze was unfocused as he stared at the floor.

Jason pulled the blanket over his grandmother up to her chin. He reached for her left hand, outside the covers. It was limp. He found her right hand, under the blanket, and took it in both of his. Her bones were like rabbit bones, so thin. And her hand felt like ice.

"Can you feel anything, grandma?"

He felt a faint squeeze. "Her right hand is moving," he said. Then he noticed her lips were, too. He leaned toward her.

"Angie?" his grandmother whispered.

"She's going to be great, Grandma," he said. Whether this was true or not, it was what his grandmother needed to hear, and he was rewarded with a weak smile as he said it.

"Jason?" Whiting said. "Somebody down in the cabin wants to talk to you."

"I'll be right back, Grandma," he said.

"Jason?" Angie said weakly. She was tucked into a cabin berth. A railing had been dropped in place to keep her from rolling out of it.

"Mom!" he said. "Grandma's hurt, but she's talking."

"Tell her I'll be all right," his mother said, stroking his face with the back of her hand. Her fingers were icy. He waited a few minutes but she said nothing more and seemed to be asleep.

The boat was rocking, moving slowly, as Jason made his way across the cabin and took the companionway stairs up to the deck.

"A rescue chopper is on the way, son."

"The kind with the big baskets and the winches?" Jason said.

"That's right, and if they have room, we'll send you with it. You need to look after your mom and your grandma when they get to the emergency room."

"Great," Jason said. Beside his grandmother, he got down on his knees. He reached under the blanket to find her good hand.

The Don Juan Con

"Grandma? I just heard from Mom. No lie. She really is okay."

His grandmother's face remained a mask, but he felt a distinct squeeze on his hand.

"Thank you God," he said as he squeezed back, "It's cool."

CHAPTER 74

As they waited on the deck for the basket to arrive to lift Angie into the chopper, Joe smoothed her matted hair. Her teeth chattered and her body shook. She clung to him.

"Can't I ride back on the boat?" she asked.

Joe put his finger to her lips, still black with cold, and shook his head. "You'll be in the emergency room in fifteen minutes. I'm going after Octave."

"Jumped off."

"He was in the launch?" Joe said, startled, as he leaned close to hear her above the chopper noise.

Her head made the slightest of nods. "Between here and the exit marker." Angie mumbled. "He said they'd be married in hell." Tears leaked from the corners of her eyes. "Planed, too fast...then it went wild. I..." she sighed.

"Take your time," he said, putting his ear close to her lips.

"Nobody on the wheel. Octave gone, swam off, just before..." Angie shuddered and closed her eyes as the sling, suspended neatly over the stern, swung like a hammock in the breeze.

They stabilized the basket across the stern of the boat, and on a count of three, slid Angie in, careful to move her as little as possible.

"Take care, love. I'll be with you as soon as I can," he said.

271

CHAPTER 75

The patrol boat eased forward, drawing a bead on the exit marker, which Joe could barely make out in his field glasses as a black spot in the distance.

"Our sweetheart's pulled his usual escape number, leaving the wreckage behind," he muttered.

"Do you think he really meant to jump? Or did he turn coward at the last second?" Whiting said.

"Look at it this way. When he slipped past your first guy out at Puffin, he knew we were closing in. But this guy doesn't run. He hides in plain sight. He'd planned to blow up the vessel with Angie and Jane aboard. Probably went out there early this morning to wait for them to get back with the launch. But for some reason, the women went back there ahead of schedule and surprised him.

"They intended to return to Friday Harbor, had to. They wouldn't have left Jason. At any rate, our friend turns really daring and decides to go along for the ride. If he can make it look as if this were a murder/suicide, he figures we won't look too hard for his body in the wreckage."

"Clever sumbitch."

"There was only one hitch."

"What was that?"

"He finally met some women who were too tough for him."

Ahead of them, a boat slowed in the channel, just beyond the marker Joe was watching.

"Hold it," Joe said. "Something's going on. Looks like another patrol boat homing in on the buoy. Hell. Octave must be clinging to the buoy."

"That must be Eddie Byers. He called on Puffin this morning. He's responding to the all points call."

Whiting picked up his mike. "Byers, Byers, man overboard ahead is presumed to be the suspect. Be advised to let us cover the rescue. Over."

"Byers? Byers? Come in please."

"Damn," Whiting said. "He's away from the radio."

"Floor it," Joe said, tossing his binoculars aside. "I just caught the big splish-splash. Byers is overboard. Tadeschi has seized his boat."

CHAPTER 76

Eddie Byers was waving his arms, practically leaping out of the water, he was that furious.

"I saw him hanging on the marker buoy," Byers said as Joe pulled him into their boat, through the transom gate. "Had his face all wrapped in his shirt. Said he was a Canadian tourist whose boat had been run down by the crazy driver of the launch that blew up. Talked good Canuck, right down to the 'eh,' they tack on the end of every sentence." Byers toweled off his spiky blond hair and dripping face, but no amount of drying off was going to wipe the beet red rage off his face.

"Hey," Joe said, "Don't be hard on yourself. The bugger's a mafia grad with witness protection status. You're lucky to be alive."

"I got the stern in close to him, so's he could step aboard real easy. I reached out a hand to him. The shirt slipped off his head. I looked right into his snaky eyes and damn but I knew I'd been had. By then he's got his feet braced on the stern. He cannonballed me right over his head."

"He didn't get your gun, anyway," Whiting said.

"Might as well have," Byers moaned as he pulled his wet weapon out of a soggy holster. "I sure as hell couldn't shoot anything with this."

"Got some spares?" Vensure said.

"That we do," Whiting said. "Take Joe below. Get him equipped."

274

"Tadeschi's gonna have all the firepower I got on my boat," Byers wailed.

"So? We'll keep him too busy to use it," Whiting said. He turned on his siren full blast and his cruiser shot forward as he throttled it.

CHAPTER 77

Chills ran down Joe's spine as the siren started up. He hated the things. They had to shout over them.

"I don't know how we'll catch the bastard. He's got every bit of power we do," Whiting said as they shot past Puffin Island and followed Octave as he bore west.

"He doesn't know these islands," Byers said. "He's on the wrong side of Wasp Island. He's heading straight into San Juan."

"We'll take North Pass. We should be able to head him off." Whiting said.

"Suppose he catches on to us? He could double back."

"You've been tailing this guy all these months, Joe. You tell us what he'll do next," Whiting said.

"He's bearing west," Joe said. "My guess is all he knows about these waters is from thirty years back. He'd kidnapped Angie Pelham and was attempting to run across the Canadian border. He'll swing north up San Juan Channel and bear west along Spieden Island. What else is he going to do this time?"

"She-it, Whiting said. "Why the hell didn't you tell me Tadeschi is Johnny Octave?"

"We haven't exactly had time for a long conversation," Joe said.

"Dammit, I was a green recruit when we chased that bastard down the first time. There was talk on the boat about how we should have just shot him by accident and let it go at that. Save us a hell of a lot of paperwork and the D.A. wouldn't have to work so hard. But no, we had to bring the dude to justice. And then Janie Pelham gets up on the stand and pleads for that sumbitch's life. Now we got to catch the dude all over again? I swear, this job makes me retch." Whiting picked up the radio. "Wait'll the Canadians hear there's another American felon trying to violate their borders. Now those fellas are equipped. Hell, they'll turn out with frigates. They ain't going to mess with any pissant Whalers."

"He's got at least five minutes on us, but the tide's in our favor. We can catch him," Byers insisted.

"Take the wheel, Eddie," Whiting said. "You deserve a crack at the dude. We want to herd him into the Speiden channel, where the Canadians can bottle him up."

They hugged the eastern shore of Wasp Island, avoiding a small sailboat and upsetting some kids on a sailboard. As Joe glanced over his shoulder, he saw a woman standing on the bank, shaking her fist at them. Just as they were about to round the tiny island, Byers throttled down.

"What are we waiting for?" Whiting said.

"We'll be about three minutes ahead of him, if he was able to maintain speed, which I doubt." Byers said.

It was more like five minutes. They heard the scream of a siren fill the channel before the boat emerged. "I hope he's having fun playing with the whistles," Joe said. Rifle—an assault weapon—in hand, he moved up to the bow as Byers pulled out and headed due north up San Juan channel. They roared alongside Octave.

"Halt your vessel. Put down your weapon," Whiting said through a bullhorn. "Stop your vessel. Don't shoot."

But Octave fired, shooting out a rear window in the cabin.

Joe returned fire, hitting the control panel right in front of Johnny. He jumped away from the wheel and hid behind a center strut in the cabin.

"He can't go long with a ghost pilot," Byers shouted.

Joe raised his head, ready to take another shot, and grunted as a bullet tore through his shoulder instead. It was all he could do to hang onto his rifle.

"Pull over," Whiting shouted as the other boat wandered toward them. Byers pulled the wheel hard over, but couldn't correct quickly enough. As the two boats ground together, Johnny was thrown forward, over the control panel, but turned to fire once more. Joe blasted the rifle out of his hands. He saw the shock cross Johnny's face. He slumped forward, over the wheel.

"Prepare to board him," Whiting said. But just as Byers reached out with a boat hook, the vessel sped away from them, tossing them in its wake.

"Stubborn boy," Byers said.

"He's bent on suicide," Joe said, as Whiting leaped for the wheel.

As the boat lurched forward, Joe was thrown into the railing. Like a vice grip, pain locked into his wounded shoulder. His body was getting the word out to his brain. Until now, he'd been too busy to notice, but this was one signal he could not ignore. He closed his eyes, gritted his teeth, and hung his head over the side.

Sara Williams

CHAPTER 78

The rescue chopper lifted off and headed east, for the hospital at Anacortes. Though he stayed well out of range, the pilot kept watch on the two vessels below.

"Hold it," he shouted to his dispatcher. "The attempt to board has failed. Patrol vessel alpha is pulling away from Whiting. Beta vessel is giving chase. Both vessels have rounded Limestone Point on San Juan. They are proceeding northwest, up Speiden channel."

"Jason," Angie whispered. "Can you tell what's happening?"

"Joe's boat closed in on Adolph," Jason said. "I could see them start to board her, but just as they did, he shot off. He must have been playing possum."

"Jason? Get in your seat, son, we're going to tail them," the co-pilot said as the chopper roared ahead, sending vibrations through Jason's every pore.

As he clung to the back of the co-pilot's seat, Jason had a commanding view of the action. The two patrol vessels screamed up the narrow channel throwing up long, feathery wakes. A tiny sloop lay ahead, skimming across the channel, sail bellied out.

The chopper pilot tried to raise the sailor on the radio, but there was no response. "I shouldn't take the chance, but I don't have room for any more casualties," the pilot growled. He buzzed the vessel. The skipper came up from below. Hearing the approaching sirens, he dived for the tiller and tacked out of the way, just as the two patrol vessels roared across his bow. The sloop's horn wailed in protest.

The two vessels shot past an oncoming ferry, dodged a fleet of fishermen in small boats, and slipped right between two big motor cruisers who were traveling in tandem. The cruisers shot apart as if stung, at the last second.

"The boats are passing the marker off Speiden bluff. Alpha vessel is heading north just off the western flank of Stuart Island," the pilot shouted into his mike, and signed himself off. "Okay. That's it, Tadeschi's fatal mistake. Or Octave's. Whatever the hell his name is. The Canadian border is just off the tip of Stuart Island. They'll bottle him up good. See that, Jason? The channel ahead is choked with vessels. The Canadians have a dragnet strung between the three islands ahead, Sidney, Moresby and Pender."

The pilot lifted his headphones and grinned as he turned to Jason. "See that big one front and center? That there's a frigate, Jason. Lookee there at the guns on that baby. See those cutters flanking her? Then come a gaggle of power cruisers and open boats. Bee-you-tee-ful," the pilot said. "Will you look at that Canadian fleet? He's in the bottle now."

As Octave's boat approached a narrow channel bristling with the Canadian vessels, it slowed down. He looped back toward Joe's boat, which fired a warning shot across its bow. Then the vessel wheeled north and like a maddened dog headed straight for his attackers.

"Hell," the pilot shouted. "He's determined to take somebody out with him."

CHAPTER 79

Joe clung to one of the stanchion posts supporting the bow rails as their small cruiser hurtled over the swells. The vessel was planing. Each time the bow hit another rise it was with the smashing force of a jackhammer on concrete: *Slam. Slam. Slam.*

He took a wave over the bow full in the face as they heeled hard to starboard, barely missing some poor bastard in a sloop, his face frozen in terror, lying on his tiller as his sail sagged helplessly. They swept past his bow with barely three feet of clearance. On the rail, Joe slid past him, rifle in hand. The skipper's eyes widened, his jaw dropped, but he stayed on his tiller, thank God.

The scream of their sirens pained his ears, and he felt, rather than heard the mournful horns of vessels responding as they passed a fleet of fishermen. Two or three guys stood up on their bows and waved like crazy, as if this were some sort of picnic. His head was pounding and his stomach was sour with the terrible feeling that some Sunday boater was going to get seriously hurt.

He felt a new vibration on the back of his neck, looked up and saw the pontoons of the rescue chopper swinging out of the channel. He was outraged. What the hell was the pilot doing? Angie and her mother were up there. They ought to be in the hospital by now.

"Channel blocked ahead," he heard Whiting bellow, over the bullhorn. "Slow your vessel. Put down your arms." The bow dropped.

281

The Don Juan Con

Their boat slowed and began to wallow in the swells. Joe propped his good elbow on a seat cushion, eased his rifle into place between the stanchions and cocked it, simply to cover the action. Just a precaution. Suddenly, Octave simply stomped on it. His boat stood on its stern and began to walk away.

"You cowardly fucking bastard," he bellowed as Johnny hurtled right for the lead vessel in the channel, a hulking Canadian frigate, its gray hull gleaming in the sun bright as a new toy wrapped in cellophane. Joe's skin crawled. No telling how many would be killed.

"Joe! Take him out!" Whiting bellowed as he gunned after Octave. As they pulled alongside, Joe rose to his knees and rested the rifle on the bow rail, hoping to get a clear shot at Johnny. Unfortunately, the cabin struts in the other boat protected him. Ahead, a wall of hulls loomed, sending up an eerie wail.

Out of options, he sprayed the hull line of Octave's boat with rifle fire. Fountains of spray rose along the black bootstrap of the boat. Then one of the bullets found its mark. There was a dull thud, a blinding ball of light. As the vessel began to disintegrate, he saw Octave stagger toward the stern. His body was on fire but his voice box hadn't been consumed in the flames. The aftershock to the blast was the banshee scream of a man coated in flames. Johnny Octave and all his aliases danced wildly on the deck, then leaped off the bow. For one crazy instant as the blackened body sank through the water, the flames seemed to sink with him, riding him straight to hell.

Do the good scream the same? Joe wondered.

Whiting wheeled frantically against the wall of water mounding toward them, but the maelstrom washed across the bow, lifting Joe clean off the deck. He hurled the rifle away and made a frantic, one-handed grab for the safety rail. His hand closed over it. He was safe for a few seconds before the force of the waves pried him free. He was sucked into a vortex of water, fire and smoke.

Going under, the water seared at the bottom of his lungs. Incredibly, it seemed even icier than it had been earlier in the afternoon. A man overboard this far north in the Pacific could die in twenty minutes, Whiting had said. But were the effects cumulative as was the case with the air capacity of divers? Panicked, he rolled over and over in the deep green water, trying to discern where in the foaming grayness there was light. When he found a trail of rays, he swam toward them, slowly, way too slowly, in a digging, one-armed dog paddle. His other arm simply wouldn't move. He tunneled toward Angie, her dazzling face. It was all he could see, or ever want to.

282

CHAPTER 80

Joe sweated with the heat, then turned so cold his teeth chattered. He lay on a gurney beside the nurses' station, awaiting entry into an operating bay. When he attempted to turn on his good side, the nearest object he could focus on was a red switch plate in the stark wall. The thing was a menace, a harbinger of medical disasters.

He rolled on his back. The glaring grid of florescent lights overhead stabbed him in the eyes. He squeezed them shut. His shoulder hurt like hell, but the carnage of the afternoon had taxed the small hospital on some other island. Fidalgo, was it? Wherever he was, he had to wait his turn.

He felt light hands pulling a blanket up around his neck and opened his eyes. It was Jason. "They put Grandma in the recovery room. She's got a blocked nerve in her spinal cord, but they think she will be all right."

"Where's your mom?"

"They are just finishing up with her. I heard the doctor say she has a concussion and a broken arm."

A door opened, Angie was wheeled out by two uniformed attendants. A nurse followed, trailing her with an IV unit.

"Angie?" Joe said.

283

The Don Juan Con

She smiled weakly as she went past. Her face was wrapped in a white bandage.

"Wait," she said, and the procession stopped.

"What happened to you?" she said, reaching out to him with her free hand.

"I had a little run-in with the bad guy."

"Yeah," Jason chuckled. "He took out four guys: Abruzzi, Tadischi, Tadeschi and Octave."

"Sounds like law firm," Angie said.

"A crooked one," Joe said. He drew himself up on his good shoulder, only to see the nurse's back.

"Hey, bring her back here," he said.

The whole entourage halted. The nurse turned back, holding the IV unit regally, as if she was some standard bearer of the medical tribe. "I'm sorry, Mr. Vensure. But Mrs. Reynolds needs her rest now."

And with that Angie and her escort swept off.

CHAPTER 81

"Mom?"

Angie woke up. Jason was leaning over her. His face was still faun-like in its innocence. How could this be after what this child has been through?

"Hi sport," she said, reaching up to pull his face down to her breast. She ruffled his hair as she heard him say, "Grandma talked to me, but I don't think she knew what she was saying."

"What makes you think that?"

"She said I ought to put more powdered sugar on the doughnuts."

"She's been under anesthesia," Angie said, smiling through the tears in her eyes. "Sometimes it makes you have good dreams."

"Joe's going in to be operated on. The bullet's in his shoulder muscle. The doctor said that if you have to have a bullet in you that's a good place for one."

"He's going to be fine, Jason."

"Mom?"

"What darling?"

"Joe sent me to ask you something."

Angie opened her good eye. "What is it, Hon?"

"He wants to know if you are ready to move upstairs? Can we, Mom?"

The Don Juan Con

Angie shook her head. The man was relentless. She flashed Jason a grin and an okay sign with her fingers, and saw his eyes startle wide in pure delight.

"I gotta go tell him, before he goes to sleep."

As Jason's footsteps faded, Angie lapsed into a dream.

She was in the water, screaming. Above her was a tower of fire. Her body was stiff with the cold.

A lone voice called to her, "Hang on, Angie."

Only this time she wasn't afraid. She felt safe, as her body floated free. Her consciousness soared above the flames, and it turned and looked down upon her as strong hands lifted her out of the waves.

"Joe. Thank God you've come," she murmured.

Look for Sara Williams' next exciting mystery-thriller

THE SERENOA SCANDAL

Summer 2004 From

ArcheBooks Publishing
www.archebooks.com

PART ONE

MAYA

PROLOGUE

Hoots of owls and the beating of wings startled Maya Menecal awake. Her eyes opened wide. Could this be possible after what had happened? After such a day? She shifted on the pillow placed beneath her thighs to ease the throbbing in her hip.

Of course.

She had awakened because the pain pills had worn off. She lay very still in her bed, considering whether it would be time to take another. Beside her, David was sound asleep, breathing heavily. The poor man was exhausted. Maya nestled beside him, basking in his nearness, afraid that if she got up to take another pill she would awaken him. So long were the months they had been apart. David with all his campaigning to bring the new university to the county. Maya knew how important it was, how much it meant, but it had taken David from her at the very beginning of their life together. She had already begun to hate the fact that he was so powerful and all his obligations.

But today Maya had triumphed.

Yes, she had succeeded in getting him alone the moment he arrived at the ranch. She had met him down at the entrance gate mounted on Fandago, the stallion he'd given her on their wedding day. David was thrilled at how she'd learned to ride. Claude Fayals rode with her on David's horse. Claude drove back to the ranch house in David's Navigator loaded with the mountain of gear David used in his campaign for the university site.

David left the other business right at the gate and turned his attention to her and Serenoa, his beloved ranch. They had ridden to the heart of the ranch where they'd dined in style on the bridge over the swamp. Maya had made his favorite chocolate molé and black beans and rice. They had danced to her favorite Cuban music and David had wrapped her in his arms and promised her their life would be different. Very soon now it would all be over. In just a few months Governor Milne would be re-elected. David would retire from public life and focus all his attention on Serenoa and on her.

"I'll be home to chase you around the dining table, Maya. Better be ready to run."

Maya had leaped on Fandango and spurred him on. David took to his big bay and came thundering after her. She headed Fandango out of the swamp, through the southern meadows and across the muddy wallow where the bison were pastured. Unfortunately, Fandango had stepped in a hole in the ooze and Maya had been thrown over his head and landed in the wallow. She'd ruined the beautiful new western cut suit she'd worn, and was more embarrassed than hurt, though she feared for her horse.

David had suppressed a grin. "I won't tell the boys at the roundup if you won't, Maya."

He'd waded right in after her. The slime and the mud roiled over his alligator boots and he'd slipped, landing beside her and they both sat laughing in the brackish water and it was wonderfully cool against the sticky heat of the day.

"In the great spas of Europe people pay great sums for mud, Maya," he'd said, holding up a handful and letting it squish through his fist. "My dear, I believe you have discovered a new profit center for the ranch."

David dredged up handfuls of mud, laughing so hard he'd fogged up his wire-rimmed glasses and his deep brown eyes were filled with tears of mirth. Out here David Menecal was not the sainted hero of Calusa County, but simply David, a country kid enjoying the forbidden pleasures of the ooze and the mire. It was at that moment Maya knew she truly loved him for himself alone, and not for all his power and all his wealth and all the stability he'd brought into her troubled life.

"It seems not the first time you have saved me from the mud," she told him when they realized she had done something to her hip and could barely walk. He'd picked her up and set her on the creek bank where they would have, if not for her throbbing hip—

A sound?

Maya heard again the cries of the owls and the beating of wings. As she moved away from David in the bed she saw a movement in the shadows on the ceiling. Her eyes opened wide and shifted toward the doorway where a beam of light gave shape to a shaft of metal.

It was the moon, focused on a gun barrel.

CHAPTER 1

Immobilized by terror, Maya drew in a breath but was afraid to expel it. Her eyes traced upward, past the gloved hand on the trigger, but the face of the intruder was lost in the darkness. She lay between this specter and David, now aware that the gun was trained not upon her but her husband.

No!

A scream stuck in her throat. Her heart pummeled the cage of her ribs. She tried not to stir, willed this apparition to go away, but something in her movement out of David's arms must have stirred him. David came awake, sat up on his elbows and saw the evil in this metallic threat.

She heard him roar, "What the—?" He reached across her body, batted at the gun barrel, pushing it away, shielding her.

A blast rocked the room, sending shards of light stabbing through her brain. She squeezed her eyes shut but sickening images pulsed against her eyelids. The stench of powder hung in the air, the acrid taste of it burning her tongue.

David's body slumped over her, shuddering and rasping. She felt the slick warmth of his blood. Pulling him close, she compressed her body into his to stanch the bleeding.

Two more shots rang out, followed by David's shuddering and Maya's gasps. She felt a searing pain in her hand and found herself gulping air. Her hands tingled painfully, like a bad electrical shock. Her ears rang and then shut down. It was as if from an impossible distance she heard the muffled demand for her murder:

"Shoot the bitch, Lew! Shoot her!" a voice hissed.

"I took care of her."

It was the timbre of the voices Maya focused on. These were *joven*. *One of them was just a kid!*

David's body jerked and gurgled, convulsing in her arms, protecting her to the end. Death was rattling, writhing, tearing at him as he lay there thrashing. David gave up nothing easily. Choking down sobs, she lay beneath her husband, blocking the wound in his chest with her throbbing hand. The stench of blood was terrible. There was no way for the murderers, these striplings, to perceive that Maya herself was neither dead nor seriously wounded. She was terrorized but alive, choking down her own fear, praying, *Dios mio,* for them to leave. But until they did, there was no way to help David. Maya willed him to hang on. She would not let him go, never. David was not dead. Not really, no. It simply could not be.

"Shee-it, Lew, you killed him," a third voice, a child's, howled. "I want outta here..."

"Shut up!" the one called Lew replied.

"You crazy, man? We get caught we'll..."

There was a sickening crack. The muffled, indefinite sound of wood grating on bone. A shocked silence was followed by moans and whimpering.

"I said shut up!" Lew said. "Sniveling little fuck. I told you to stay back at the car. Now where's the payoff?"

A search proceeded. They were tearing the room apart. The closet doors were flung open; drawers were opened and tossed on the floor. Maya lay on her back, the weight of her husband squeezing the air out of her. She watched flashlight beams dart across the darkened ceiling while this band of idiots carried out their murder and robbery. They moved into the alcove adjacent to the bedroom and rifled David's desk. But the sniffling and the sobbing of the terrified child only became louder. His whimpering distracted the other two. They never checked again to see that Maya was alive.

And then it came, across the distance, a howl from the kennels. It was the baying of Regent, David's beloved hunter, the demanding red dog that thought he was David's alter ego. Regent had been banished from the house because he had not been all that friendly to Maya. Regent's howling told Maya what she didn't want to accept. Had David's soul departed? Had he drifted past the kennel to say good-by? Maya's spirits plummeted. This was the end. David was gone. Beneath the covers, wracked by silent sobs, she clung to his final warmth.

More dogs yipped, then chorused in a primitive wail, as if they had reverted to a feral state.

"Shee-it!" It was the voice of the leader. The one called Lew. "We gotta get the hell out of here."

Blessedly, they were gone, clattering into the hall, dashing down the stairs. Maya eased out from beneath David, grabbed the bedside phone, and tried to call out. The phone was dead. Moaning with despair, she threw the receiver to the wall. The ranch was twenty-five miles from town. It would take forever for an ambulance to get here. Then she remembered the radio, downstairs in the kitchen.

David lay face down, ominously still.

Maya rushed past him. She would put a call out. Someone would help her. She hobbled down the stairs, her injured hip jolting her at every step. At the window in the landing she could hear the commotion of the fleeing murderers. Something splashed in the pond at the foot of her rose garden. Beyond that she heard the distant sound of a truck grinding to life down by the bunkhouse.

"Claude, thank God," Maya whispered. Claude Fayals, David's trusted foreman, had a sixth sense when it came to trouble. He would know something was wrong. He would be arriving any second.

"David, don't leave me," Maya sobbed as she hobbled across the hallway to the kitchen. "Come back to me. I can't lose you. I can't bear it. Please. Not this. Not now!"

Printed in the United States
24975LVS00002B/190-198

9 781595 070111